I0600415

SWEAT
Jonah Yorke

Copyright © 2025 by Jonah Yorke

All rights reserved.

No part of this publication may be reproduced, distributed, or transmitted in any form or by any means, including photocopying, recording, or other electronic or mechanical methods, without the prior written permission of the publisher, except as permitted by U.S. copyright law. For permission requests, contact Jonah Yorke at jonahyorke.com.

The story, all names, characters, and incidents portrayed in this production are fictitious. No identification with actual persons (living or deceased), places, buildings, and products is intended or should be inferred.

Cover Art and Design by Rachel Sierra

First edition 2025

For Melvin

Contents

Note To Reader

Please be aware, this book deals with challenging topics such as internal and external homophobia, including use of the f-slur by queer characters as an expression of internal struggle. Additionally, expect mature discussions that include but are not limited to grief, depression, suicidal ideation, and past childhood trauma. Please prioritize your mental health while reading.

This book is intended for readers age 18 and up. All depicted sexual scenarios are between consenting adults. Related content warnings include but are not limited to:

A sex act between a protagonist and someone other than his eventual romantic partner (no cheating, no love triangle).

Unprotected sex.

Affectionate teasing/name-calling.

Power exchange.

1

Tommy

There's no feeling quite like being called *faggot* at age twelve by the kid you worship like royalty. Even at fourteen, people called Rowan Hughes the next Beckham, the next Messi. I believed it. Still do. Especially now, as he's racking up insane stats as captain of the Sacramento State Hornets.

I played against his team in youth soccer back when. I'd just made it into the age bracket, and Rowan was on his way out, half a head taller than everyone else on the field. Sparred with him a little in the second half when Coach finally put me in. It was the best moment of my life, playing on the same field as Rowan Hughes. Even if we were opponents. Even if it was only for five minutes at most.

His team kicked our asses, and as we all shook hands after, he gripped mine tight enough to crackle my bones and send a shiver up my spine. He looked me dead in the eyes, his face still beet red from earning that win and sweat still rolling down the sides of his face. At the same time that I chirped, "Good game," he snarled, "Suck my dick, faggot."

I watched him walk off the field where all the parents were, and I don't think I spoke one word the whole rest of the day. Until then, I never had two thoughts in my head about the concept of gay or straight, but there was a hole carved out of me that's stayed hollow all these years. Funny how four dumb words exchanged between near strangers can change the whole way someone navigates life. Then again, maybe I'm just too sensitive.

Annalese always calls me sensitive, and it's always a bad thing when she does, like I'm letting her down. Ever since Rowan called me...that word, I've tried to be hard, but it's...hard. It's gotten a little easier since starting college. People aren't as up in my business all the time. I'm not constantly on guard like I used to be, especially now I'm not playing soccer anymore.

But today...right now...it all comes crashing back. That hollowness Rowan carved out of me is still there, but everything else in me fills with pure, full-throttle rage.

It began as a simmer almost an hour ago when my boy, Malik, texted that one of his buddies thought he saw Annalese fucking around at some party she had tried dragging me to last weekend. That simmer turned to a boil when Malik sent receipts. A grainy pic of a packed apartment living room, where I see clear as day my girlfriend pressed up against some guy who looks awfully familiar.

"Word is she was all over him before they disappeared together for a good minute," Malik tells me when I call, and I'm already seeing red.

"Who?" is the only word I can get out of my throat without screaming.

"Rowan Hughes, man. Fuckin' team captain. On him like a groupie."

I hang up after Malik makes me promise not to go ape shit, but I'm damn near close to flying off the handle when I call Lese up and ask her straight up if she's fucking around again. Takes some prying, but once she starts crying, I know what's up. Now, she's sobbing through the phone, saying the same shit she said last time. *It was an accident. It meant nothing. I'm sorry. I love you. I'm coming over.*

"Don't you fucking dare," I tell her, because I can't look at her right now. I can barely see my steering wheel, and I'm staring right at it. Still parked in my space outside Ma's house, because I can't go inside like this. Heated and ready to punch something.

Lese is bawling the way she only does when I catch her acting out, and she's pleading with me to "just listen," but I'm done listening. Maybe it would be okay if it wasn't with Rowan fucking Hughes. I didn't get this crazed the other times, about the other guys, but this one hits different.

It takes some calling around, but I find out where Rowan hangs out on Tuesday evenings. I drive straight there. All the red lights blur in my vision, but I make it to McKinley Park without running myself off the road. I take it as a sign I'm doing the right thing. Finally standing up for myself. Things are done with Lese—for good this time—but the humiliation will devour me if I don't take action. Maybe things haven't been great lately. Maybe I've had my doubts for a long time. But she was my girlfriend, and I won't let Rowan get away with hollowing me out all over again.

There's some kind of pickup match going on at the far right soccer pitch, and I'm out of my car, marching across the field with my fists clenched. I haven't been face to face with Rowan in years, but I watch enough of his film to pick him out among the other bodies sparring on the field.

He's no longer the tallest guy out there. Peaked around sixteen at just under six-foot, but he commands every second of field time with the way he blocks, the way he moves with the ball, the way his body is built, and the way he carries what God gave him. My eyes find him immediately, and he's the only thing I see as I get closer and closer. My heart races with adrenaline, and I'm sweating in the cool air. *Do not chicken out.*

I can't remember the last time I knocked someone's lights out, but I won't chicken out. I don't care that he's probably going pro with the next draft.

A second after he shoots a goal, his head turns across his shoulder, and I swear his eyes stare right into mine.

Closer and closer.

He's shirtless, lean, cut and glistening, chest heaving, lips parted. He's staring right at me, but there's not a hint of any definable expression. No confusion. No realization that I'm here to fuck his shit up.

Closer and...something blunt crashes into the side of my face.

It's not Rowan, though. *What the fuck was that?*

I'm on the grass, shoulder aching, and the left side of my face stings like I was hit with a hot iron. No, a soccer ball. It rolls off toward the side of the field. I flop onto my back, feeling wet grass through my shirt and suddenly dizzy as hell.

"What the fuck?" someone says from a few yards away, or maybe that's just the voice in my head asking the same question.

I'm blinking up at the dark, cloud-stripped sky. *What the fuck, and where am I?*

It all comes back to me when I'm suddenly blinking up at Rowan Hughes. He's standing over me, staring with his black brows lowered. He licks his lips, and they plump up, a shade pinker than his sweat speckled face.

"Hey, man. You good?" His voice vibrates deep, tickling that emptiness inside me he left there a long time ago. It feels strange. The first time he's spoken right to me since middle school.

The pain in my face subsides quickly, but I'm too out of it to nod. Am I good? Something about getting knocked on my ass stole my fury, and now I'm left racking my brain for what to do next. Can't fight a dude when my back is on the grass.

"C'mon," he says.

Rowan gives two taps to my bicep before wrapping his hand around it to help me up. The gesture adds to my confusion, but I've got enough sense left to shrug him off once I'm on two feet.

More sense comes back to me, and I notice the other guys circling. Some of them, I recognize from the Sac team. Some, I don't recognize at all.

They're all looking at me, looking more confused and annoyed than Rowan does.

I clam up, realizing what a dumb idea it was to want to throw down with Rowan in front of witnesses. I can't beat a dude without telling him why, or else I'm just a deranged wackjob fit to be cuffed, but I also don't want all these dudes knowing my girl stepped out on me. Deep down, I know it's not my fault, but at the same time, maybe it is. Lese is always saying I don't pay her enough attention. Don't text her enough, don't go out with her enough, don't buy her things enough, and don't touch her good enough. It's humiliating.

The really sad thing is, I'm not even sure I can blame her for fucking Rowan. I mean, he's Rowan Hughes.

"You look familiar." Rowan's voice fills the feet of space between us, low and even spoken. "You play soccer?"

I surprise myself when my voice makes sounds, even more so by how calm I stay as I look into his gray eyes. "Used to."

Finally, there's a hint of expression on him. The slight lift of one corner of his mouth. "How old are you? There's no *used to*. Either you play or you don't."

"Yeah, I play."

He sizes me up slow. "Tommy, right?"

My name in his voice is disarming. There's no reason he should know my name. We grew up in different neighborhoods. Never went to the same schools or played for the same team. Only times we ever interacted were on the field. Does he remember that day eight years ago the same as I do?

Thinking it'll save me some face, I answer, "I go by Tom now, mostly."

"No, you don't." His half smile grows to a smirk. "You're too young to be a Tom."

"I'm twenty."

"You've got a babyface. Tommy suits you. Like Tommy from *Rugrats*."

"What?" Takes me a minute to remember what *Rugrats* even is, then I'm sort of offended. Speechless, mostly. The moisture in the air must be collecting in my ears, because my head is full of fog. Not sure which way is up anymore.

Rowan tips his chin to one side. "Levi's team needs an extra midfielder. Stick around."

"I don't have cleats."

Already jogging backwards and swishing a finger through the air as a cue to his buddies, Rowan answers, "Make it work, babyface."

That's how I, once again, wind up scrimmaging against Rowan, just like old times when his school would play mine. I made varsity as a sophomore at Johnson High, and we had three matches against McClatchy High when Rowan was a senior. Back then, I thought he looked like a soccer God, chiseled from marble and brought to life for the sole purpose of being the best.

Now, the only thing that's changed is four years and some hair on his chest.

The few inches I have over him didn't diminish Rowan's power on the field when we were in high school, and it doesn't now. Even in a pickup match at a public park after dark, Rowan is the conductor. The gravity we're all floating in. A few times, I try to escape it. I throw a shoulder and fish the ball from his cleats, but Rowan moves like water and blocks like a brick wall. He dribbles the ball like it's a dance, and he kicks with power. Undoubting.

He's confident in everything, but unarrogant in the ways that matter. He's not a ball hog. He lasers in on the best possible play and makes sure the ball gets to the right person at the right time. He communicates with his team and has their backs while keeping one eye on the opponents. It's mesmerizing and infuriating.

He scores a goal, and he grins like his team won the cup or something. Then he turns around and jogs back to center. I'm heaving, lungs on fire, hands on my knees. It's been so long since I played, I feel weak as shit.

"That all you got, babyface?" Rowan taunts me.

Remembering how much I hate the fucker, I find enough adrenaline to get my body back in the game, but my head has switched back to revenge. As good as it feels to play again, on the same field as Rowan no less, it would feel a heck of a lot better to make him eat crow.

Next time Rowan has the ball, I'm on him. At first, it's still about the game, needing the steal and needing a score, but then his elbow jabs my stomach, and I shove my foot between his. The ball gets loose, goes foul, and Rowan hits the grass.

"You good, bro?" I ask him, my chest puffed up like I'm hot shit now.

One of his teammates helps him up, but Rowan's eyes never leave me. They don't burn with rage the way mine do. They size me up again like he just learned something new about me. Hopefully that something is that I won't take his shit just because it comes out gold.

"We playing, or what?" he asks.

"Let's do it."

I lay in wait a couple more minutes, but next time Rowan has the ball dribbling between his cleats with a clear path to the goal, I run him down, and I don't quit until he's back on the ground.

The back of his head thuds on the grass, and that's when I see it. The rage. Not a lot, but just enough for him to grit his teeth and say, "You got balls, babyface."

"Don't call me that."

One of his buddies checks me back while Rowan pulls himself up.

"You gonna cry about it?" Rowan asks. "Huh? Like a fucking baby?"

"Fuck you." I start at him, but his buddy checks me again, like Rowan's personal bodyguard. I can't help but laugh.

"We got a problem?" Rowan asks.

"Yeah, we got a problem."

"Think good on it. Just 'cause you're built like Captain America doesn't mean I can't fuck you up."

I stiff arm the bodyguard and charge Rowan. Get right up in his face, chest to chest. I press my forehead into his and steal his body heat to fuel my anger.

It's true I'm built. The time I used to spend on a field, I spend lifting now, and I'm bigger than I've ever been. Big enough to wallop Rowan into the ground, if that's really what I want. A guy as lean as Rowan shouldn't intimidate a guy as big as me, but life ain't that black and white, and Rowan doesn't back down.

His eyes don't blink as they stare into mine. He licks his lips, and it breaks my focus for the millisecond it takes for Rowan to smirk like he just won something.

I let it get to me even though I shouldn't, and I let myself get flustered enough to shove him back. Not hard enough for him to fall, but hard enough to concede how intimidated I really am by him.

Still smirking, he says, "Spit it out, baby boy. I take your parking spot or something?"

"You fucked my girlfriend, dickhead."

I'm too caught up to appreciate the falter in Rowan's bravado or the way his eyes finally shift from mine, like he suddenly cares about the others around us.

"Nah, man," he says. "You're looking for someone else."

"I'm looking for you."

"I don't hook up with girls with boyfriends."

"You hooked up with Annalese Smith."

"I don't know who that is."

This fucker. Can't even man up to his own bullshit. King of confidence here, but he's just as big a fraud as Lese. I dig my phone from my joggers, swipe the photo Malik sent, and turn the screen to Rowan.

"What the fuck is that?" he asks.

Grumbling, I zoom in on the image until Rowan and Lese are front and center, then I show him again.

"Shit." The moment the word breezes past Rowan's lips, I know we're finally on the same page. His eyes widen a touch, then flit from my phone to me. "She never said anything about a boyfriend. I'm sorry, man. I really am." His hands raise up in surrender, almost convincing me he means it. Right up until he smirks again. "But your girl gives trash head."

Whether it's rage from his jeer or humiliation from his buddies snickering behind me, I finally snap and do what I came here for.

Next time Rowan's back is on the ground, it's right after I drive my fist into the side of his face. It's the first time I've socked someone since middle school. It feels damn good. Rowan is a groaning mess on the grass by the time I step over him and march back to my truck.

So much for being able to fuck me up.

Then again, as soon as I'm back in the Tacoma with my adrenaline running on fumes, I realize how fucked up I already am because of him. There's just something about him. The way he stands, the way he speaks, and the way his eyes consume me like he can see me from the inside out. Any delusion I had that Rowan Hughes may have grown out of being a dickwad douchebag is completely dispelled.

I must be real goddamn pathetic, because as badly as I want to hate his guts, I just can't. I couldn't hate him when I was twelve, and I can't hate him now. Why? Because he's Rowan Hughes, and he was right about what he said all those years ago. I am a fag. At least, sort of. Enough that when he admitted to hooking up with Lese, the thing that pissed me off the most was how jealous I was my girlfriend got to be alone in a room with the most freakishly perfect human I've ever met. Enough that the memory of Rowan licking his lips three inches from my mouth makes my dick twitch in my joggers.

The entire trip home, I'm white knuckling my steering wheel with one hand and palming my cock with the other. By the time I'm pulling back into Ma's driveway, I'm so shamefully hard that I have to tuck my boner up into my waistband.

To make matters worse, I get inside and Lese is there on the living room sofa playing Mario Kart with Maverick. It all looks like a riotous good time until I shut the door behind me. Then, Lese becomes sheepish as Mav torpedoes himself from the sofa to my hip.

"Tommy, Tommy! Guess what we did today?!" he starts in just like he does every time I come home after dark. It's easy to ignore Lese and focus on my nephew as I scoop him up and carry him with me toward the dining room where there's still one place setting left uncleared.

Mav is halfway through a babbling tale of going to the plaza and seeing ducks in the wishing fountain when Ma pokes her head out the kitchen to scold me for missing supper. She follows it up with bringing me the plate she kept warm in the oven for me, proving once again I don't deserve her. As soon as Mav tires himself out, Ma starts in on the interrogation.

"So, where were you?" she asks, hands on her hips. "I texted you dinner was at six."

"I'm sorry. I was at McKinley."

"What were you doing there?" She asks like I was buying crack or something, even though she knows McKinley is in a decent neighborhood. Rowan probably grew up around there, in one of those swanky two-story houses on a full acre with a pool and maybe even his own personal soccer pitch. Dude sweats entitlement. Dude just sweats in general. His pores were weeping tonight, his black running shorts sticking to his quads. Under the solar park lamps, his whole body glistened.

Lese is watching me from the sofa, so I can't tell Ma the truth, not that I ever would. Even if I wanted to tell her about Lese cheating again, I can't tell my mother I got into a fight. She'd beat my ass. Actually, she'd just give me one of her looks and one of her lectures, and I'll feel beaten down all the same.

Moving my fork through Ma's signature chili casserole, I say, "I was, uh, just kicking a ball around with some guys from school."

The tension leaves Ma's body with a sigh. Her hands leave her hips as she says, "You're playing again?"

"It was just for fun."

She puts her hand on my shoulder. The one that still aches from when I fell sideways like a domino. Makes me wonder how much Rowan is hurting right now. Hopefully, a ton.

"I need you to fix little man up for bed once you clear that plate," Ma says.

I'm already nodding when Lese jumps up and announces she'll handle bathtime, but her eyes won't meet mine. As annoyed as I am that she's here at all, she is great with Mav. Sometimes, I think he prefers Lese over me, but that might just be because she's a pretty girl.

Vibrating with excitement, Mav squeals, "We can play Aquaman!"

"Hell yeah, little dude." Lese races up to the table and tickles Mav's sides with her long acrylics. "I'm Aquaman this time, though."

Mav giggles like mad in a way that's usually music to my ears, but I'm too busy being pissed at Lese to appreciate it.

She smells like that cupcake-y body spray she hoards from Bath & Body Works. I used to love that scent. Always made me kind of hungry. Lately...I don't know. Smelling like a cupcake just isn't enough to make me want to put up with her shit anymore.

"Don't you two go getting water all over the place again," Ma says before laying her hand on Lese's head and saying thank you. That's how I know Ma thinks of Lese as her own. Ma only ever lays her hand on top of her kids' heads to tell them thanks or I love you. First time Ma did that was a year after I started dating Lese, and it made me feel weird then same as it does now. Like that hand on her head is a commitment I'll have to uphold somehow. Like I'm not allowed to really end things with Lese now that she's basically family.

But I never asked for her to be my family. All I asked was that she quit riding other dudes' dicks.

Ma puts her hand on my head next and reminds me to say goodnight to Erica before I turn in. Just the fact Ma is reminding me at all says Erica isn't doing any better today than she has been.

After I finish supper, I dip into Ma's bedroom that's been Ma and Erica's bedroom for the better part of a year. When Erica got sick, she and Mav moved back in, and Ma shoved her bed against the wall to make room for Erica's medical one. It's a narrow bed, but the chemo's thinned her out so bad, it's not a thing when I fit myself beside her. She's got some nighttime soap opera playing on the TV, but she's dazed. Half-dead looking, if I'm honest. So bad it hurts to look at her sometimes without crying, so I stare at the TV instead.

A sharp cheek bone rests on my shoulder while a skinny hand lies on my leg. Erica's hoarse, tired voice asks, "Was that Annalese I heard?"

I clear my throat like that'll harden me as I put my hand over Erica's, feeling how cold she is. "She's giving Mav his bath."

"She'll be a good mom someday. Maybe someday soon?"

The hope in Erica's voice nearly breaks me. Seems like the only hopes she has these days are about what a great man Mav will grow up to be, and what a great wife Lese will be to me. It's as if she spends all day now imagining our happily ever afters. Happily ever after has never really been my thing, though.

"Not with me," I say, because I'm too grouchy tonight to lie. Too selfish to play into my bed ridden sister's fantasies.

"Don't be cynical. She's good for you."

My eyes well up, and I don't know whether to agree or disagree or which one would be more truthful. Lese will be a great mom one day, and she might even make a great wife if I could get over the fact she can't keep it in her pants. Honestly, I don't even care that she screws around. It's the humiliating way she does it that hurts the most. Throwing herself at Rowan Hughes at a party full of people I go to school with is about as bad as it gets.

"Maybe it doesn't feel like she's your soulmate, but that stuff is only in movies. Real love isn't always a transcendent, passionate affair. Sometimes, it's just knowing you're better together than apart. Sometimes, love isn't as much a feeling as it is a choice to take care of someone and to be taken care of by them."

"I get it."

Erica lifts her head. "I'm sorry."

"Don't be." I finally look at her, my heart breaking a little to see how sunken her eyes are, how bloodshot and glossy. Maybe love isn't always a feeling, but my love for Erica is as close to transcendent as I can think of. My big sister. My rock. The only person I ever let see me cry, because when she cries, I can't hold mine back.

"I just want you to be happy."

I frown, feeling like a failure that I can't honestly swear to her I'm happy, or that I even can be happy. Happiness isn't meant for me. The best I can manage is content, and maybe that's what Erica was getting at with the whole *love can be a choice* thing.

If I choose to love Lese even when I don't feel it, is that happiness?

"I just want you to get better," I tell her, because I'm a selfish little brother who can't just let her rest.

She frowns, like I'm accusing her of not trying hard enough, and I hate this. Sweating, chest aching, eyes leaking. I'd rather feel nothing than feel this way for another second.

Even if it's a lie, I promise Erica I'll be okay, and when she puts her cheek back on my shoulder, I stay put until Mav slips into the room dressed in dinosaur jammies.

"Come say goodnight to Mommy," I tell him as I scoot off Erica's bed. I hoist Mav up under his arms and put him where I just was.

Lese lingers in the doorway, and I figure I better walk her to her car before she tries to stick around.

The air outside is colder now that I'm not consumed with rage. I shove my hands deep into my pockets and lift my shoulders. I look straight ahead and let the silence between Lese and I fester while we walk at a snail's pace down my congested street.

That little silver hatchback Lese's dad bought her after high school glints under the last streetlamp. Before we get to the corner, she tugs on my arm and forces me to look at her.

"I fucked up, Tom," she says. "I'm a selfish, stupid slut sometimes, but I love you. You're the only person I've ever loved, and I'll never love anyone but you. I just get so lonely sometimes. You know how lonely I get. I'm clingy, and you're the opposite, but I feel like if you loved me as much as I love you—"

"What? If I really loved you, I would have gone to that party with you? Is that what you think love is? Me ditching all my responsibilities to watch you get shit faced around a bunch of people I barely know?"

"If you loved me, you would want to do more with me than watch me babysit your nephew and do chores for your mom."

"I never asked you to do any of that."

"You don't need to ask. I do that shit because I love you, and I love your family, and I want to feel like you want me in it."

"Maybe I don't."

In a flash, Lese's face drains of life and her eyes go as dull as I feel. "Fine, then," she mutters before picking at the clasp on the charm bracelet I gave her for her twentieth. She forces the silver, jangly thing into my palm, then goes rummaging through her giant purse. Some cheap keychain, a Bic pen, and a vape battery amount to the whole of our four-year relationship when she puts them into my hands.

"You're being dramatic," I tell her.

"You're done with me? Then, take your shit."

"Whatever." I cradle it all in my hands and watch her march past me toward the last street lamp.

She makes it a couple yards before switching around and saying, "I don't know if it's erectile dysfunction or depression, but I never woulda stepped out if your fucking dick worked right."

Yeah, well, you give trash head, I almost say, but what's the use? I let her go, and it's the easiest thing I've done in a long time. Hard, because I don't want to have to tell Ma, Erica, and Maverick I failed. Easy, because being alone makes more sense than trying to keep Lese and me afloat.

When I get back inside, Ma is still tiding up the kitchen and Mav is still with his mom, so I sneak to the bathroom for a shower among Mav's many bath toys.

I lock the door, switch on the fan, get the water going, and while it's heating up, I open an incognito browser tab on my phone and type in my go-to Pornhub search. My pants are already tenting from the thumbnails alone, and I strip naked quickly before tapping on a video.

Every time I failed at maintaining an erection for Lese, I could've flung myself off a tall building. But it's not because of E.D. or depression. It's because the only thing that'll keep me rock solid is something Lese doesn't have.

Sitting on the cushioned toilet seat, I stroke my dick to a muted video of a dude my age doing the exact same thing.

I used to get by fine on straight porn, but once I realized I paid way more attention to the dicks than the pussies, I switched to male masturbation porn. Somehow, it hadn't really felt gay, even when I clicked on sites called GayTube and GaysGoneWild. I told myself it was just to better my personal technique. Even now, I mimic the actions of the man on my phone screen. The way he cups his balls, the way he pinches his cockhead, and the way he grips himself at the base and wags his dick like a tail. I do everything to my cock that this random cam boy does to his own, chasing whatever he's feeling, desperate to come as hard as I know he will.

But I'm also desperate to see him come. Desperate to see how much spunk shoots from that red tip as his large, hairy-knuckled hand tugs on his shaft. I want to see his balls get tight and his abs flex. If I'd thought to bring my earbuds in, I could even listen to his deep groans and grunts while he unloads.

The video frame cuts whoever-he-is off at the neck so he's all body and no head, but everything I see is pretty close to perfect. Maybe a bit too skinny for my taste. Lean is good, but I like muscle. Not too much. Not like me, beefed-up and too lumbering on my feet to come close to besting Rowan on a field. No, someone like Rowan... Dreamy eyes, chiseled jaw, svelte body, and running shorts so sweaty they stick to his body like paper mache.

Did he call me *baby boy*?

What the fuck?

I come into my hand with my head cranked back and my eyes squeezed shut. No need for the video when I see Rowan so clearly in my head now.

The shame sets in as my dick softens, and I swipe away the incognito tab with my dry hand before disappearing into the shower to wash myself clean. No matter how hard I scrub, desire remains.

Yeah, I'm a fag alright, and maybe that's not Rowan's fault, but I've gotten pretty good at blaming him over the years, and that's not about to change tonight.

2
Rowan

I make it three steps out of the locker room before Coach says my name like a command, stopping me dead. Guess I was too optimistic thinking I could get through practice without him noticing the glaring shiner shadowing the entire upper left quadrant of my face.

The look he gives me is damn near fatherly, but Coach is a hard-nosed, my-way-or-the-highway type dad. Shoulders back, arms crossed, mouth teased and brows knitted. If I was one to be intimidated by older men, maybe I'd be quaking in my cleats right now, but even as a freshman, I found Coach McDonough more comical than threatening.

"What happened?" he asks in a tone that allows the *and don't lie to me* part to go unspoken.

Still, I shrug a shoulder and say, "Fell out of bed last night."

"Yeah? Fell out of bed and onto someone's fist?"

I crack a smile as Levi and Raisel come out of the locker room. I lift a hand and dap them both as they go past. The snicker those two share reminds me they know exactly why I'm black and blue, and that won't do me any favors with Coach right now.

"Rowan," Coach brings my focus back to him, and I swear his eye is twitching.

"It's nothing. I went to a party over the weekend, hooked up with this chick who, as I learned last night, has a boyfriend, so..." I finish the story with a shrug.

"I'd expect this from someone like Levi. Not from you."

"Shit happens, right?"

Coach shakes his head and uncrosses his arms to un-tuck his clipboard from his armpit. Nodding toward the locker room, he says, "Go put some runners on. You'll be doing laps through practice."

"You're messing with me."

The look Coach gives me is blunt as a baton to my side. "Not messing with you."

I toss my arms up. "What happened to boys will be boys?"

Coach steps right up close to me, head tilted down because the old dude is like six-foot-six. "You want to be a boy? Then you can turn that captain's patch in to me before August so I can give it to someone ready to be a man."

The tide inside me shifts to where I no longer feel the late spring breeze against my skin or hear the far away chatter of my teammates already stretching for drills on the field. I'm steel now. Hard, immoveable steel that locks my jaw and keeps my eyes glaring into Coach's. Just tough love maybe, but it's still bullshit. No one on this team practices more and parties less than I do, but all McDonough sees in me are coattails to get him coaching pro.

He needs me, but he's too macho to admit it, so he pretends I'm a problem athlete he's got to whip into shape. Truth is, I've never needed him for jack shit. Okay, maybe he's come in clutch from time to time, but all in all, the dude is a dud.

"I want your ass on that track in five minutes," he says.

It takes all the restraint I can gather not to curse him out and throw my jersey in his face, tell him to find a new striker, a new captain, a new future-cash cow. Fuck this place, this school and this polluted city.

If only I didn't love this sport so much. If only I didn't give a full-blown shit about my team. So, I swallow my pride and do what the tyrannical prick says, change into my New Balances, and get my ass on the track.

I can't run for shit with my phone on me, and my Bluetooth buds won't work between my locker and the track, so the only thing I have keeping my mind company is my own grating inner voice. While I sweat my weight out and kill my calves on the packed dirt, I'm cursing McDonough's life over and over and the lives of my so-called teammates who whistle at me as I loop the field, chanting "Run, Rowan, Run!" and "Faster, faster, faster!" Dumbfucks.

I run for an hour and then some, until my legs give out, and I scrape my knees and the heels of my hands on the dirt. My clothes are soaked through. My head is killing me under the high sun. What does McDonough do? Walks me over a plastic bottle of room temp water, then tells me to move my ass.

"Screw you," I mutter, because I literally cannot keep it back to save my life.

"When's the next party?"

I flip him off, grab the bottle and start on running again. I might feel half-dead, but I'm not dead yet. If Coach wants the death of a twenty-two-year-old on his hands, he's going to have to wait a while longer.

What's really unfair is that I didn't even want to go to that party. When Levi and Raisel rolled up to my place, they said we were just going to play Madden at Zeke's apartment. They didn't mention the thirty odd other people who would be there acting foolish.

My lungs are burning to crisps, and for what? So I could drink trash beer around trash people and get a trash blowie from... What's her name again? Anna-Maria? Margarita? I don't know or care. I didn't even want her on my dick at all, but she made a big show of fangirling all over me and not taking no for an answer. It started looking weird that I wasn't jumping on the sure thing.

If I hadn't downed three beers out of boredom alone, I probably could've come up with some excuse to stiff arm her, but I took the path of least resistance instead. Let her take me into a walk-in closet and fuck around with my dick while I imagined she was someone completely different.

All I wanted to do was play Madden, and now my muscles feel as battered as my face looks. Tommy really knows how to lay into a punch, that's for sure. Not surprising given the mass of the dude. The Tommy Mathison who used to play against my team in high school was one step up from scrawny. I've noticed him around campus from time to time, and noticed his gains, but it's different when he's bumping those hard muscles into me with a purpose.

As big as he is, he's good on his feet, and he's fast in quick bursts. If he wasn't so caught up hounding my ass, he might have been able to put those muscles to good use. Instead, I kicked his ass, and he settled for decking me in the face.

Got to admit, the fire in his eyes nearly got to me. If I thought his muscles weren't all for show, I probably wouldn't have ribbed him so bad. I assumed he was just there to play. Thought he wanted a challenge, and I was down to provide. I didn't realize until it was too late that he was there to literally beat my ass.

No matter why Tommy came to McKinley last night, he played, and he played like it was his lifeblood, distracted or not.

He's rough, no doubt, but he's better than most of our second stringers. Or he could be, if he evened out that gym rat bod and tempered his anger to a manageable simmer.

Coach's whistle blows, and it wakes me from my plotting. He hollers at me to quit running, and he doesn't have to tell me twice. I make it half a step onto the grass before I collapse onto my back. Starfished and heaving so hard I could puke, I stare up at the clear blue sky and wonder if Tommy really hates my guts now. He never seemed to be my biggest fan as teenagers, but sticking my dick in his girl's mouth might have put me on his permanent shit list.

"Fuck!" I squirm away from the sudden downpour of water sluicing across my bruised face. I shield myself with my hands until it quits, then I swipe the water from my eyes to find Coach standing over me with an empty water bottle in his hand.

"Just making sure you're still kicking," he says.

"I'm gonna kick you!"

He chuckles at that. A fucking sadist in the body of an obscenely buff sixty-year-old. Man looks like an aging gay porn star, like he should be bottoming for hung twinks in his office between practices. The thought gives me shivers, and not the good kind. He crouches down next to me with his knees spread wide and his shorts stretched to the limit over whatever he's got packing. I have to force myself not to look. I'm only human, designed to be curious, but the consequence of sating my curiosity might just make me ill. It's McDonough, after all.

"Seriously, you okay?" he asks.

Forcing my eyes above his dick print, I notice his whistle isn't around his neck anymore. Coach-mode over.

"Peachy."

"You get the shiner checked out?"

I scoff. "It's a shiner. What's there to check out?"

"You know, if you'd have shown up to a match like this, I'd have benched you."

"I didn't know the chick had a boyfriend! A boyfriend built like Thor, no less."

"I'll tell you what I tell my kids. Make better choices, and I won't have to humiliate you in front of your friends."

"Father of the year," I mutter, but I take Coach's hand when he offers it. Mostly because I'm not sure I can get up on my own even if I tried.

My trip back to the locker room is slow and limping. Each step feels like sticking my foot into a wood chipper, and I need a Gatorade out of the team fridge like I need air to breathe. I swear, the first sip of cherry Gatorade fresh out of the door hits like an instant dopamine high. I need a shower, but our backup goalie, Malik, just came back from there with a towel around his waist, and I zero in on him.

"Yo." I nod to him, making sure he knows I'm talking to him. "You went to Johnson, right?"

The fear flashing across his face is both comical and annoying. My tone wasn't harsh, I'm just impatient, but Malik straightens up like I caught him texting during a huddle.

"Uh, yeah. Why?" He looks confused, probably because we've hardly exchanged words before beyond a cordial *wassup* in passing. I know everyone on the team's name by heart, the schools they came from, and their start-of-year stats. Starters, backups, second string, third string, everyone. Doesn't mean I want to bro out with them or start a book club.

"You play there with a guy named Tommy? Tommy...something or another. Shredded guy. Baby face?" I'm trying to play it cool and inadvertently announced to this backup two things I can't keep out of my head about Mr. Mathison. That hard body and that soft, doe-eyed face. Because Malik is in only a towel, and nearly as shredded as Tommy, I face my locker and focus on getting it unlocked.

From a few locker spaces down, Malik says, "Tommy Mathison? Yeah."

"He good?"

"Good? Like, good with a ball? Yeah, he's great. Was, I mean. He left the game behind after high school."

"Why?" I get my locker open and stick my half-downed Gatorade into it before tugging off my shirt.

"Dunno."

Balling up my shirt, I eye Malik like I know he's lying. Guy doesn't trust me, I guess. Funny how all these dudes trust me with their lives as soon we're on that field, but off of it, I'm like their parent, stuck in a revolving door of anxious half-truths.

Am I scary or something?

"You know where he hangs out?" I ask.

"You lookin' for revenge or something?"

I fling my shirt ball into my locker and finally allow myself to sit on the long bench behind me. "What? Oh, that." I roll my eyes and tug at my shoelaces.

"He really clocked your ass, huh?"

Now I'm hoping the glare I shoot Malik scares him, but all it does is make him fold his lips and hold back the laugh vibrating his throat.

"Not looking for revenge," I say, but now I sorta want it. Maybe I'll save a piece for Malik too. "Just wanna chat about his glory days a little."

"You fucked the dude's girl, man. I don't think he wants to chat with you about dick."

"I didn't—" I stop myself from arguing the different between head and fucking, because it's a moot point that would only raise more questions. Like, why didn't I fuck her? Aaliyah, or whatever her name is, must be pretty hot if Tommy is wasting time on her, and she was majorly down-to-fuck. Like Levi said, only a homo would turn that pussy down. "I didn't know she had a boyfriend."

"It's all good. Annalese just been doing Annalese past couple years. Maybe now she's dipping her pen a little too close to home, Tommy will get it through his head that she's not wife material. Woman just wants to party."

Seems like Tommy hates partying even more than I do. I pry his routine out of Malik and it's monotonous as hell. Gym, classes, work, gym, home at dusk, lights out before midnight, rinse and repeat. No one sees much of him except in passing, and his social media presence is scarce to none. I'd think a gym rat would be posting reels of his reps on the daily, if only for the boost in quality DMs. It's the dude version of thirst-trapping.

It takes a week for me to spot Tommy. He's leaving the Humanities building at the same time I'm waiting on an order of corn dog bites at the Quick Stop window outside the Student Union. These deep fried babies are an integral part of my weekly cheat day, so I give it a few seconds, and as soon as I've got my dogs and a handful of mustard packets shoved into my sweatshirt pocket, I bolt down the East Quad steps and snake through the counter-current of late morning foot traffic.

"Yo!" I holler, clipping some rando's shoulder as I keep my eyes trained on the tip of Tommy's head poking out from the crowd. His honey-brown hair wafts upward in the breeze, and his backpack has a teal water canister shoved into the side pouch.

I get closer, and the crowd size dissipates as Tommy turns onto a wider thoroughfare. "Yo, babyface!"

The big dude slows, but he doesn't stop. He glances oddly over his shoulder, spots me, and that odd expression turns downright startled.

"Damn, Tommy." I catch up to him, laughing at how quick he is when he's not even trying. "Almost lost my dogs chasing you down."

"What do you want?"

The coarseness in his voice quickens my heartbeat, but it's the softness in his tone that has me pulling my focus off my corn dogs. Only difference between Tommy at night and Tommy in the daylight is that the sun makes his hair glow golden on the ends, and it's easier to see how blue his eyes are and how smooth his face is. He sure as hell isn't the lanky kid I played against in high school anymore. Now, he tilts his chin up and looks at me from the bottoms of his eyes, like he wants me to know I'm shorter than him. As if that's not obvious.

There's still a timidness to him, though. Something tells me it's so ingrained in him he'll never grow out of it, whether by age or by reps at the gym. When I ask him what he's doing tonight, he grips the straps of his backpack like it's a jetpack and glances left and right, like I've got him on candid camera or something.

"Why?" he asks.

"You know the intramural field next to the campus gym, behind the psychology building?"

"Yeah?" He draws out the word like he's not sure, but it's probably just that he doesn't trust me.

"Be there at seven."

"Why?"

My eyes roll, but I sort of like the skepticism in his voice. Skepticism means his mind's working, and if his mind is working, that means it's not made up yet. "Either you play or you don't. Or are you still on that *'used to'* nonsense?"

One step shrinks the gap between us by half, and Tommy softens his chin down while hardening his stare. "Is this a trap or something?"

It's actually endearing how young he looks when he's trying to look tough. It's a struggle to keep my eyes locked on his when they're so intense, so I trail mine down for a temporary reprieve. My eyes catch on the two small bumps of his nipples peaking through the white tee he's wearing. Maybe bringing him around isn't such a good idea, but right now, it feels like the best idea I've ever had.

"August will be my last season here," I say as soon as I drag my eyes off his chest and back to his face. "I got to ramp everything up to a hundred-and-twelve if I'm gonna get drafted. You weren't much of a challenge last week, but you gave me a good workout. Think you can find some cleats by seven?"

"Maybe," he mumbles, looking even more skeptical now with his eyebrows wrinkled.

"See you tonight then, babyface."

My hands are busy, popping one of these corn dog balls into my mouth, or else I might try to shake Tommy's hand. Amends, or whatever, for what I did at the party, even though it totally wasn't my fault. I walk away backwards, in case Tommy has any parting words for me. *Fuck off,* maybe.

All he does is stand there wearing a dopey look like he just woke up in Narnia. He must really think I'm luring him into a revenge trap. That or I just made his damn dreams come true. Either way, his parted lips and blue-eyed stare have me wondering how the hell someone could cheat on him.

3
Tommy

After my shift at the deli, I eat Ma's supper like it's a race before I track down the tote in the garage with all my old soccer gear in it. I must be out of my mind even thinking about going to meet with Rowan tonight. For all I know, I'll get there and he and his buddies will wallop on me into looking like a car crash victim. I did lay into Rowan pretty mean last week. Took my knuckles days to quit hurting, and from the state of Rowan's face yesterday, he's still healing from a gnarly bruise.

It's selfish too. Cutting out on my family just to get a taste of what I've been missing since high school. I should be helping Ma. The dishes need doing, laundry needs folding, Mav is too scared to bathe on his own, and someone's got to make sure he's brushing those teeth right. Lately, Erica needs the same sort of help, but it takes longer when I'm trying not to hurt her anymore than she's already hurting. She needs her meds when the timers go off, and she needs someone to talk to who isn't our mother or a six-year-old. She needs me, and I want to be here for her, but it's soul crushing watching her get worse and worse and not being able to do shit about it.

At least being scorned by Lese and worrying over Rowan's intentions has been a change of pace from the slow-brewing tragedy constantly hanging over my head.

"Where are you going?" Ma asks, clearly perturbed by me moving around the house like it's about to flood.

"Just going out." I go into my room to change into shorts and long socks. It takes longer with all Mav's stuff filling my closet and scattering the floor between our beds.

Ma watches me from the doorway. "With Annalese?"

"Told you. It's done with Lese."

"I don't know why you can't work things out. She's a good girl. Someday, you're going to have to learn how to work through conflict and not run at the first sign of trouble."

I roll my eyes, but only because my head is so deep in the closet, Ma won't see it. Last thing I want is her knowing the "conflict" I can't work out is Lese's cheating. Ma is old-school. She doesn't want to hear about how I couldn't satisfy my girlfriend, and she really doesn't want to hear the reason why.

"I need your help here, Tommy," she says, hands on her hips and giving me that tired look that reminds me how much she sacrifices on the daily.

Another reason to get out of the house. Too much fucking guilt. Guilt for being the healthy sibling. Guilt for not being able to fix anything. Guilt for being another person Ma has to cook and clean for. Now, guilt for breaking up with someone who actually wants to help Ma out. Lese may have a plethora of flaws, but she was right when she said she loves my family. This past week, I've wondered if that should be enough for me.

I shove my cleats and shin guards into my backpack and join Ma in the doorway long enough to kiss her cheek and promise, "I'll be back in a couple hours to help put Mav to bed."

"He's not getting enough sleep," she says like she's scolding me. "His teacher says he's been taking naps during recess."

"It's his recess. He can do whatever he wants during it, right?" Maybe that's flippant, but it's ten minutes to seven, and something about Rowan tells me he doesn't enjoy tardiness. Besides, I promised Mav I wouldn't tell anyone about the nightmares that wake him up in the middle of the night. Something else to feel guilty about...that no matter how hard Erica's cancer has been on me, it's a drop in a bucket compared to what it's doing to her little boy.

Like the selfish fuck I am, I interrupt Mav's TV time to ask him if he'll help Ma out with the folding. "I'll let you have a candy out of my secret stash if you do."

That's got him giddy and trotting toward the laundry closet. That kid is too good for this shitty world, and that's the biggest tragedy of all.

I park at the gym lot and walk over with my pack slung over my shoulder. The flutter in my gut reminds me of the kiddie birthday parties I used to go to when I was Mav's age. The ones where the entire class was invited, and I didn't know what to expect or if I was even walking into the right house.

This is the right place, but that realization isn't calming me none. Unlike last week at McKinley Park, all the men here are Sac State first stringers. An unofficial after-practice practice, I guess, but why the hell would Rowan want me here?

Everyone's stretching still, chatting some, not paying me more than a glance as I cross the lawn. So, safe to say they aren't about to jump me.

Still, my anxiety doesn't waver. It only travels up to my chest when I see Rowan on the grass in a hamstring stretch. Both hands around a cleat, chin nearly touching his leg. He peeks up when I get close, just watching me until I drop my pack in front of him.

"Hope you got cleats in there," he says, coming out of the stretch slowly. Spreading both legs in front of him, he looks me up and down. Part of me wonders if he'll send me packing if he doesn't like the clothes I'm in.

Then, he nods to the side. "You remember Levi? You're on his team again."

Levi is the blond guy with the full beard shooting the shit with a guy I think is named Raisel Cruz. Hearing his name draws Levi's attention. "'Sup, Tyson?" he says to me, but it feels rhetorical the way he doesn't wait for an answer before jogging toward the far goal.

Tyson? Oh...the knockout.

"Everyone here is a starter," I say.

"So?" Rowan answers. "You intimidated?"

"No." But of course I am, and it's probably written all over my face.

"Good." He climbs to his feet to size me up eye to eye. He pulls his t-shirt up and over his head and flings it onto a gym bag I assume is his. "Get your shit on and stretch up. You're late."

So he is a stickler for punctuality. Got to remember that in case I live through this scrimmage.

I nod to the last guy still stretching on the sidelines and ask him what the foul rules are. He snorts and says, "Don't worry. If you stay down, we'll drag you off the field before you get trampled."

"Great."

Try as I might to switch my mind into competition mode, most of the first half I'm just a little fish in shark-infested waters, struggling not to be eaten alive. Even the dudes on my team give me a run for it, shoving me out of the way when I'm in it and stealing the ball from me if I'm taking too long. Half my team keeps calling me Tyson, which is throwing me off.

"Pick it up, Tyson!" Levi snarls after I completely fuck up a pass. The few times I manage to keep the ball, I can't do a damn thing with it without Rowan or one of his midfielders running me down like they might actually want me dead.

The third time I'm knocked to hands and knees, I think about what that one guy, Connor, said. If I just stay down, they'll drag me off the field, and I can spend the rest of this hellish practice counting stars.

"You crying, baby boy?" Rowan's deep, panting voice above me is laced with enough sarcasm to bring me back to life.

"Fuck you." I pick myself up and glare at his smirking face. The devious prick somehow figured out the only thing worse than being beaten up is being beat. No one likes to lose, but it's another thing to be a loser. "Did you invite me here just to humiliate me?"

I'm pissed, but I don't expect Rowan to care. I don't expect that smirk to slip from his face and for his eyes to harden the way they do.

"I invited you here to play," he says, "so are you gonna play, or are you gonna cry?"

Jesus, who raised this guy? I imagine a cross between a pride of lions and a sewer of rats. If he has siblings who treated him like this growing up, I should feel sorry for him.

A guy I think is named Zeke throws from the touchline, and the match is back on. Whether Rowan is trying to be an ass or just is an ass, he does get me focused. Focused on doing everything I can to keep the ball from him.

I fail spectacularly, and Rowan's team wins 4-1.

As soon as I leave the field, my legs turn to jelly and I'm on the grass, crawling the rest of the way to my bag. I turn onto my ass and chug half my water in half a minute. I count it out in my head. Thirty chugs. When I'm through, I barely have the strength to unlace my cleats.

"Good work out there, Tyson."

I look up and see Levi towering over me, reaching down his fist.

Dazed as hell, I mutter a thanks and dap him up.

"Yeah, man, good job," Raisel says next, reaching down to pat my shoulder before they both walk off.

Maybe I wasn't as big a train wreck as I thought. We lost, but that's not all on me, right? Any team going against Rowan has the odds against them. That's just smart money.

Even so, when Rowan crouches down beside me and tells me I did good, I dismiss it with a scoff.

"For real?" I ask, putting my sights on his face for any hint of deception.

Dude is as stoic as they come, though. The muscles in his face seem soft while the look in his eyes digs into me deep. His lips fold like he's mad for a second, but relax again in the next. The way his tongue slips out to wet his lips stirs something in me that I really don't want to be feeling right now, in front of everyone.

"For real," he says. No deception detected. "How long's it been since you played?"

I sigh, dropping my shoulder and curving my body until the top of my head touches my lap. I wait for the sound of my back popping, then I straighten up some. "Two years about."

"Why'd you quit?"

"Personal shit."

He nods, accepting my vagueness. "You wanna un-quit?"

"What?"

Before my scrambled brains can fully process Rowan's question, he's answering mine. "There's just over four months 'til August. I can get you on the team if you really want it."

Despite the burn in my lungs, I laugh. "You're joking."

"I'm not."

Again, no deception detected. Then again, Rowan is a superstar. I shouldn't put it past him to be a superstar liar too.

"So, what? I'll kill myself and ignore all my responsibilities just to sit on a bench every match come August?"

Rowan's face hardens up. "I don't waste my time on bench-warmers."

I study Rowan closer. Not for deception this time, but for motive, because none of this makes sense. "You think I can be a starter in four months?"

"I think I can make you a starter in four months."

I want to laugh again, but all I do is smile at the arrogance. The fact Rowan Hughes is taking any sort of interest in me at all has my inner fanboy reeling. The fact he's still shirtless is doing things to me too.

"I don't know," I tell him. "I'll have to think about it."

"Meet me back here tomorrow night. Same time. Don't be late again."

By the time I've slow-blinked myself into the realization Rowan means to train me personally, he and his bag are already gone.

This time, I don't tell Ma where I'm heading out to after supper. I've got a feeling she'll be mad, and it's easier to ask forgiveness than permission. I don't know yet if trying to make the Sac team is worth it in the end, but I'm sure about meeting up with Rowan tonight. Even if it's just for another grueling scrimmage, it's an opportunity I can't wuss out on. It's a taste of something that used to be my everything. Plus, it's Rowan fucking Hughes.

I had a dream about him last night. It wasn't a nightmare, but I woke up sweating and panting all the same. Thank God Mav was fast asleep. He's too young to know why guys sometimes have to change their pajama pants after certain kinds of dreams. It took me an hour to fall back asleep, and I spent all that time watching YouTube clips of last season's Sac State matches, clicking on anything and everything with the name Rowan Hughes in the title.

It's safe to say I've got a major boy-crush on the guy, if that's even a thing. Maybe it means I'm not straight, but does it have to mean I'm gay? Am I gay just because I get off to wank porn and have wet dreams about Rowan pressing his hard, lean, sweaty body against me? I had a girlfriend for four years, for fuck's sake. I loved her once, I think. Liked her, at least. I'm aware she's beautiful, and she was fun to be around when she wasn't upset over dumb shit, like me not wanting to have sex all the time.

We could have sex sometimes, like when I was high on edibles or in one of those moods where just about anyone would do. I guess that's not very romantic of me, but I've never been good at romance either. Probably because I'm gay but have only dated girls.

Shit.

I can't meet up with Rowan tonight. What am I thinking? I know next to nothing about him save for his talents and the one time he called me a slur after a game. Could he tell I was gay then, when I had no idea? Can he tell now, when I'm only half aware of it myself?

"Where you heading off to?"

My sister's voice breaks me from my silent freak out. I'd come into her and Ma's room to say goodnight in case she's asleep when I get back, but I ended up staring at the wall beside the TV, forgetting to breathe.

"Huh?" I ask.

"You've got your backpack on," she says. "Where you headed?"

She's got a hopeful look in her eyes, like she wishes I could take her with me. I wish that too. Maybe if Erica came along, Rowan would be on his best behavior, or he'd just taunt me mercilessly about bringing a chaperone to whatever training session he has planned.

"Just gonna meet a," I falter, "friend."

"A friend?" That hopefulness grows. "Like, a date?"

"No." I nearly choke. "Absolutely not. Just a dude from school who thinks I maybe have what it takes to get on the soccer team in time for next season. I'm going to work out with him."

A wide grin stretches across her pale face, and she reaches a hand out toward me. "Good. I'm glad. You used to live and breathe soccer. You never should've quit."

I take her hand, holding it with all the gentleness I would an injured bird, and I lean down to touch a kiss to the top of her head. "Love you."

It's five before seven when I get to the field beside the gym. Rowan is already here, stretching his hamstrings on the grass, alone this time. It's early enough in the evening there's still a bit of sunlight lingering in the dusk, and there are still a few students strolling past the field to and from the gym.

"You're late," is the first thing Rowan says when I drop my bag next to his, before he's even looked up at me.

"No, I'm not." I check my phone just in case, and it's still three before seven.

"On time is late. Fifteen minutes early is on time."

I laugh, thinking this one's got to be a joke, but he tilts his head back and treats me with a look that's serious as sin. "Alright then, should I leave?"

The corner of his mouth quirks up, like maybe it was a joke after all, or maybe he just gets off on confusing me. Nodding to my pack, he says, "Put your cleats on and meet me at the goal line."

I rummage through my pack and shove on my cleats while Rowan chides me from a few yards away for taking so long.

"Hurry up! You've got two and a half minutes to put them on, or else you're *late* late!"

I roll my eyes and shout back, "You're neurotic, dude!" But I pick up the pace anyway and jog over to him.

Tonight, he's in those same black shorts from when I decked him and a sleeveless tee that bares his arms to the chilly evening. I stare long enough to notice goosebumps under a dusting of black hair.

"You should take that off."

I blink and lift my eyes to connect with his. "What?"

"Your hoodie. You won't have time to take it off by the time you're desperate."

While I shuck off my sweater, I ask, "What are we doing?"

"Suicides."

"For real?" I chuckle, because only a psychopath would choose to run suicides.

"You're too big."

"S'cuse me?" My heart is racing, partly from how comically weird and cryptic Rowan is, but also because he's standing two feet from me, running his eyes all over me like I'm wearing new skin. I want to tell him nothing's changed since the last time he sized me up, but maybe I have changed and just don't realize it.

"You're too bulky." He meets my eyes, and I like this too. "All that muscle is gonna slow you down and make it harder to get out of a jam. From now on, less weights, more cardio. You should be training at sixty percent cardio every day."

"Beckham was bulky."

Rowan balks at that. "You want to be Beckham, baby boy? You've got to get on a fucking team first."

"Bro, why do you call me that?"

The way Rowan's brows lower a touch tells me I asked the wrong question, or maybe it's the *bro* part he doesn't like. "I'm gonna run, and you're gonna run along with me, like a baby glued to his daddy's side. When I go, you go, and you better get back at the same time I do, because I'm not gonna wait for you. We run until I feel like stopping."

"So, we're just going to run all night?" I'm exhausted just thinking about it, but I'm also shivering now, so a few sprints sounds alright.

"Not all night. Just for as long as I feel like it."

"Alright well, I can't be out too late."

Rowan licks his lips, a slight smirk still playing on them. "Why? Got a date with your girl?"

This dude must love getting punched. "You're messed up, man."

Still smirking, he gets on his mark and checks his watch. I get set, too, ready to prove I'm not some wuss afraid of a few suicides.

"On my go," Rowan says. "Don't lose me when we've only just begun."

I lose myself a little in the way he stares so intensely in front of us, like his enemy is standing at the opposite goal line, and Rowan is out for blood. I stare at the thick ridge down the side of his neck long enough that when Rowan says "go," I stumble on the jump.

Off to a miserable start, just like that.

The first sprint is cake. I get back to the goal line perfectly in sync with Rowan, and the time he gave us feels like more than enough to catch my breath. Long enough that I have to force myself not to spend the extra time staring at Rowan.

He doesn't look at me once, and he never says *"go"* again. He just goes, and I follow. Like his shadow, I'm right there with him, and I'm determined not to let him see me struggle. I even try chatting him up a bit between sprints, like that'll show how little I'm struggling.

"I broke up with her, you know," I tell him a dozen minutes in.

He doesn't say one word back. Doesn't acknowledge me at all. He goes, and I go, and when we get back, I say, "It's not the first time she's done something like that. I guess I'm sorta pathetic for sticking around so long."

Nothing.

He goes, and I go.

"Just letting you know the sorta girlfriend she is," I tell him. "In case you're trying to start something with her."

Nothing. Brick fucking wall.

He goes, and I go.

My lungs burn, but I keep my heaving to a minimum. "You're right about her head game being trash, though. Her pussy's nice."

Finally, I get a reaction out of Rowan, but it's only a single sidelong glance that makes me feel like a real jackass. *Her pussy's nice?* What the fuck does that even mean? I mean, it's not bad. Not gross or anything, and it felt good around my dick those times I was high or desperate. It's not Lese's fault I couldn't appreciate her enough.

He goes, and I go, but now I'm really pushing to get back at the same time he does.

"She's a good girl. I mean, if you're actually interested. She's a good person despite the cheating."

He goes, and I go, and my chest aches with how hard my heart beats.

"Maybe I shouldn't have ended things. It's hard to find a good person. Someone who puts up with you and your family."

He goes, and I go, and I'm two steps behind him to the goal line, breathing hard.

"Besides...monogamy is...old-fashioned anyway. Maybe I'm a...pussy for giving a shit."

He goes, and I go, and my lungs are on fire. I have to put my hands on my knees to keep from collapsing. My head is spinning, and whatever I want to say doesn't make it up my throat before Rowan goes again. He's a good six feet ahead of me the whole way, and my side is cramping. He's already on his mark when I'm still running, and he's glaring at me.

He goes, and I turn right back around.

Before I make it back, Rowan is already on his next sprint.

I stop, because the pain is too much. My knees drop, and I heave stinging breaths down at the grass.

"If you'd been on time, you could've stretched with me." Rowan's voice barely cuts through my rapid fire heartbeat, but the fact he's not ignoring me anymore makes a tiny bit of the humiliation subside.

When Rowan touches my hand, I'm too out of it to think much of it. He picks my hand up and hooks two fingers under my wrist, pressing them over the vein there. He studies his watch, tutting under his breath.

"You need to lose weight," he says.

"You know...it's not...cool anymore...to body shame." My words slur together like I'm drunk, and the sight of Rowan under the stadium lights looks like he's being rained on by golden stardust.

"Only thing your current workouts are good for is looking fuckable, but for soccer, you're out of shape, and you're never going to make the team unless you shed bulk."

Looking *what?* I guess that has been the point of the daily lifting sessions. Make Lese want me, even though I constantly disappointed her. Make girls around campus interested in me while I grow less and less interested in them. Now that I'm single, what's going to be my excuse when they ask for my number? That I'm gay? Just start blurting it out like it's the truth, even when I'm not sure that's what's really going on? I could be bi. I could meet a woman tomorrow who finally makes me passionate about women. God knows I'm not ready to walk into a gay bar and start picking up dudes. I don't know the first thing about fucking a dude, and I sure as hell don't want any dudes fucking me.

Dry humping sounds nice, though. Grinding my cock against another one and feeling a hard body against me, a deep voice in my ear, and a stubbled jaw tickling my face.

"Are you gonna puke?" Rowan asks, vacant of any genuine concern.

"Maybe." I stick my forehead to the grass and sway like the motion might soothe my mind, steady my stomach, and force my dick not to get hard.

Rowan walks off, and I roll onto my side, already accepting that he's probably leaving. Wouldn't blame him. I don't know what he saw last night that made him think I could play on the same field as him and the other starters. If this whole thing is just to give him a laugh, I sure walked right into it.

But, he comes back. He sets an unopened bottle of cherry Gatorade on the grass beside me and tells me to, "Drink up, babyface."

It hurts just to turn onto my ass. When my swollen hands can't get the bottle cap off, Rowan snatches it back and cracks it open with one quick twist. He pockets the cap and hands me the bottle.

"Thanks." I tip it back, glad it's not cold, for the sake of my throat.

"We've got a lot of work to do to get your endurance up to where it needs to be."

The exhaustion in Rowan's tone rubs me wrong. He's not my daddy or my coach. What business does he have being disappointed in my endurance?

I don't tilt the Gatorade bottle back down until half its contents are swimming down to my gut. "Who cares? I'll work out with you from time to time if you want, but I'm not making any team."

"When did you become such a loser?"

"The fuck?" I use what little strength I've regained to shoot him a glare.

Rowan squats down, making it easier for me to glower into his dark, heartless eyes. "Guy I used to know wouldn't have lied down for anything. Definitely didn't peg him for a quitter."

"You didn't know me. You never said more than four words to me." *Suck my dick, faggot,* to be specific.

"I knew you on the field. I remember playing against you in high school. Season before I graduated, you were a sophomore, right? You may have looked like a kid, but you didn't play like no kid. You were a pain in my ass every time we were on a field together. In a good way. In the way I wished you were on my team instead."

Am I high? Was there something in the grass I huffed up through my desperate heaving? "Really?" My voice cracks, and I bet my face looks as dumb as I feel. Never in my life did I think Rowan Hughes had wanted me for a teammate. If I'd grown up just a couple miles west from home, I would've been in Rowan's same school zone. Life didn't plot my path out that way. It gave me to Johnson High, and then it gave my sister cancer.

Rowan's expression hardens. "I'm not looking for a damn workout buddy. Either you want to play or you don't. Figure out what you want, and how bad you want it. If it's anywhere close to how bad I want it, meet me here tomorrow. Same time. And, for the love of God, put the weights down and start running."

"Okay."

I think that's the end of it, but Rowan lingers. Watching me drink his Gatorade until it's empty.

"Another thing..." he eventually says. "Anyone who fucks around behind your back isn't a good person. You were right to dump that girl, and I don't want jack shit to do with her."

4

Tommy

In fourth grade, I had a crush on a boy named Anthony. Only, I didn't know it had been a crush until I was twelve and Rowan called my entire identity into question. Way back in Miss Katanjian's class, I didn't know why I was so obsessed with the gangly, gap-toothed kid who sat across from me. Figured it was a mix of jealousy over his height, the structure of his face, and how popular he was with our classmates.

When Anthony invited me to the arcade after school one day, it felt like I'd already won something. I thought about him constantly. Never anything strange, just a deep desire to be next to him whenever I could. I loved the idea of him and me being two parts of one whole. We weren't 'I's' anymore, but 'we's.'

"We're hungry."

"We need to go to the bathroom."

"We didn't finish our assignment."

Best friends... That's what we were. It was all I wanted to be, forever.

I'd seen other best friends kiss each other on the cheek. Erica would kiss cheeks with her best friend, Sky. They'd even hold hands and sit on each other's laps sometimes. That's why I did what I did. Because I thought it was normal, and because the pull to do it was too strong to ignore.

We were at recess, playing Magic cards on the cafeteria steps, but we took a break because Anthony was upset over the other boys picking on him. Eventually, he'd stopped being as popular as he was before we became best friends. He spent all his time with me, and his other friends twisted that into something bad.

He looked so sullen, brown eyes glossy with the tears he tried not to shed. They filled me up with sympathy and longing to take that pain away, and to make Anthony see he didn't need those other kids. Even if it was only ever the two of us, I could be enough.

So I laid my hand on top of his the moment before I pressed my mouth to his smooth, salted cheek.

"Stop!" he immediately shouted. He tore his hand from under mine and shoved me so hard my back hit the stair. "What's wrong with you?! This is why no one likes you!"

Just like that, *we* were shattered. Anthony never spoke to me again, and that afternoon, the other boys from class jumped me on my way home. They tied me to a tree with their sweaters knotted together into a rope, and they threw rocks at me until I cried and a neighbor lady scared them away with a Mary Poppins umbrella.

When I told Ma what happened, she said cheek kisses are only for girls, and I needed to stop spending all my free time around Erica. She said I needed to spend time with boys and men to see how I'm supposed to act. The very next week, she took me to my first soccer practice.

I cried myself to sleep for weeks over Anthony and the throbbing pain in my chest.

Now, it feels like history repeating itself, except that I'm sexually mature now, and half the time I'm thinking about Rowan, I'm rock hard. It doesn't help that he seems intent on spending every single evening with me, getting me literally hot and bothered with all his workouts and patronizing name calling.

Two weeks pass like a shooting star across my eyes with Rowan's face engraved into its core. He times my mile and berates me for being slow. He makes me do drills I did as a kid, but insists I do them "his way." Wind sprints, more sit-ups and push-ups than I can remember, and we do so many burpees I puke up Ma's cooking behind a lamppost.

"I'm going to have to put you on a meal plan," Rowan says as he studies my barf like it's an archeological wonder.

"Are you a sadist?" I ask, hands still on my knees, drooling down my chin.

It's the first time I hear him really laugh, but by the time I lift my head enough to see his face, any smile he had is gone. He slaps my back and asks if I'm good.

"I'm good." I stand, wipe my face, and remind myself that no matter what Rowan puts me through, I'll always be taller than him.

"You look good." He takes me in the way he likes to. Slowly. Stoically. He didn't shave this morning. There's black stubble across his jaw. I wonder if it's long enough to scratch me if I rub my face against his. He's shirtless again, cut and slick with sweat, little russet nipples tightened up to pebbles. "Losing weight."

I roll my eyes, because that's easier than letting them linger on the dusting of dark hair below his navel. When I was younger, I hated body hair. I thought it was synonymous with being dirty, and I would've shaved my whole body if I was skilled enough with a razor. Now, I can't quit wondering how much hair Rowan has in places I can't see. Is it soft? Does it smell as good as the buzzed hair on his head?

Thank God I wore tight boxer briefs, because as my mind wanders, so does my dick.

"Rowan!"

I look over my shoulder where two girls I don't recognize are walking down the cement path. The one waving has her hair in a ponytail with a pink headband.

My head whips back to Rowan quick enough to see a slightly crooked grin stretch across his face. An imperfection that only proves how perfect he is.

"Yo!" he hollers back before starting a jog across the field.

Not knowing what to do, I follow him. He's always telling me to follow him, *like he's my daddy*. Talk about wet dream fuel. So, I walk, staying a few steps back in case he doesn't want me in his business.

The way he hugs the girl stirs insecurity in with my infatuation. Just one arm before using the other to dap fists with the girl's friend. But Rowan doesn't strike me as a guy who gives away hugs willy-nilly, no matter how many arms he's using.

"Ugh, God!" the girl with the headband laughs, shoving Rowan back a step. "You smell like man sweat!"

It's true. He's glistening with sweat from the nape of his neck to the small of his back, but where this girl pushes him away, all I want to do it glide my hand up his slick spine and kiss him someplace I know I shouldn't.

Rowan laughs and calls headband-girl Thalia. They chat like they know each other, but there's more to it too. They seem friendly. She mentions a party, and it reminds me of the photo evidence of Lese throwing herself at Rowan. He said he doesn't want jack shit to do with Lese, but he still hooked up with her. Was it just because she's cute? He's into cute women with long hair and small waists? This girl, Thalia, fits that bill.

Are they dating?

That hollowness inside me Rowan has been filling with training sessions opens up again.

"Hey," the girl beside Thalia says to me. It's the first time she's spoken, and she sends me a little smile to go with the greeting.

"'Sup?"

That gets Rowan's attention enough for him to remember I exist. He introduces me to Thalia and her friend, Eve.

"What are you two doing?" Thalia asks Rowan. "Working out?"

"Trying to get him in shape," Rowan answers.

My face heats. Doesn't help that Eve's eyeing me like I'm a hot fudge sundae. Unlike Rowan's stare, Eve wears her intentions on her sleeve, nearly chomping at the bit.

"He looks in pretty good shape to me," Eve purrs.

"You should see the gruel he just barfed up."

"Well, they don't call 'em burpees for no reason," I say, sending Eve a wink that makes her suntanned face go pink. I know how to flirt with girls. Just never like doing it. I did it for Lese, because I cared about her for real for a long time, and I knew how badly she wanted to be with me.

For a split second, I'm thinking about Lese and Anthony at the same time. But when Rowan's incomprehensible stare is on me again, all I'm thinking about is him.

"Wait," Thalia says with a snap of her fingers in my direction. "Tommy? This is the guy who gave you the black eye?"

"It was nothing," Rowan mutters.

Shit... If Rowan is dating Thalia, does she know about him hooking up with Lese? This would be the perfect opportunity for revenge, but I'm not that spiteful. I'm not spiteful at all, really. Just jealous.

"It was a misunderstanding," I say. "We're cool now. He even has cute little nicknames for me. Calls me babyface."

"Oh, fuck!" Eve swoons. "You totally do have a baby face!"

I frown while Rowan quirks one of those sneaky smirks that's gone in a flash.

Eve asks if I have Instagram, and I feel too put on the spot to lie. I let her add me, but my profile is public, anyway. Not much to hide except the shit that stays in my head behind an airtight seal.

"I'll see you around." Rowan gives Thalia another one-armer before turning around and heading back to where we left our bags in the grass.

Following close, I channel all my uncomfy feelings into a question that comes out awkward as hell. "That your girlfriend?"

The look Rowan pays me shrinks me down to pea-sized. Wish I could learn to just shut my mouth. Surprisingly, he actually answers.

"No. Connor Whitlock's girlfriend. We went to high school together."

"Oh." The relief I feel is tantamount to euphoria. "Do you, uh, have a girlfriend?"

The more I talk, the more I hate myself. Rowan crouches at his bag and pulls out a flipbook and pen. "No girlfriend, babyface. Here." He hands over the notebook and pen. "Write down everything you've eaten the past seven days. Every Dorito, every jelly bean, every fingernail. Got it?"

No girlfriend? Got it. I grin as I toss the notepad and pen back onto his bag. "I'm not dieting. I drink the protein shakes, and I eat my veggies. No Doritos. Sometimes jelly beans, but only the Trolli ones. They call 'em Sour Brite Eggs. You ever try 'em?"

"Can't say I have."

"Dude, you're missing out."

"I doubt that." He finds a shirt in his bag next and pulls it on before standing. "You remember McKinley Park?"

"The park where I punched you in the face?"

Rowan exhales a short chuckle, like it's all water under the bridge. "We're doing another pickup match tomorrow. Meet there instead of here. Same time."

"Okay."

He must see my anxiety, because he says, "Don't worry. Half the guys there are chumps. You'll be fine. Just...don't be one of the chumps."

"Don't be a chump," I mutter. "I'll try to remember that."

Rowan smirks and says, "Good boy." It goes straight to my dick.

"We should exchange numbers, yeah?"

"We should?"

"In case I'm late tomorrow, or—"

"Don't be late."

"Or in case I get sick, and I can't show up one of these nights."

"Don't be sick."

I toss my head back and laugh. "Do you, like, not have a phone or something?"

His brows wrinkle, staring at something in the middle of my body. One of the many sweat stains on my shirt? Before I can figure out what it is, Rowan dives back into his bag, this time taking out his phone. He gives it up, unlocked and vulnerable.

The home screen is a landscape shot, a beach at dusk. Spotify app, Kindle, Wordscapes, a guided yoga app. Nothing exciting. I tap on the phone icon, program my number, and send a text to myself so I can save his number later. I send the first emoji in Rowan's recents. The fingers-crossed one. Feels fitting.

"I'm going to talk to Coach McDonough about you," Rowan says, standing now and slipping his phone from my hand. "Try to get you on the team in time for summer training. Just have to find the right time. McDonough is a fucking meathead."

"Well, even if it doesn't work out—"

"Don't be a quitter."

I'm in awe of how stern Rowan looks when he's actually being nice to me. "Let's see. Don't be a chump, don't be late, don't be sick, and don't be a quitter. The Rowan Hughes guide to success."

He smiles. "Exactly."

5

Rowan

Giving Tommy my number makes me anxious. Makes me even more anxious that I've got his number. I'm still not one-hundred on why I'm trying to get this beefcake on my team. We're stacked. A few weak points here and there, but nothing Tommy can obviously fill. He was a thorn in my side during some pretty big matches back in high school, but he's rusty as hell and his endurance is shit.

The pickup match at McKinley proves Tommy still has skill, though, and he puts his broad chest and thick arms to good use from time to time. Nearly trips me on my ass a couple times, pushing that hard body against me when it's the difference between winning and losing.

At one point, he gets his foot between mine at just the right time and pops the ball right out of my command. If he were anyone else, I'd cuss him out, but the adrenaline coursing through me just wants to go again. I could spar with Tommy all night, maybe let him win a time or two just to keep his spirits up. The way he lights up when Levi kicks a go-ahead goal has me feeling like a proud papa.

Zeke throws the ball out, then Connor bats it down with a chest shot and passes to some doorknob named Bartlett who kicks the ball foul. Raisel takes possession, aiming the ball over his head and eyeing my availability.

My boy Tommy has the right idea to put that body in front of me. The way his ass bumps against my hip makes me snicker. If I wasn't positive he's straight, I'd think he's trying to rile me up. Maybe he's still trying to rile me up. Wouldn't be the first time a straight guy baited me, but I learned a long time ago never to fall into the trap, no matter how convincing.

"Don't lose me, baby boy," I tell him close to his ear before I swerve out from behind him. A hip check disorients Tommy long enough for Raisel to toss me the ball and head knock it to a kid named Gimenez.

We win by one, but by the looks of the field after time winds down, Tommy's the winner. He's quickly passing Levi, Raisel and Connor's sniff test, at least. They're seeing what I see. They're living what I remember from high school, during those matches where Tommy made it his singular mission to keep me and the ball as far apart as possible. He rarely succeeded, but damn, he made me sweat for it.

"Yo, Tommy." I drop my shin guards on my bag and join the guys in their little bro huddle.

The way my voice draws his attention immediately is an ego boost. Whenever those blue eyes fix on me, it's like I've got him. In what way, I'm not sure, but there's ambition in those eyes. He knows I'm helping him, even when he's fussy. He rakes his honey waves off his wet forehead, greasing the strands to make them damp too.

"You looked good." I hold out my fist and he taps it with his.

"Yeah? You still kicked my ass." The smirk on his plump lips is enough to make my cock twitch, but it's the tenor of Tommy's voice that has the power to drive me completely mad. Deep. Like he's a grown ass man and not just a green, baby-faced twenty-year-old. There's power in a voice so tantalizingly deceptive.

What else about Tommy is deceptive?

His compliments are too close to teasing for my comfort. I never know if he's seriously cool with me or if he's just wanting what I'm offering. The self-deprecation has to be a show. No way a guy like Tommy Mathison is insecure about anything. Even when he's on hands and knees, puking up Mommy's supper, he's stunning.

Not since he marched onto this very field last month, out for blood as it turned out, have I been able to stop thinking about him. This isn't the first time I've been infatuated with a guy. Happens way more often than I'll ever admit, but when I spend hours of every day around fit dudes in shorts, there's no way it won't seep into my fantasies.

That's all it ever is, though. Fantasies. Quick glances at body parts that I commit to memory and replay at night when I can take care of myself secretly and not do something reckless. Something like put my dick where I shouldn't.

I want Tommy on the team because he deserves to be on the team, and it's bullshit he ever quit. I also want him on the team because I want him on *my* team. Finally.

But not yet. He's got to earn it first.

"We gonna be seeing more of you?" Connor asks Tommy, patting his shoulder like they're pals now.

Tommy only shrugs—that fake bashful shit—so I interject. "We're going to get him on the team. Retire your ass."

Connor laughs and scrubs his palm across my scalp the way a brother might. It makes me feel weird. A bad weird, but I shrug it off and tell everyone to take it easy before I dip.

Half way to my car, I hear Tommy's deep voice behind me asking me to hold up. I don't turn around, but I slow down and send him a glance over my shoulder so he knows daddy's listening.

"You think it's a good idea telling the guys I'm trying to get onto the team?" he asks, more bashful now than I've ever heard him.

Maybe it's not all bullshit. Maybe my boy really is insecure about something. Might be better that way. Insecurities make people defensive, and if Tommy is going to be on my team, I need him defensive.

"They're gonna find out soon anyway," I tell him, "when you start coming around to team practices."

"You think I'm ready for that?"

"No. You will be, though. Once you—"

"Lose weight. I know," he chuckles. It's hollow though, like all my talk about his body gave him something else to be insecure about. That one's no good. Last thing I want is Tommy feeling down about how he looks.

We get to my car, just an old Subaru Legacy I found on Facebook Marketplace once I saved up the cash, and I turn around to face my new project. "I was gonna say, once you want it bad enough."

He frowns, a little wrinkle forming between his brows. "I do want it."

"You need to want it bad enough you'll bulldoze over anyone to get it, because if you're on that field, it means someone else isn't."

Thankfully, Tommy shrugs a shoulder. "That's the game, right?"

"Right."

That should be the end of things, but Tommy lingers, shifting on his feet like a nervous teenager. "Can I ask you something? It's not a trap."

I can't help but chuckle, since Tommy is very much a trap, even if he doesn't know it. Especially if he doesn't know it. "What's on your mind?"

"What, uh—What exactly did you do with Lese?"

"Lese?"

"Annalese. My girl—My *ex*-girlfriend."

My lungs deflate, and my mind curses this boy for reminding me about that night yet again. "You want to punch me again?"

"Told you. It's not a trap."

Oh, but it is, because I can't exactly tell him the truth. That I couldn't keep it up inside a woman's mouth because all I want is a man's. But I also can't tell him what everyone thinks I did with his ex, in case he changes his mind and punches me again.

"Why does it matter?" I ask, wishing I wasn't so agitated.

"I guess it doesn't."

"I don't have any STIs, if that's what you're worried about."

He shakes his head, but it's dripping with as much disappointment as sweat.

It kills me. The bashfulness, the insecurities, the disappointment. This dude has everything, and he doesn't even know it. He's got a mom who cooks dinner for him every night, for fuck's sake. He shouldn't have one negative emotion in that perfect body.

"Look, dude," I start, catching his eyes and holding onto them, because this is the last time I'm ever going to talk about that night again. "I was sorta drunk and kinda out of it. She went down on me for like two minutes, but I wasn't feeling it, so I dipped. Didn't even nut. That's it. That's the truth."

"You weren't feeling it?"

"I was drunk." Not that drunk, though. Three beers alone in a room with Tommy, and I'd never go soft. "And she's not my type."

He nods, almost like he gets it. The softness of his eyes negates that deep, haunting voice that asks me the most dangerous question of all. "What's your type?"

I smirk and say the first thing that pops into my mind. "I like blonds." Then, I cut and run before Tommy can lay more bait in the trap.

Later, while I'm beating off in bed to a video of two beefed up jocks sucking each other off, my orgasm is delayed by a text notification from a name that has my balls tightening. I thought the straight boy had an early bedtime, but it's nearly eleven and he's texting me a fucking YouTube link. Since chances are slim to none Tommy is texting me gay porn hotter than the shit I've already got going, I swipe his notification away and work my cock until I'm spent all over my stomach.

I clean up, tuck myself under my comforter, and open Tommy's text with a clear head.

Tommy

> Found this searching through my sister's fb

I tap on a link attached to the text, and it brings me to a video posted four years ago. A playoff match between McClatchy and Johnson. The tickle in my chest makes me chuckle as I watch Tommy come into a match I remember winning in overtime. There's my boy, on my ass like I jacked his wallet. Back then, though, he really was just a boy. Sixteen, probably. I remember thinking he was like a six-two chihuahua, nipping at my ankles and never giving me a moment's peace.

Tommy

> Cute right? Maybe I wasn't half bad back then

I watch the entire video. All eight minutes until I'm sleepy enough to blacken my screen and roll over to sleep. But as I bask in the silent darkness of my room, my mind wanders before I even get to dreamland. Thinking about soccer, thinking about workouts, thinking about summer try-outs, and thinking about Tommy.

Thinking about earlier tonight and how Tommy's style hasn't changed much since we were teenagers. He was still on me like a hungry cheetah, ass grinding against my hip, locking me in, fucking owning me for all of those seconds before I showed him how easy it is for me to slip from his hold.

"Fuck," I sigh into my pillow as my dick tries to get hard again.

Why do I have to like straight dudes so much? Why can't I be into those flashy twinks always making eyes at me at Mustache Jack? Why can't I be into those goober daddies always hitting me up on Grindr? Sure, they would be fun in the moment, and it would be a nice change of pace to come into something other than my hand, but they don't live in my head the way guys like Tommy do. The way Tommy does.

I bury my hand back inside my boxers and fist my cock, wet with residual cum I already spent. Takes only a few minutes to get close, my balls as tight as my pelvic muscles.

In this vulnerable state, I'm possessed to do something risky. I dig my phone out from under my pillow and text Tommy back with my free hand.

Me

> Very cute. Now go to sleep baby boy

My impulsivity pushes me over the edge. I wet my comforter with what all my cock spurts out, but I'm too dazed to care. I roll onto my side, tuck my phone back beneath my pillow, and pass out before any reply comes in.

6

Rowan

With finals coming up, I'm working double my usual hours at the tutoring center. My boss likes to pass me all the student athletes. He thinks I have some innate ability to meet them on their level. I don't mind it. The fact I've tutored a fourth of Sac State's varsity athletes only bolsters my persona on campus. Not only am I needed to win matches, but I'm single-handedly keeping a handful of the school's biggest star athletes from falling under the minimum GPA threshold.

All these extra hours mean rescheduling a few of mine and Tommy's training sessions. He just loves that.

Tommy

> Too busy to train? Sounds like a quitter's spirit to me

I reschedule on him again tonight, but I send him a workout set list I want him to get through at the gym without me. All cardio and balance. I considered adding time on the rowing machine to the list, but I'm not sure he knows the equipment, and using a machine improperly is worse than not working out at all.

Me

> Meet 6am tomorrow at McKinley

I'm heading into a tutoring session with a varsity volleyballer when Tommy answers.

Tommy

> 6am?? On a Saturday?? Your nuts

Using the wrong "you're" makes me chuckle. Also makes me think he might not be doing awesome in his writing intensive classes. If he's going to be on my team come August, he'll need to keep up with the sports department's rules for academic success.

Me

> Don't pout

I have to force myself not to add "baby boy" to the end. It's so easy to tease Tommy when he never challenges me. The next time he tells me to stop, I will, but he hasn't. He asked me why once, and it made me so defensive and flustered that I doubled down harder than I should've. Still, Tommy took it without question.

Tommy

> Not pouting. Looking forward to it. Your still nuts

Is it a bad sign that I'm blushing? The volleyballer notices, because he tips his chin at me and asks if I'm texting my girlfriend. Why does everyone assume I should have a girlfriend? Even if I was born with the inclination to desire a girlfriend, I've got way too much shit on my plate to worry about getting into a relationship. People on the internet love to wax on about how relationships take work. Well, I don't need more work, unless it's the kind that puts food in my mouth and gas in my car.

"I don't have a girlfriend."

"Boyfriend?"

I look up from my phone, halfway through a text instructing Tommy to time his mile speed on the treadmill. The way this freakishly tall blondie is smirking at me makes me want to give him the old Tommy "Tyson" Mathison treatment. With folded arms, he's lounged back in the desk chair like this is his mommy's house and not a private study room.

"You wish," I tell him in a hard tone that hopefully conveys how he should mind his fucking business.

Oscar is the dude's name, and he's got a slight Scandinavian accent to go along with the inflection in his vocal cadence that makes me think he's *gay* gay. The sort of gay who owns it as part of his identity and not just a porn preference.

"Actually," he says, drinking me up with crystalline eyes like he's trying to picture me naked, "I'd much prefer you to be single, but I'm not picky."

"Nothing against you, man, but I don't swing your way."

Oscar's smirk widens as he pushes himself forward, elbows on the table to lean closer to me. "I've seen you before. At Moustache Jack."

Shit. I knew going there was a bad call, but I figured it's far enough from campus it'd be reasonably safe. It's not like I do anything there besides sip sissy cocktails and people-watch until my anxiety reaches max capacity. I've semi-flirted with a few older guys who flirted with me first, but no one I'd actually be interested in has ever approached me. Had Oscar approached me, I'm not so sure how I'd feel. He's *gay* gay, a little too tall, a little too blond, and a little too smug. But he's cute, muscular, and my age.

"That wasn't me," I lie, because my current anxiety dictates it.

Oscar's tongue runs along the seam of his mouth, adding shivers to the churning feeling in my gut. "Maybe not. But if it was you, it wouldn't be a big deal. A lot of people are gay now."

"Good for them."

Finally meeting my stalemate, Oscar pulls his gaze from mine and pushes Krakauer's *Where Men Win Glory* across the table toward me. "My English Comprehension paper on this book is due tomorrow. Heads up, I never even started reading it."

Just like that, my shivers turn to annoyance, but at least I've read this book before.

"Get me an A, and I'll buy you a drink sometime," Oscar says as he scribbles ten numbers onto the top of his tutoring slip. A phone number. He pushes the slip toward me, and it takes everything inside me not to get up and leave.

Dawn at McKinley Park, the sky is a gray-blue, and the air is hazy with a thin layer of late spring fog. It's cool enough for long sleeves, but I tell Tommy to take his hoodie off after we finish stretching.

"Suicides again?" he asks, his face doing that puppy dog thing where his eyes get round under a furrowed brow. His hands are on his hips like he's already exhausted. It's kind of adorable. That thin veil of indignation before he submits to whatever tickles my fancy.

"Nah, we're just gonna run," I say. "Cross-country style. We'll run the perimeter of the park until eight."

"Two hours?"

"Stay at my pace. Don't fall behind. Whatever you do, don't stop. I don't want to see your ass on the ground before eight o'clock unless you need an ambulance. Got it?"

His head shakes, worry drawn all over his face, but he soon says, "Okay. Let's do it." The acceptance alone makes my balls tingle, but I can't let Tommy's readiness blow my head up too big. I didn't become the captain by being a hard-ass. That's more McDonough's style.

"Don't worry." I slap my palm behind Tommy's back, and it makes a deep, blunt sound. "You got this. Just, don't—"

"Don't lose you." Tommy smiles. "I'll try."

It's unclear whether the goosebumps covering my arms and legs are from Tommy or the chill in the air, but either way, it's nothing a long run can't right. I program my watch to chart our mileage before giving a three-two-one count off.

For Tommy's sake, I keep the pace moderate. A little quicker than a jog. Tommy sticks by my side, even when the sidewalk goes narrow. Every time his bicep grazes mine, I feel the heat from his skin like touching a hot stove. I want to wince away, but it's too intoxicating. I keep forgetting to check my watch.

When I catch him slipping, I throw out some encouragement. "Stay with me."

"Trying," he grits.

Next time his arm brushes mine, he's damp and red-hot. I look sideways and catch his face sweating bullets. His t-shirt is damn near soaked.

"Push," I say. "Half hour to go."

Saying the time may be what does Tommy in. He huffs a sigh that comes out a whimper that sounds a hell of a lot like defeat.

"Push, Tommy."

"I'm gonna die," he whines.

"You're not gonna die."

I shift my gaze between the path ahead and the boy beside me. He does try, I'll give him that, but he's unstable now. Staggering, wheezing. He veers off the sidewalk, cursing under his breath, and falls to his knees in the dewy grass.

"Don't call an ambulance!" he says, crawling a few strides before rolling over onto his back. "Just got a cramp."

My own body burns with fatigue, but Tommy looks wretched. I slow up and jog in place while I look him over, trying to ease my heart rate down slowly.

"Where are you cramping?"

"My leg," he groans. Lifting himself up on an elbow, he rubs at his right quad.

"Let me see." I put my own knees to the grass and straddle his right leg. As soon as Tommy's hand leaves his thigh, I put my own hands there.

"Fuck," Tommy hisses when I put pressure on the muscle group.

I feel their stiffness. Hardly any fat between them and Tommy's heated skin. I knead his leg from the top of the knee to the upper part of his thigh, pushing his shorts up a few inches as I go. Enough I can tell his underwear is light gray. The brown hair on Tommy's thigh is so light it's nearly blond. The skin above the tan line is white as cream. I press my fingers in and feel how supple and strong he is.

Another groan fills the calm air between us, but it doesn't sound so pained anymore. Somewhat strained, but there's a contentment in Tommy's tone now. Nearly pleasureful.

He groans again when I glide my fingers higher, barely beneath the bunched leg of his shorts.

"Rowan." My name from Tommy's deep voice entrances me. I lose myself in it, and in the feel of him below me.

"That feel good, baby boy?" I murmur, inching my hand higher.

"Rowan." Tommy's hand lands on mine, squeezing it hard enough to ache.

I blink, staring at our joined hands until it finally registers in my head what I was doing—what I was about to do.

While one hand stays on Tommy's firm quad, the other hand snuck so far beneath Tommy's shorts, my fingertips were only an inch from his prominent bulge. My gaze falls to it, examining Tommy's dick print in complete awe. Heart racing and my own cock swelling, I watch Tommy's bulge long enough to notice how thick and long it is, pushing against his shorts to make them tent.

In a flash, Tommy pushes me back and climbs to his feet.

Still dazed, I watch as he digs his hand under his waistband to adjust his placement before tugging his shirt down over his crotch.

"Sorry," he grumbles. "Just really have to piss."

Before I can say one word, Tommy marches off toward the park bathrooms. Part of me wants to follow him. Part of me wants to dig a deep hole and die in it.

What the fuck is wrong with me?

Crushing on straight guys is one thing. Trying to massage their cocks is another.

I trek back to where we left our bags and spend this time reconsidering my whole life. If I wasn't so sexually repressed, maybe this wouldn't have happened. Maybe if, just once, I loosened up enough to do the things I fantasize about, I wouldn't be this reckless.

Just because I have sex with a guy doesn't mean I have to suddenly be *gay* gay, right? I can still be me. I wouldn't even have to tell anyone. It could be something for me and the other guy to take to our graves.

One guy. That's all I need.

Not Oscar, though. He goes to my school, probably knows some people I know. A rando would do. Someone from the bar or off Grindr.

"Hey."

I flinch at Tommy's voice above me while I'm stooped beside my bag, catching my breath before I completely panic. I stand up and give Tommy a once over, seeing a portrait of discomfort.

Eyes not meeting mine, Tommy says, "I'm sorry about that, man. Since breaking up with Lese, I've been kinda pent up, and—"

"I get it," I interrupt, if only so I don't have to hear about how much Tommy misses his cheating ex. "It's normal. Don't sweat it."

He nods, and we fall into an awkward silence while he scoops up his backpack and slings his hoodie over his shoulder. "I'll, uh, see you."

"Yeah."

He walks away again, and I can't follow him. What would I even do if I could?

I get home just after eight. Park the car at the curb and use my key on the wrought iron gate across the driveway. I'm halfway to the garage side-door when the backdoor of the house opens up, and Matt steps out onto the stoop in pajamas and flip-flops.

"Went for a run?" he asks after we exchange good mornings.

"Yeah." I fiddle with my keys between my fingers, not in the mood to make fun of Matt for his lame Mickey Mouse pants.

"Xiamara is about to fix breakfast. Take a shower, then come on in."

"I've got finals shit to work on."

He shrugs. "You've got all day. C'mon, Rowan. Family time."

Family time. Always sounds nice on the surface, never feels quite right in practice, but homemade breakfast sounds great nonetheless.

First things first, I head into the garage, strip naked in the backroom that's been my bedroom for nearly four years, then slip into the three-quarter bathroom for a shower.

My phone buzzes on the pedestal sink just before I step into the narrow shower stall.

Tommy

> One day we'll laugh about how you ran my ass so hard I popped a boner

I want to smile, but it's hard when I know Tommy knows that boner had nothing to do with running and everything to do with my traitorous hands. He's saving face on my behalf, and I don't know why. The only person who should have apologized is me.

But I can't.

Before I figure out what to say, Tommy double-texts.

Tommy

> Messaged that girl Eve. That should help the problem lol

I swallow, and my saliva sinks like a stone into the pit of my gut. It almost hurts too much for me to consider jerking off, but only almost.

7

Tommy

I don't hear from Rowan the rest of the weekend, and by Monday, I'm panicking that he's through with me completely, and that would fucking suck for multiple reasons. For one, try-outs for the soccer team are this coming Saturday, and it would feel strange trying out without Rowan in my corner.

Just when I thought the Tommy and Rowan duo was fit to take off, my dick went and outed me three feet from his face. In the middle of a public park, no less. Thank fuck it was early enough in the morning that there wasn't anyone else close by.

After dropping Mav off at school, I drive to campus for my first final of the day. Statistics. Takes nearly the entire three-hour class period for me to finish, and by then I'm famished. After lunch, I wait in line outside my English class to drop off my paper. While I'm waiting, my phone vibrates, and Rowan's name across the screen has my body temp rising and my heart beating funny.

Rowan

> Come to the gym. Room B. 12:30

The time in the top left corner of my phone reads 12:13, but there's still a few people ahead of me in line.

Don't be late.

But the dude gives me 17 minutes' notice. That's messed up. Not as messed up as my nerves, though, wanting to get there as soon as possible.

What if it's a trap? What if Rowan rounded up the other guys from the team, the guys still on the fence about me, and told them all I'm a fag? What if they're waiting for me in Room B, ready to jump me like it's elementary school all over again?

Man up, Tommy. You're six-two and two-hundred pounds.

After I hand my paper to Mr. Pratt, I jog across campus and get to Room B of the student gym at three past 12:30.

And...it's the opposite of what I thought I'd be walking into.

A curvy, bleach blonde woman stands barefoot at the head of a class of equally barefooted students, all standing with their toes at the front edge of their respective yoga mats. The woman sends me a pointed look when I accidentally push the door shut so hard it echoes through the quiet room. No one says a word, but some sets of eyes land on me while I scan the room.

I lock eyes with Rowan. My tummy flutters like something's tickling it from the inside, and I sidle down a narrow path between yoga mats toward the empty one laid out between Rowan's and a mirrored wall.

"You're late," Rowan mouths. No sound passes between his lips, but my mind processes the words in his voice. His eyes flicker to my feet, and he mouths, "Shoes."

I tug off my Vans and socks and shove them against the mirror along with my backpack. I scoot my feet to the top of my mat, and when the blonde instructor gently commands us all to raise our arms above our heads as high as we can reach, I do that too.

Seems odd now that I've never done yoga before. It always sounded like a chick thing. Actually, everyone in this class is a woman, aside from Rowan and me. Between poses, my head keeps straying sideways, drawn to Rowan's profile like there's a magnetic field between us. Something doesn't jive between my memory of him snarling a slur at me and him taking a majority-female yoga class on a Monday afternoon.

Is this what being secure in one's identity looks like?

The poses start off easy-peasy, like the shit Mav does during P.E. But, while the poses are simple, it's holding them that starts my adrenaline going. Lunging deep, flexing my muscles and holding steady for minutes at a time. Reaching up to the heavens, breathing deeply from my core. Stretching my legs farther than I thought they could go and leaning into it, reveling in the burn. It's relaxing and strenuous all at once, and I'm sweating bullets in the air-conditioned room.

We end on the floor in what the instructor calls *savasana,* which is a fancy way of saying "lay on the floor and chill." It's more special than that, though. I lay there so long my limbs feel like jelly and my mind feels like I took an edible. Legs parted, arms out, the backs of my hands rested on the sleek wood floor.

I look at my left hand and notice Rowan's hand lying limp an inch away. If I only had the courage to stretch my finger out, I'd be touching him right now instead of just thinking about touching him. I want to *savasana* on top of him. I'll breathe deep for him, and he'll breathe deep for me. Maybe we'll meld together and become one. Tommy and Rowan.

That magnetic field tugs on my eyes again, lifting my chin to find Rowan staring back at me, expression unreadable. It quickens my breath.

His dark eyes flit down my body. A black brow quirks, and his mouth screws into a funny smirk.

I look down, and the enchantment shatters. I jolt upward, bring my legs into a pretzel and lay my forearms over my lap before anyone notices I'm hard as a rock. Why did I have to wear boxers and basketball shorts today?

A second later, the instructor brings everyone out of *savasana*. As they all stand up and roll up their mats, I'm stunned rigid, forcing my mind onto anything that might quell my raging boner. My life is a pretty good start. Erica's chemo side effects and how she's getting sicker every day. Mav having to watch his mother deteriorate. Ma constantly on edge and expecting me to pick up all the slack.

"Here."

Rowan's voice takes me out of my melancholic detour, and I look up. He's standing beside me, holding a sweatshirt down to me.

"Thanks." I ball it up and press it onto my lap, which covers me up enough that I can stand. My reflection in the wall-to-wall mirror does wonders softening me up.

Rowan rolls up my mat for me. Takes both to the door across the room. A closet, I guess. I put my shoes on, grab my backpack and follow Rowan out of Room B. It opens up to the second floor of the gym. To the left is the weight training wing, and to the right is the indoor track.

"Things didn't go well with Eve, then?" Rowan asks, heading for the stairs.

"What?" I follow alongside him, noticing he hardly broke a sweat. He must do yoga often. Could be why his body is so lithe and taut. "Oh. We were going to get together last night, but with finals this week, it didn't work out. We put a pin in it."

It's not a total lie. I never planned on messaging Eve, but I got paranoid Rowan would somehow find out I fibbed about messaging her, so I messaged her to keep my story straight. I was the one who blamed finals for not being able to get together last night. We did put a pin in it, but it's a pin I hope to keep firmly inserted.

Rowan smirks. "Ah, so you're still aching."

I chuckle, because at least Rowan seems to buy my lame ass excuses. "It is what it is. My dick still thinks I'm a teenager, I guess. That instructor in there was pretty hot too."

Is she hot, though? I don't even know, but she looked like the sort of woman that a guy like me would find hot, if I weren't so fucking gay. She's the sort of woman Lese would act huffy over and half-jokingly tell me not to talk to. Lese's jealousy was always a good indicator of whether I was supposed to find a woman hot or not.

Rowan stops on the landing between the first and second floor and nods back up to the second. "You want me to grab her number for you? Maybe you could do a three-way with her and Eve. That should take care of the problem, right?"

Halfway through laughing my ass off, I realize Rowan looks as serious as I've ever seen him. My laughter turns to an awkward chuckle, then a meek sigh. "Yeah, maybe. You've, uh, done a three-way before?"

Rowan doesn't answer. Just folds his lips and carries on down the stairway. "Your finals going okay?"

"So far, I think. I had a Statistics exam this morning. Just hoping for the best on that one."

"You're not a math guy?"

"No," I snort. "I'm, uh... I don't really know what kind of guy I am."

Rowan smiles like I'm a tad bit mad. "You're an athlete. Aren't you?"

"Ask me again next week."

"You're going to make the team, Tommy."

I sigh, trying not to swoon. The way my name sounds on Rowan's tongue gives a whole new connotation to the syllables. Still, nothing beats *that feel good, baby boy?*

Why did he say that?

I've gone back and forth on it. The conspiratorial side of me wonders if Rowan wanted to rile me up, like trying to get me on the team is just a backdrop for a long-play to prove once and for all I'm a homo. What better proof than making sure I'm hard every time Rowan enters a room? Rowan wouldn't do that, though. He called me a faggot once, but that was a long time ago. I said some dumb shit when I was a kid too.

"You need to study tonight?"

I hand him back his sweatshirt when we get to the main doors. "You got an alternative?"

That smirk comes back to Rowan's face, the sort that says he's got an idea, and it just might make me puke my guts out.

"Drink this." Rowan hands me a plastic flask out of his gym bag like it's the most casual thing in the world to get toasted in the middle of Douglas Field with a women's rugby practice going on behind us.

"Uh...what is it?" I take it because it's Rowan giving it to me, but I'm hesitant to unscrew it. I'm not big on liquor, and I hadn't pegged Rowan for a booze hound either.

In front of me is an intimidating tower of concrete steps and aluminum bleachers. Rowan's ass is on the lowest bench, tying his New Balances as he says, "Just drink."

Usually, I'm pretty good at dodging peer pressure, but this is Rowan we're talking about. If he ever jumps off a cliff, I'll find it just so I can jump after him. Maybe that should embarrass me. It does embarrass me, but it's still true.

I unscrew the cap and toss back a swig. The tang and salt hits my tongue like a bolt of electricity. I come out of it coughing.

"The hell? Is this pickle juice?"

Rowan's expression is downright maniacal. "It'll help with the cramps."

"You're fucking with me," I laugh, handing him back the flask.

"Swear to God. Pro athletes drink it. Tyler Glasnow drinks it."

I consider Rowan's argument with a low hum and a peek down the barrel of the flask. Fuck it. If a major league pitcher vouches for pickle juice, I'm sold. I throw back another swallow, and whether or not pickle juice really staves off cramps, it's at least helping to keep my dick soft as Rowan sheds his muscle shirt in front of me.

"How long are we running for this time?" I ask, tossing the flask onto Rowan's bag.

Hopping to his feet, he says, "This time, we're gonna race."

"Race?"

He nods toward the top of the bleachers, high enough I have to crane my neck to see the summit. "First to touch the railing wins."

"Let's do it." To even the playing field, I pull off my shirt and drop it onto my backpack. The slight breeze in the early evening air tightens my nipples. I look down at Rowan's chest and see his little nips hard as beads. "What do I get if I win?"

He tips his chin. "What do you want?"

"Buy me dinner." God, I hope that didn't sound as gay as I think it did.

"Didn't you just eat at Mommy's?"

"What can I say? I'm a growing boy."

"So I've seen."

I laugh to mask my embarrassment. Before I can pop another woody, I tell Rowan to get set and begrudge that he has to leave my side in favor of the next aisle over.

"On one," he calls back to me as soon as he's on his mark. "Three. Two. One."

We bolt. I keep my eyes on the steps in front of me, focus on my breathing, and I dig the fuck out of the concrete.

At the top, I snatch the railing like a lifeline, my chest buzzing and my calves howling. But not even my adrenaline can convince me I won when I saw Rowan reach the pole a second before me, and the first words out of my mouth are a string of curses. I keel forward to catch my breath while Rowan paces with his hands on his hips, heaving toward the starlit sky.

"You good?" he asks, just like he did the night I got knocked on my ass with a fly soccer ball.

When he stops in front of me and holds his hand down, I take it. The way he pulls me upright says the dude is stronger than he looks, but I could still toss him over my shoulder if I ever want to. The thought makes my dick twitch.

"I'm good."

"Loser." He smirks.

"Fucker," I mutter through a goddamn blush.

"Is that what I win?"

"What?" Was that meant to sound as gay as I think it did?

He laughs, slaps my back and says, "C'mon, man. Best two outta three."

Best two out of three becomes best three out of five, and so on. Eventually, I realize this is less to do with racing and more to do with bolstering my subpar endurance. After my fifth loss, I feel like I'm letting Rowan down. He's right about me needing to lose muscle mass, and I'm already feeling lighter than I did when he had us running suicides until I collapsed.

We walk down the bleachers together, chug from our respective water canisters, make a couple cracks about the pickle juice, then take our marks for round six.

When we reach the top, I realize I won.

"Fuck, yes!" I cheer between hard panting, my heart beating a mile a minute.

"Whatever. I tripped," Rowan mutters.

It's adorable seeing him lose. The wrinkle between his brows and his lips disappearing into a thin, downward line. Clearly, this is not something he's accustomed to.

"Don't pout," I tell him, throwing his own teasing back at him while I revel in my victory.

"I'm not—" He pauses, likely noticing the demonic grin on my face, and he just laughs instead of arguing.

On the march back down the bleachers, I notice Rowan's steps are a little uneven, like he's favoring one leg. "You alright?" I ask him. "Need some of that pickle juice?"

"Just tweaked something. I'll be fine."

"Where?"

Back on the grass, Rowan rubs the hamstring of his left leg, lifting the leg of his shorts enough to show taut muscles, a tan line and more fine black hair.

My mind wanders to what his skin might feel like there and farther up. How firm is his ass? How round? How hairy? My cock swells in my shorts, and it's got a direct line to my mouth now, when I tell Rowan to lie on his back.

He chortles and goes to his bag. "You're going to have to try harder than that to get me on my back."

"How hard?"

He scoops up his shirt, but stalls slipping it on to look back at me with those dreamy eyes and parted lips.

"C'mon," I say. "Lay down. I'll stretch you out."

Rowan's expression is painfully stoic. It's unnerving, but also incredibly sexy.

Finally, he pulls his shirt on and walks past me a few strides, patting my chest twice with his palm as he goes. "Alright, baby boy. Stretch me out," he says before dropping his ass to the grass and lying back with his arms folded under his head. The black hair under his arms radiates a tantalizing mix of musk and some sort of piney deodorant. His nipples poke at the thin fabric of his muscle shirt.

This is a mistake, but no matter how many times I chant that phrase in my head, my actions don't comply. I lower to my knees between his legs and lift his left leg under the calf muscle to rest it against my shoulder. My right side flush with his leg, I press forward and down, pushing Rowan's knee closer and closer to his chest. It's incredible how flexible he is, and it's equally incredible how composed he looks while my bulge thickens against his upper thigh.

"How's that?" My face inches closer to his as my body nearly folds him in half.

"Good," he answers quietly through a steeled jaw.

"You're flexible." I press firmer, and his knee nearly touches his shoulder.

"You're heavy."

"I've lost weight. Thought you'd like that."

"It's not about what I like. It's so you'll be lighter on your feet."

That answer only begs the question, *what do you like?* The other day he said blonds. I'm not blond, but my features are on the lighter side, especially when I'm getting a daily dose of sun exposure. Then again, I'm pretty sure he meant blonde women.

His dark stare trails down between our bodies, and I have a sinking feeling of what he sees. Turns out, pressing my body against the body of the boy I'm obsessed with is a surefire way to pop a massive boner.

"Sorry." I scramble off him and to my feet, shoving my hand into my shorts to flip my dick up under the waistband of my boxer briefs to prevent a full-on tent.

One would think I'd be used to humiliation by now, but when Rowan chuckles and says, "I'm starting to think you like me, babyface," the panic building inside me puts me into a frenzy.

"Fuck you," I spit down at him. "I can get any pussy I want. I don't need yours."

My moment of shameful rage quickly turns to fear when Rowan's countenance darkens. His eyes turn haunting, his lips pressed firm and his nostrils flare. When he stands, I get flashbacks to the time I called Ma a bitch in the heat of a pre-teen tantrum. Boy, did I pay for that fuck up.

I'm still as a frightened statue as Rowan marches across what little space is between us until his chest is nearly grazing my own. His eyes hold mine hostage, and just when I think I might drown in his stare, I feel Rowan's hand clutch my balls.

My breath hitches, and I choke on a startled cough. Pain and something so much better courses through me as Rowan squeezes me through my shorts. It swells my cock to a painful thickness, and each pulse feels like an impending orgasm.

"Get a fucking grip, Tommy," Rowan mutters.

"Mhm," I whine from my throat, nodding quickly in supplication.

Rowan releases me, and the relief is near euphoric. Shame commingles with my regret when Rowan packs up his bag like he's late for something.

"I'm sorry," I say, even though I'm pretty sure he's equally the asshole in this scenario. I just don't want him to leave. I'd rather he punch me. Even us out and wipe the slate clean so we can get back to training.

Without paying me one look, Rowan hoists his gym bag onto his shoulder and walks off.

"Rowan!"

He keeps walking, fading into the shadows where the park lamps don't reach, and I curse under my breath for doing the same thing with Rowan I did with Anthony. Except with Anthony, he left me because of how I admitted my affection. Now, Rowan's leaving because of how I'm too afraid to admit it.

Only good thing about being rejected is it's as frigid as a cold shower, and my dick goes limp on my way to the parking lot. I notice Rowan's Legacy a few spaces down from my truck, taillights on. Part of me wants to stand in the red glow and make sure he can't leave, but then I can't think of anything needier, or creepier.

I get into my truck, already preparing myself mentally for the inevitability of losing Rowan before we could even become something. What though? Best friends? Does a guy like Rowan even *do* best friends?

I turn my key in the ignition, and the FM radio switches on with the engine. The local rock station is doing their nightly countdown. Right now they're playing some trendy alt-rock hit. I'm not sure I even like it, but it's catchy, and it takes my mind off other things, if only a tiny bit.

I jump when the handle of my passenger side door rattles like someone is trying to break in. It's locked, though, and whoever is outside knocks their knuckles on my window. I hit the window button and roll it down a couple inches.

"Unlock your door," Rowan's voice breezes through the gap in the glass, so deep it sends a shiver down my spine.

Heart racing, I hit the unlock button and let Rowan inside. He shuts the door behind him and rolls up the window.

"Rowan—"

"Shut up," he says, staring at my windshield.

Shutting up, the only other thing for me to do is stare at Rowan, amazed he's even here. Screw best friends. We're barely even friends. Acquaintances and workout buddies, maybe. Mentor-mentee if I'm nasty. That's it.

So why is he here?

His arm moves, and my eyes fall to where his large hand rubs at his crotch. His shorts are black and the interior of my truck is kind of dark, but by how curved Rowan's palm is, I'd say he's got quite the bulge going.

My cock wakes back up, and by the time Rowan turns his head to blink those dark, dreamy eyes at me, I'm weeping in my underwear.

"Relax," he murmurs, then runs the tip of his tongue along his lips. "It doesn't have to be gay."

I gulp, anxiety building from that one word being spoken aloud. It feels forbidden and dirty, and I have to rub my bulge to soothe the overwhelming ache in my balls.

Rowan pulls off his shirt and drops it by his feet before reaching his hand into his shorts and grabbing what's inside. His waistband slips far enough to free the first few inches of his cock, but his stroking fist blocks any detail from view.

He works the head in steady, rolling pumps, and it gives me permission to follow suit.

It's like the porn I watch, but a million times hotter, because it's real, right in front of me. It's Rowan.

I do what he does. Peek my cock up from my waistband and stroke the head. It's already wet, and my strokes get quicker from the slickness.

"That's it, baby boy," Rowan murmurs.

How can this not be gay?

My eyes flit between Rowan's lap and the serenely wanton look on his face. He licks his lips again, and I can't help imagining what that tongue might feel like licking at the tip of my dick, tasting my pre-cum and telling me if he likes it or not. I hope he'd like it.

The truck fills with the scent of our cocks and all the heat and fluid that comes with. Rowan's heaving kicks up to rapid, and his abs tighten intermittently. His eyelids slouch as he moans curse words under his breath.

As beautiful as his chiseled jawline and his furrowed brow are, I glue my gaze to his lap, so desperate to watch his cock erupt that I'm squeezing my cockhead just to keep from blowing first.

His knees spread wide, and he presses the back of his head to the headrest, eyes slipping shut. "Fuck," he moans, stroking harder and faster.

Yes.

I stroke harder and faster too. I keep time with him as best I can, trying to time this perfectly.

"That's it," he breathes while my mind tells him, *come for me.*

The second Rowan turns his head and sets his eyes on my dick, I can't hold it anymore. My balls tease up and my cock jumps in my hand, spurting gobs of cum all over my bare chest and abs. Through dazed, half-lidded eyes, I watch a stream of fluid spill over Rowan's fist from the little slit at the tip of his plump, purple cockhead.

We stay like this for a while. Not sure how long. Eventually, Rowan takes his hand off his cock and grabs his shirt from the floor. He wipes the spunk off his hand and dick with it then tosses it to me. My mind is too mushy to think to do anything besides scrub it across my body, cleaning up some of my jizz while leaving some of Rowan's behind. Before I can finish, Rowan is out the passenger door and pushing it shut behind him, leaving me to stew on this development alone while an ad for life insurance buzzes from the radio.

8

Rowan

I'm not ghosting Tommy. Swear to God. It's just that, every time I try to come up with something to say to him, in text or in person, I find myself needing more time.

It's been three days since we jerked off together, and I can't stop thinking about it. Too stuck in the memory to consider damage control, so I abscond from Tommy. Not on purpose. I just don't know what else to do. He texts me, and I don't know what to say. He asks if we're meeting up, but I'm not ready to face him yet.

The fact he's still speaking to me should be a positive sign. If I were a more optimistic person, I'd focus on that. Tommy never mentions what we did in his truck, so it's safe to say he'd be cool with pretending it never happened. I'm not sure I can.

The past two nights in a row, I haven't worked out at all. Just laid up in bed, signed into Grindr and letting any dude within a 25-mile radius proposition me. A few gym rats twice the size of Tommy sent pics of their monster cocks, telling me they'd like to split me in two. *Hard pass.* A lot of older and probably married men wanting to come over and exchange blowjobs. Last night, some flamboyant muscle daddy offered to pull up and suck my dick in his Porsche. Didn't even want anything in return. It's the only offer I seriously considered, but the dirty talk was enough to get me off solo, and I fell asleep with the app still open.

This coming weekend, I decide I'll finally pull the trigger and pop my gay cherry. Not sure I'm ready to fuck, but a no-strings-attached blowjob is sounding more and more like exactly what I need.

Until then, I burn away my desires at practice, at the gym, and at the pitch behind the Psychology building.

I don't invite Tommy to the scrimmage tonight, but I brought him to the last five. Every Thursday at seven. It shouldn't surprise me when he saunters up fifteen minutes til.

"Tyson!" Levi hollers, jumping up to clap Tommy on the back.

Tommy grins like he's into the nickname, and he huddles with some of the guys, catching up like they're all good buddies now. It makes me wonder if Tommy is texting with them all, maybe hanging with them when he's not with me. Would he tell them what we did? What I instigated?

His head turns, eyes landing on me for all of a moment, and the pensive look on his face has my stomach in knots. I haven't eaten enough the past few days, but I've forced down the protein shakes and hard boiled eggs, and I had half a pre-packaged salad for dinner.

When it's time to hit the field, Tommy jogs straight to me, finds my gaze and asks, "We good?"

It's the last thing he texted me too. **Hey, are we good?** Now, I tell him what I should have texted back.

"Of course. Why wouldn't we be?"

He still has my shirt. The one I wiped my cum onto. I guess I should forget about it, because asking for it back would only lead to questions from Tommy, like *why did you do that?*

I'm off my game. Partly because I'm as mentally fatigued as I am physically, but it's also because whenever Tommy gets within a few yards of me, my heart feels like it's going to explode. In a twist of things, I have my shirt on and Tommy is bare chested. Broad, smooth, and pink from heat and exertion. Every time he knocks into me, I think about how his balls filled my hand, and I want to grab him again, this time with nothing between my skin and his.

A small cluster of girls walk by the sideline, and they're staring. I can only assume they're staring at Tommy, since he's the most beautiful guy here. Dude could be an underwear model, or the star of some cringe teen soap opera. He's got the soft floppy hair, the blue eyes and plump lips, and abs that would probably turn me gay if I were ever straight to begin with.

"Hey, Rowan!" one girl calls out.

It takes my mind farther off the game, because now I'm looking at them and wondering if I've met any of them before. A couple wave at me, and I wave back. *I don't fucking know.*

Something hard clips my shoulder. It's Tommy, jogging past with his chin tipping toward me. "Quit flirting, superstar."

Something about that has me laughing. Trying to get my head into the game, I call out to Raisel that I'm open. As soon as he passes the ball, Tommy is on me, and the motherfucker won't let up. He better not, because when I'm in it, I'm in it, and Tommy can't be on my team unless I know he has what it takes to beat me.

As hard as he tries, I still make my shot, but he makes me lose focus enough that I miss the goal by a foot.

"There he is," I tell him, smirking at how delicious he looks when he succeeds. "Keep doing that, baby boy, and you'll be a starter this fall."

Tommy's smile is short-lived, turning pensive again. At halftime, he comes up to me while I'm chugging my weight in Gatorade. "You still cool with me trying out?"

I lower my bottle and squint at him. "Doesn't matter what I'm cool with. What matters is if you want to play or not. Haven't I told you that a hundred times already?"

His eyes shift down to the ground before lifting to something to the side of me. "I'm gonna try out. Just wanna make sure you've still got my back."

So bashful. I can't stand it. It's too adorable, and it's too diminishing of Tommy's talent. He shouldn't give a fuck what I think or want.

"I got you," I tell him, and I mean it like a promise.

Tonight, Levi's team finally pulls off a win, and while I hate losing, I'm proud of Tommy. The way he mops up his sweat with his balled up t-shirt reminds me of how I left him Monday night. Reminds my cock too, which hops a little in my underwear.

"You hungry?" I ask him before I can chicken out.

He looks up at me from where he's sitting on the grass, knees up and parted enough that I have to force my gaze to stay on his face.

Looking a little dazed, he says, "I dunno."

"You won. I owe you dinner now, right?"

A smile comes onto his face, and his eyes shift shyly. "Uh, yeah. Okay. Whatcha have in mind?"

We take my car to the south side and hit the Sonic Drive-In. Tommy acts like I've gone mad, but it's not like I can survive on protein shakes and grocery store salads alone. Gotta treat myself now and then. We order Coney dogs, tots, and giant slushies with crunchy candies in them that make my teeth tingle. We eat with the AC on and my phone plugged into the aux.

"What is this?" Tommy asks with his mouth full of chili dog. He reaches over and turns the music up a few notches. "You a hip-hop guy?"

It's one of a few Kembe X songs I have on my driving playlist. Not everything is hip-hop, but it is one of my go-to genres.

"Surprised?" I ask.

"Maybe," he chuckles.

"What did you think I was into?"

"I have no idea," he chuckles more. "You're, like, the most enigmatic dude I've ever met."

"Really?" I'm not sure if that's a compliment or not, but I'm too into this slushy to care much. It cools my insides while the AC cools my outsides.

"Yeah, really. You're a total mystery. Like if an Agatha Christie novel were a person."

That makes me laugh. "What? So, one of my personalities has murdered another, and the remaining personalities have to figure out who done it before they're next?"

"But, the killer-personality offs the rest, one after the other, until all that's left is him and the little softie hiding somewhere inside that tough exterior of yours."

I lose the humor, and now I'm just thinking. "What makes you think I've got a little softie inside me?" I ask. "And don't make a dick joke."

Tommy snorts and laughs some more. A real laugh. The sort that should embarrass him if it weren't so cute. When he settles down, he answers, "I think everyone does. Some people just hide theirs better."

That means Tommy has a soft side, but that doesn't surprise me at all. The more time I spend with him, the more genuine I find his gentleness. That almost needy side of him. A gentle, needy straight guy... My dick is already half hard under the tray in my lap.

I'm doomed.

"So, who do you think is gonna win?" I ask. "My baddie or my softie?"

"Hm." He ponders, then sends me a dangerously pretty grin. "I think they should both win. Maybe they can work together, like teammates."

I shake my head, masking my blush by taking a huge bite out of my Coney. With a full mouth, I say, "You're a fucking poet, babyface."

"I have to come up with a pet name for you," he says.

"Call me your dad."

He snickers, calls me a weird-o, then shuts up long enough to finish his tots.

There's a Coney left on my tray, but my appetite slips from my tentative grasp as I watch Tommy suck ketchup from his thumb. He never put his t-shirt back on, opting for a thin hoodie he leaves unzipped. He smells like all the things I associate with manliness. Sweat, musk, grass, and Old Spice. This sugar-on-sugar drink I've been sipping on has me craving the salt that likely lingers all over Tommy's body. I've never wanted to lick a man as badly as I do him.

The yearning drives me mad enough to say something I shouldn't. "You still have my shirt."

"Huh?" He lifts an eyebrow at me before his expression softens into understanding. "Oh."

"Where is it?"

"I, uh—I was gonna give it back, but I figured you'd want it back washed."

"You letting Mommy wash our jizz rag?"

The shade of red tinting Tommy's face is new. "No, uh...honestly, it's still in my truck somewhere. I can give it back to you when you drop me off."

"Keep it," I tell him, too lost in his eyes to rein myself in. "You can think about me the next time you nut all over yourself."

The way Tommy exhales is something akin to an incredulous chuckle, but his mouth forms something like a frown. It's got me paranoid until I figure out what he's thinking. I watch him stick his hand beneath his tray and tug at his shorts.

What's a straight boy doing getting hard over me and my bullshit?

Facing forward, Tommy clears his throat and says, "Those girls back at school were checking you out."

If they were checking me out instead of Tommy, they're blind. If Tommy thinks I give a shit about girls checking me out, he hasn't spent enough time around me yet.

Breezing past this subject, I ask if he's finished with his tray, then I take both his and mine and all our trash to the can beside our parking spot.

I drive us back to school. The whole while, there's a tension in the air between us I can't quite place, but it makes my heart beat fast and my dick throb. We're silent, save for the music, and it's a struggle not to stare at Tommy at every red light.

Halfway back to campus, I chance a quick glance at him, but when I see what he's doing, I can't tear my eyes away. His hand is on his crotch, gripping his erection through polyester shorts. The barely there movement of his knuckles suggests he's squeezing his cock in soft pulses. The sort of shit I'd do while edging myself through an hour long porno, waiting for the action to get good before committing to getting off.

I look up, and our eyes meet.

His hand flies off his lap, and he looks sideways out the passenger window, a look of shame on his face through the side-view mirror.

The light turns green, and a car honks behind me to get my ass moving. I step on the gas a little too hard, caught up in a flurry of conflicting emotions. Last thing I want to do is take advantage of Tommy, but a close second to that is I can't ruin my future over some baby-faced beefcake who can't control his dick. Yet, I'm sick and tired of controlling mine. I'm twenty-two, about to enter my last year of college, a virgin in all the ways that matter to me, and I've never been with anyone I actually liked before.

At the next red, I hold my foot on the brake pad like if I let off even slightly, we'll teeter off a cliff that exists only in my mind. I stare at the road ahead, and I reach across the center console.

Last time I touched Tommy, it was out of anger and self-loathing. This time, I glide my palm over his bulge and hug it gently, feeling how thick he is. I stroke him slowly, feeling how long he is. Even restricted, he feels massive.

I hear his breaths over the music, hard puffs forming a steady beat. I feel his eyes on me, but I refuse to turn my head. I find his cockhead poking at his waistband, and I pinch it between my fingers.

He moans, and I feel him pulse in my hand. My own dick swells in my shorts. I press the heel of my free hand into it.

The light turns green, and I tug both hands away and plant them on the steering wheel before stepping on the gas a touch too hard.

This is it, I think. No matter what comes next, certain death is the only outcome now, but God, I just want to keep touching him and never stop. Not just touching. I want to look at him. I want to see all of him, and I want to watch him get off knowing that I'm the one making it happen.

Speeding down the sparse highway, I feel a hot palm skate across my thigh, sneaking under the leg of my shorts. My breath hitches along with the shiver rushing down my spine, and I take one hand off the wheel to slap it onto Tommy's hand.

Holding onto it, I say, "Wait 'til I park."

His hand slithers away, and I'm scared I just ruined the only opportunity I'll get to experience his touch. I'll have to settle for the Grindr randos, or chance it back at the gay bar, hoping that d-bag, Oscar, won't be there to wreck my vibe.

When we get back to campus, it's late enough that there isn't anyone around, and when I park beside Tommy's truck, ours' are two of the only cars in the lot.

Tommy unbuckles his belt quickly, but instead of getting out, he puts his hand back onto his lap, rubbing at his bulge.

I take that hand and move it over the console so it's rubbing mine instead.

At first, he pets me like a cat, like he isn't sure what he's doing, but the fact he's touching me at all is sign enough that this doesn't have to end in disaster. Maybe death isn't so certain. Maybe this can just be a secret thing between us that no one ever has to know about.

I reach over and tug on his waistband.

Tommy takes his hand off me long enough to push his shorts and underwear halfway down his thighs. His cock juts straight up, tapping against his abs. A pale veiny shaft leads to a raging head, glistening with fluid. It looks hot, and when I wrap my fingers around it, I feel just how hot he is.

I stroke him while I shove my own shorts down my ass, far enough to free my dick to open air. Thank fuck Tommy grips it quickly. I'm already close, and I want him to get me there while I get him there. I stroke him the way I like it, and I swear he's mimicking everything right back on me. When I squeeze my fingers under his cockhead, he does the same to mine. When I drag my thumb up and down the thick vein under his shaft, he does the same to mine. When I roll my fist over his tip to collect the pre-cum beading from his slit, he does the same to mine.

"Fuck," I moan, watching my ministrations while reveling in the pleasure his gives me. "Holy fuck, baby boy. Don't stop."

Tommy moans through his hard breaths, and he changes the game on me, stroking fast and gripping firm.

"Oh, fuck." I mimic him this time, finding his pace and pumping him just as quick.

"Row," he groans. "Row, I'm—" His words become a low, guttural moan before a thick rope of cum ejects from his tip.

The sight does me in. My muscles tense and my eyes roll as I release into Tommy's large, hot hand. "God, fuck me," I moan, pressing back against my seat and lifting my hips, chasing more pleasure than I deserve.

Eventually, it's too much. At the same time that I still my hand around Tommy's leaking cock, I snatch Tommy's wrist to keep him from pumping the life out of me.

I come down. The fog clears from my mind slowly. "Shit," I sigh as I open my eyes. Carelessly, I turn to check on Tommy and find his big blue eyes blinking back at me. His lips are parted, still catching his breath. I look at them and wonder what it would feel like to kiss him. But that's too much. A can of worms I can't risk opening.

We take our hands off each other, and I pull off my shirt to wipe the fluid off me. I fold it once, then reach over and wipe down Tommy's body from those projectile shots. Dude comes like a cannon, and his cock is as thick as one.

Why the hell would that Annalese chick need to step out on Tommy and his massive, insatiable cock? If I were Tommy's girlfriend, I'd never want to leave his bedroom.

That's not true... I'd want to leave his bedroom, but only to play the game we both love. Together. Maybe even on the same team.

9

Rowan

There's a jizz stain on my car's ceiling. *Fucking Tommy.* I notice it two days after making him come, as I'm sitting in the parking lot closest to the team stadium. I scratch at it with my thumbnail, but it's going to need a spot treatment or a Tide pen or something.

The dude can really blow. Makes me think that if he ever comes in my mouth, he'll bust a hole in my throat. But I'm trying not to think about shit like that. I've decided that being *gay* gay is chill, as long as I'm discrete. Messing around with Tommy is the antithesis of discrete, especially since he's going to be on the team now, assuming he nails tryout weekend.

I spot Tommy's truck in my rearview, and I climb out of my car in time to watch him park. He's exactly fifteen minutes early, aka on time, so we're off to a good start.

"Don't be so nervous," I tell him as I walk him straight to McDonough's office. Fuck the process. I'm taking my boy straight to the guy who calls the shots around here.

"Trying," Tommy says, looking like he could faint at any moment.

McDonough's door is open, and he's standing behind his desk, shuffling through a sea of loose papers and random tchotchkes. He knocks over a Deadpool figurine trying to get a legal pad out from under his keyboard.

"Coach." I tap my knuckles on his open door.

His head snaps up, and his face washes with relief. "Good, you're here. Help me find my whistle."

Swear, the dude can't coach without a whistle. I roll my eyes and reach behind the door, where I know there's a hook Coach hangs his coats and his—*bingo*.

"Here." I toss him the whistle, then motion for Tommy to come in. "Hey, Coach, this is my boy, Tommy. He's trying out today."

Once the whistle is around McDonough's thick sun-browned neck, coach-mode is in effect. His face hardens and his arms cross over his chest. "Your boy?"

I steel my jaw to keep from frowning. Forgot how inept Coach is with any type of slang that came out after the nineties. "My friend."

"Nice to meet you, sir." Tommy reaches his long arm across Coach's desk.

Probably impressed by the *sir* bit, Coach shakes Tommy's hand good and firm. "Rowan is going pro next year," he says. "In the thirty years I've been coaching, I've never had a more talented player than him, so if he says you can play, you must be something special."

The bashful dork he is, Tommy stammers. "I, uh, I—I don't know about—"

"He's special," I say. "He can play."

"You're big for a freshman," McDonough tells Tommy, sizing him up like he's sure he'll find a flaw. *Good luck.*

"I'm a Sophomore. A Junior, I mean, in the Fall."

McDonough nods like that's the flaw. *Asshole.* "So you haven't played since high school?"

"No—"

"He plays," I interject, "with me and with some of the other guys. Just not officially."

Tommy adds, "I played at Johnson for four years. Varsity for three. Captain my senior year. I actually had a scholarship to play at San Diego, but I had some family stuff come up and had to put soccer on the back burner for a minute."

A scholarship to play in SD? It makes sense with how good he was at Johnson, but why the fuck would he give that up? I know why I stuck around in the ball-sac of California, but why did he?

"Huh." McDonough twists his lips and puckers his brows the way he does when he's using that meatball brain for actual thinking. "Alright well, go out there and give it what you got. I'll be sure to keep a close eye on you."

"Thank you, sir." Tommy shakes McDonough's hand again before slipping back out into the hall.

I'm halfway out the door when Coach tells me that since I'm here, I can help him and the assistant coaches manage tryouts. Not my idea of a good time, but at least I'll be able to keep an eye on Tommy.

This whole affair begins with a tedious seminar where Coach brags about Sac State, the team, and his extraordinary coaching skills to a group of around sixty kids. Not actual kids, but more than half of them are fresh out of high school, so they may as well be kids. Toward the end, Coach parades me in front of everyone like some sort of living after-picture. As if I'm what these chumps will turn into if they're privileged enough to be coached by the great Hank McDonough.

Nah. I'm what I am because of willpower, diligent training, and the expertise of better, and worse, coaches than McDonough ever will be. I'll let McDonough think he's the shit today, though, if it'll help give Tommy a leg up.

"Couldn't have done it without this guy right here," I tell everyone, slapping my palm behind Coach's shoulder. "Coach McDonough is like a father to me. You can be sure he'll always have your best interest in mind, and he would never push you to do something you aren't already capable of."

The proud look on Coach's face is nauseating, but he lets me sit back down after that, so it's worth it.

After all the yapping, Coach dismisses everyone to the field and tryouts officially begin. The assistant coaches lead everyone in stretches before dividing the crowd up into four "teams" according to the positions they wish to try out for. Tommy's a center-midfielder. He'll be the best one the coaches see today.

He wears a practice jersey with the number 19 on it. The assistant coaches don't know I brought Tommy. They talk to me like I'm one of them, asking my opinion and letting me know their thoughts. Whenever they bring up number 19, it's either to comment on how good he is or how big he is. I want to tell them Tommy's slimming down, but I also don't want to blow my cover.

Watching him lift his shirt up to clear the sweat from his face, I realize what a tragedy it is that he should have to lose an ounce of weight. Not sure I've ever seen a more perfect body.

When I think I can get away with it, I show Tommy a thumbs-up to let him know he's doing great and to relax a little. He won his scrimmage match 4-2, and after a rest break, the coaches mix up the teams and have them go again. Again, Tommy's team prevails, this time 8-0. A bloodbath.

I knew he could do it, but seeing it with my own eyes is a whole other feeling. Pride, but something else too. Arousal. Every time he steals a ball, every time he kicks a goal, my cock twitches against my fly.

Tommy is wilting by the end. The sun is high, and it's hotter than hell out. He's used to evening trainings, not mid-day scorchers. His fair skin in pink all over, and he's sweating enough to water the lawn. *Poor thing.*

As everyone's leaving, McDonough pulls Tommy aside and chats him up. It must be good shit, because the hand-shake after is even firmer and lasts twice as long. Plus, Tommy is smiling like he just got engaged.

"Told you," I say, meeting him halfway as he walks off the field. Most everyone else is gone by now, so I don't care about keeping a cover anymore.

"Yeah," he sighs, all smiles. "I think I might die, though."

I laugh while he limps and breathes heavy. "It's that endurance, babyface."

"I didn't know we'd be playing two matches."

"C'mon." I pat his back, t-shirt soaked through with sweat. "Time for daddy to take you out for ice cream."

"I gotta hit the gym first for a shower." He wears a grim expression, like if the workout doesn't kill him, his body odor might.

If he only knew how sexy he smells to me...

"Shower here." I nod to the team locker room entrance before trying the door. It pushes open, unlocked.

"Is that...allowed?"

I send him an amused look. "I'm the team captain. You're fine."

We share a locker room with the basketball team, but everything is quiet now that the semester is finally over with and summer practice not starting up for a couple weeks. I grab a couple towels from the linen closet and show Tommy the showers.

It's not like in gay porn where there's one big tiled room with a dozen shower heads for the entire team to soap each other up under. It's like the showers in the student gym. A long aisle dividing two rows of shower stalls, each with half-panel walls and their own curtains. A narrow bench splits the aisle in two lengthwise, and that's where Tommy sets his bag and where we stack our clothes as we strip.

"You're taking one?" Tommy asks, eyes on my chest after I shed my shirt.

I shrug. "Not gonna just twiddle my thumbs out here while you shower."

"Okay," he chuckles, pushing down his shorts and underwear before pulling off his socks.

Either his dick is both a shower and a grower, or he's half hard. I hope it's the latter, because it'll make things less awkward when he sees I'm half hard under my jeans.

I'm not planning on showering with Tommy. That would not only be *gay* gay, but super weird. My cock seems to love the idea of weird, though. It hops under Tommy's gaze, and my foreskin slowly shortens as my cock swells.

Tommy is cut, his bulbous head fully exposed.

"You looked good out there," I tell him.

He smirks a little, says "Thanks, man," and tugs on his cock a few times before slipping into the first shower stall.

Don't fall into the trap, Rowan.

I hear the water turn on. The top of Tommy's head peeks out from over the curtain, his feet showing below it. I slip into the second stall, turn my water on, and as I wait for it to warm up, I fist my cock and stroke it to full mast.

All that's between me and Tommy is a single aluminum panel, yet he feels too far away. Especially when he's naked and just as horny as I am. This is the exact shit I told myself to stop thinking about. There are other options. This city is full of gay dudes who would suck me off whenever I need it, but I don't want any of those men. Not right now.

Maybe Tommy isn't totally straight. I'm not sure if that's a good thing or a bad thing, but it would explain why he came so hard when I jerked him off. It would explain why he's hard after all our workouts, and why he stares at me like he's star-struck. Maybe that's it... He thinks messing around with me will make him more like me, like he can absorb my talent and my discipline through my hand wrapped around his dick.

Why is that idea only making me want him more?

If he wants my talent, he can have it. I've got enough for the both of us, and when he's got all the power he can handle, he can fuck me with it.

Get a fucking grip, Rowan.

But I'm already done for. I leave my shower before I've even wet my hair and slip into Tommy's stall.

He's facing the faucet, back to me, and his hand is in front of him, arm moving. He's pumping that big cock of his under the water spray. *Little devil.* I don't even bother shutting the shower curtain. I press myself to Tommy's back, wedge my cock between his firm ass cheeks, and snake my arms around his waist.

Dude doesn't even flinch, like he knew I was coming, like he had me in his trap before I even knew it myself.

Finally, he moans when I replace his hand around his shaft. I splay the other across his abs while I stroke him good and steady. Touching him feels like the most natural thing in the world while also feeling wronger than wrong. Can I be the one taking advantage of him even when he's the one laying traps?

I touch my chin to his shoulder and murmur into his ear, "Tell me to stop, and I'll stop."

"Don't," he groans. One hand covers mine on his abs while the other braces on the wall in front of him.

The shower spray dries him out, so I squirt body wash into my palm from the dispenser mounted on the wall and bring it to Tommy's cock. I make suds with how quick I stroke him.

"You may need to slim down for soccer, but your body is perfect to me. So fucking beautiful. Makes me hard just looking at you." I grind my hips against Tommy's ass, gliding my cock up along his crack.

"You're not gonna fuck me, are you?" he asks, his voice doing that meek whiny thing my dick loves. "I can't do that."

As hot as fucking a straight boy sounds, that's not my M.O. "I just wanna get you off, baby," I tell him. "Wanna make this big cock erupt."

He moans, loud and hot. The distance between his feet widens, and he puts both hands to the wall, like I'm arresting him. He tucks his chin down, watching what I'm doing to him, no doubt. Trying not to miss a single beat, I pump his shaft quickly and polish his head. I swipe my thumb over his slit to mix pre-cum with the soap bubbles.

"You got your jizz on the ceiling of my car," I murmur, the tip of my nose buried in the wet hair above the nape of Tommy's neck.

"I'm close," he huffs.

"You gonna come for me, baby boy?"

"Fuck," he whimpers, body shivering. He moans low and grunts hard. His hips jerk against me, and his cock pulses in my hand.

"Good boy," I huff like a maniac.

I stroke him as he softens, and I rub his abs as they heave. He touches the top of his head to the wall under the water faucet and releases a haggard sigh.

A feather's touch will get me over the edge, and I have to back away from Tommy before I accidentally come all over his ass. I take care of my needy cock back in the second shower stall with the curtain shut, and the post-nut clarity is a beast this time. Not only am I regretting how aggressive I was with Tommy, but I'm replaying everything I said to him in my head and realizing I'm totally screwed. I told him I get hard for his body, that it's *beautiful*. I told him to come for me. What was I thinking? I was thinking he's beautiful and I want him to come for me, always.

Fuck.

When Tommy gets out of the shower, I'm already halfway through dressing. I went to my locker and got a Hornets shirt and a clean-ish pair of joggers for Tommy, so he doesn't have to put his sweat-soaked clothes back on.

Shit is awkward now. Awkward for me, at least. I don't know what Tommy's thinking. Either that I'm a predator using him, or that I'm a loser being used. No matter which, the cat's out of the bag how obsessed I am with him.

"Rowan?"

I'm forced out of my thoughts as Tommy laces up his Vans, staring up at me through his eyelashes. His towel dried hair is still damp and tousled. I have to shove my hands deep into my pockets to keep from raking my fingers across his scalp and planting a kiss on his forehead.

"What?"

"I just..." Tommy sticks his elbows to his knees, my t-shirt stretching across his broad shoulders. "Thank you."

"For what?"

"For everything. For helping me."

"I didn't do anything."

He scoffs like I'm nuts while his eyes stare at me like I'm superhuman. "You got me this far. I'm probably making the team because of you."

"I didn't do anything. Your life isn't my responsibility."

He frowns. "I know that, but—"

"I got shit to do, Tommy. I'm sorry." I ball my hands inside my pockets, nails digging into my palms. "I'll just see you back here tomorrow for round two, alright?"

Leaning back and sizing me up, Tommy asks, "What do you have to do?"

"Stuff," I say. "I got to...clean my place. You know, clean environment fosters a clean mind. And I gotta scrub your jizz out of my car."

He nods slowly, Adam's apple bobbing with a hard swallow. "Look, Row. It's like you said. It doesn't have to be gay. I'm not gonna tell anyone, if that's what you're freaking out about."

Freaking out? I'm not freaking out. Who the fuck is this guy to accuse me of freaking out? And when did I give him permission to call me *Row?*

Doing my best impression of someone who is not freaking out, I say, "I'm cool."

"So, you're not gonna ghost me again?"

My eyes roll involuntarily, and I realize I need to get out of here before this turns into a conversation I seriously cannot have. "I'll see you tomorrow, Tommy."

I skip round two. I planned on being there, swear on my life, but I can't. Instead, I go for a long run, then hit Santa Anita Park with some of the guys for frisbee golf. Tommy texts, but I swipe away the notifications without reading what all he sends. I'm getting texts from other men too. Men off a couple gay apps who I gave my number to last night when I was at a low point.

This must be how women feel when trying to meet men. Give a dude their number, and suddenly their inbox is full of dick pics and dirty talk that makes their bones shiver. It's disgusting, but everything they send goes straight to my dick. By the end of Sunday, I'm seriously considering meeting up with one of them.

I go for another run instead.

I text some suburban looking dad named Greg that I'm busy training for a marathon. An hour into a lung-piercing run, Greg texts back that he can come meet me where I am and suck me off in my car. My car, that still has Tommy's cum staining the ceiling.

Greg

> Say the word and I'll make up an excuse to slip away for a bit

> Just can't be gone too long or my wife will ask questions

> I need your cock in my mouth so bad

I want to tell him to fuck himself. I want to tell him to come here so I can fuck his face behind the bathroom.

I leave him on read, silence my phone, and run hard for another hour until my leg bones feel close to splintering.

It isn't until I'm hyperventilating against the hood of my car that my mind is clear enough I can read Tommy's messages.

Tommy

> Running late, huh? Tsk tsk

Tommy

> You ok?

Tommy

> So much for "I'll see you tomorrow" huh?

Tommy

> It went well. Coach wants me there for start of summer training.

Tommy

> How did cleaning your place go?

On Tuesday, I skip the pickup game and go to Mustache Jack. It's karaoke night, which is as terrible as I expected. Even when someone is singing well, the song choice is nauseating. Is this proof I'm not actually gay? That I can't stand 80s pop karaoke and none of the dudes here turn me on?

But none of the women here do either. Funny enough, they're all dressed skimpier than the women I've seen in straight night clubs. Lots of fishnets, mesh tank tops and exposed underwear. Actually, a lot of the men here are dressed similarly. Meanwhile, I'm in cargo joggers and a Raiders t-shirt. I order a blackberry margarita with sugar on the rim, and that feels pretty fucking gay.

I never replied to Tommy. I can't deal with that boy yet. Once I get laid, I can stop drooling over him like he's the last meal on death row.

"Well, well, well!"

Shit. I'd know that crooning Swedish accent anywhere. I don't even try to mask my groan when Oscar slides onto the stool beside me. Weeknights are usually safer than this, but I forgot to account for summer break.

I roll my eyes at Oscar's smug, angular face. "I'm just here for the karaoke."

"Sure you are." Oscar waves toward the bartender and tells the bearded man he'll cover my check.

"You don't have to do that," I say in a tone I hope convinces him to fuck off.

"I got an A on that paper you wrote for me, so I owe you a drink. Looks like you picked a good one." He leans over and sucks up a sip from my straw. "Blackberry. Yummy."

"I'm not gay," I tell him, and the words sound as hollow as they feel.

"If you weren't sitting in a gay bar, I might actually believe you." He slaps my shoulder and leaves his hand there too long. "Between the outfit and your sour look of contempt for everyone here."

"That's not—I don't have contempt—"

"Relax." He squeezes my shoulder, expression softening to something more friendly. "I'm not going to hit on you or try to convince you of something that only you can determine, but if you're looking for places to go where you won't be noticed by someone from school, there are other places. I'd just hate to see you go that route. Those places aren't for people who want to have fun and make connections. They're for desperate people with no other choices."

"Maybe that's me," I mutter, swirling my skinny straw around in my drink until it's cloudy. "No fun and desperate."

"Come on." Oscar's hand travels from my shoulder to my bicep and gives it a tug as he stands.

I pull my arm back. "No."

"Come on," he says more pointedly.

"I don't wanna fuck you, dude."

He howls with laughter, pale face turning red. "I'm going to take you over there to meet my friends. Then, you are going to have fun with us. No fucking. Fun. Okay? Come on."

I relent, if only to not feel so cornered. Once I'm on my feet, I can slip away easier. Go back home and beat off to jock porn like I should be doing now. But Oscar's grip is firm on my arm as he pulls me through the bar, across the dance floor and to a half-moon booth against the far wall.

One by one, Oscar introduces me to the four people at the booth. Cleo, Indy, Jake, and Trenton. I don't recognize any of them, but they look my age, and Indy is wearing a rainbow Sac State pin next to one that says *they/them*.

"Everyone, this is Rowan. He's captain of the varsity soccer team."

Welp, this is the exact opposite of discrete. "I'm not gay," I tell them, and they all just snicker and size me up oddly.

"Yes, he's not gay," Oscar says, patting my back like we're friends. Inwardly, I want to beat his ass, but if I did that here, it might be a hate crime. I don't hate him because he's gay, though. I hate him because he sucks. "He got lost on his way to go hook up with all the girls who always throw themselves at him. That's all."

"Hey, you think y'all will win the championship this year?" the normie-looking dude at the table asks. Jake? "Heard this coming season will be the best chance we've had in decades."

"For sure," I nod. "We're pretty stacked. Been trying to fill in the weak points. Get new talent onto the starting roster. Some guys that aren't really on anyone's radar yet."

Guys meaning Tommy. My ace in the hole. *God, that sounds gay.*

"Jake played soccer in Stockton," Oscar says before nudging me into the booth. He wedges his towering body in right after me, and now I'm more cornered than before. "So you see, soccer players can be gay."

While I'm glaring at the blond buffoon, Jake says, "I wasn't very good. I'm more just a fan."

Sounds like something Tommy would say, but I have no desire to find out if Jake is just being humble. He's not bad looking, but he doesn't look athletic. He's average. Bland. He seems nice, but he's not special.

Everyone talks, jokes around, and makes references I don't understand. They ask me questions sometimes, and I answer honestly, for the most part. I don't know what Oscar thinks he's doing. If he's trying to convince me gays are just like everyone else, I already know that. I'm not a bigot. The only person I can't accept is myself.

"I gotta go," I tell Oscar, only because I need him to move his body so I can leave. "Got an early run in the morning."

Oscar had been in the middle of a conversation about some TV series I've never watched, but dips out of that to tell me, "You should come back sometime. We're here all the time. I can introduce you to more people."

"Maybe."

"You still have my number?"

"Maybe."

Oscar reaches down and shoves his hand down my pants pocket. It freaks me out, and I shove him back, but he manages to fish my phone out of my pocket. Chuckling, he swipes my phone unlocked, because I'm a careless dumbass who doesn't lock his phone.

"Hm. Someone named Tommy keeps texting that he misses you, Rowan."

"What?" I reach for my phone, ears burning, but Oscar slips from the booth and finishes typing his number into my contacts before handing it back.

I close the contacts page and open my texts, skimming everything Tommy has sent me since Sunday.

Tommy

> I'm sorry man. Whatever I said or did to piss you off

Tommy

> Are you sick?

Tommy

> Can we meet up? I'm free whenever

Tommy

> I'll leave you alone til then

Tommy

> Kinda worried tho ngl

"You're a dick," I tell Oscar before leaving, even though I'm pretty sure I'm the real dick.

On Thursday, I show up for the pickup match on campus as usual. Half of me hopes Tommy will be there, and half of me hopes he won't. In the end, he doesn't show, and when the guys ask me where Tommy is, I tell them the truth. "No clue."

Saturday night, family man Greg texts me while I'm on my way to the gym. Somehow, being in my car already, relatively clean and chronically horny, I'm convinced to bypass the gym and drive to McKinley. I park in the lot on the other side of the fence from the nature reserve. It's more secluded here, shadowy and discreet. But that just makes it feel sketchier. More wrong.

It doesn't hit me that I don't want to be here until Greg pulls up in a minivan. I'm standing against my car door, hand near the handle in case I need to get out of here quick. The guy rounds the van, and he looks the opposite of intimidating. He looks like the sort of dude you'd see cheering in the stands of a Little League game. Probably twenty years older than me, average height, slender but out of shape, dark hair beginning to thin.

"Wow," he says when he sees me. "You're the real deal."

"Am I?" I ask dully.

Hands in his khaki chinos, silver watch on his wrist, Greg says, "You're beautiful."

"Nah." If I looked like Tommy, I'd be beautiful. I'd be perfect.

"So, uh..." Greg glances around us, but I already know there's no one around. I've been here for fifteen minutes. "You want to do this in my car or yours?"

Like hell am I doing anything in someone's family's mini-van, but I don't really want him in my car either. I nod toward the darkness between the trees. "We can do it over there."

Good ol' Greg looks scared, which makes me feel a little less scared. If he thinks I might jump him, he won't try to jump me. If he tries, he'll be dead in a minute. So, I lead the way into the shadows, where there's just enough light from the moon and the streetlamps cutting through the branches that it's not pitch black.

I press my back to the trunk of a large tree and palm my dick through my joggers.

"Get on your knees," I tell Greg, like I'm a seasoned pro at getting public blowies from random men.

After an awkward chuckle, Greg lowers his knees to the dirt in front of my shoes. He reaches for my waistband, but I slap his hand away.

"Don't touch me." I push my pants and underwear down to my ankles, then fist my cock until it's throbbing. I shut my eyes and think of that hard, flawless body I'm obsessed with. When I feel lips on my cock, I imagine they're Tommy's. When I'm sucked in fully, I wonder what it would feel like to take Tommy into my mouth.

"That's it," I groan, steeling my jaw and breathing through my teeth. "Suck my fucking dick."

I grip the back of Greg's head and imagine I'm fisting Tommy's hair when I hold him down on my cock as far as his throat will allow. I empty my balls into Greg's mouth, grunting and panting and longing for someone else.

At least I could get off. As if that's my life's objective. Everything would be so much simpler if that were the case.

When Greg is through choking down my cum, I pull away from him and put my wet dick back into my pants.

"That was so hot," Greg heaves with a giddy exuberance that only makes me pity him as much as I pity myself. He's still on his knees when I walk away.

10

Tommy

Summer practice kicks off two weeks into June. Feels weird, being here when I'm not sure if I have Rowan's blessing anymore or not. Then again, he did tell me what he thinks doesn't matter. It shouldn't. I shouldn't care what Rowan thinks about me, but I do. I can't help it.

Took nearly a week of him ghosting me to accept he's done with me. I hated myself for crying over him. I just don't know how he can do and say all of that only to give up on me at the drop of a hat.

I'll see you tomorrow. That was the last thing he said to me, over two weeks ago.

Now, I'm in the team locker room for the first time since Rowan jerked me off in the shower. My locker isn't anywhere near Rowan's, though. Coach has me segregated to the third string block. Not even second string, which is where I assumed I'd go until I could prove myself.

Even though Rowan doesn't care anymore, I still feel like I let him down.

It was so hard to get this far, but now it all feels pointless. Summer training is no joke. Grueling daily practices under a blazing sun. Hours of drills, running, scrimmaging and mandatory gym time. I still follow the gym regimen Rowan gave me when he was training me, and I've lost ten pounds since we started.

Because third stringers don't interact with the starters very often, I don't even see Rowan until the third day of summer training.

He looks exactly the same, and I'm not sure how I feel about that when his absence feels like a Rowan-shaped hole carved out of my chest. I stare too long at him from halfway across the stadium field, and he turns his head like he can feel my eyes on him. For a moment, I think to wave, but all I do is look at him, and all he does is look back at me.

That's it.

Where did I fuck it all up? I didn't try to kiss him. He's the one who came into my shower stall. I told him after that it was all good, and I didn't think he was gay or anything. *Is he gay?*

I told him I didn't want him to fuck me when his cock was grinding against my ass like it was dying to get inside. I was just afraid. Afraid it would hurt, afraid I wouldn't like it, afraid I'm not ready for all that. Maybe Rowan thought I meant that I'm only interested in him getting me off. But there's so much more I want. To hold his hand. To hug him to my chest and kiss him until we run out of air. Maybe I'm not ready for all that either, but right now, I want it more than I even want to be on the team.

Erica is getting worse. Half the time, she can't eat, and what she does eat comes right back up. She's constantly medicated, and she sleeps most of the day away. She tries, though. Takes walks around the house and talks to Mav for as long as she can keep her head up. The doctors say we need to let the chemo do its job, but it's hard to be positive when it looks like my only sister is on a fast track toward death.

When I'm on campus, I know I should be home instead. I should be the one taking Erica to her appointments, giving her her meds, and helping her bathe. Ma doesn't need all that on her shoulders alone. I should be there for Mav too. It's not fair he should have to go to day camp all summer instead of spending as much time with Erica as possible.

Then again, it wouldn't be healthy for Mav to be stuck inside that house watching his mama struggle. He needs to cherish this time with Erica in case the worst happens, but he also needs to be a kid. Run around outside, make friends, and discover the good parts of life.

When I told Erica I made the team, she made it sound like I deserve to be a kid too. But I'm not a kid anymore, and I can't be selfish like one anymore.

Rowan is always one of the last guys to leave practice. I know that because I sometimes wait in my truck, watching the stadium doors until Rowan comes out.

This time, I wait in the locker room. I tell people I'm hanging back to speak to Coach, but really, I just want to talk to Rowan.

When the place is empty, but Rowan's stuff is still in his locker, I go looking for him. I find him in the outdoor lifting gym of all places, shirtless on the squat press.

Sculpted, sun-kissed and sweat-speckled, Rowan's body is a work of art. His shorts ride up with each press, quads pulsing, and it's only because his eyes are shut that I stare as long as I do.

"Thought you didn't believe in weight training," I say.

His eyes pop open, falling to me as he holds his position longer than normal. Jaw tight, he says, "Told you. Sixty percent cardio. Forty strength."

I sit on the barbel bench in front of Rowan, straddling the end. "Can we talk?"

He finishes his current rep with a groan, then climbs off the machine. "I have to shower."

"Rowan." I stand so he knows I'm not about to let him go that easy. "I know you don't give a shit anymore, but since this was your little brain child, I thought I should tell you in person that I'm gonna quit the team."

The edges of Rowan's face clench, and he stares into my eyes with an intensity like I slighted him. "Don't quit," he says.

I shrug. "It's too much. I got other responsibilities. My family counts on me for—"

"Your responsibility is to yourself."

"That's not how it works."

"Yes, it is." He halves the distance between us, enough I can feel the heat radiating off his damp body. The musk of a day-long workout surrounds him like an aura. "The only person you should be worrying about is you."

I exhale a humorless chuckle. "Maybe there are more important people in my life than myself."

"There shouldn't be," he says firmly. "Those other people don't have to live inside this body every second of every day." He touches two fingers to my chest, and it stuns me like a bolt of electricity. He touches those fingers to the side of my head next. "They don't have to wake up every day inside this mind. What's the first thing you wanna think about in the morning? Regret? You wanna think about all the shit you gave up for other people just to make their lives a tiny bit more convenient? 'Cause you're not gonna be the first thing they think about. They're gonna be thinking about their own miserable lives and everything they wish they coulda done different."

Maybe it's how hard Rowan's tone is, how close he's standing to me, or how deeply his words settle into my soul, but my eyes water on their own, and my heart beats nearly as loud as Rowan's voice.

"This is your only chance, Tommy. Your only life. You only get one. Don't let anyone else let you feel like it's ever okay to give up on yourself."

I reach out, snatch the back of Rowan's neck, and I press my mouth to his. All salt and stick and his stubble tickling my chin. He's stiff against me, not breathing. I let him go, and he blinks at me in haunting silence. I lick my lips and taste his sweat.

Then he leaves. Doesn't even take his shirt from where it's draped over the dumbbells. He leaves from my view, and it hurts like a bomb shot straight to the chest. As I struggle not to cry, I realize he doesn't feel gone yet. I turn around, and he's still here, standing before the gate, back to me like he isn't sure if he should keep on walking or not.

"Don't lose me," I say, and he turns his head over his shoulder. "That's what you told me. I'm just trying not to lose you. Whatever way you want me, I want that too. It can be whatever we want it to be. It can mean whatever we want it to mean, but if you want me at all, in any way, I want you too."

He turns fully, but he doesn't speak for what feels like a long time. He breathes hard from his nose, walks closer, and grouses, "Don't quit. I don't fuck with quitters."

"Okay." I nod, prepared to agree to just about anything if it means Rowan gives me a chance. Even if I only ever get the one.

The gap between us closes, and just when I think Rowan is going to kiss me, he grabs my shoulders and shoves me back until my ass hits the gym wall between two shabby looking boxwoods. His eyes are like smoldering ash, and his hot palms singe my jaw as he covers my mouth with his, all power and rigidity. I grab his wrists and pry his hands away, giving me room to move with him. Holding his wrists, I part his lips with my own and breathe into his mouth until his lips feel less like a plea and more like an offering.

I give him my tongue, awakening his own, and they move together in a tantalizing dance between slow smooches to each other's lips. His are thinner than what I'm used to, and the quiet noises his throat makes are so deep that even with my eyes closed, I can't escape the fact I'm making out with a man. I don't want to escape it. I want to bask in it. I want to crawl into Rowan's masculine mouth and bathe in his deliciously low moans.

His hips touch mine, and our crotches press together so firmly I gasp into his mouth.

My body melts between his and the wall I'm against. My hands relax enough that Rowan's wrists fall from my grasp, and the next thing I know, his hand wedges between our bulges, kneading my cock in slow yet firm squeezes.

Panting into my mouth, he says, "You ever kissed a boy before?"

"No," I murmur, looking into his eyes half-lidded. "You?"

Instead of answering, he locks our lips again and sweeps his tongue across mine until they're dancing again.

I feel him unbutton my pants, and I feel him drag the zipper down along my bulge. He steps back, breaking our kiss to push my pants and boxers down my hips until the stucco wall scratches at my naked ass.

Without a word, Rowan sinks to his knees right here, and I gasp when his mouth closes around my cock. One hand holds me at the base while the other cups my balls in an electrifying grip. He sucks my cock better than he kisses, dragging his tongue around my shaft and sucking on the head. He strokes me and licks me at the same time, swirling his thumb over my frenulum while his tongue laps at the slit where pre-cum is already leaking.

"Holy shit, Row," I moan, head in a flurry as I watch him. I lay my hands on his head, just petting his scalp with almost no pressure at all. Don't want to scare him or mess with his control. I felt it when he kissed me, before I got him to relax. He's pent up with something that makes him need to act tough as nails. Maybe it's the same thing I'm pent up with.

He pumps my cock and tilts his chin, looking up at me like he's making sure I'm still here. Where else would I ever want to be? Then he slurps me up again. Deep, then deeper. He plants his hands on my hips and bobs his mouth on me.

"I—I'm gonna come," I warn him with my last breath of clarity before I crumble to bits right here in the outdoor weight gym.

Over the sound of my own grunts and whimpers, I hear Rowan's throat at work, swallowing around me in a feeling that is wholly indescribable. It's so intense, I have to grab Rowan's shoulders and push him off before he gives me a literal heart attack.

"Fuuuck," I moan, cum still drooling from my slit.

Rowan swallows hard and licks his lips. He rises to his feet, as wobbly as I feel. Before he can even think about leaving, I pull him against me and palm the tent in his shorts.

Forehead rested on mine, Rowan murmurs, "I gotta shower, baby boy. I reek."

"I don't care." I reach my hand under his waistband and grip his heady cock.

He shimmies his shorts and underwear down his ass until his cock pops free, and I stroke him the way I'd stroke myself.

I look between us, watching my hand pump his foreskin up and down, revealing that plump, purple head with each downstroke. It's wet with pre-cum, fucking glistening. Swiping my thumb across his slit makes Rowan shiver and his cock throb in my hand.

"Harder," he breathes close to my ear.

I hold him firmer and jerk him faster until he's grunting against my cheek and balling his fists in my shirt.

Clear fluid geysers from his tip, spilling over my knuckles as Rowan shudders. I quit stroking and just hold him until he pulls away and fixes his shorts.

Unsteady on his feet, Rowan walks to the barbells and brings back his shirt only to mop my cummy hand with it.

"Rowan."

He blinks those dark eyes at me, glinting steely gray in the sunshine.

"I have to pick my nephew up from his day camp," I tell him. "I'm gonna text you tonight. Promise me you'll text me back."

It's not a question, because I don't want Rowan to think it's a question. I don't care what we are so long as we're something. The two of us. We can't be anything if he keeps burying me with the silent treatment.

A slight smirk crawls across Rowan's face. "I'll text you. Promise. And don't worry, babyface. We're going to get you onto second string in no time."

I nod, and he slips away, leaving me to trust that he'll keep his word.

Later, five minutes after I text Rowan asking about his weight routine and just as I'm sitting down for dinner, he fulfills his promise by texting me a picture of his swollen cock laid along his hair-dusted abs.

I shove my phone under the tablecloth so quick I hit my knuckles on the table and wince. While Ma busies with carving up Mav's burger patty, I turn my phone over and study Rowan's erection long enough for my own to grow in my jeans.

Rowan

> Not as big as yours baby boy, but thinking about sucking your cock makes it the biggest it's ever got

A second later, he double texts a link to a Google Doc with his entire gym regimen plotted out with meticulous notations.

My body jitters with excitement and nerves, wondering what sort of worm can I opened today when I kissed Rowan and told him we can be whatever he wants.

For starters, I'm beginning to think Rowan Hughes might be gay.

We're back.

The Tommy and Rowan show has been officially renewed for a summer season, and now I have to decide if that's a good thing or not.

It's good for my game, one-thousand percent. As a trainer, Rowan is half-neurotic drill sergeant and half-mischievous fuckboy. Between runs, weights, and nonstop drills, Rowan runs my ass into the ground damn near every evening. Tears me down to my fundamental parts until I swear I can feel each one of my muscles working independently of the others. Until I feel more human than I ever have before, and more pissed off. Some nights, the way Rowan rides me makes me want to kill him, but he's always right there with me. He never makes me do anything he won't do as well.

Every time we're together, I dedicate myself to keeping up with him, or at the very least, not letting myself fall too far behind. I realize I desire his approval even more than I desire his body, but the adrenaline and endorphins his workouts illicit in me lower my inhibitions enough that, afterward, I can't keep my hands off him.

"Push, Tommy!" Rowan hollers back at me, but I'm only trailing him by a stride or two. So easy, a stride or two can turn into a wide valley, so I ignore the ache in my legs and dig.

"To the tree!" Rowan says, and I see the tree. The tree beside the park path where we began what feels like hours ago. I don't even know the mile count around the perimeter of McKinley, but if I can make it to that tree, I will have run it faster than I ever have. I want to finish with Rowan. This is his pace, and I want to show him I can handle it. That I'm not the little weenie I was when we started this thing almost three months ago.

I push, or maybe Rowan lets up a little at the end. Either way, I swear my right leg crosses that tree at the same time Rowan's does, and the euphoria eclipses any throb of pain in my muscles.

I don't collapse or puke. I plant my hands on my knees and laugh as sweat drips from my nose onto the pavement.

"You good?" Rowan's palm slaps my spine, coaxing me to straighten up. He grabs my shoulders from behind and kneads his fingers and thumbs into my flesh, hard enough to make me moan and my dick to throb. "You're so fucking wet," he murmurs behind my ear.

I breathe another chuckle, letting my eyes slip shut. I know he's referring to my shirtless, sweat-drenched torso, but I think I finally get why Lese loved it when I told her how wet she was. Rowan could murmur just about anything in my ear, though, and I'd swoon.

Hands on my shoulders, Rowan turns me around, then his palm is flat against the middle of my chest. "You feel that?" he asks. "That's what it feels like when your heart is working for you and not against you."

My tongue swipes at my lips, tasting my sweat when I want to taste Rowan's.

When my heart quits beating a mile a minute, I grab Rowan's wrist and pull him off the path and under the shadow of our marker tree. I hook my fingers in the waistband of his shorts and tug his hips against mine. The pressure of his crotch against my growing bulge makes us both moan.

"You feel that?" I huff.

With a devilish smirk, Rowan says, "How can I not, big boy?" His palms skate across my body, fingertips grazing my nipples.

My clothed cock twitches against his as I hold his hips in place. "It's for you."

"Yeah?" He leans in and drags his tongue up the side of my neck, ending behind my earlobe. "Don't give me something unless you want me to keep it."

"Fuck," I moan low, rubbing my cheek against his as I grind myself against him. "Want you so bad, Row."

He glances left then right, checking our surroundings before putting his mouth on mine. Lips soft but not loose, he kisses me with more passion than I've ever experienced with a girl's mouth. Between Freshman year of high school and now, I've made out with four girls, including Lese, and while there was always an initial excitement over the novelty of behaving slightly naughty, I never really enjoyed kissing until Rowan kissed me like he meant it. Powerful and vulnerable all at once, with that subtle tickle of his stubble that never lets me forget it's a man I'm kissing. Doesn't get naughtier than that, and now that the shame has worn off, it's all excitement filling me up.

The way his tongue plays with mine weakens my knees more than that run could. It makes me wonder how many men he's kissed. How many women? Did he kiss Lese before she attempted to suck him off? I hope he didn't.

"We need to cool you down," Rowan says against my mouth.

"Cool me down in your car."

He chuckles from his chest.

"Or we could go to your place." There's a small niggle in my gut at this being the first time I've suggested getting an actual room with a bed in it. It would open up a lot of possibilities—possibilities I'm not sure I'm ready for, but maybe if we were lying down and comfy between four walls, I'd feel more open to them.

But he gets a look on his face like that's the worst idea ever. "Nah."

Trying not to take it personally, I ask, "You have roommates?"

"Sorta," he says. "What about your place?"

"I share a bedroom with a six-year-old."

Rowan laughs so suddenly the back of his head taps the tree trunk. "Jesus, baby boy. No wonder you're so pent up. Can't even jerk off in your own bed."

My face gets hotter. "I usually do it in the bathroom while the shower warms up."

Shaking his head, Rowan pats my chest and tells me to "C'mon."

I'm limping a little on our way to the parking lot, but all in all, my body feels better than it has in a long time. Like I'm capable of just about anything. I feel lighter, more agile, and happier, because when I'm training, I'm not thinking about anything besides my body and what I can do with it. When I'm alone in the Legacy with Rowan, it's the same, except I'm also thinking about his body and what I can do with it.

So far, all I've done is jerk him off. If he asks me to go down on him, I probably will, but I'm still too chicken to go for it on my own. Me and oral never really melded right, but that was when I was going down on girls. I just don't want to make a fool out of myself, especially when Rowan is so good at giving head.

I shove my shorts and underwear down to my ankles, then I push the passenger seat a few notches back while Rowan pumps his fist around my shaft.

He picks a knee up onto his seat with an elbow on the center console, and he takes me into his mouth like he's been craving me all day. He's shirtless, and I run my palm along his spine, from the nape of his neck to the top of his ass where his waistband rides low. My other hand finger combs his sweaty scalp below bristly hair he keeps buzzed short.

He takes me deep enough to gag. Deep enough that I swear I can feel the back of his throat. He bobs and sucks, and he swishes his soft tongue under the ridge of my cockhead in a way that makes my thighs vibrate.

"So good." I try to relax into the pleasure while Rowan does everything to tighten my abs and curl my toes. "Getting close."

He eases off, like he wants to make me last. He holds my cock in a loose grip and lowers his mouth to my balls. The soft licks and kisses he leaves there make me shiver. He flattens his tongue and drags it from my scrotum to the tip of my cock, then laps at my pre-cum.

"Please," I pant, pushing gently on the back of Rowan's head.

He opens his mouth and sinks down onto me again, surrounding me with his wet heat. He bobs faster, sucking harder, tongue caressing me firmer.

I come whimpering, but I don't care. When I'm hooking up with a man, I figure it's okay to let my softness out from time to time.

Like every time Rowan goes down on me, he chokes my cum down his throat before pulling off. Maybe it's because he's the first person to swallow for me, but the naïve part of me romanticizes the action. Makes me feel like Rowan wants some of me with him after we part ways. It's also just sexy as hell.

Everything about Rowan is sexy as hell, even when he taunts and teases me and infantilizes me with a wicked smile on his face.

"Where did you learn to suck cock like that?" I ask as my body melts to my seat. It's a compliment more than a question, and as soon as I ask it, I realize I don't really want the answer. I know Rowan has hooked up with women, but I'm not sure I can handle hearing about him hooking up with other men when he's the only man I've done anything with.

Shifting back into his seat, Rowan says, "I dunno. Porn, I guess."

I laugh, finding more comfort in that answer than any of the alternatives. "Gay porn?"

Rowan doesn't answer. Just stares at me, running his eyes over my body and my cock that softens on my pelvis. Takes me a few seconds to realize I spoke the forbidden word aloud. No one ever said *gay* is forbidden, but it seems to be a word Rowan doesn't enjoy being associated with.

It's hard for me to believe any man who loves giving blowjobs as much as Rowan does can convince himself he's straight, but what do I know? Rowan is a steel vault that seldom opens, and when he does, it's usually related to soccer or our dicks. For all I know, Rowan is a straight arrow who only bends for me. He did tell Coach I'm special, but *that* special?

To ease the tension, I reach over and palm Rowan's bulge. "Your turn," I tell him and watch his smirk reappear.

11
Tommy

The Friday smack in the middle of July, Coach tells me to move my stuff to a locker among the second stringers and that I'll be scrimmaging with them against the starters on Monday. First thing I do, even before moving lockers, is find Rowan at his and tell him we did it.

Not sure what I expect, but I'm a little disappointed when his reaction is to tell me, "This is just one more step. We still got a lot of work to do," between chugs of Gatorade.

Some of the other guys overheard and are much more enthused. I get pats on the back from the Thursday night scrimmage crew, and my Johnson buddy, Malik, says he'll buy me a beer tonight. That prompts Levi to say there's a party going on tonight at his girlfriend's best friend's house. Some girl on the golf team with rich parents who left her unbridled access to the house while they're out of town.

"You in?" Levi asks, meeting me eye to eye with his typical macho intensity.

There are a lot of reasons going to a party tonight is not a good idea, but they elude me now, and I end up looking to Rowan to fill in the gaps. But he just stares at me with his own subliminal sort of intensity.

"Awe," Levi coos as he slings an arm around Rowan's neck in an annoying, brotherly sort of way. "You need permission from your butt buddy over here? Please, Mister Hughes, can Tommy come out and play?"

While my instinct would be to shove Levi against the lockers and tell him to eat a dick, Rowan flashes a charming grin and laughs.

"You keep partying while Tommy's training, and you'll be out of a job come August," Rowan teases his friend.

"What a relief!" Levi chortles. "You know how long I've been waiting for someone to usurp my throne? So many have tried, but none have succeeded. I could use a break. It's exhausting being this naturally gifted."

"So whatcha say, Tyson?" Raisel asks as he slaps a hand on my shoulder. "You in?"

Looking between him, Levi, and Rowan, I can't think of anything to do besides shrug. "Yeah, sure."

"Cool." Levi releases Rowan to point an earnest finger right at him. "Captain is the designated driver. He'll pick us up."

The last party I went to was with Lese, and it sucked. She kept slipping away to the bathroom with her girlfriends, even after I told her to cool it with the coke. She called me a party-pooper, and on the drive home, she went on a whole diatribe about how lucky I am that she stayed with me after high school. If I wasn't such a loser, I would've dumped her that night, but it took until she fucked around with Rowan for me to commit.

I wonder how many beers it would take for me to gather up enough courage to pull Rowan into a walk-in closet and eat his dick. Oral is a far cry from fucking, but it's close enough that it feels like a significant threshold in my sexual awakening, and the more I want to cross that threshold, the harder it is to pull the trigger. At the heart of it, I just don't want to give Rowan trash head.

Not sure what to wear, I settle on something I think Rowan might like me in. He likes my body, so I wear fitted jeans and a two-year-old henley shirt that suddenly fits me again, just barely.

Rowan

Otw

While I wait for Rowan to pull up, I fold the laundry Ma left on the living room sofa. She's in the bathroom, scrubbing Mav's fingers with nail polish remover. When I picked him up from day camp, his short nails were painted sparkle-purple. He said his friends, Brenleigh and Aurelia, were painting their nails and they offered to paint his too. When he asked me what I thought, I wasn't sure what to say, so I told him what I figured Mav would tell me if I painted my nails. "It looks awesome."

Ma didn't agree. She balked when she saw him, like he came home with a fresh neck tattoo. Had me start on dinner while she wrote an email to the day camp that it was irresponsible of them to allow two girls to paint her grandson's nails.

"He's six!" I shouted through the walls while Mav sat teary-eyed on my bed, thinking he was in trouble. "It doesn't matter! He was just playing with his friends!"

Because I know how much Ma hates shouting, I wasn't surprised that she stormed into my room and gave me a piece of her mind. Some bullshit about how boys need to be friends with boys, not girls.

"He can start hanging out with girls when he's old enough," she said. As if the only reason a boy should ever spend time with a girl is to date.

I comforted Mav as best I could while tending to supper, and as soon as the food was on the table, the subject was dropped. Straight after, Ma took Mav into the bathroom to clean his fingers.

I hear him sniffling through the open door now, and it breaks my heart a little. Makes me wonder what Ma would think if I told her I like men, and that I'm probably gay. I don't think I'll ever have a desire to walk around with sparkly nails, but I have an overwhelming desire to roll around naked with the men's soccer captain. What's gayer than that?

Two quick honks from the curb interrupt my thoughts and my folding. I shout to Ma that I'll be home late. Before she can come out and scold me for it, I grab my keys and dip.

The Legacy is full of starters: Rowan behind the wheel, Levi in the passenger seat, Raisel and Connor in the back. Connor shoves over into the middle seat, and I squeeze in to the right of him.

"'Sup, Tyson!" Levi greets me with his typical bluster. He grips the safety handle above the passenger side window like it's an ejector lever. Above his head is a small stain from when I came so hard I shot a glob onto the ceiling.

"You good?" Rowan twists his body to look at me between the front seats, one hand on the steering wheel.

"Yeah, I'm good." I click my seatbelt under Connor's ass, and Rowan shifts into drive.

Rowan's wearing a Nipsy shirt, of all things, and black jeans that hug every inch of his lean, muscular legs. I keep two paces back from him as the five of us walk into this house party as a unit, and I lose myself a little in the scent of his cologne. He's got his smart watch on, black like his Adidas, and his face is clean shaven.

It's the first time I've been around Rowan when he's this put together and my cock is swelling because of it. When we're both filthy with sweat and grass stains, the fact we're hooking up doesn't seem super shocking, but right now, I'm dumb-struck to think someone as cool as Rowan has literally sucked my dick.

I'm forced to quit staring at him when we walk through the front door and end up in the thick of a rager. What I consider a rager, at least. Music so loud the walls rattle. Clearly inebriated twenty-somethings laughing at the top of their lungs and tossing themselves on top of each other. Beer bottles rolling across the floor and red Solo cups in everyone's hands. People dancing, grinding, taking turns off each other's vapes. Just the sort of shit Lese used to beg me to come to. The sort of shit I wouldn't be caught dead at. Even when I was willing to get high and grind on Lese, I wouldn't do it in front of a hundred half-strangers.

When I look back to Rowan for guidance, he's slipping away with Levi and Raisel, deep into the current. He's a flash of black clothes, then gone.

"C'mon, man!" Connor plants his hand on my shoulder and squeezes. "Let's get some drinks!"

With Rowan gone, I stick by Connor like a scared puppy, but while he's whipping up a Connor-Deluxe party cock-tail into a cup for me, he spots his girlfriend through the kitchen window. I think to follow him out onto the back deck, but the last thing I want to be is the third wheel to a couple making out and whatever else.

I stay in the kitchen and sip on my drink, wondering where Rowan went. Leaned against the counter, I take out my phone and text him.

Me

Thx for ditching me bitch

He'll laugh at that and tease me about it later. Hopefully soon.

In the meantime, I end up scrolling Reddit until I remember how many gay porn subs I started following, and I close the app in a flurry.

"Tommy?" a slightly familiar voice chimes in my ear like the high chirp of a morning dove.

I look up from my phone, and a curvy blonde is smiling back at me, a hard seltzer in her hand and the outline of a heart drawn onto her cheek in permanent marker. Eve, it dawns on me. I never got back to her about meeting up, but I still follow her on Insta and tap on her stories now and again.

"Hey." I tip my chin, but she comes in for a hug.

I give up one of those one-armer hugs like Rowan gave to Connor's girlfriend the evening I met Eve. When I take my arm back, though, Eve stays glued to me, arms cinched around my middle and swaying like she's trying to slow dance with me.

"You been drinking?" I ask, chuckling through the awkwardness.

"Just this." She uncurls one arm to lift her can to her lips and sip. "I ate a brownie, though."

"Ah."

"You never texted me back." She blinks up at me like she's trying to fan my face with her eyelashes.

"Sorry. Got distracted with finals, then soccer."

"Did you make the team?" Her face sparkles like she knows the answer already.

"Second string, as of today."

"Oh my God!" She literally hops with excitement, grinning big and rubbing her tits against my side. "That's amazing! You're gonna play with Connor and Rowan and that miserable fuckface Levi!"

I quirk an eyebrow down at her.

"We had a thing, but that was a long, long, long time ago."

"Ah," I chuckle.

"I have to pee!" she declares. "Do you wanna come to the bathroom with me?"

"Uh…" Trying not to cringe, I look at my phone, relieved to see Rowan texted back.

Rowan

In the basement babyface

"This place has a basement?" I ask aloud, not used to basements in Sacramento.

"Yeah, you wanna go?!" Eve asks, hopping again.

"I thought you had to pee?"

"Oh. Yeah."

"I have to go find Rowan."

"Rowan," she groans animatedly. "Everyone is so obsessed with Rowan because they think he's gonna be famous one day. So fucking fake. I know for a fact half the guys on his team hate his guts. There's a rumor going around among the girls that he's gay, but I just think he's autistic or something."

This is the first time I've heard someone talk critically about Rowan, and I hate it. It's also the first time I've heard that anyone besides myself has questioned Rowan's sexuality. My mood sours, and I'm tempted to tell Eve to fuck off with her speculations—to tell her Rowan is none of her business.

"Don't tell him I said that!" Eve whines, throwing her arms back around me and laying her cheek on my chest. "You're warm."

"Where's the basement?"

Once I've got directions, I find the basement stairwell and take it down into a wide, dim-lit den. There's different, more subdued music playing down here, and there's a second makeshift bar set up on an actual bar top. A beer pong tournament is in full swing, an A's game on a flat screen, and half the starting lineup squeezed onto a long sectional with a handful of girls I've only seen in passing. There's one girl standing behind the sofa in spikey heels and a crop top, and she's draped over Rowan's shoulders, talking in his ear while he sips from a tallboy.

"Tyson!" Levi exclaims from his post at the beer pong table. "Don't worry, man! We checked, and Rebecca over there promises she's not your girlfriend. She's just a slut!"

The girl falling all over Rowan jolts up to pelt a half-crushed beer can at Levi's head. "Look who's talking, slut!"

"Men can't be sluts, Becky," Levi chortles, ducking under the pool table just in the nick of time. "That's called being men!"

"Can't argue with that," Rebecca mutters with a heavy eye roll that brings her focus back to Rowan.

I take a long swig from Connor's concoction to mask my discomfort.

Jealousy. It's not a feeling I'm accustomed to. With Lese, I felt anger, resentment, even possessiveness, but never anything like this. Like I'm watching someone take something precious right out from under me. As a guy, it's easy to beat up another dude who comes after what's mine, but when it's a girl, I don't know what to do. I don't think there's anything I can do.

"Make room for my boy," Rowan says, shoving over the starting sweeper beside him.

Just like that, jealousy turns to an anxious paranoia that someone in this room will interpret *my boy* as something naughty. I love it, though. Whether Rowan means it like "friend" or "baby boy," my tummy swirls with pride that he wants to be next to me at all.

I wedge myself between his hip and the sweeper's, and Rowan's arm swings around my shoulders. I turn my head and blink curiously at him, wondering what he's up to. All my pride turns to fear that Rowan is high already and about to do something careless. But when his gaze meets mine, he just smirks and says, "Sorry for ditching you. Thought you were behind me, but then you were gone."

"It's all good."

His head cranks back over the top of the sofa as Rebecca's manicured nails rake across his scalp. Fear circles right back around to jealousy when I watch Rowan's eyes flutter shut and a moan ripple from his throat. "That feels so good," he murmurs while shifting his ass to lounge deeper on the sofa. His shirt is long enough that I can't tell if he's popping a woody, but it sure looks like he's enjoying himself.

Before I can do something careless myself, I stand up and leave for the stairs. Rowan doesn't follow. Doesn't even call after me. I'm so concerned with not losing him, I wonder if he'd even care if he lost me.

I come out of the stairwell into a frenzy of body heat and a nauseating bass note rattling my skull. Shouldering through the crowd, my heart aches so bad I could cry. *Get a grip, Tommy.* He's not even mine. Not really. We're something, but what? Whatever Rowan wants us to be... Because that was the deal I offered up on a silver platter out of my desperate, gay as fuck longing.

The back deck offers fresh air, but it also proves I was right about what Connor was going to get up to with Thalia out here. He's got her pressed up against the railing, her skirt hiked up and her knee glued to his hip.

They're what Lese wished we could've been. She wanted to be my arm candy at these shitty gatherings and revel in being dry humped in front of everyone. Seems like a fun way to live life, if only I could do it with someone I actually want to be with.

I leave the deck and wander into the backyard. The vibe is calmer out here. The music isn't so loud, and people are chatting at normal volume. A few pairs are making out by a firepit, but everything is dim enough that it's easy to ignore.

Like a loser, I spend this time Googling stupid shit on my phone.

'Am I gay?'

I tap on a quiz, and it asks me all sorts of damning questions. Questions about my sexual preferences, my romantic preferences, my friendship preferences, and what sort of life I want for myself in the future. I want Rowan, but do I want a boyfriend? Do I want a husband?

Do I?

The results come up: **It is possible you're gay, but your identity is something only you can determine.**

Well, fuck.

When my head is clear enough to accept that even if I'm one day the husband of a husband, he won't be Rowan, I head inside to let him know I'm going to order an Uber and split. I make it halfway between the back door and front door when my ear buzzes with the sound of Rowan's voice cutting through the music, shouting my name.

I turn toward the sound, and he's in front of the dining table, recoiling away from a girl who looks a hell of a lot like my ex.

His eyes connect with mine, and he shouts, "Can you come tell your girlfriend to get off my dick?!"

I want to roll my eyes, but all my jealousy and anxiety comes rushing back to flood my head with a fog of anger, and I end up shooting Lese a mean glare.

"Tommy?" She jumps in surprise, looking me up and down like I'm a ghost come to haunt her or something. "N-no. Tommy, I wasn't—"

I turn on my heel and march toward the front door.

"Tom!" Thin fingers grip my arm and tug me back with such little force I could walk right out of it if I wanted to, but I suddenly have something to say.

Switching around, I tell her, "Fuck with whoever you want, Lese! I don't care! You don't mean anything to me anymore!"

As soon as I let the words out, I feel like an asshole. Even if she was a cheater, I'm just as big a liar. Her big brown eyes well with tears, but no matter how bad I feel, I don't have it in me to apologize. Not now.

I turn back around, but instead of going for the door, I walk into the raucous cluster between the living room sofas, shouldering my way to where Eve is Stevie Nicks dancing. As soon as she's within reaching distance, I circle my arm around her waist and bring her against me. I hear her squeak my name before I press my mouth to hers, then her arms swing around my neck to keep me captive in my decision.

Her mouth tastes like alcohol and chalky lipstick, and her kisses are sloppy. Not sloppy the way Rowan's are, passionate and purposeful. Just...sloppy. Somehow too needy and too gentle all at once, and she hangs onto my neck like she's waiting for me to pick her up and take her to a bedroom. I'd rather die.

Self-loathing sets in too late to undo anything, and when I finally squirm away from Eve, Rowan is staring at me from the mouth of the dining room in his stoic way where I can't tell if he's studying me or judging me. I open my mouth like I've got something to say, but even if he could hear me over the music, my mind is mincemeat.

While Eve paws at me to kiss her more, Rowan breaks our shared stare to do what I was planning on—marching out the door.

"Tommy!" Eve whines.

Once I shrug her off, I race after Rowan. I shout his name as I jump down the front stoop. I shout it again as I chase him down the sidewalk in the direction his car is parked. It isn't until Rowan is beside the Legacy that he turns to face me. A deep set frown and an anger line between his brows replaces his stoicism.

"What do you want?"

Skidding to a stop a few feet from him, my mind is still tossed, and I end up asking, "Are you drunk?"

"No. Are you?"

"No."

"Huh." He nods. "Then why don't you go back inside and screw your new girlfriend?"

Wincing from the verbal slap, I argue, "I don't wanna—I was just—I was jealous, okay? And upset."

Halving the gap between us like he wants to grab my nuts and squeeze until they pop, Rowan seethes, "I told you. I don't want jack shit to do with your stupid ex."

"I'm talking about the basement. That chick was all over you, and you were lapping it up. Fucking moaning for her like she was rubbing your dick. How's that supposed to make me feel?"

The veins in Rowan's forehead define as fire brews in his dark eyes. "I'm not your boyfriend, Tommy. I'm not a faggot."

All I can do is blink while my heart cracks deeper than it ever has. It hurts. A palpable pain spreads through every inch of me, making me want to puke, or cry, or punch his windshield. Instead, all I do is blink and watch the strange work of art that is Rowan Hughes shift before my eyes. His anger sobers to something downright morose as he looks left and right. The whites of his eyes turn pink as he fumbles with his keys like his hands are shaking on their own.

Suddenly, he can't look me in the eye. He looks off toward the road when he says, "Get in the car."

Something about this shift in persona aches my heart in a different way, but I can't quite place it.

He rounds the hood. "Tommy, get in the car. Please."

I get in the car, and Rowan cranks on the ignition. He drives us two minutes from the house and parks in a little lot behind a Dairy Queen.

When the engine cuts, everything is silent. Rowan stares at the brick wall in front of the windshield for a while before clearing his throat. "You said we could be whatever we want."

It's not just that he can't look at me. It's that his tone is so unusually quiet, voice breaking a bit on the word *said*.

Hollowed of any emotion but my ever-present longing, I softly say, "I need to know what that is. You have to tell me how you feel about me."

"Isn't it obvious?"

I almost want to laugh, because nothing about Rowan is obvious to me. "I think I'm gay," I confess, if only to judge his reaction. To save face, I add, "Or, bi. Maybe."

He stays staring out the windshield, one hand gripping the bottom of his steering wheel while the other picks at the frayed upholstery on the driver's side armrest. "Well...I won't tell anyone."

"I know." I blink and discover tears in my eyes. Being gay would explain how sensitive I've always been. "Is it just sex? If it's just sex, you can tell me. I won't be scorned or anything like that, but I need to know so I can manage my expectations."

"I can't—" He closes his lips, breathing deliberately through his nose as he presses the back of his head into the headrest. "I can't... I can't be in a relationship. I need to focus on soccer."

"You think I'd ever try to come between you and soccer?"

"It's—" He shuts his lips again. The bottom one plumps as his breaths harden and his eye leaks a tear down his cheek. Voice good and broken, he says, "Can we not talk about this right now? Can we just put a pin in it? Please? I'm sorry I let that girl touch me. It wasn't like that. Sometimes, I just let people do things. I don't know why."

"It's okay, Row." I reach over and clamp my hand over his, the one gripping the steering wheel like he's trying to split it in two. "I overreacted. I'm sorry. I'm sorry I kissed Eve."

"You should kiss her. You should kiss whoever you want."

"I only wanna kiss you."

His lips fold tight together. He doesn't say anything else, but he turns his head and finally looks at me. The sight of him makes me want to pull him to my chest and never let go. Screw a relationship, screw a five-year plan, screw gay or straight or bi, or whatever. All I want is one more moment with Rowan Hughes. Moment after moment after moment.

"Do you wanna go somewhere?" I ask. "You could sneak me past your roommates. I could crawl in through the window."

His head shakes again. "I can't."

I nod behind us. "We could get some ice cream."

He sniffles and swipes at his cheeks with the hand not secured beneath mine. "I got you something. For making second string."

"You did?"

"It's in the glove box."

Reluctantly, I take my hand from his so I can turn forward and rifle through the glove compartment. Among schoolwork, pieces of mail, and a lot of rubber bands, there's a narrow box with the sticker seals still on it. The box says FitBit on it with an image of just that, black like Rowan's clothes.

"I noticed you never use one," Rowan says. "Figured you don't have one already. It'll help you with your workouts, especially when I'm not there."

The sweat on my fingers wet the sleek box. "Rowan, this is a lot."

"You've made a lot of progress."

I look at him. Just stare at him for a few long moments before I drop the box on my lap and hold his face instead. I kiss him, and this time, the salt I taste isn't from sweat, but tears.

When he kisses me back, I feel like everything's going to be alright. Whether or not that's true, I'll leave for the universe to decide.

"C'mon," I say after a good minute of my lips pressed to his. "Now I have to buy you ice cream."

12

Rowan

Tommy lets me off the hook for not being able to give him any real answers, and that only solidifies my opinion that he's perfect. Better than I'll ever be, that's for sure.

Just like every party I've been dragged to, I didn't want to go to this one tonight. I wanted to celebrate Tommy's progress by making him run suicides with me again. Then I figured I'd give him the FitBit before or after giving him head. Still can't believe Tommy didn't call my ass out when I lied and said I'm not gay. Even after he came out to me, I couldn't return the favor, but we're just two different people. I don't know how to be like him.

Knowing for sure Tommy is gay, or bi, changes things. Makes everything feel more like something real. I'm not sure if that makes things better or worse, though, since I don't have a clue what to do with something that's real.

I've never been in a relationship before. I've never had someone I like like me back.

What am I going to do?

Nothing, for now.

I eat this Oreo Blizzard with my ass on the hood of the Legacy, eyes on a brick wall while Tommy smiles at me like I'm not just a high functioning train wreck.

"Do you have any idea how beautiful you are?" he asks.

I scoff, but with how warm my face is in the cool air, I'm sure I'm blushing like crazy. Tommy's one to talk. When he walked out of his little suburban bungalow earlier looking fresh as fuck, all I wanted to do was climb him like a tree. He's lost a bit of muscle mass, but the muscle he's retaining is more taut and defined now, like he's sculpted from stone. His shirt and jeans do little to hide how incredibly built he is.

I stab my plastic spoon into my Blizzard, prepping for a monster bite. "Thanks, gay boy. Or, bi boy? Gay boy has a better ring to it."

Tommy snorts, full lips glistening with a sheen of ice cream residue from the milkshake he's been sipping on. "Kinda like *baby* boy the best."

"I knew you liked that. Saw it in your eyes the first time I called you it. Like you wanted to eat me."

"I wanted to kill you."

Recalling that evening on the McKinley soccer pitch before Tommy introduced his fist to my eye socket, I chuckle. "That too." I pop my monster bite into my mouth and savor the icy rush down my throat. Not nearly as tasty as Tommy's jizz, but it's a pretty great consolation prize, considering what a chump I am.

"You know," I say, "I think this is the first time I've ever liked a guy who isn't straight."

"You're the one who made me realize I'm not straight."

There's a smile on Tommy's face and a lightness to his tone, but it's still hard to hear something like that. I don't ever want to force anything onto him. I can be domineering and impatient, but I never want to hurt him.

"I'm sorry."

His head shakes. "Don't be. It was always there, even before I knew who you were."

He's brave. Brave, beautiful, and a good person who deserves to be with someone just as good. All I'm good for is helping him come to terms with himself while I continue to deny who I am. I'm good for getting him off and letting him experiment with touching a man. I'm good for training him to get onto first string where he belongs. Tommy could go pro, too, if he doesn't quit.

"I'm sorry about Rebecca. I didn't realize I was making you jealous. I didn't really think I could."

"It's okay, Row."

"You're the only person I like touching me."

He smiles like I complimented him. "You're the only person I wanna touch."

It does feel an awful lot like a compliment. Dirty, but sweet.

I finish my small Blizzard and leave the empty cup on my hood until Tommy finishes his giant milkshake. Before he does, he wraps my hand up in his own and presses his plump, cold lips to my cheek.

13

Tommy

First day on second string, we scrimmage against first string, which means scrimmaging against Rowan. Feels a lot like what we do on Thursday evenings, except all the starters are on one team, and all the people Rowan would call "chumps" are on my team. The second stringers are good, but there's a reason they aren't starters. They don't do me any favors, and defending against Rowan is more arduous when our offense is lagging.

What we lack in finesse, we overcome with little-brother-syndrome determination. I realize we all have what it takes. It's just a matter of building body discipline and mastering technique. The starters have those skills in spades.

We score one goal, but we're decimated in the end. It's demoralizing, made worse because I can't even debrief with Rowan straight away like I'm used to. He'll taunt me mercilessly on the field, but afterward he's a walking pep-rally, bolstering me up and half-convincing me I'm hot shit. Then, of course, he gets me off in the front seat of his car. Who wouldn't love that?

But at practice, we have to be cool. He keeps his teasing to a few murmured comments when no one's looking, and we try not to stare at each other too long when the shirts come off in the blistering heat. If I let myself watch Rowan spray

Coppertone all over his body, my boner might just tear a hole in my shorts. We hardly talk at all during practice, and that sucks, but I get it, and we both agreed laying low in front of everyone is what's best.

Off the field, it's still the Tommy and Rowan show.

After coming out to Rowan as maybe-gay, I had a small panic attack thinking it would change everything. Like maybe Rowan was only into me because he gets off on turning straight guys on. He did say he'd only ever liked straight guys before. But if Rowan feels less into me now, he doesn't show it. He still sizes me up like I'm hot apple pie, he still goes for my cock after a grueling workout, and he still sends me dick pics during his nightly wank sessions. Only thing that's changed is that he'll sometimes call me "gay boy" instead of one of his many other nicknames for me, but he saves that one for when we're perfectly alone.

It feels nice actually, as if every time he calls me "gay boy," it's another step toward associating myself with something that feels true. Not just true, but fun. I have fun with Rowan, between sweating out my body weight and feeling like my bones are going to splinter out from under me. I love doing gay shit with Rowan more than I ever liked having straight sex.

Kissing him, touching him, sucking on his Adam's apple while I hold his cock in my hand. I keep waiting for him to ask for head, but he never does. He must be waiting for me to do it on my own, but I'm too anxious. I want to be bold, as bold as Rowan was that day in the outdoor weight gym under a scorching sun, but Rowan and I have nurtured a dynamic between us where he's the leader, and I follow wherever he takes me. That's not very alpha of me, but not every guy is born with that alpha mentality. I sure as hell wasn't, and I don't want to dominate Rowan. I just want to make him feel as much pleasure as I can give him.

The student gym still holds morning yoga classes during the summer session, and Rowan takes me whenever I'm not working a shift. Not only does it help stretch me out for practice, but I've noticed a difference in my balance on the field. I'm moving better on my feet, and it helps me mentally wash away the stress of home so I can show up to practice focused and ready to work. It also always, without fail, makes me incredibly hard by the end, but I've taken to flipping my dick up into the waistband of my underwear and wearing a loose muscle tee that drapes over my crotch.

If the gym is empty enough when the class finishes, we go to the locker room together and share the wheelchair accessible shower to beat each other off. It's always nice when I don't have to show up to practice with blue balls.

Sometimes, on weekends, Rowan takes me swimming. But it's not the backyard pool party kind of swimming or beach day road trip kind of swimming. The student gym has a natatorium with twelve lanes, a ten-person hot tub, and three diving boards. Rowan refuses to go into the hot tub with me. Says it's like sitting in a hot broth of human skin and body oil. No matter how revolted he is by the idea, I still want to know what it's like to chill in a Jacuzzi with Rowan Hughes. Call me romantic, I guess.

Rowan is a skilled swimmer. Even wears those regulation Speedo shorts the competitive guys wear. He strips bare ass naked in the gym locker room, and I drool over how his cock twitches with life in between tugging off his boxer briefs and pulling on those skin tight swim shorts.

"Take a picture, it'll last longer," he tells me while sliding his palm purposefully inside his shorts to position his half-chub just right.

He's bolder in the student gym locker room than he is in the team locker room. Lets himself check me out while setting himself up to be checked out. It helps that, here, we can choose lockers right next to each other. I'm sitting on the bench beside him, a perfect line of sight to his crotch, but I let my gaze drink in the whole of him too. Not just his bulge and the way his shorts sit low enough on his hips to show off the top of his ass. I may have been gay before Rowan was ever a blip in my universe, but I've never been so drawn to a man's ass until him.

"I already got about sixty of those pics in my phone, actually," I answer, glancing around us to see if the coast is clear. When I don't notice anyone around, I stand up and press my bulge against the Rowan's ass, the same way he did to me the first time we were naked in a shower together.

"You're welcome," he chuckles before shoving me back and tossing me a towel from his gym bag.

"You know, I've been thinking…" I scrape my teeth across my bottom lip and wiggle my brows.

Rowan smirks. "Oh no, baby boy's been thinking?"

"Sex can be more than just a cooldown from a workout. It can be a workout in itself."

"Is that what you think we're doing? Having sex?"

"Well," I step real close, enough to lean my mouth inches from Rowan's ear, "More than half the time, I finish inside your body. I'd call that sex."

"You calling me a bottom bitch, Tommy?"

The heat in Rowan's eyes is chilling. It sends a shiver down my spine that resonates in a throb of my growing cock.

"Either that or a cum addict," I tease.

"A cumaholic?"

I snort and plant my hands on his hips, gliding one over his ass. I want him so bad it hurts. My abs flex with how badly I want to grind myself against him.

Rowan's hand dips between us, palm grazing over my clothed erection. "It's not my fault you taste so fucking good, baby boy."

I press my nose to the side of his head and moan into his ear.

Giving my cock a firm squeeze that turns my moan into a whimper, Rowan says, "Get it together. You get a day off when I say you do."

He parts from me, then puts so much space between us I could scream. It leaves me with two options. Go jerk off in the bathroom or follow Rowan to the pool and let the cool water shrivel my hard-on to something I can swim with. Do I need to even say which one I choose?

The atmosphere in the natatorium is warm, humid and reeks of chlorine. We're two of only a handful of people here. All but two of the lanes are empty, and there's just one girl in a Staff t-shirt and short shorts straightening things up around the perimeter of the pool. For her benefit, and the benefit of my pride, I hold my towel so it hides my erection until I think no one is looking, then I fling it onto a bench and dive into the cold, clear water.

When I crest, Rowan tosses me down a pair of goggles before slipping his own on and pencil diving into the open lane beside mine. I nearly laugh at how, even when we're working out together, we still end up in separate lanes. I guess I'm just a clingy bastard, wanting to be as close to Rowan as possible at all times, but it's not my fault that his aura is so enticing and his body is so inviting. As Lady Gaga sang, I was born this way.

Shit, I really am gay.

Rowan warms us up with a steady one-hundred meter swim, then we work a little harder with a manageable ten fifties on the minute. I stick to the technique Rowan taught me. Three strokes for every breath. Chin down, hips up, kick small and fast, stretch long and reach far.

When I start lagging behind a couple seconds, Rowan flips his goggles up and tells me, "Gonna have to pick it up."

I nod, and I pick it up. Rowan's right about swimming being the ultimate full-body workout. Before he started bringing me around to the nat, I didn't know it was possible to sweat so much while submerged in water.

We spend a good forty-five minutes doing laps at various paces and intervals, then we cool down with another lazy one-hundred. And boy is mine lazy. I swim so slowly, I almost sink a few times. By the time I'm back to the gutter, Rowan is sitting on the lip of the deck, legs dangling over the side. I don't have clearance to ogle at the way his knees are parted and his abs are flexing with each breath, because he's chatting with the staff girl in the short shorts like they know each other or something.

Don't be jealous, Tommy.

It would be easier if Rowan would just tell me he's gay, but that's not really how it works. Like that dumbass internet quiz said, his identity is something only he can realize for himself. For now, I just have to exist in perpetual anxiety that Rowan might just be a sex fiend, and I'm just his latest fuck buddy.

But what about the night he cried in front of me?

When I get the water out of my ears, I realize Rowan is talking to the girl about soccer. Clinical, like the sports nerd he is, dropping stats on her that are making her eyes glaze over. It's adorable, actually. Kind of fucking hot.

I lift myself out of the pool with what upper body muscle Rowan allows me to maintain, and I sit my ass on the tiled deck.

"Now *you*," the girl points down to me, "look like a swimmer. Don't swim like one, though."

She and Rowan both giggle at that while my face reddens. *I see how it is.*

"You think he's big now, you shoulda seen him a few months ago." Rowan reaches over and squeezes my shoulder.

"You a starter too?" the girl asks. There's a Sac State lanyard around her neck where an ID badge dangles. The name on it looks like Sage.

"He will be," Rowan answers before I can, because I would've just said no.

The way she smiles at me reminds me of how Eve did the night I met her, and she flits her wistful gaze from me to Rowan. "Is he single?"

My chest gets tight for a second, wondering what Rowan will say and which of the many options would embarrass me the most. He promised he wouldn't tell anyone I'm gay, and I trusted him when he said it, but now my anxiety is working on overdrive, second guessing myself.

"He's single, technically," Rowan answers in as casual a manner as he would order food at a drive thru, "but he's preoccupied, if you know what I mean."

Her eyes roll like she's heard that line before, but that smile is still there, dripping interest. "What about you?" she asks Rowan, and now my gut feels tight too. Even if Rowan isn't interested in Sage, I hate how easy it is for people to throw themselves at him. Like, just because he's beautiful, he must be fair game.

"I don't do relationships," he answers.

"Yeah," she sighs. "That's what the word on the street is. Well, I'm single and wouldn't mind staying that way so long as I'm preoccupied. You two seem like good buddies. Maybe you want to have some fun later, and we can all preoccupy each other?"

The discomfort in my gut quickly morphs into a knee-jerk laugh. It comes out so suddenly that I think I might blow a lung out of my nose. Did she just offer what I think she just offered?

I look to Rowan so we can share in this absolute bonkers twist in the conversation, but he looks the very opposite of amused. His expression is all baddie, steeled jaw and sharp eyes squinting up at the girl like she just outright called him a fag.

"Don't you have some towels to fold?" he sneers.

Sage balks. "Thought you were a closet man-whore, Rowan. Not a total prude."

"Just 'cause I don't wanna fuck you, doesn't make me a prude."

"Maybe your friend does."

"He doesn't," Rowan says with a look in his eyes like that should be the end of the conversation, for everyone's sakes. To me, he says, "Let's go, Tommy. There's not enough chlorine in this pool to mask the stench of desperation in the air."

"Asshole," Sage mutters as Rowan picks himself up and leaves for the locker room as fluidly as someone who hadn't just worked the hell out of their muscles. "Is he always such a brat?" she asks me while I ungracefully pick myself up.

Ignoring her and the No Running sign, I chase after Rowan. I might have slightly longer legs, but the dude can really book it. I catch up to him at our lockers, and it looks like the steam has left his ears at least.

"You good?" I put a hand on his back, but he shrugs it away.

"I'm fine." He rifles through his locker, finding his t-shirt and tugging it on over his head, quashing my hopes of an after-swim shower. "I just wish people would leave me the hell alone. Like, what is it about me that suggests I want to fuck every girl who speaks to me?"

"You're hot."

He blinks at me like I'm full of it.

"I'm telling you, Row, you're hot. That's just how it goes. It's one of the main perks of having a long-term girlfriend. Women gradually stop hitting on you."

"Yeah, well, I'm not interested in having a beard." The slight twitch of Rowan's eye after he spoke suggests regret.

Likewise, I'm a little stunned he said that out loud. Calling a hypothetical girlfriend a beard would mean he's gay, after all, and that's still a forbidden word, if only when regarding Rowan.

"Do you think, maybe, we spend too much time together?" Rowan asks in a quieter tone.

"No."

There's a lull of silence that threatens to eat me alive. *Don't do this, Rowan. Don't leave me high and dry again.*

Leaning my back against the lockers, I say, "We're friends. I'm your friend. Friends spend time together. They do shit together, help each other out and have each other's backs. That's us. I got your back. If anyone sees a problem with that, they're just jealous no one gives a shit about them enough to have their back."

Thankfully, Rowan nods at that. "Okay."

This time when I rub the back of his shoulder, he doesn't flinch away. "You hungry?" I ask, because there's still over an hour until practice.

After a heavy sigh, Rowan nods. "Whatcha have in mind?"

"In-N-Out?"

He half smiles, laying those dreamy eyes on me again. "So basic."

Now, I'm balking. "You don't like In-N-Out?"

"I didn't say I don't like it. I said it's basic."

"Whatever, weird-o." I roll my eyes, but I'm all smiles, just glad for the simple pleasure of Rowan not running away from me. "Can I take you somewhere first?"

The black FitBit on my wrist tracks my steps as I take Rowan on a meandering trail through campus. He asks multiple times where we're going, but I let him be the follower this time.

I take him past the science building to the seldom noticed horticulture building. Around the back is a fence covered in ivy and morning glories, and I push open the unlocked gate. A placard on the gate reads CLOSE AFTER ENTRY, so I keep a hand on it while Rowan comes through, and I make sure it's latched when I shut it behind us.

"What is this place?" he asks with a tone of wonderment and an amused smile.

It never ceases to amaze me how few people know this place exists, especially students who've been full-time here for years. Then again, the only reason I know about it is because Erica used to bring me here on weekends back when she was a Sac State student and I was in middle school.

"It's the school's garden for the horticulture program."

"So, like, plants and shit?"

I chuckle and pat Rowan's back. "Yeah, c'mon."

It's nearly an acre of winding pathways lined with native plants and small informational placards. We're not the only ones here. It's open to the public, and people like to bring their kids. There's a chicken hatchery in the west corner, and a few of the hens run free across the paths. The first time one bumbles from the brush in front of us, Rowan gasps and curses under his breath.

"Fuck me in the ass," he mutters. "There's chickens here?"

Wide eyed, he follows the chicken now, who leads us to the hatchery.

"The hell?" he mutters.

I laugh and put my hand on the hatchery gate. "You wanna go in?"

He looks awestruck and slightly anxious. "Like, to pet them?"

There are already a couple kids in the hatchery, timidly patting the more sociable hens. I open the gate to let Rowan in first.

It's adorable, watching him be as timid and tentatively giddy as a child the way he scopes out the friendliest chicken and goes in for a gentle swipe of his palm down its back. The way he grins and breathes, "Holy shit," makes me think he's never been to a petting zoo before, like this is all a brand new experience. Makes me glad I brought him here.

"I can't believe I never knew this place existed," Rowan says as we leave the hatchery to continue exploring the garden.

"I would come here a lot when I was depressed. Always kinda cheered me up."

Rowan looks sideways at me. "You get depressed, baby boy?"

I shrug one shoulder, trying not to blush under Rowan's uncharacteristically soft stare. "Sometimes. Everyone does, right? Sometimes?"

Maybe not Rowan, but if the night Rowan cried to me in his car is any indication, he at least knows what it's like to feel confused, overwhelmed, and maybe a little lost.

He doesn't nod or say anything in agreement, but he walks close enough that his arm brushes mine, and he says, "Don't be depressed," like it's that simple.

I crack a small smile. "Don't be depressed. Another Rowan Hughes rule for success?"

"Nah. Just, a favor? As a friend?"

Friend. A term that sits so oddly in my stomach that I'm not sure if it's a step in the right direction or the wrong one. I'm not even sure what the right direction is with Rowan, but so long as we're friends, we can be together without scaring Rowan off and without making promises and commitments neither of us are ready for.

"I'll try, but it's not really something I can control."

"Well, you can talk to me if you want," he says, eyes on the path ahead of us. "I got you."

14
Rowan

The next "family time" is dinner at Dominico's Pizzeria. I don't really want to go, but it's important to Matt and Xiamara. Not sure why. I'll never sneer at a free plate of Dominico's spaghetti with meat sauce, but it's hard not to feel like an interloper. Too old to be Matt's son but too young to be his brother, and I'm the only one named Hughes. I don't know what people think when they see me tagging along with him, his wife, and their three little ones. Chances are good that no one is thinking anything at all about me and them, but it's something that lingers in my mind no matter what.

As awkward as I feel on the inside, I don't mind spending time with them. I like Matt. I like Xia. Olive and Lena are by far the most tolerable children I've ever been around, and baby Bruno is fine when he's not shitting himself.

Mostly, I like that they let me talk about sports all the time. Soccer mainly, because Matt is almost as obsessed with the game as I am, but I sprinkle in some baseball talk and even MMA.

It's a Friday, so the place is busy. We wait fifteen minutes for a five-top table and high chair, then it's a bit of a wait to get everyone's special orders in. I realize before our food arrives that I need to text Tommy and let him know I'm hung up. Part of me thinks I should just postpone tonight's training, since

Dominico's nights on Matt's dime are nights I stuff my face. But I want to see Tommy. Even if we're not training. Even if we're not messing around. I just like seeing him when I don't have to pretend he's *just* my friend.

> Out to dinner rn. Don't know if I can train tonight

"Ah, ah, ah!" Xia chides me with her cat eyes and a manicured nail pointed at me from across the table. "Phones away. You know the rules."

I hit send before shrugging. "I was gonna work out with a buddy before tonight became family night. Just gotta let him know."

"Mm," she hums, lowering her lined lids in her perpetually suspicious way. Xia may not be my mom, but the way she treats me, I swear she's convinced she gave birth to me. She would've been sixteen at the time if so, but she looks younger than her thirty-eight years. Everyone always says so. "All you do is work out. You need to relax sometimes."

I smirk a little at the irony of Xia telling me to relax while bringing me to a noisy family restaurant with three kids under ten.

"This that Tommy kid?" Matt asks, one hand holding a crayon he uses to help color in Lena's illustrated paper placemat.

"Yeah."

Xia shoots me a glare when my phone vibrates, and I just chuckle at her intensity. She might be the only person I know more intense than I am, but she's also the kindest person I've ever met. Even kinder than Matt, since there's no way Matt would've done everything he's done for me if Xia weren't egging him on in the background.

Tommy

> Out to dinner? Damn ok meanwhile I had hotdogs and Kraft

Me

> Rest assured, I'd much rather be eating your hotdog rn

I'm either blushing while typing or smirking like a fiend, because as soon as I hit send, I look up to find Xia's suspicious expression has only grown more suspicious. Lips pursed, brow ticked up, and a subtle bob of her head like she knows something she's not supposed to. Xia always thinks she knows everything, and unfortunately, she's usually right. Seems I can lie to everyone in the world, but never to Xia. The mom instinct, she calls it. For a long time, I thought that didn't apply to me, but I guess it does.

"How's he doing?" Matt asks, still keeping his eyes on his and Lena's artwork.

I haven't told him much about Tommy. Just that he's some kid I was helping make the team. I showed Matt a few videos of Tommy's playing time at Johnson, and Matt agreed Tommy was talented and that it was a shame he quit.

"Got bumped up to second string," I tell Matt, flipping my phone screen-down on the table. "So he's practicing on the big boy field now. Just have to prove to McDonough he can hold his own competitively."

"He hasn't played in a long time," Matt answers, sounding like McDonough.

"I train with him nearly every day. I see him at practice. He does well when we scrimmage. Defense is great. Working on offense. He has what it takes, and he loves the sport. He just needs to keep working hard and believe in himself more."

Matt exhales a chuckle. "Well, if you think he's got what it takes, he must be the greatest thing walking."

"He's good, and he's cool to train with. Doesn't complain. Well, sometimes he does, but he doesn't quit."

"Sounds like you really like him," Xia says while tearing up bits of soft breadsticks for Bruno to nom on. Her knowing suspicion is replaced by a knowing smile—soft and accepting in a way that darkens my mood like rain clouds opening up over my head.

"Xiamara," Matt mouths to his wife, but his warning reaches just close enough to a whisper that I hear it.

"What?" she asks him at full volume, animatedly tossing up her bread filled hands. "I think it's nice. He needs a good friend. Everyone does." She turns her rounded eyes to me. "Do you two do anything together besides train?"

Well, there's Sonic, Dairy Queen and In-N-Out. There's the party where Tommy fractured my soul by tongue kissing that chick, Eve. There's the horticulture garden where Tommy goes when he's depressed. I don't ever want him to be depressed, though. I don't know why he ever would be, unless he's struggling more with the gay thing than he lets on. Then, of course, there's all the gay shit we do that's made me the happiest I've ever been. Not just the sexting, the handjobs and the way I take him in my lying mouth whenever I can, but the soft stuff I let Tommy do to me sometimes. Like when he put his hand on mine and kissed my cheek with milkshake lips.

"No," I lie. "We just train."

Xia doesn't believe me. I can tell because when my phone buzzes, she doesn't make a single grunt of objection when I check Tommy's text.

I blink my screen on and immediately, my eyes feast on the gloriously shocking sight of Tommy's veiny, raging cock. Tucking my phone right up close to my chest, I skim the message while struggling not to drool over how pink and wet his flared head looks, like he's already been stroking. Background suggests he's sequestered in the family bathroom.

Tommy

> **Room for dessert later?**

The implication has my body temp rising. Hooking up without the pretext of working out would just be hooking up. Like what I did with minivan-guy.

Another text appears while I'm caught up in my nerves.

Tommy

> **Please? Wanna taste you too**

My dick swells. How can it not? I've wanted to feel Tommy's mouth around me almost more than I've wanted him on first string, but I've been too paranoid to coax him down on my lap whenever my cock is out. Paranoid that it'll feel too much like something sick and desperate. Paranoid that Tommy won't like it, or that he'll like it too much. Paranoid that I'm corrupting him, turning him gay and taking advantage of him.

He's only two years younger than me, but that baby face gets to me sometimes. So pretty and flawless. Coming in his hand is one thing, but coming in that perfect face is a game changer. Just the thought is enough to push me over the edge when I'm beating off solo, but there's guilt laced in my desire to follow through.

I don't decide until Xia says, "You should go out with him later. It's Friday night. Have some fun."

"Can I go too?" Olive asks, hopping in her chair and grinning like the answer is already yes.

"No," Xia tells her.

Me

Did you cum yet?

Tommy

Not yet. I'm close

Me

Don't cum. I'll pull up in an hour and a half.

Tommy

I can cum again

Me

Do as daddy says

Tommy

Fuck

Ok

You better not be late

Is it possible to blush while smirking like a fiend? If so, I'm pretty sure that's what I'm doing until Xia snaps again and tells me enough is enough with the phone.

I know I always say fifteen minutes early is on time, but when little kids are a factor in my timeliness, there's only so much I can do. When Tommy drops into my passenger seat, he pays me a look that is almost pained. The little sadist in me finds it adorable, and when I reach over and feel Tommy's lap to find his cock is still hard as a rock, I'm beyond pleased.

"Mmm," I moan, feeling my own cock press against my fly. "You were a good boy, weren't you?"

"I hate you," he says, nostrils flared. He presses his hand on mine, and that rigid tool in his pants throbs against my palm.

Laughing, I one-handedly zip from the curb and head east toward Douglas Field. McKinley would only make me think of that seedy, down-low blowjob I let myself get roped into, and I don't want that to be mine and Tommy's story. I got paranoid after that night and got tested, so I know I'm clean, but there are more ways to protect someone than making sure I don't give him an STI.

I park at the very end of the lot, where there's enough tree cover to block out most of what the streetlamps produce.

Tommy is on me from the jump, like a cat in heat as soon as I get the keys out of the ignition. He makes out with my ear before I turn my head and let his wet kisses devour my mouth. His hand is on my bulge, stroking me to full mast through the thin fabric of my joggers.

I moan around his tongue and push on his shoulders. "Slow down, gay boy. Wanna get in the back?"

"Okay." He's out the passenger door quickly, but I save time by crawling back through the front seats.

When I get my ass in the backseat before him, I say, "I win," with a devilish smirk that I hope conveys so much more.

He's on top of me as soon as the backdoor shuts, kissing me and tugging at my shirt. He gets it off me before pulling off his own, and we kiss with our bodies flush and our erections grinding together.

The back of my head is on the door armrest, one foot up on the seat with Tommy fitted between my legs. He kisses my mouth, my jaw, and my chest. He even touches his lips to my nipple and swirls his tongue around the beaded nub. I moan, back arching into the unfamiliar sensation.

Sitting up, Tommy hooks his fingers into my waistband and tugs down my joggers, making my cock spring free and nearly slap him across the chin.

I grip the base and hold it toward Tommy's mouth while I run my fingers through his soft hair. I don't push. This needs to be his decision, but I'm also too naughty for my own good.

"You wanna suck my dick, baby boy?" I murmur, wagging my cock a little.

"Mmm," he hums before replacing my hand around my shaft. He strokes me slow and agonizingly soft, moving my foreskin over my crown and milking pre-cum from my slit.

"Fuck, baby," I moan. "Give it to me."

My fingers stay threaded in his hair while he lowers onto my lap.

First, it's a tentative lick right on top of my sensitive tip, then he pumps his fist nice and slow around my shaft while closing his lips around my head.

I see stars as every nerve in my body alights with a warm euphoria. I lose myself in the wet, velvety feeling and push down on Tommy's head until he's swallowing half my length into his mouth.

He shifts his hand lower, off my cock and over my balls, dancing his fingers around my scrotum in a way that has me crooning. He takes me down far enough to gag, and it startles him enough to pull off completely. A thick line of drool tethers his lips and my cock while his doe eyes blink up at me.

"Is it okay?" he asks, so bashful I could melt into a puddle right here and now. I still might, if he puts his mouth back on me quick.

"Don't stop." I push his head back down with minimal pressure.

He takes me back in, bobbing now and dragging his hot tongue along my length as he goes. I lift my hips and he gags again, but he ignores the discomfort this time and keeps going.

"Fuck, fuck, fuck," I chant when I'm dangerously close. I cup Tommy's head and lift him off me just as the first spurt of cum pulses from my cock.

I frantically grab my dick and pump the jizz from it, trying not to shoot on Tommy's face, but he opens his mouth and licks at the underside of my head while I'm still gushing, capturing my cum on his tongue and even lapping at the rest.

I groan low from my core, eyes half-lidded but watching Tommy intensely. "You like that, baby? You like making me come in your pretty mouth?"

Flickering his eyes up to meet mine, Tommy gobbles my cock down his throat and swallows around me, sucking up every drop that my soul has to offer.

"Shit," I hiss when it starts feeling so good it stings. I push him off again, but this time I hold his face, sit up, and plant my mouth on his cummy lips. I've tasted myself before. It's no big deal. But tasting myself on Tommy's tongue is a new level of delicacy.

"Was it okay?" Tommy whispers against my mouth.

Breathing a laugh, I speak something too true to ever take back. "You're perfect."

Before I can overthink what I just confessed, I nudge him back against the seat and fold over him. I press my face into his lap, dragging my nose and mouth along the thick bulge straining his twill shorts. I bare my teeth and gnaw his cock through the fabric.

"Please, Row," he exhales. One of his hands is between my shoulder blades, gliding along my spine, and the other is un-buttoning his fly. "I'm gonna come in my fucking pants."

The devil in me loves that idea so much my dick actually twitches back to life, but I want his cum for myself. I sit up and help him shimmy his shorts and boxers down to his ankles un-til his bare ass is on my black leather seat. His balls are already tight and lifted, and his head is glistening in the moonglow coming in through the windows.

Licking my lips, I wrap my hand under his scrotum and grip his balls and cock in the same grip.

Tommy's breath hitches, fingertips digging into my back while he looks at me with pleading eyes.

I lean in nice and slow, nudging the tip of my nose against his before I poke my tongue out and lick his parted lips. His tongue is quick to meet mine amid our comingling breaths, and I take my time petting his tongue with mine.

"Please," he moans, and I glance down at his lap to see him pump his cockhead in his fist.

I release his balls to tug his wrist away. "Did I say you could touch yourself?"

He whimpers in a way that goes straight to my swelling dick.

"You wanna come, baby boy?" I ask him.

"Mhm."

"Ask me."

He licks his lips, eyes going half-lidded. "Can I come? Please?"

I lean down, pucker my lips, and blow a steady stream of air over Tommy's raging tip.

"Fuck!" his hips buck like I just shoved a finger up his ass. "Please, Row?"

I lean farther down and touch the tip of my tongue where Tommy's scrotum meets his shaft, and I trace the thick vein all the way to his little pinhole slit, catching a bead of pre-cum on my tastebuds.

Moaning, Tommy puts his hand on the back of my head, but he's not bold enough to push me onto his cock. I'm almost disappointed.

Tilting my chin up, I look into his hypnotic eyes and say, "Call me daddy."

"No," he half-moans, half-laughs. "Too fucking weird."

"I thought you wanted to come."

"Rowan," he whines, cock throbbing and tapping my lips.

"Go on, baby boy. Ask daddy nicely if you can come, and I'm sure he'll take good care of you."

Groaning, fingers scraping my scalp, Tommy mutters, "Can you please make me come...daddy?"

The title drips from Tommy's deep tenor like a warm compress to my balls. I have to reach beneath me and stroke my cock while I give Tommy his reward.

My boy is huge, I have to drop my jaw to keep from scraping him with my teeth, and by the time my nose touches his pubic hair, I'm gagging around him. But I stay low and suck hard, gliding my lips and tongue along his shaft in quick motions that turn Tommy into a quivering, panting mess.

"Fuck, fuck, fuck," he chants through choked breaths.

My throat fills with heat. There's hardly enough time to register Tommy is coming before my throat contracts, and I choke down every spurt. I bob off and latch my mouth onto the soft part of his inner thigh, sucking and biting with my cheek pressed under Tommy's balls. Like I want to eat every inch of him.

Tommy becomes putty against the seat, closed eyes and humming low-droning moans while his wet cock softens.

I turn onto my back and bend my knees, laying my head on Tommy's lap. I shimmy my pants back up my ass and let my dick go limp as Tommy's fingers trace my abs.

Blinking up at his drowsy face, I ask, "So, what do you think? Feeling more gay now, or less?"

He hums. "Definitely more."

I don't know why, but I smile like that's a good thing. It's a good thing for me, I guess, since the gayer Tommy feels the more likely he is to keep wanting to waste time on me. "It was good?"

"Crazy good. Wanna give you head again. Just give me a minute."

When I realize how wide I'm grinning, I suck my bottom lip into my mouth to rein myself in.

Soon, Tommy reaches his hand under my waistband to knead my soft dick back to a half-chub. "Who did you go to dinner with?"

"No one. It doesn't matter."

Tommy goes silent, his hand stilling on my cock. The jealousy radiates off him stronger than his pheromones.

I sigh, dick going limp again. Even though it feels like a lie, I say, "My family."

"Your parents?"

"Sorta kinda." I don't want to lie, but it's hard not to when the truth is so muddy and depressing. To make up for it, I tell Tommy something I know is true. "I missed you."

"Really?" He smiles down at me. "I missed you too."

"I could tell how much you missed me from that pic you sent."

Tommy chuckles. "It's kinda weird, huh? Hooking up when we're both clean and not drenched in sweat..."

"I wasn't gonna let your first time sucking my dick be when I smell like ass."

His laughs harder. "Oh, no. Do I smell like ass when you go down on me?"

"Nah. You always smell baby fresh."

"Weird-o."

I smirk up at him, and I swear he's blushing. I probably am a weird-o. It would only make sense, but being a weird-o is better than being a deviant, right? So long as Tommy's okay with the way I am, I can be okay with it too. Maybe.

15

Tommy

Ma texts me halfway through my shift at the deli to bring home a package of thin-sliced turkey for Mav's lunches and a pound of ground beef for dinner tonight. She says Erica is planning on fixing her signature taco salad. She's been feeling better lately, slowly but surely, and now she's well enough to cook.

With soccer season right around the corner and things with Rowan as confusing as ever, the fact that Erica's chemo is finally working has me thinking life is about to take a lucky turn. Not only will I get my sister back in full force, but I'll power my way onto first string, and I'll somehow convince Rowan to quit keeping me at arm's length. Sometimes I wonder if the two are connected, like Rowan's trust will come as a reward when I accomplish what all we've been working toward since April.

I still don't know for sure if Rowan is gay or not, or what he wants from me in the long run. Still don't even know where he lives or the names of his roommates. I don't know the names of his parents either, or how his relationship is with them. It took until a week ago to figure out what his major is. Communications, ironically. Says it's for when he goes pro and has to sell himself as a charming, picture-perfect sports diplomat.

"Yo, Mike!" I call to my boss as I sift through the freshly packaged pats of beef. "We got anything leaner in the back?!"

Normally I wouldn't care, but when I'm not getting burgers and milkshakes with Rowan, I've been trying to eat lean.

Coming out the back office, my stocky, gray-haired boss grunts toward the overflow fridge and says he just stuck some 90% lean in there.

While I'm looking through, the doorbell chimes behind me, and Mike asks whoever it is the usual, "What can I do ya for?"

That's as much as I hear before my mind fills with my inner voice, mulling over the look of each packaged pound of beef. I'm not picky, just indecisive. Maybe that's why I haven't pressed Rowan too much for commitment. I'm not sure I want commitment either.

What would that even look like? Rowan...my boyfriend? The thought gives me giddy goosebumps all over my body, but it also churns an anxious sickness in my gut, because *boyfriends* is as real as it gets. *Boyfriends* isn't simply out of the shadows and having sex somewhere other than our cars and the gym showers. It's a promise.

The next time I'm a boyfriend, it won't be like when I was Lese's boyfriend. The next time I tell someone I'm in it, I'm going to be fucking *in it*. Can I be in it with Rowan? Better question...can Rowan be in it with me?

"Can I see some ID?" Mike asks the customer as I finally settle on the best looking beef. I move on to the sandwich meat display.

"Uh, okay." The customer sounds confused. I glance over my shoulder and see they aren't buying any alcohol. Just a couple pounds of something wrapped in paper.

When I come back around the counter to ring myself up on the open register, the customer is passing Mike her ID.

Or...his? A brief glance at the customer doesn't tell me one way or the other what their gender is, and it's no skin off my back either way. I've always hated using *ma'am* and *sir* anyway. I only do it when I think I have to, but I'm more than happy to leave gendered monikers by the wayside.

"This is your ID?" Mike asks, flitting a disapproving look between the customer and their ID in Mike's hand. He hands it back. "No, I don't think so."

"What?" asks the customer asks, rightfully bewildered.

My first thought is that Mike thinks the ID looks fake, but then he hands a credit card to the customer and says, "We can only process credit cards from the cardholder. It's store policy."

Huh? Tell that to the guy Mike rung up this morning who used his boss's card to pick up a tray of sub sandwiches for some office function.

"I am the cardholder," the customer says, an uptick of annoyance in their husky voice.

"Your name is Jennifer?" Mike asks, an edge to his amused tone.

The customer tosses their hands up. "Yeah, it is. Why does it matter?"

"What matters is that the picture on that ID is of a woman, and you don't look like a woman to me."

My eyes go wide and the back of my neck sweats the way it does when conflict is imminent and I'm right in the line of fire. I'm not sure what's going on, but I know what Mike said is only going to escalate whatever situation this is.

"I am a woman, actually," the customer states, showing her anger by folding her arms across her chest and pursing her lips. It's a lot more restraint than I would've shown if some jackhole deli owner insisted I'm not a man.

"Whatever woman you are sure ain't my definition of a woman."

"Ha!" the customer laughs humorlessly. "And who made you the arbiter of what the definition of a woman is?"

"God gave me eyes, and that's license enough. He also blessed me with the means to own this store and the agency to decide to deny service to whomever I please."

Looking between Mike and Jennifer, I feel like a total door-knob. The noble side of me thinks I should tell Mike he's being a fuckhead, but the side of me that needs a job says to keep my mouth shut. I end up frozen like a deer in headlights, waiting for Jennifer to leap over the counter and throttle Mike. I sure as hell wouldn't blame her if she did.

Instead, she uncrosses her arms, shoves her cards into her pants pocket and storms out without her meat.

Mike laughs when she's gone, shakes his head toward me and says, "Can you believe that?"

No, I really can't. In all my cowardice, the only thing my mouth challenges Mike on is, "Since when do we check IDs for credit processes?"

Mike adopts a perfunctory look as he saunters up and plants his heavy palm on my shoulder. "You're young, Tom, but as you get older, you'll realize that the only way for society to function is if people know they can't act however they want in public without facing consequences."

"How was she acting?" I ask, too dumbfounded to read between the lines of Mike's bullshit.

Mike chuckles. "Let's just say, if you ever showed up to work in a dress and makeup, I'd fire your ass just to teach you a lesson, and you'll thank me for it too. Whatever that chick does in the privacy of her own home is her business, but she damn well better look like a normal person around me."

Even though I'd probably never wear a dress anywhere ever, I can't help but feel personally slighted. Oh, right...it's because I'm gay. Still getting used to that. And this right here is another reason not to commit to Rowan. Because once I do that, being gay is no longer just a private, personal identity, but a way of living, and life happens in public. Life happens in front of people. It's brought up in conversation, and it's how I make decisions that affect people other than myself.

I get to my truck and text Rowan, because even though he's not my boyfriend, he's sort of become my best friend. He may not tell me much of anything, but he'd never betray my confidence, and even when he teases me, he has a way of making me feel supported.

Me

Bad day at work):

Before I shift out of park, my phone buzzes in the cupholder.

Rowan

What happened

Me

Nothing really. Just my boss is a dick. Going home now tho. See you tonight?

Rowan

I'm sorry babyface. Nothing an hour of suicides can't fix

He's actually insane, but he's got me smiling again, which is exactly what I wanted. When I get home, Erica is on the sofa, dressed and watching Mav play Mario Kart. Another reason to smile. Life is good sometimes, bigoted bosses be damned.

"Got your meat," I tell Erica as I move toward the kitchen. I unpack it on the counter, then notice Erica crossing the living room in my path. Though she's moving around on her own more, she's still unsteady enough to freak me out whenever she walks without assistance. I rush to her side and take her elbow, just in case.

"Thanks, little bro," she chuckles. "Help me with dinner?"

"Of course. Where's Ma?"

"In your room, getting a load of wash together. Hope you hid all your unmentionables."

"She still in her mood?" I whisper in case Ma really can hear through walls. For a couple of weeks now, Ma has been unusually terse. Sometimes it's like I'm talking to a wall the way she pretends I'm not there. Can't think of anything I've done wrong. Can't imagine she's upset over something Erica's done either when all she's done is finally feel better than dying.

"Don't worry about what you can't change," Erica says with a small, crooked smile.

Halfway through prepping supper, Ma storms through the kitchen, not even saying a hello to me. Just, "Whatever mess you make in here, you're gonna clean it up. I don't care where you're heading off to tonight, but this kitchen better be spotless."

"Sure, Ma," I say over the sizzle of the meat in the skillet. I share a look with Erica, who's chopping lettuce at the peninsula.

My pocket vibrates, so I lay down the spatula and dig out my phone.

Rowan

This guy's dick reminds me of yours

Under, is a link from a gay porn site Rowan watches a lot of for someone who still claims not to be gay. The video heading is *Axxxel Stallion Jerks Giant Cock to Explosive Orgasm.*

Fucking Rowan Hughes.

"Who is she?" My sister's voice coaxes my focus off the ridiculous video thumbnail and onto her sneaky expression.

"What?"

She nods to the phone in my hand. "Every time you look at your phone, your face gets all red and dopey."

"Dopey?"

"Come on, Tommy. Who is she?" Erica tosses a tiny sliver of lettuce at me that only makes it half the distance between us. "You getting back together with Annalese?"

"Hell no," I balk and shove my phone away.

"Well, who are you texting? The same girl you're always sneaking out of here to see?"

"Sneaking out?" I laugh. "I leave through the front door. And I've told you. I've been training to make the team at school."

"You're training for soccer every night? Every Saturday night?" She pays me a look that says I'm full of shit, but I really am training most nights, including Saturdays. That's not all I'm doing, but as cool as Erica has been my whole life, I'm not ready to risk altering her entire perspective of me. Especially now, when I'm finally getting her back.

I'm bought some time when Erica calls out to Mav to set the table for supper. For six, he's pretty good at putting the plates and utensils where they belong, but he's not quite old enough to be trusted with the glassware.

Once Erica has passed everything along to Mav to put on the table, she's back down my throat. "So? What's her name? Tell me!"

"It's, uh..." I keep my eyes on the meat, stirring it while it reduces. "It's Rowan." I'm not good enough of a liar to think up a fake name, but I'm too cowardly to say Rowan is a guy.

"Rowan." she parrots. "That's a pretty name. I used to know a girl named Rowan. Wait. You're not dating Rowan Keiner, right?"

"No."

"Good. She's too old for you, and kinda nuts. So, what's your Rowan like?"

My Rowan. Why does my heart beat so quickly when those two words are paired together in my mind? If he's my Rowan, does that make me his Tommy?

"Hh—She's, um..." I clear my throat and lower the heat on the burner. "Weird. Intense. Funny. Loves soccer even more than I do."

"So, the opposite of Annalese?"

I chuckle at just how accurate that it. "Yeah. Rowan is...unique. Could be the best thing that's happened to me in a long time." I look back at her and smile. "Besides you getting better."

She smiles back, but there's something behind her eyes that doesn't seem as hopeful as I'd think she would be. "Can we talk?" she asks. "After dinner?"

16

Rowan

On my ass at McKinley Park with the evening sun lingering enough to make me sweat, I check my watch and see it's five after seven. Tommy isn't just late. He's *late* late. Just as I'm about to text him, I notice his truck pulling into the lot.

"You're late!" I call out to him before hopping to my feet. "You know what that means!"

No stretching. These suicides were already going to hurt, but now they're going to *hurt*.

"I know," he mutters, dropping his backpack on the grass after yanking his cleats out. He looks like someone just shat in his Cheerios. A mix of exhausted and pissed off.

"You good?"

"Peachy." He toes off his sneakers and pulls on his cleats, not paying me one glance. The first time he looks at me is when he's at the goal line, taking his mark. He tips his chin at me and asks what I'm waiting for.

Hmm. I can't think of why he'd be mad at me, but only because I'm very careful not to share anything too personal with him. Tommy can be jealous, but I haven't even looked at another guy since letting that pathetic dude suck my dick behind the bathroom. Did Tommy find out about that? I don't know how he could have.

Was it the porno I sent him? He knows I watch porn. He even knows I watch gay porn. I didn't even wank it to the video I sent him. I just wanted to make him laugh.

Maybe it's not me. Tommy did say his boss was being a dick today. Probably because he wanted me to comfort him. I'm just not good at comforting people. I don't know what to say or what to do.

The best I come up with is, "You sure you're good?"

"Are we gonna run or what?" Tommy shoots back, his typically smooth voice turning coarse as loose gravel, like he'd been screaming earlier. Or crying.

"Yeah, man. Let's sync up."

Once our watches are on the same timer, I give a three count, start my watch, and run.

When I texted Tommy about running suicides for an hour, it was only to mess with him. I figured we would do a few dozen then switch to technical drills, but Tommy is on another plane right now. He stays at my pace, but other than that, it's like I'm not here. Usually, Tommy rambles between sprints, wasting his air like a dumby, but not tonight.

"Last one," I tell him, the first words we've spoken between us since the timers started. I'm out of breath, calf muscles howling, and my clothes soaked through.

He doesn't answer. Doesn't pay me one look. We run the last suicide, and I plant my hands on my knees, sweat dripping from my nose to the grass below. I haven't stopped my timer yet, and when it gives a soft-tone beep, I notice Tommy going again.

After that, he goes again.

I watch him from behind the goal line, not sure if I'm witnessing a Rocky moment or a mental breakdown.

"Tommy!" I shout after he goes a fifth time past when I stopped.

He doesn't answer. Doesn't look my way. Doesn't stop.

In the few seconds' rest between sprints, I tell him, "That's good, Tommy. You can stop." But he goes again without so much as a grunt of acknowledgement.

Fed up, I march to the center of the field. As Tommy barrels toward me, I shout, "Stop!"

At the last second, Tommy swerves around me, then carries on like nothing's amiss.

Dude is a runaway train. Or...an updating laptop stuck on a perpetual restart loop. I don't fucking know, but it's freaking me out.

"What's going on?" I ask from the center of the field while he passes me at a strained sprint. "What happened? Are you pissed at me? Did I do something? Is this about your boss? Are you okay?"

Nothing. Like I'm talking to thin air.

Annoyance mixes with concern, and I come up with a stupid plan that might work to shake some reality back into Tommy's noggin. The next time he comes sprinting past, I lunge at him and sack him linebacker-style, dragging him down by the waist and landing on top of him when his back hits the grass.

"What the fuck?" he finally speaks while trying to buck me off him.

I steel myself, like I can make myself heavier with sheer will alone. I grasp Tommy's wrists before he can push me off, and I hold them to the grass.

"Yeah, what the fuck?" I ask through gritted teeth while trying with all my might to hold Tommy down.

He bucks and pushes, not going easy on me, and when I falter for just a moment, Tommy shoves me off him and turns the tables.

Now he's the one holding my wrists to the grass. His knees dig into my thighs, his ankles cuffing mine with how much pressure he's able to put on me, even after the weight he's shed.

"Tommy," I hiss, because the pain is real and so is the fear. Adrenaline pumping my heart like a speed bag. I don't like being afraid of Tommy. It doesn't feel right—those baby blue eyes full of rage and hatred. Then again, I've seen it before.

I fight against Tommy's weight, but the more I do, the weaker I become. In a last ditch effort to break through to him, my macho jock brain decides to challenge him. "You wanna fucking hit me again, motherfucker?! Do it!"

Something flashes across Tommy's face, making it crumble from his fiery bluster to something sad and hopeless. His sneer morphs to a pouty frown, and his eyes well up with tears. He goes from overpowering me to burying his face in the crook of my neck and latching himself around me so tight my lungs can hardly expand enough for me to murmur his name.

"Tommy," I choke. "It's okay."

His knees shift off my legs to straddle me instead, and as I rub my palms along the back of his sweat-stained shirt, his body quivers against me. Something wets my shoulder. Tears. Tommy's soft, whimpered groans aren't anything like his pleasured ones. These hurt even worse than that punch to the face did.

"It's okay," I repeat, but nothing feels okay. Tommy is clearly not okay, and I can't be okay until I figure out what's wrong.

Do I want to know what's wrong? As indestructible as Tommy seems to think I am right now, I'm not a rock for people to take their emotions out on. My own emotions are hard enough to handle without me trying to take on the responsibility of another's. Just another reason in a very long list of why I can't do a relationship.

"Tommy, please. I can't breathe."

Finally, Tommy's hold relaxes enough that my ribs quit aching and I can take in a full breath. I use it to ask, "What's wrong?"

"I'm sorry," he whines with his forehead pressed to the center of my chest, his soft hair tickling my chin. I lay my hand on the back of his head and run my fingertips along his damp scalp.

"It's okay, baby boy."

After a minute of him catching his breath against my skin and relaxing those intense muscles of his, Tommy rolls off me. Onto his back on the grass beside me. His hand finds mine without looking, and he holds it almost as tight as he squeezed my body against his own, like he's trying to absorb me into him or the other way around.

He has a way of holding my hand where I can't hold his back. It's probably because he thinks I'd pull away if given the choice, but I think I could hold his hand. It's not that big of a deal.

Dumbly, I ask, "You okay?"

His head shakes, eyes to the sky.

I should ask what's wrong again, what happened, or if he's mad at me, but now that he might actually answer, I'm too afraid to ask.

Soon, though, he answers on his own. "My sister is gonna die."

That isn't what I expected him to say, though I'm not sure what I expected. I didn't even know Tommy had a sister. Or did I? Maybe he told me and I forgot, because my head is so compartmentalized there's no room for anything besides soccer, school, and getting off. I started building a new com-partment just for Tommy, but it's still under construction, and I'm not sure it'll ever be stable enough to shelter him full-time.

"Do you, uh...wanna go somewhere and talk about it?" Part of me wants him to say no and let him deal with it on his own, but the thought of him leaving me now fills me up with more dread than I can stand. I want to be there for him. I want to want to be there for him, at least.

He doesn't answer for a while. Long enough for me to wonder if he's stuck in another loop of blinking up at the sky. But then he turns his head, blinks glossy blues at me, and says, "Okay."

We take my car to a 24/7 diner I like because the décor makes it feel like a cozy den. The mood is always chill, and the bacon is always perfectly crispy. I order us both chocolate milkshakes and a plate of double bacon, and Tommy tells me everything without qualm, as if the four-top booth we're tucked into is our own private confessional.

He talks and talks, and I try to process everything as it comes. I try to focus more on the words Tommy says rather than the way his mouth moves, and I nod when I'm supposed to and ask questions when it seems appropriate. Active listening, and what not.

What I hear is fucking heartbreaking. It explains why Tom-my quit soccer in the first place, and why he still thinks he should. I've never loved someone so much I'd give up soccer to be there for them. The concept is difficult for me to un-derstand, but Tommy's not me. Tommy is warm, thoughtful and compassionate, and his heart is ten times bigger than those muscles that crushed me to the ground so easily.

"So, she's decided to just give up," Tommy says, frowning morosely at his fingers while they crumble a piece of bacon into chunks. "Told the doctors she doesn't want the chemo anymore. I thought she was feeling better because the chemo was working, but it's because she stopped treatment two weeks ago. Didn't even tell me 'til tonight. Ma knew, and she didn't tell me. They haven't even told Maverick yet. How do you do that? How do you tell your six-year-old you're choosing to die and leave them parentless?"

A question I can't possibly answer, but the way Tommy pauses makes it seem like he expects one.

"I don't know," I tell him, wishing I could say more.

"She tried making it sound like she was doing me a favor." Tommy scoffs down at his bacon crumbs. "Like, I wouldn't have to do so much now that she's feeling better, and she could come to my soccer matches, as if I'm ever gonna get actual playing time. It's bullshit. Sure, she'll be better for now, but in six months...maybe a year...she'll be in hospice, and it'll be too late to do anything. She'll just be gone. None of us are gonna be better off with her gone. It's fucking selfish."

He's angry, but the tears that slip down his cheeks before he can swipe them away don't feel like malice. Feels like grief, and maybe that's what he's really pissed about. That he has to grieve his sister before he's ready.

"What do you think?" he asks, like he's begging me to validate or invalidate him. He trusts me, I guess.

"I don't know."

"C'mon, man. You're always telling me not to give up. She's giving up. Trading the possibility of a long life with her family and her kid for...what? Six good months? Six months of playing Mario Kart with Mav, helping Ma with dinner, and watching me sit on a bench? That's enough for her apparently, but it's not enough for us. It's like she just decided we're not worth it anymore."

He blinks at me expectantly, forcing me to speak, but I know that no matter what I say, it's going to be the wrong thing.

"I always tell you not to give up on yourself," I say. "You can give up on anyone else whenever you want." *Including me.*

"How is letting yourself die not giving up on yourself?"

"Because people don't chase life, Tommy. They chase happiness. For most people, life is essential to the experience of happiness. For others, sometimes, that's not the case. Sometimes, life can feel like more of a barrier than a pre-requisite to happiness. Maybe your sister reached her barrier."

His Adam's apple bobs as his throat contracts. "How do you know that?"

Looking at the table, I tell him something I never planned on telling anyone who doesn't already know. "There was a time—a couple times—when I hit that barrier. The first time, I told the doctors I accidentally took too much Tylenol because of muscle pain after a match. They believed me, because I was thirteen, and they bought that a thirteen-year-old would be stupid enough to take a toxic amount of Tylenol because their back hurt. The second time... Well, no one bought that that was an accident."

Tommy's face looks like heartbreak, like I just told him I'm dying. "Row—"

"I'm okay. I'm fine. I got past the barrier, and I'm fine now. I didn't tell you so you'll worry about me. I told you so you'll know that I've been there. In a way, I get it, and I'm telling you that Erica's decision has nothing to do with how she feels about you and everything to do with how she feels about her own life. She could love you more than anything in the world and still make the same decision."

"Okay, but..." Tommy's voice cracks and he rubs his wrist under his nose. "What am I supposed to do?"

"I don't know."

He drops his face and cries quietly into his hands, and it breaks my heart thinking I only made things worse for someone I care about more than I thought I could care about anyone.

We head to my car after I pay the bill, and I drive us back to campus where Tommy's truck is still parked by the intramural field. I pull up beside it, but Tommy doesn't get out. Doesn't even click his seatbelt off.

"I can't go home yet," he mumbles through his sorrow, staring at the glove box. "I can't look at Erica right now. I can't look at Mav, knowing what I know."

I didn't think so, but I've been waiting for him to say it. "Do you...wanna stay with me tonight?"

His head turns, eyes meeting mine, and I'm glad to see they're dry at least. "That's okay?"

No.

Maybe.

"Yeah, it's okay."

17

Tommy

At the very least, discovering where Rowan lives is a slight distraction from the darkness swirling around in my head. He parks at the curb in front of a nice, average house with a pitched roof, a picket fence, and a gate across the driveway. Instead of going to the front door, Rowan guides the way through the driveway gate using a padlock key off his keyring. There are two cars parked between the gate and the double garage door. A minivan and a four-door sedan. Rowan takes me to a narrow door off the side of the garage and opens it without a key.

"Be careful," he says low. "There's a ton of junk everywhere."

Taking heed, I follow a half-step behind Rowan, and I don't shut the door behind us until a light flickers on.

The place looks like a garage full of junk. Like literally just a garage full of junk. There's a washer and dryer against the back wall next to a big basin sink, and after that are two white doors, one half open to reveal a small bathroom.

Rowan holds the next door open for me, and I step through into a room no bigger than an office. The large desk that takes up a fourth of the room suggests it used to be just that. The desk is piled high with folded clothes, and the swivel chair is pushed against the opposite wall stacked with textbooks and spiral-bounds. A twin-xl bed is wedged between the front of the desk and a wall, underneath a long window fitted toward the ceiling. The bed is dressed in a fitted sheet and rumpled comforter, storage bins tucked beneath the frame, and all that's left is a sliver of floor space just large enough to do push-ups. No closet, no ceiling light. Just a floor lamp wedged behind the door and a small window AC Rowan has to climb onto his mattress to switch on.

"This is your room?" I ask, taking everything in like I just walked through a portal in *The Twilight Zone*. Wherever I'd imagined Rowan living, it wasn't here.

"What, you don't like it?" he asks once the AC is whirling on low.

"It's just not what I expected."

"What did you expect?"

I keep looking around like there's so much to see in this prison cell sized room Rowan somehow makes do in. My bedroom is tight, but only because of Mav and his things. It's still homey, though. Still has my posters on the walls, my souvenirs in the bookshelf, and my teenage growth spurt documented in permanent marker on the closet door.

"I guess I pictured something more...sterile."

"Sterile?" he chuckles.

"Like, neurotically clean. Some sleek apartment in white and gray tones with exactly one potted plant that you treat like a pet. I don't know. I always thought you had money."

I look at him, sitting on the side of his bed, and even though he's smiling, I can tell he's insecure. A hint of emotion in his eyes that he rarely shows. "I've got my own room and my own bathroom, so it could be worse, right?"

He's got a point. Most days, I would kill to have my own bathroom, especially with Mav's hour long bathtimes.

Rowan's smile fades until all that's left is insecurity. "I'm sorry."

"Don't be."

"We can go somewhere else."

"This is fine. I'm sorry. I'm just fucked up right now. I'm sorry I said that. I'm sorry I hurt you."

His lips fold and his eyes intensify. "You didn't hurt me." As ardent as it is, it still feels like a lie. As badly as I want to believe Rowan is made of steel, there's fragility under that tough façade. He stands, toes out of his shoes, and asks if I want a shower.

"Probably should," I say, figuring I'm pretty ripe from all the running and the full-blown panic attack I had all over Rowan. How humiliating. I'm surprised he's even letting me in his place. Also surprised he didn't boot me out when I couldn't think of anything nice to say about his living arrangement.

Among the stacks of laundry on the desk, Rowan pulls out two folded towels, and I follow him out of the room just to circle into the next one over.

The bathroom is small; the two of us just barely fit in it together, but it's clean and updated so far as it reminds me of a bathroom in a cheaply flipped home. There's a pedestal sink and a toilet with a few shelves above, and instead of a bathtub, there's a narrow shower stall with a clear curtain.

Rowan drops the towels on the toilet seat and asks if it's okay that we shower together.

I scoff, partly because I don't know if we'll both fit in the shower, but also because I can't imagine *not* showering with Rowan. "Of course."

Once the water is warm and our clothes are in a pile on the sink, I find out how two grown men fit into a shower so small. I circle my arms around Rowan's body and hug it against mine.

I put my cheek against his stubbled jaw and run my hands all across his back and shoulders. All soft skin and hard muscle. In my arms, he feels smaller than he is, like I could carry him around with me forever.

Being flush against him, my cock naturally responds. Even with how dark I feel inside, my outsides feel warm, comforted, and enchanted by the feel of Rowan's nakedness against mine. As I swell up, my cock digs against Rowan's hip.

"I'm sorry," I whisper.

"Don't be sorry, baby boy." He sweeps his palms along my spine and says, "I got you."

Rowan reaches for a bottle on the small alcove in the wall, a Pert 3-in-1 that he snaps open and squeezes into his palm.

"Couldn't find a six-in-one?" I ask. "Shampoo, conditioner, body wash, toothpaste, laundry detergent, drain cleaner—"

"You motherfucker," Rowan snickers, a wide grin stretching across his face while smearing the green soap across my shoulders and down my chest. "Here I am, trying to take care of your ass, and you act like a little brat."

I kiss his water speckled forehead and revel in the feel of Rowan's large, slightly coarse palms soaping me up. I reach for the bottle myself, squeeze out a hardy amount, and spread it down Rowan's back and all the way up to make suds in his short hair.

His eyelids lower as I massage the 3-in-1 into his scalp, a soft moan rumbling from his throat. I look down between us and watch his cock jump, grazing my balls in a sensation that only hardens me more.

I smooth a soapy palm down his chest and abs to wash his junk as gently as I can. His cock thickens in my palm, and I stroke his shaft nice and slow until he's as hard as I am.

Another moan breezes past Rowan's parted lips, and a moment later, I feel my cock wrapped in the snug embrace of Rowan's slippery hand. I kiss the moan from his lips and taste shower water amid the lingering milkshake taste on his tongue.

We get clean and leave the bathroom with towels around our waists like skirts, my dick poking at the fabric.

As soon as we're shut up in his room, I take my towel off and drape it on the doorknob while Rowan hangs his on the corner of his headboard.

"Want boxers?" he asks, sifting through his clothes stacks.

"Row." I take his hand, guide him from the desk-turned-dresser and turn him to face me.

Washing my eyes over every inch of him, I find his beauty helps to quell my fucked up thoughts. Like resenting my dying sister for not loving me enough. I don't want to be that selfish. I don't want to prefer her suffering to me not losing her. I don't want Rowan to think I'm that needy, even though I am needy. As needy as Lese was with me, I think I might be that needy with Rowan.

I take his tapered hips and kiss our cocks together.

Sweeping a palm through my damp hair, Rowan tells me to get into bed.

I touch my forehead against his, grinding our hips together. "Call me baby boy."

Against my mouth, Rowan murmurs, "Get into bed, baby boy, and I'll make you come."

I obey, arousal and affection eclipsing my sorrow just enough to stir some excitement into me. Chasing happiness, I guess.

The closest, purest source of happiness I can get my hands on climbs onto the narrow bed with me, pushes aside the comforter and straddles my thighs. His balls sit on top of mine, his cock crossing with mine, and all I can do is stare at his sharp jaw and parted lips while running my hands over every inch of his toned body—his rippled abs, pebbled nipples, and the black hairs across his chest.

I put my hand around his cock and stroke it until a dribble of pre-cum drools onto my own cock.

"Fuck," Rowan sighs. He plants his hands on my shoulders and rolls his hips like he's riding me.

I fit both our cocks in a loose fist and give something for Rowan to fuck. My other hand reaches around to squeeze his ass and tug at the cheek, curious about that part of his body but too nervous to try anything.

What are the chances Rowan would ever bottom for me?

One of us will have to, the way we're going, and I really hope it's him.

He sits up, points his nose down and drools a long dribble of saliva onto our cocks, until they're both slippery in my palm.

We're both moaning, AC still whirling, and the bed frame creaking in time with how Rowan grinds his balls against mine. Lost in the euphoria of it all, I do something reckless. I bring a hand to my lips and push as much saliva onto my fingers as I can. Some of it drips onto my chest as I bring my hand back to Rowan's ass, but I smear most of it down his crack and around his tightly puckered hole.

He folds over, putting his hands on either side of my head and tucking his mouth against my ear. "You wanna fuck me, baby boy?" he murmurs.

I whimper involuntarily, my cock throbbing like mad. I massage Rowan's hole firm enough to feel the muscled ring relax. "Just wanna feel how tight you are."

Rowan's hot, wet tongue swipes across my ear. "If you put that finger in my ass, I'm gonna come."

"Oh fuck," I groan and press my finger in to the first knuckle. I press firmer until Rowan's ass loosens, and I sink all the way in.

Rowan's face drops to my shoulder, mouth open and moaning against my skin. His hips move quicker, like he's fucking himself on my finger.

I'm in heaven, thinking the only thing better than this right here would be if it was my dick inside Rowan's asshole. Just his moaning alone is enough to get me close, but his grinding is making me see stars.

I pump my finger in his hole, but it's tighter than tight, and I could sure use some actual lube right about now.

Rowan reaches back and captures my wrist, pressing my finger as deeply as it'll fit inside him and holding me steady there.

"Slow," he says.

When he lets go, I move my fingers in small, steady motions while Rowan humps my body and wets our bellies with his pre-cum. His mouth latches onto my neck, tickling me with his stubble and riling me up with his tongue and teeth.

I'm panting, bucking my hips up to meet Rowan's hips. "Rowan," I moan.

"Fuck me," Rowan grunts before groaning a string of incoherent pleasure-sounds.

I feel him come. The way his body shakes and my abdomen feels warm and wet.

"I'm coming," I cry, squeezing our cocks together hard enough to make us both gasp before orgasm ripples through me.

I take my hand away and slap it down on Rowan's ass I'm still knuckle deep in, and I let the pressure of Rowan's body pressed flush against mine coax me through a slow-rolling climax that seems to last even after my balls are empty.

Can't think of the last time I came so hard from dry humping. If this could even be called that, when everything is so fucking wet.

As soon as Rowan calms on top of me, he grabs my wrist again and guides my finger slowly from his ass. He slips onto his side, tucked between me and the wall, and he reaches across my head to grab his towel off the headboard. He cleans himself of our fluids, then me, but my erection isn't going down.

I turn on my side and press my body back against Rowan's, where it belongs. "You're so hot," I murmur before colliding my mouth against his.

A chuckle rumbles from Rowan's mouth into mine. "Thanks, gay boy."

"How did I know you were going to say that?"

"'Cause you're my gay boy."

Dancing my fingers along Rowan's hairy thigh and smooth hip, there's no doubt in my mind that I'm gay. But *his?* My heart flutters at the thought. And when I look into Rowan's eyes, it's like the world around us melts away. There's nothing else.

His hand touches my face, tracing my brow, my cheekbone, and the slope of my nose. "You gonna be okay?"

"I dunno," I answer honestly. "Don't think I've been okay for a long time. But right now, I feel okay. With you."

I want to cling to him so badly, but how do I cling without being clingy?

The way he touches his lips to mine almost convinces me I can. When he pulls away, I miss him, but he puts his mouth on my chest next. He nudges me onto my back and kisses the narrow valley between my abs. His hand lifts my cock, and his mouth envelopes me in a wave of heat and comfort.

I open my legs for him and lay my hands on his head. I watch him for a minute before letting my eyes slip shut, and I swear the orgasm he sucks out of me takes my soul along with it.

And the next time I open my eyes, it's morning.

I'm wrapped around Rowan, nose in his hair, arm slung around his waist and my knees tucked behind his. He must've switched off the AC some time after I passed out last night, because the room is quiet and warm enough I consider un-furling myself from Rowan, but that's the last thing I want.

My dick is hard against his ass. I hold him tighter, and he lets out a sleepy groan. I kiss the top of his shoulder before drifting back to sleep.

I don't know what time it is when I next wake up, but Rowan is still asleep, and the ache in my balls is now an ache in my bladder. It forces me to leave his bed, and I steal a pair of boxers from his clothes pile before slipping out of the room.

Our workout clothes are still in the bathroom sink. I pile them on the floor to wash my hands and snag a swig of Rowan's mouthwash.

I leave the bathroom just as the side garage door opens, and I freeze. Light from the backyard streams into the musty garage, and a slender woman with thick, curly hair comes through carrying an overloaded laundry basket on her hip.

She gasps a little when she sees me.

Realizing I'm wearing nothing but Rowan's boxers, which are a size smaller than I usually wear, I wrap my arms around myself like that'll make all the difference.

"Hi," the woman chirps at the same time I say, "I'm sorry."

I clear my throat, looking around like Rowan might manifest beside me to explain why a strange, mostly naked man is standing in the garage.

"No, no," the woman says. "I'm sorry. Rowan is normally out on one of his morning runs by now." She hefts the laundry basket up on the washer before extending her arm toward me, face alight with a cheery, pearly grin. "You're Tommy, right? I'm Xiamara."

"Uh, y—yeah. Nice to meet you." I uncover myself with one arm to shake her hand.

If Xiamara is Rowan's mom, it would explain his dark hair and lean build, but she would have to have been really young when Rowan came along. Could explain why he doesn't talk about his family. Ma had Erica when she was young, and Erica always says it made things between them off, like Erica was more of an annoying baby sister to Ma than a daughter. But all that resentment went by the wayside after Erica's diagnosis.

"Do me a favor and let Rowan know I'm about to start on breakfast. I want both of you at the table in twenty minutes, alright?"

I say the first thing that will get me out of the conversation and back into Rowan's room. "Sure thing."

As soon as I'm back in Rowan's room, I remember how warm it is in here. Careful not to step on the sleepyhead, I climb onto the mattress and fiddle with the window unit until it's humming a cool breeze.

Rowan's body shifts between my feet. I look down, and he's on his back, blinking a confounded expression at me. "Are you about to shit on me?"

I laugh and wink. "Want me to?"

"Please don't," he groans before rubbing his eyes and letting out an adorable yawn. "What time is it?"

Lowering to my ass, I stick my back to the wall and drape my legs across Rowan's. "Almost eight-thirty." I skate my palm across his torso and swirl my fingers through his body hair.

"How did you sleep?" His eyes drift shut as his hand comes to lie upon mine, stilling it above his navel.

"Good. I think I held you all night."

"It's okay," he says, like I had apologized for it.

"How'd you sleep?"

"Surprised I slept at all with your horse cock stabbing at my ass all night."

"That's completely out of my control," I chuckle.

Peeking his eyelids open, Rowan pushes my hand down his body until the comforter lowers and I'm palming his hot, swollen cock. "That's in your control," he murmurs.

My chuckle turns breathy as my dick perks to life in these tight boxers. "Rowan Hughes giving up control?"

"Happens more often than you think." He props himself up on his elbows and sets his drowsy gaze on what my hand is doing to his cock. "Do you mind I'm uncut?"

"No." In a gentle grip, I make his foreskin move over his crown and back down. "I like it, actually. It's like I'm playing peek-a-boo with your boner."

"Fuck off," Rowan laughs, snatching my hand off his dick and pulling me over him.

I nestle myself halfway on top of him, hugging his waist and draping my leg over his hip. The best part is when Rowan curls his arms around me and hugs me back, then when he nuzzles his nose against my forehead before kissing it. His guard is down, even after how I acted last night. After how I put a look of genuine fear on his face.

"Am I crushing you?" I murmur.

"Huh uh. Feels nice. Heavy, but nice. I guess, now we know for sure which one of us would win in a fight. I'm not too proud to concede."

"I'm sorry." I hug him tighter, turn my face and bury my nose under his arm, smelling one part musk and one part Pert.

"Shh. You have no reason to be sorry."

"Yes, I do."

"Well, I don't want it. Besides, I'm the dumbass who tackled you to the ground. Guess I forgot why I quit football in pee wees."

"Thank you." I lift my head to look him in the eyes, and I hope he doesn't mind I'm pouting.

"I didn't do anything," he answers in his typical stoic way.

"You did a lot. You do a lot for me, Row. More than you've ever had to. I wish there was a way for me to tell you how much you mean to me without it fucking everything up." *Like that I need you. That I want to be with you, even if it means people find out I'm gay and can never see me the same again.* I stare at his throat and watch the knot move as Rowan swallows. "What you told me last night...about how you tried to—"

"Don't worry about that. I'm past it."

"Still." I force my eyes back on his, suffocating a little in the intensity. He doesn't like talking about himself, especially when it's serious, especially when it'll make him seem fragile. "Promise me you won't try anything like that again. Promise me you won't give up."

"Tommy—"

"Promise me."

"I promise," he whispers, sweeping his hand around my back like he wants to warm me up. "And I know I said I don't fuck with quitters, but if you ever need to quit the team, I'll still fuck with you."

So I won't bawl all over him again, I preoccupy myself with nipping at his frown until he kisses me back.

When Rowan asks if I want to go for a run, I think he's trying to preoccupy me too, but it just makes me laugh against his cheek.

"Actually, before you woke up, while I was coming out of the bathroom, I ran into...Xiamara—"

"What?" He blinks wide, fully awake now. "What do you mean? What happened?"

"Nothing. She shook my hand and told me to tell you we have to be at the table for breakfast in twenty minutes. Which was about fifteen minutes ago."

Rowan is silent for a few seconds, his expression losing the morning-magic glow to adopt his more typical grimness. "Shit," he mutters. "You can borrow my clothes."

The clothes Rowan lends me fit, sort of. Enough that I won't look like a dumbass in front of his mom again. I decide that if she asks, I'll say I crashed on the floor, and I slept in boxers because my clothes were filthy. Innocent enough, right? At the very least, it might save Rowan from an inquisition he doesn't want.

Then again, Xiamara knew my name already, which means Rowan must have told her about me. That's a good sign, right?

Rowan is tense heading into this. He has his hands in his pockets from his room to the main house, and he only takes one out when he has to pull open the back door and let me inside.

The first thing I'm hit with is the scent of home cooking as I step into a galley kitchen and come face to face with Xiamara again, posted up at the stove flipping pancakes.

"Oh, good!" she exclaims over the sound of something jaunty and animated playing on a TV past the kitchen. She skitters away from the stove long enough to pull me into a hug that startles me. Rowan shuts the door, and Xiamara rustles her hand across his bristly head and tells him good morning.

A young girl races into the kitchen and flings herself against Xiamara's side just as an even younger girl races after her.

"Mom, she's trying to glitter glue me!" the larger one whines.

"Lena!" Xiamara points at the littler girl. "What did I tell you about the glitter glue?"

Stopping in her tracks, the little one hugs a bottle of blue glitter to her chest and says, "Glitter glue is not makeup."

"Go put it back, then wash up for breakfast." Xiamara pets the bigger girl's dark hair. "Olive, go help your sister wash her hands."

"She's not a baby!" Olive exclaims. "She can do it herself!"

"Help her anyway," Xiamara says in a firmer tone, leaving Olive no choice but to unstick herself from her mother's side and comply. As she goes, she casts a long look over her shoulder at me, eyes a little wide but unquestioning of my presence.

Rowan has sisters. *Little* sisters. Somehow, I always pegged him for having youngest-child syndrome.

"Matt!" Xiamara hollers through the wall. "Breakfast is almost ready!" She quiets her voice to tell Rowan and I to head to the table.

Rowan leading the way, I'm shown a family room open to a dining area where a table is made with six place settings. Butter, syrup and jam already in the center of the table. Between the sectional and the TV in the living room, a man with graying blond hair changes the diaper of a toddler-age boy laid out on a towel on the rug. The boy's brown curls and Cars t-shirt remind me of when Maverick was small enough to still wear diapers.

Rowan pulls a chair out for me, like I'm his date or something, but I think it's just so he makes sure I sit in the correct seat. Families always have their own personal spots at the table. But before I can sit, Rowan's dad pops up from behind the sofa with the tiny one on his hip and says, "You must be Tommy."

To be polite, I leave Rowan's side to shake his dad's hand. "Nice to meet you, sir."

"Call me Matt," he says. "Rowan's talked a lot about you."

"He has?"

"He said he's been training you to be a starter. Had a late night?"

"Oh. Yeah. I, uh, crashed on the floor."

He gives a casual nod, hopefully believing me. "Have a seat. We'll have plenty of food to go around. Hope you're hungry."

"Thank you." I do as I'm told and sit in the chair Rowan pulled out. He sits in the one beside me.

This feels weird. Weird-good, because I love homemade breakfast, but also weird-scary. I barely told Erica about Rowan last night, lying about him being female even, but Rowan's parents know about me enough to assume any random guy appearing in their home must be Tommy. I'm sure they only know of me as Rowan's friend, but I know we're more than that. Especially after last night. I know we didn't fuck, but the way our bodies melded together as we came at the same time was such a mind-fuck that it feels like we consummated something. And I was inside him, for crying out loud! Just a finger, but still. The way he responded to it, it may as well have been my dick.

Sex aside, I talked to Rowan about something I never thought I'd be able to. Not only did he listen, but he took care of me. Took me home, cleaned me up, calmed me down, and let me spoon him despite my pesky boner poking him in the back all night. He told me things too. Things I can't minimize or forget. Things that make me worry about him while also tethering my heart tighter to him.

I look sideways at him, and I can tell he's in his head. Pensive and chewing on the inside of his cheek. Under the table, I lay my hand on his leg long enough to give it a reassuring squeeze. Thankfully, he responds by sending me a soft smile that's almost reassuring back.

The girls come back to the table and sit across from Rowan and me. The younger one, Lena, quickly starts up talking to Rowan the same way Mav talks to me, rambling and overexcited about even the most mundane activities. It's cute to see how unintimidated the little girl is of Rowan, and how sweet Rowan is back to her.

Meanwhile, Olive won't quit staring at me, and when I smile at her, she goes beet red and looks away.

Matt sticks the toddler in a high chair beside one head of the table before joining Xiamara in the kitchen. They both come out a minute later with platters of breakfast foods that turn my nervousness into hunger.

As soon as everyone is at the table and piling their plates, Rowan starts in talking to Matt about sports. Catching up on the latest MLB news, commenting on the recent NBA draft, and discussing our upcoming soccer season. It's nice Rowan can nerd out with his dad about the shit he's passionate about, and Matt seems to know a lot about soccer. Not just fan stuff but minute details about the sport, how it's played and how to train for it. It takes minutes for me to realize he's wearing a faded McClatchy High Men's Soccer t-shirt.

"Okay, okay, that's enough sports talk," Xiamara interjects, waving her hands as if to waft the subject into oblivion. Turning a giddy grin to me, she asks, "What do you do, Tommy?"

"Uh." I clear my throat. "I play soccer."

Rowan chuckles beside me as Xiamara's expression turns pointed and unamused.

"Sorry," I say. "I, uh, work at a deli part-time. Go to school. Help take care of my sister and my nephew."

"You're close with your family?" she asks me.

"Yeah. I think so. They're, like, the most important people in my life." *Besides Rowan.*

She nods, sending a smile at Rowan. "He gets along with his family."

"Yeah, I know," Rowan replies with a slight edge of annoyance to his tone.

I look between the two of them, kind of confused, but I know as well as anyone how complex the mother-son relationship can be.

Looking back at me, Xiamara asks, "So how long have you two been, you know...friends?"

"Uhh." Between the manner in which Xiamara said *friends* and the sparkle in her eyes, I'm guessing she gleaned something intimate from how she met me in the garage. The strangest thing is that she doesn't bat an eye at the idea Rowan would be involved with a guy. In fact, her eyes are wide open, scintillating for details like she's been waiting her whole life for Rowan to bring a boy home for breakfast.

"Xiamara," Matt says with a small warning in his tone.

I look between the two of them before looking at Rowan. He's staring at his plate, not touching a thing despite the bacon being extra crispy, just the way he likes.

Do his parents know he's gay? If they know, and they don't mind, why the hell does Rowan have such a hard time admitting it?

"Well, listen," Xiamara says, reaching over to rub my shoulder. "You are always welcome here, and don't think you have to stay out in the garage. You and Rowan can use the house whenever you want. Use the kitchen to make food or the living room to watch movies—"

"Thank you," Rowan interrupts, sounding like he really wants her to quit talking.

"He's a good one, okay?" she tells me, pointing at Rowan. "People act like all he's good for is kicking a ball around a field, but he's a good man without all that. Remember that, Tommy."

"Chill out, Xia," Matt tells her. "You're making Rowan uncomfortable."

"No, I'm not," she argues, but when I look at Rowan, he looks upset. I want to put my arm around him and tell him his mom is right. He is a good man, with or without soccer.

"Tommy, how's practice going?" Matt asks me. "Finding your footing alright?"

"Yeah, it's been alright. Don't think I could've made it this far without your son's help, though."

"My son?" Matt chuckles, laying a hand on the head of the babbling toddler in the highchair. "Did Rowan tell you we're his parents?"

"No," Rowan answers for me, quickly and firmly. His face is red, and he looks more embarrassed now than when Xiamara insinuated that we're more than just friends.

Shit. "I'm sorry. I assumed—"

"It's okay," Rowan tells me.

"Matt was an assistant soccer coach at McClatchy when Rowan was there," Xiamara says. "He's been living with us since his senior year of high school. He's pretty much family now. If I weren't too young, Rowan could be my son."

"You would've been sixteen. It's not too young," Olive objects.

"Yes, it is," Xiamara tells her pointedly. "Sixteen is too young. Way too young."

"Not for *Gilmore Girls*," Olive argues.

"I knew letting you watch that was a mistake."

"Just saying!" Olive exclaims. "Rowie can be your son. You're not too young."

Rowie? That's hands-down the cutest thing I've ever heard, but I'm too confused to fully appreciate it. Rowan lives with his high school coach's family? Where is his actual family?

Trying to change the subject for Rowan's benefit, I ask the two girls how old they are. Lena proudly says six, and Olive clams up, letting her little sister announce she's nine.

"My nephew is six. He's the coolest little dude in the world."

"You should bring him over," Xiamara suggests. "We grill in the back sometimes and invite friends. You can bring your whole family."

"Thank you. That's..." I feel my whole countenance dim as the realization hits that if Rowan's pseudo-family knows he's gay and we're more than friends, I can't bring my family around them. Erica thinks she can die happy now because I've got a new *girl*friend, and Ma is...Ma. I can't even bring Mav around, because he'd parrot back anything he sees and hears to Erica and Ma. "Uh, that's really nice, but it probably wouldn't work out. There's usually a lot going on, so..."

"That's alright," Xiamara says. "Just keep bringing yourself around."

"I'll try." Not like that's my decision to make, and when I look at Rowan, he's stuck in stoic mode. Unreadable.

This is too much for him, I can tell, but these people seem amazing. At first I felt sorry about Rowan's living situation, but now I see how good he has it. His chosen family seems to really care about him and want him to feel included. Matt even says they're all planning on coming to the first match of the season to watch Rowan play.

After breakfast, I offer to help with the dishes, and Xiamara eagerly accepts the offer. She looks so happy that it's hard not to smile when she flips up the sink water and asks, "How long have you two been seeing each other?"

I exhale a chuckle as my face goes hot. I'm overwhelmed and flustered, sweating despite the central cooling.

"It's not... We're just..." My mind goes back to the first time I kissed him, when I swore I'd be happy so long as we're *something*. I still don't know what that something is, only that being here makes me feel more comfortable than ever about the idea of having a boyfriend. Not just having a boyfriend, but having Rowan as my boyfriend. "Since spring, I guess, but it started with him just wanting to help me get on the team and kinda evolved from there."

Nodding, Xiamara starts on rinsing the dishes for the dishwasher. "The only really positive role models Rowan ever had in his life were his coaches. Matt coached him from when he was a kid, and now he's part of our family. If Rowan is putting so much effort in to help you train, it's because he cares about you. It's not always all about soccer. Not even for Rowan."

I glance back toward the family room, where Matt and Rowan have switched the TV channel to college basketball. Even in his semi-uncomfortable, just-rolled-out-of-bed state, Rowan makes my heart pump quicker with how stunning he is. Clearly, I'm very attracted to the male form, but there's something about Rowan specifically that almost makes me feel lucky to be gay.

"It's not just about soccer for me. Even when we first started training together, it wasn't. I think it's always been about him for me."

I look back to Xiamara, and she's grinning ear to ear, her eyes sparkling with something that looks a hell of a lot like pride.

18
Tommy

Rowan has been going easy on me. He's not running me as hard, pushing me as much, or chiding me when I'm whiny or lazy. He's giving me days off out of the blue, or picking me up just to take me to Sonic. I don't complain, because who doesn't love eating Coney dogs and being lazy? But my game is slipping, and Rowan's might be too. Coach is yelling at him a lot more at practice, and second string won the last two scrimmages. Failing is one thing, but I don't want Rowan failing because he thinks I'm too depressed to train the way we were.

Mentally, I'm a wreck. Even though Erica is feeling okay, tensions at home are high. The better Erica feels, the shorter Ma is with her, like she's trying to punish Erica for choosing the path she has. I'm trying to be accepting. As accepting as I'd want her to be of me if I had enough courage to tell her the truth.

Rowan knows I want to date him for real. Not because I told him that in so many words, but because it's pretty glaringly obvious. That might be another reason he's going easy on me, like sucking my dick and buying me junk food is his form of a consolation prize. Again, it's a tough thing to complain about, but we're well into August now, and the first match of the season is only two weeks away.

Coach pulls me into his office after Friday's practice and tells me straight up I'm plateauing.

"I've got Rowan in here nearly every day telling me you belong on the starting roster, but I'm just not seeing what he sees in you. You paying his rent or something?"

"We're just friends," I say, hanging my head a little. It's embarrassing the way Rowan pushes me to Coach like an overbearing parent, but then I think back to what Xiamara said about how Rowan shows affection, and my heart swells a little.

"Rowan doesn't have friends." Coach shoots a wad of paper into a wastebasket like it's a three-pointer, misses, then drops heavily into his desk chair. "Rowan is a machine. Crank the pin in his back, and he goes. Last thing someone like him needs is a friend."

"Well, I'm his friend and he's mine. If I'm plateauing, it's not his fault."

"Is it your fault he's slipping?"

"What?"

"How would you feel if I benched Rowan for the first match of the season because you want to take him out partying, or line-dancing, or whatever kids do these days?"

My ass scoots to the edge of my seat, probably looking like a deer in Coach's headlights. "Rowan is getting benched?"

"You tell me." Coach puts his focus on his computer monitor, like he's said all there is to say. He cued the rain cloud and leaves me stranded in the downpour with a dry mouth.

"Listen. Sir... It's true our training has slipped, but it's only because I've got personal stuff going on at home, and Rowan's been trying to help. It's my fault."

"I know it's your fault. That's what I said."

"My sister only has six to twelve months left to live," I blurt out, only because it might aid Coach's opinion of Rowan.

"She has stage four pancreatic cancer that's spread to her lungs. She stopped treatment last month. Rowan's been... We don't party, sir. We just get food, listen to music, and talk."

Taking his focus from the computer, Coach sizes me up silently while his countenance softens bit by bit until he gently says, "I see."

I walk out of the meeting with the realization I need my neurotic drill sergeant back, not just for my sake but for Rowan's. I go straight to his locker and tell him everything Coach said, and everything I said back.

"Fuck McDonough," Rowan responds, whipping off the towel around his waist and shoving it into his locker.

To stave off a public boner, I avert my eyes. "He sounded real serious, man. I think we need to drill in."

"Let him bench me," Rowan mutters. "When we're losing miserably to the Gators, he'll be shitting himself to put me back in."

"Rowan, I'm okay. I wanna train. I wanna be on that field with you. I want Erica to see me play."

Rowan pulls on his underwear and shorts in silence, brows furrowing contemplatively.

The locker room is still half full, so I put my back to the lockers and lower my voice real quiet when I say, "But you're the daddy, so I'll do what you say."

Got him with that one, but I mean it. I will do whatever he says, but if it's not what I think is best, I'll speak my peace. He sticks his shoulder to the locker and leans in close. "You ready to grind, babyface?"

"With you?" I smirk. "Always."

Rowan chuckles at that, face turning a shade pinker than what the sun did to it. He sticks his head halfway into his locker so no one notices, but I see him nod, and I hear him say, "Game on."

And for the next week, we grind. Early morning runs before work, yoga before practice, and grueling drills after dinner that make it all come up more than once. Reps in the gym, laps in the nat, and more fucking running. We stick to Rowan's diet plan with minimal detours, drinking chalky protein shakes and green smoothies, and eating baked chicken and hard boiled eggs every goddamn day.

It makes me push harder when Rowan calls me names, like I'm some sort of masochist. But it's all for the game. Okay, it's not all for the game. The harder we grind, the harder my cock is by the end of the night, and the better the orgasm when Rowan drains my balls.

After collapsing in the middle of McKinley Park well after sundown, my heart beating a mile a minute and my dick throbbing like mad in my shorts, Rowan collapses right beside me and jerks me off right here. Firm grip and quick strokes. His eyes staring into mine, neither of us speaking a word that isn't a pleasured moan. I spurt all over my abdomen with my hands fisting the grass. When I'm spent, I take my shirt off and clean myself up with it, toss it to the grass and tell Rowan I'm ready to keep grinding.

"I think that's enough for tonight." He wipes his hand on the grass before slapping it into mine so I can help him to his feet.

"You tired?" I ask.

"It's almost ten, and classes start tomorrow. Baby boy needs his beauty sleep."

I grab his hips and tug them against mine, crashing his hard-on against mine. Something about this man and his workouts won't allow my cock to go soft. I slip my hand under his waistband and grab his firm ass. "Baby boy needs to fuck his daddy."

The moan that rumbles through Rowan's throat has me thinking I can tug him into the dark side of the park and shove my fingers in his ass. No such luck. Rowan takes my wrist and pulls me out of his shorts. "You wish," he murmurs against my ear.

Rubbing my cheek against his, I say, "I wanna get inside you so bad. Just my fingers, I swear. I'll rub your prostate and make you leak all over my cock just like last time."

"I knew letting you do that was a mistake."

I chuckle from my chest, pressed flush against Rowan. "You fucking loved it."

When Rowan answers by sucking my earlobe into his mouth, I know I'm right. His tongue is like a wet, warm snake made of velvet, slithering over the ridges of my ear and even dipping inside like it's full of nectar.

"Fuck, Row." My dick thickens, desperate again.

His teeth graze my lobe. "Tell me what you want, baby."

My eyelids flutter as Rowan's mouth moves to my neck, slurping at my skin like I'm soft serve. "Wanna go back to yours. If we wake up early, you can drop me at my place before I have to go to my first class."

"I have a better idea." Rowan reaches between us to squeeze my balls hard enough to make me gasp. "You're gonna drive home, and when you get there, you're gonna go into your bathroom, lock the door, and turn the shower on. While the water heats up, I want you to beat your big dick for me until you come all over yourself, and I want you to film it for me so I know you're being a good boy."

"Fuck," I sigh, both disappointed and excited as hell. As badly as I want to get off with Rowan, I want to obey him.

"Tell me you'll be a good boy," Rowan says, inching his hand up to squeeze my shaft. Too soft to hurt, but hard enough to make me whimper.

"I'll be good."

"And don't forget to send me your class and work schedule so I can organize our workouts."

"You gonna make one of your sexy Google Drive spreadsheets?"

"Of course." His hand jumps from my cock to my hand, wrapping it up in an equally gentle embrace. His gray eyes soften to that look he pays me often, ever since learning about my sister. Like he's searching my own eyes for a reason not to worry himself to death while we're apart. "Good luck tomorrow."

Squeezing his hand, I say, "It's just school. I've been doing it since I was, like, five."

"Let me know if you need help with anything. You need to keep your grades up for athletic eligibility."

"I know. I'll let you know." I kiss him, and he kisses me back, but it's not a sloppy, heat-of-the-moment kiss. It's so tender it tingles my spine in a way that's more comforting than arousing. I want to keep kissing like this. Just stand out here all night, kissing until our lips go numb and our legs fall asleep.

When Rowan pulls back, I lean in and touch my forehead to his. I whine from my throat, because I'm a whiner now. He gives me so much, yet it's never enough. There are never enough minutes in the day for me to ever tire of him.

"C'mon, gay boy. I'll see you at practice tomorrow, and we'll show McDonough you're ready."

By the first Monday of the Fall semester, there's a huge banner hung across the Eastern side of the Student Union building, right over the Quick Stop window where I buy a Red Bull between classes. YOUR SAC STATE MEN'S SOCCER TEAM, reads the banner in comic book style letters. To the right of them are suave shots of Levi and Raisel in Hornet's green, and to the left is an enlarged mugshot of Rowan, his eyes-on-the-prize expression. Hard and confident, just like his boners.

I lift my phone, take a pic of the banner, and attach it to a text to Rowan.

Me

> Is it just me or is campus looking a lot better this year?

I'm paying for my Red Bull when my phone vibrates.

Rowan

> It's just you gay boy

Me

> How did I know you were going to say that

My afternoon class is a three-hour lecture on extreme weather. When I told Rowan I still need a science class to fulfill my general education requirements, he suggested meteorology with a specific professor. Word on the street is the dude is an easy grader with a cool personality, and he shows a lot of crazy videos of tornadoes.

Just my luck, I walk into the classroom and see Lese sitting at a middle row desk. Hoping she doesn't see me, I beeline for the closest vacant desk, but it's only two slots away from her.

Great.

She's been messaging me enough I considered blocking her, but I still feel bad about what I said to her at that party during my moment of weakness. I just wish she'd get the hint I'm not interested in fixing what ought to stay broken.

Because my neck is a traitor, it turns my head to check if Lese notices me. Lo and behold, she's staring right at me. She lifts a hand and sends me the meekest wave I've seen out of her.

I wave back, because I've decided holding resentment toward someone I don't even miss is dumb. If anything, I should thank Lese for inadvertently thrusting me into Rowan's orbit. Or is he in my orbit? Somehow, the longer I play by Rowan's rules, the more powerful I feel. I never felt half this powerful when I was with Lese.

What makes me feel itty bitty is when I'm thinking about being the reason Rowan doesn't have the best season of his life.

After class, I fast-walk back toward the Student Union, but when Lese is bound and determined, she puts those petite legs to work.

"Tommy!" she calls after me.

I don't have enough care left to try ignoring her, so I slow down enough to let her catch up. "What?"

"I'm sorry," she quickly says, like her very presence is a burden to me, which it kind of is. "I just wanted to know how you're doing. How's Erica?"

"Do you wanna know how I'm doing, or how Erica's doing?"

"Both."

"I'm fine." I leave it at that, because Lese doesn't need to hear about Erica's prognosis.

"Yeah?" she asks, like I'm lying to her. "It wasn't how it looked at that party. I don't know why that Rowan prick said—"

"Lese." I stop in my tracks and turn to face her. "It doesn't matter. I'm seeing someone else."

She stops with me, blinking big, wistful eyes up at me. "You are?"

"Yeah."

"Who? That chick from the party?"

Ah, so Lese saw me acting out too. I was too busy chasing after Rowan to notice. For a second, I think to lie and say I'm dating Eve. Easier than saying I'm in an unofficial and undefined relationship with the guy she cheated on me with last spring, but I'm so disinterested in Eve that even talking about her would give her too much value in my life.

"Someone else."

"Oh." Even if I was in outer space, I could see the heartbreak on Lese's face. She looks away and asks, "What does your mom think of her?"

"They haven't met."

"Is it serious?"

"It is what it is, Lese. It's none of your business. All you need to know is I'm focused on someone else now. We had a good run, but it's over now, so go do whatever you want."

I'm about to walk away when Lese whines, "But I miss you. Can't we...be friends, or something? We were friends, you know, before we started dating."

After taking a few moments to pretend to consider it, I shake my head. "I got too much going on. I'm on the soccer team now, working on getting some playing time this season."

"Really?" Her countenance brightens up. For all her faults, Lese was like Rowan in that she never wanted me to quit soccer. Then again, that might be because she clearly has a thing for soccer players. "You know that Rowan is the team captain, right?"

"No shit. He's been training me all summer. Helped me get on the team."

"You're buddy-buddy with Rowan Hughes now?" She sounds shocked. Offended even.

"I don't got beef with him. You're the one who betrayed me." When it looks like she's about to sob in the middle of this busy thoroughfare, I quickly say, "But it's fine. Like I said, I'm seeing someone new, and you're free to do whatever you want with whoever you want. Everyone wins."

"If this is winning, I'd rather lose." She mopes in a way that I'm trained to want to fix. Even now, I hate to see Lese so upset, especially when it's not all on her. She may have been the cheat, but I was lying to her just as much. I used her to help bury myself in a lie, and that wasn't fair to either of us.

Part of me considers telling Lese the truth, but at the crux of it, I can't trust her. Never could. If she blabs to anyone associated with the team, they could all find out, and if the team finds out I'm gay, they'll be a small step away from realizing Rowan and I do more than just train together. It's one thing if I inadvertently out myself. It's another to inadvertently out Rowan. I'm not sure he'd come back from that.

"You'll be fine," I tell Lese, a little too curt, but it is what it is.

Thankfully, she doesn't keep following me. If she did, she'd see I'm on my way to meet Rowan at the gym for a pre-practice yoga class.

On my way through campus, I wind up smack in the middle of a club fair pitched between the Student Union and the library. I thought about joining a couple campus clubs back when I was a freshman. Something to help ease the heartbreak of quitting soccer, but my head wasn't in it. Aside from Lese and the rare meetup with my Johnson friends, I didn't have it in me to socialize for a long time after Erica's diagnosis. Still don't feel like a social butterfly, but there is one booth which catches my eye, if only due to its flamboyancy.

It used to be easy to ignore gay pride shit. Told myself it didn't apply to me since my gayness only existed in fantasies and barely realized crushes I learned not to act on. I figured every guy wondered what it would be like to have sex with a man, and that it was only gay if I wanted to actually go through with it. Now, I think about having sex with men almost every second of the day. One man, really, and he's about as manly a guy as I've ever fantasized about.

It isn't just the sex I'm obsessed with, either. It's also the soft stuff I've somehow coaxed out of Rowan over the last couple months. His kisses, his gentle touches, his hand when it holds mine back, and his voice when it goes breathy, telling me I'm beautiful and perfect until I half-believe it. Even more than I want to fuck Rowan, I want to press my face in the crook of his neck and inhale him.

"Would you like a pin?" a small, skinny girl in a denim vest asks when I unintentionally stop too close to the Queer Alliance booth. She rattles a shallow basket between us that's full of small pins. Each one titles a different pronoun set, from *she*, to *he*, to *they*, and all of the above.

My reflex is to chuckle awkwardly and joke, "I think it's pretty obvious I'm a dude."

The girl blinks slowly, half-smiling despite how clearly unamused she is. "I didn't ask if you're a dude. I asked if you want a pin."

On the spot now, I say sure and pick a *he/him* pin out of the basket.

"Not everything is as obvious as it seems," she tells me, "and not everyone has the benefit of being easily understood by society at first glance."

As I'm nodding, trying to process, I realize the person in front of me is wearing a pronoun pin on their vest lapel that says *they/them*. So it seems my assumptions and I are part of the problem. I'm just glad I noticed the pin before saying something to them that could be accidentally hurtful.

Nodding to the brightly decorated booth, I ask, "Do you have to, like, *come out* to join your club, or...can people who aren't really open about themselves join too?"

Their smile widens, genuine this time. "You don't have to do anything to join. You just show up when you want and be respectful. Everyone else will respect you back."

By the time I'm back on the move toward the gym, I've signed my name to an email list and have a folded up events calendar shoved in my pocket.

I semi-decide not to tell Rowan I'm thinking about joining a campus LGBTQ club, in case it freaks him out. But in the locker room after yoga, when we're putting on fresh deodorant and talking about grabbing food before practice, Rowan notices the pin I stuck to the front pouch of my backpack.

"Wait, you've been a boy this whole time? I had no idea," he jokes.

I laugh and swat at him halfheartedly before shutting my locker. The start of the semester has packed the student gym and the locker room, so we have to keep our voices down.

"You know, not everything is as obvious as people think, and not everyone is lucky enough to be easily understood by society."

"That's beautiful," Rowan chuckles, leaning his back against his closed locker. Lowering his voice to a whisper, he asks, "Is it obvious I wanna suck your dick?"

The question stirs the erection I worked so hard to turn limp after another glorious savasana. "If you had asked me that four months ago, I would've said no. But, now that I know you, it's the most obvious thing about you. I'd even say it's one of your defining characteristics."

"Little bitch," he snickers before rubbing his hand on my head, messing up my hair as penance. The blush I put on his face is totally worth it.

I've watched Rowan Hughes play more times than I can count, but this is the first time I've watched him from the sidelines, wearing a jersey with the same name across the chest. Coach calls Rowan a machine, but he's more like a dancer to me, moving to the rhythm of the game like it's embedded in him.

When he digs, he digs hard. When he stays back, he's like a panther lying in wait. When he's got a Gator on his ass, he's a runaway train, and when he's got a clear shot, he's an assassin. He makes the opposing defense look like chumps, and he quickly becomes the opposing goalie's worst nightmare.

We're up 5-0 by the half, and Coach brings Rowan out after a solid hour of playing time. He's still sweating while he pumps the guys up to clinch the win, radiating an intensity that goes straight to my dick. As badly as I want Coach to put me in, there's nowhere I'd rather be when Rowan whips his shirt off, hikes up the legs of his shorts and plants himself on the bench right beside me. Wedged up so close to my side that I can feel his body heat through my fresh-out-the-package jersey.

Ignoring the crowd and our teammates and the blistering August sun, I look beside me, and time slows. A droplet of sweat rolls down the slope of Rowan's nose. Rivulets flow down the side of his face, and a glistening sheen covers his lean body like a sugary glaze I want to taste. His eyes meet mine, dark and glinting in the sun. His blazing hand clasps my knee as a smirk crawls across his clean shaven face.

"How'd I look out there?" he asks.

I can't answer honestly. Not here. I can't tell him he looked like a walking wet dream. Can't tell him my arms are folded on my lap because seeing him so capable, confident, and *hot* has me fully erect. I can't tell him he's the most stunning person I've seen in the flesh.

"Great," I say, the word coming out like a low hiccup from all the butterflies swarming in my gut.

He exhales a chuckle before taking his hand back and turning his focus back to the field. It hurts just to keep myself from snatching that hand and pressing it onto my aching boner. It hurts not to press my lips to his and taste the way his sweat mixes with the sweetness of his tongue.

As lucky as I feel to have Rowan in my life, I can't help but want more. I want all of him all the time. I don't just want to be his. I want him to be mine.

We win 6-1, and by we, I mean the guys who actually played. In the locker room after, Rowan promises me "we" are going to get me off the bench.

We. Tommy and Rowan. Rowan and Tommy.

"Hey, butt buddy!" Levi's obnoxious voice bounces off the locker room walls as he pops up behind me and slaps his hand so hard on my back, I flinch. "Lunch at Walker's Tavern. You in?"

And there's the reason I need to quit staring at Rowan with heart-eyes all the damn time. *Tyson* is hokey, but at least it isn't *butt buddy*. Clearly, the team thinks Rowan and I spend too much time together. At worst, they think I'm some sort of submissive pet. It's only when I'm hard and we're alone that I don't mind the thought of being Rowan's pet.

"Don't call him that." Rowan challenges Levi with that hard stare.

Levi sticks his hands up in surrender. "Relax, Cap. I'm just playing with the kid."

Since I told Rowan about Erica, he's also been noticeably more defensive when the guys tease me. Can't say I mind, but I also don't want to be the reason team morale slips. I still think about what Eve told me at that party while she was high. That half the guys on the team secretly hate Rowan. She also said there's a rumor going around Rowan is gay, and I know for a fact Rowan still isn't ready to accept that part of himself.

Trying to make light of Levi's humor, I send a half smile up to him and say, "Don't think I burned enough calories today to warrant tavern food."

"Eh, don't worry, dude. It's the first match of the season. You'll get some playing time before too long." Levi pats my shoulder gently this time. "And then, you'll be drowning in so much pussy, you won't have time to follow Cap around like a little puppy dog."

"Shut the fuck up, man," Rowan spits before slamming his locker hard enough to draw the attention of half the starters. The hardness inside him shines from his eyes like lasers, not just to Levi, but to everyone bearing witness. "Tommy's off-limits. That goes for everyone. Maybe if you all trained as much as him, we'd have gotten more than one goal in the second half."

As sexy as Rowan is when he's defending me, the tension he brings to the locker room has my anxiety heightened.

Levi breaks it with one of his smug chortles, clapping Rowan on the shoulder. "No need to go all mama dog on me. Tommy knows I'm his number one fan. You in for Walker's?"

"Can't. Going to Olive Garden with my family."

"Olive Garden? That's bleak, bro, but I fuck with those breadsticks."

As soon as Levi is gone for the showers and everyone else is back to paying attention to anything other than us, Rowan asks me, "Hungry? You can come along, if you want."

"That'd be cool?" I ask, filling with hopeful jitters. I'd much rather pull Rowan into a shower and devour him, but the fact he's inviting me around his family again feels like a good sign. Then again, he might be asking only because I already told him I've got a shift today. "Can't anyway. Gotta work."

But then Rowan asks if I want to come over tonight to watch film from the game.

"I can come over after dinner."

"Stay the night?" he asks, a slight sneakiness to his tone.

Hell yes.

He picks me up at half to eight and we don't make it a mile down the highway before my hand is sneaking up the leg of Rowan's cotton shorts. He spreads his knees just for me, smirking at the road ahead while I knead the pale, soft part of his thigh. My fingers find Rowan's coarse pubic hair, and I cradle his balls in my hand, lifting and compressing them.

"Commando, huh?" I ask Rowan's profile.

"No point in putting underwear on just to pick your ass up and take you to my bed."

Sneaking my fingers low, I rub the flat under Rowan's scrotum. "Thought we were gonna watch the game film."

"We are. I'm gonna make you watch the entire match while I play with your body."

With my free hand, I flip my boner up under my waistband to keep from making a wet spot in my pants. "Do you have any idea how hard I was watching you play today?"

Moaning, Rowan shifts in his seat to give more clearance to where I really want to go. "I always know when you're hard, baby."

My fingertip finds the small pucker past his taint, and I rub it slowly until Rowan squirms and takes a hand off the wheel to grip the hard rod tenting his shorts.

Giving himself a few firm tugs, he tells me I better stop what I'm doing before he crashes and kills us both.

A couple more miles, and I'm back at that cute house on a quiet street, following Rowan through the garage and into his office-bedroom.

Rowan wasn't joking when he said he would make me rewatch the entire match, and he wasn't joking about what he'd be doing while I watch. He sets his laptop up on a short stack of textbooks propped on his desk chair and presses play on the game film while I'm lying bare ass naked on his narrow bed.

Lights dimmed, laptop sound up, AC humming, and Rowan stripping down to his birthday suit in front of me, I'm lulled into a hypnotic state with Rowan's hard cock as the pendulum, swaying between his legs. Dude loves to talk about how much bigger my dick is, but it's not all about inches, which he has plenty of. He's thick as my wrist, veiny and drooling from a fat, purple head peeking out from his adorable foreskin. I grab his shaft and roll onto my side, feeding that plump head into my mouth.

"Ah, ah, ah," he chides, pushing on my shoulder until I'm flat on my back again. "Eyes on the screen, and tell me what you see."

He's killing me. What sort of freak is Rowan to deny himself a blowjob just to tease me mercilessly? I'll let him fuck my face if it means having his tangy jizz on my tongue.

"I see the sexiest dude I've ever laid eyes on whooping the Gators' asses like it's nothing. Now, come here." I snatch his wrist and tug him on top of me.

Straddling my hips, he takes my face in his hands and leans down close enough for me to feel his breath against my lips. I part mine and prepare for his, but he cranks my head sideways and latches his mouth over my carotid. Sucking and gnawing at my flesh like a vampire trying to taste blood, but all my blood rushes to my raging cock. If he's trying to mark me, I'm game. Let the other guys think I spent the night with a hotter girl than they could ever dream of snagging. Maybe then they'll quit thinking I'm Rowan's pet, even though that's exactly what I want to be.

It's scary actually, how desperately I want to belong to him. I never wanted to belong to Lese. Never wanted to belong to anyone before, except maybe Anthony, way back when, and in a much more innocent way.

Rowan nips at my neck and slurps up the saliva he leaves behind, then he tucks his mouth beside my ear and murmurs, "Tell me what you see."

I swallow, forcing my eyes to refocus on the screen. "I see...that the opposing defense doesn't know dick about defending against you."

"Good boy." Rowan shifts lower until his hot mouth hovers over my nipple. One featherlight kiss to the beaded nub has me dazed. "What else do you see?"

"Fucking...*unnggh*," I moan as Rowan flickers his tongue over my nipple, something no one else has ever done before. "I see...Connor's follow through is weak. He finds the shots, but fails to capitalize. He's...nervous."

"That's it, baby. Tell me more."

I keep my eyes glued to the screen, watching for any and all weaknesses to our lineup. Meanwhile, Rowan shifts so he's lying halfway on top of me, one leg pressed between mine as he swirls his tongue across my nipple until I'm shivering from the sensitivity.

"I see..." I moan, eyelids fluttering. "I see Levi veering to the left side of the field too much. The Gators were on to him in the second half because of it."

"That's my good boy," Rowan growls against my chest. He drags a fingertip along the underside of my cock from base to tip, stopping to massage my tiny slit and spread pre-cum around my crown.

"I'm gonna come," I whimper, turning my gaze down to Rowan's ministrations like I might catch myself spurting against either of our wills.

Immediately, Rowan pulls his hand away, leaving my cock to hop and throb and weep for attention. "Relax, baby boy. You'll come when I let you."

I groan from my trembling belly when Rowan mashes my balls up against my cock and grips both firmly. "Keep watching," he says, "and tell me what you see."

"I see you," I whine, one hand fisted in the comforter below me and the other squeezing Rowan's firm ass. "I see how fucking flawless you are."

Looking into my eyes, Rowan quietly argues, "I'm not. If you watch closely, you'll see that."

"You move like an ice dancer. No one can touch you."

He squeezes me harder, swelling my cock to an impossible thickness. "I only want you touching me."

I gasp, body spasming as Rowan ducks down and takes me into his mouth. Deep. Chin on my balls and his nose in my pubic hair. I feel my tip hit the back of his throat, and I feel him gag around me.

"Fuck, fuck, fuck." My body temp skyrockets as the need to climax reaches great heights. I become almost fearful of my release. "Fuck, Rowan. I need to come. Please."

The second his grip softens around my balls and the base of my cock, a flood of pleasure rushes up my spine to flood my brain with dopamine. I climax while shouting expletives and digging my fingers into the muscles behind Rowan's shoulders as his head bobs on me and his throat swallows around me.

He sucks me dry until I'm spent and panting, sweating on his comforter and fucking trembling. His mouth is what heaven feels like, I decide. There's no other way to describe it. He releases me, and it feels like he just spun me into gold.

As I come down from the high, I'm possessed by a frenzied need to claim Rowan somehow. He only likes it when I touch him, which means there's a decent chance no one has had his ass before. I dream about how tight his anus felt around my finger, and how powerful I felt being inside him at all.

Before Rowan can tell me to put my attention back on the game film, I jolt up and maneuver behind him. I push him toward the headboard and bend him forward.

"Tommy—" he starts like he wants to object. He must feel how firmly I'm rubbing his little hole with my thumb, hard enough to nearly breach that tight ring, because the next time he says my name, there's a slight warning edge to it.

I won't fuck him, though, as badly as I want to. I hunker down, lying on my stomach with my knees bent, and I pull Rowan's hips down until my face is between his firm cheeks. I lock my lips around his asshole and sweep my tongue across it.

"Oh my God," I hear Rowan sigh, voice dripping with hazy pleasure.

Propped on my elbows, I lift a hand to wrap around Rowan's cock. As I pay Rowan's ass all the wet kisses it deserves, I stroke his cock downward, so the tip touches the soft comforter with each of my steady tugs.

"That's it, gay boy. Fucking eat my ass 'til I come," Rowan moans, the filth of it all sparking my cock to plump up under my abdomen.

As I lap at his hole, I'm most shocked by how delicious he tastes. Not rank or fowl, like how I'd typically expect a grown man's ass to taste. Rowan's tastes like the rest of his body, silken and salted and devilishly musky. I make out with it like I would his throat, and I stiffen my tongue enough to wiggle the tip through his puckered ring.

Moaning low, Rowan's hips rock between my mouth and my hand, still stroking him nice and slow. I notice his arm reaching back, and I feel his hand behind my head like he needs to make sure I don't part from him until he's good and ready.

"Fuck me, baby, I'm so close," he mewls. If I thought for a second he was being literal, I'd shoot up to my knees right now and shove my dick in his ass as far as it'll go.

He begs me not to stop. His thighs twitch and his knees inch wider apart. He murmurs curse words that turn to gibberish when his cock spurts a puddle onto the comforter.

I keep stroking until he's so spent he's whimpering into his pillow and flattening his body to the mattress. I stay over him, keeping his cheeks spread and lapping at his asshole like it's my new favorite dessert. Rowan doesn't mind; he moans softly like he would if I gave him a gentle back massage. So I keep eating him until my jaw gets achy and my dick is soft enough that I can crawl up Rowan's body and cuddle against him without stabbing him with my erection.

A couple minutes pass before Rowan finds the strength to pick himself up enough to fit his body against my side. Eyes shut, cheek on my chest, and his arm curled around my waist. It's the way Lese always liked to cuddle with me, but it feels so much righter with Rowan, and so much more victorious.

Found my softie.

Sweeping my palm along his hip and back, I whisper against the top of his head, "Mine," and the small hum that leaves Rowan's throat in response sure doesn't sound like an objection.

19

Rowan

My body comes alive before my mind does, jolted by sensations that are equal parts arousing and painful, like an electric eel snaking up my thigh, and—

"Stop!" my mouth speaks as soon as my mind comes to. The word comes out choked. Not enough air in my lungs. My eyes open at the same time I sit up and push the intruder off me.

The lamp is still on low, enough light to remind me I'm in my room and that the man I just shoved isn't an intruder. It's just Tommy. Naked Tommy, his mouth slack and his eyes as wide as mine feel, unblinking.

"I'm sorry," he says quickly, breathlessly.

"What are you doing?" I ask, my voice coming out meek and whiny. I fucking hate it. My heart is beating a mile a minute, and I have my knees to my chest with crossed ankles like my half-conscious reflexes thought I needed to shield myself from Tommy, of all people—from whatever he was doing to my junk that felt both good and scary.

"I was just touching you. I'm sorry. I'm a dumbass. I thought you'd like it if you woke up to me—I'm so sorry."

"It's okay." I intentionally lower my voice until it sounds close to normal, and I relax my body like I try to relax my mind.

"No, it's not."

"It's okay. You just surprised me. I'm not..." I take a deep breath that helps me fully adjust to reality. Enough time has passed that the video on my laptop has ended and the screen is black. My comforter is in a heap at the foot of the mattress, and the AC has been on long enough for the room to feel cold. "I'm not used to having someone sleep over."

"Well, yeah. Your bed is tiny."

Cracking a smile, I forgo the low hanging jokes in my head and ask, "You okay? Did I hurt you?"

"I'm fine," he answers with a soft chuckle before scooping his arms around me and pulling me back down to lie against him.

"I liked it," I say, because it's true. If I had known it was Tommy from the get, I would have leaned into it instead of shoving him away.

"Your dick seemed to like it. Just gotta remember to ask the rest of you if it's okay first."

God, I feel like a weenie. Tommy can do whatever he wants to me. I don't want him asking permission every time he puts his hands on me. I want his hands on me all the time. Like now, with his strong, warm arms wrapped around me like I deserve it.

Takes me longer than it should for me to realize we're cuddling. Not just spooning, like what Tommy did to me the last time he stayed over, but actually cuddling, like what actors do in movies after they make sweet, passionate love to an R&B song. Feels weird. I never pegged myself for a cuddler, but Tommy and I fit like two complementary puzzle pieces. Someone could shake me, and I still wouldn't slip from Tommy's embrace.

His nose pecks my forehead until I lift my chin, and that's when he lays his mouth on mine. His pillowy lips fill me with a tantalizing warmth, like my insides have turned to honey.

"I'm glad you were my first guy-kiss," he says.

First... As beautiful as the word is, it's laced with a foreboding I'm too insecure to shake. If I'm the first, it stands to reason there will others. Fuck that. I stare at a freckle just below Tommy's left eye, wanting to kiss him there.

Surprising myself, I admit, "You were my first kiss."

"With a guy?"

"With anyone."

Tommy goes silent for a bit, his eyebrows hopping a fraction and his mouth twitching with the promise of a smile. "Really?"

"Thought it was obvious," I mutter, remembering how stunned I was the first time Tommy pressed his mouth to mine, and how awkward and bumbling I was when we made out a minute later.

"What about... But, you've hooked up with people. Girls..."

I'm glad when Tommy stops short of speaking his ex's name. I don't care about that girl, but I do think about her from time to time in the context that I wonder how Tommy could give years of his life to her. Was it really just so he'd have an excuse to keep other girls away?

"Here and there," I say, "but that's just hooking up. I never liked any of 'em. Never wanted to kiss 'em."

"You've never been in a relationship at all?"

"Nah. Never even been on a date, except hanging out with you."

Tommy goes quiet again, long enough for me to wish I'd kept my mouth shut. I'm usually good at that, but cuddling has turned me soft as pudding.

"I'm not exactly Mister Romantic," I say.

"Open your mouth."

"What?" I chortle.

Tommy's pouty lips finally form that big smile. "Open your mouth."

I'm skeptical, but I roll onto my back—just enough room to do so without falling out of bed—and I open my jaw real wide toward the ceiling, like I would if reclined in a dentist's chair.

"Not like that, you weird-o," Tommy laughs, turning on his side and propping himself on an elbow. He pinches my chin and turns my head so our noses touch. "Relax the muscles in your face and let your mouth open naturally."

Just the deep tenor of Tommy's voice is enough to give me goosebumps. I consider defying him, feigning playfulness when I'm really just a scaredy-cat. But I give up a bit of control for the sake of him, and I calm my face and part my lips.

"Relax, and follow my lead," he murmurs.

The second Tommy's lips graze mine, my eyes drift shut. I feel his tongue dip into my mouth, probing slow. My tongue responds, lifting to slide against Tommy's and savor the taste of his saliva setting my tastebuds ablaze.

His hand touches my chest, palm skating across my body like he's trying to memorize my form, and it's not long until I'm moaning into his mouth. I knew Tommy was a softie, but I'm the one turning to mush. Even if Tommy is the gayest boy who ever lived, I don't know why I turn him on so much, but I can feel his cock twitch against my hip.

Keeping our lips locked, I shift onto my side, pressing my body flush with his. I glue us together with an arm around his back and a leg hooked over his hip.

Our hips find the languid rhythm of our mouths. Our cocks mimic our tongues, pushing and sliding together, and it feels like pure bliss.

It's everything I've ever craved come to fruition. Not just sex with a man, but sex with someone who craves me as much as I crave him. Sex with someone who cares about me like I care about him, even if I don't deserve it. Sex with someone who touches me like he wants to understand me, even though he never can.

If I were a better, less broken version of myself, I would ask Tommy what he wants from me and give it to him on the spot. I'd tell him the truth—the things he wants to hear and the things he doesn't—and I'd promise to always take care of him if he'll let me. I'd be capable of taking care of him. I'd give him everything.

Instead, I give Tommy what I can, which isn't much. I train him, because I understand soccer better than I understand anything, and I make him come, because we both need it to stave off insanity.

Our one long kiss finally breaks when Tommy needs to lick the drool off his lips, and I use the time to say, "So that's what you did to my ass, huh?"

He snickers before relocking our lips. His hands roam my back and tug at my ass, skimming my crack and tickling my hole. I think he wants to fuck me for real, and it scares me how into that idea I am. I let him give me a finger once already, because I've fingered myself before and knew what to expect, but one finger is a far cry from the ball bat Tommy calls a dick splitting me in two.

"I'm so fucking hard," Tommy grumbles.

"I feel it." I reach between us and curl my hand around us both. Our pre-cum smears together as I roll my fist over our crowns.

Lips back to pouty, Tommy asks, "Why did you offer to train me for the team?"

Stroking the top inches of our cocks in unison, I answer, "Because you're my baby boy, Tommy."

His hand jumps from my ass to the back of my head as he presses his forehead to mine. Eyes half-lidded, he breathes, "I want us to come together, at the same time."

"Tell me when you're close."

"I'm already close."

I stroke quick, my hand half-mooned around us and slick with our natural lube. The quicker I pump, the harder Tommy huffs against my mouth like he's trying to resuscitate me. Everything he breathes into me feels like pleasure, seeping deep into my bones and radiating through every nerve in my body. It makes me sweat, and it makes my heart beat wild. I realize we're moaning in sync, filling each other's mouths with the sound.

I'm waiting for it. Holding out against all odds, until Tommy whimpers, "I'm coming," and I completely unravel.

Jizz sluices from my tip, coating my hand and Tommy's cock while it pulses ropes of white that paint both our bodies.

"Oh, fuck," Tommy whines before flipping us and covering me with his body.

I move my hand from our wet cocks, and Tommy presses his face into my neck. His hips rut against me like there's still fluid left in his balls to milk out. The sensation has my body sizzling and my cock staying hard even after I'm spent.

I sweep my hands across Tommy's muscled back and tell him, "Let it out, baby. That's it. I got you."

When he's finally sated, his body melts over mine, dead weight that makes me wonder how nearly suffocating can also feel soothing. Even if Tommy had the strength to move, I won't let him. I hug my arms around him, tell him he's a good boy, and when his long breaths turn to quiet snores against my neck, I shut my eyes and drift back to sleep.

This time, what stirs me awake is a pesky knocking sound like knuckles on a bedroom door.

Shit.

It's morning, and Tommy is still on top of me, pinning me to my mattress in a way that felt incredible until someone started knocking on my door. I pick up his arm and shimmy out from under his weight until I'm slipping to the floor and landing on my ass.

Not only am I naked, but I'm caked in half-dried spunk and smell like an orgy.

It's got to be Matt or Xia knocking, but whoever it is doesn't need to see me like this. They think it's funny that I'm gay. Especially Xia. She thinks it's adorable I'm a dude who has no interest in women, like it makes me more interesting or more relatable to her. I don't know. I'm happy she likes Tommy, but it's not right for her to put it into his head that we can be boyfriends just because Xia thinks we look cute together.

If it's Xia behind the door, I don't want to let on that Tommy stayed the night.

They knock again, and I scramble to smear deodorant all over my jizzy body and dress myself in what I wore to pick Tommy up last night.

I open my door a crack just large enough to stick my face out of.

It's Matt in his silly Disney pajamas. "Come in the house."

I squint. "Why?"

An incredulous grin spreads across his bearded face. "You're on ESPN."

As quick as I get my feet into a pair of slides, I beeline for the house and enter through the kitchen where Xia is putting a kettle on the stove. "There's Mister Big Shot," she says as I pass her for the living room. Olive and Lena are on the sofa, still in jammies, bickering over which Disney movie to watch before breakfast, but Matt has the TV paused on a morning talk-segment of ESPN. He hits play.

"Next up on our college athletics watchlist is twenty-two-year-old senior, Rowan Hughes, out of Sacramento State University. We've seen this kid do some great things on the field, but if the first match of this season is anything to go off, I wouldn't be surprised if he's a first round draft pick. It's only a matter of which team is going to be lucky enough to scoop this kid up."

They show a montage of my best moments from yesterday's match, moments where all I see are things to improve upon, but the analysts talk like I'm hot shit. I've got goosebumps, and I don't think I've taken one breath since Matt hit play. I'm torn between jumping for joy and puking my guts out.

"This is it," Matt tells me, a hand on my shoulder I'm too numb to feel. "This is what you've been working for. Get your degree. Get drafted. Get out of Sacramento. Live a good life."

After a minute of the analysts discussing a gymnast in Virginia, I somehow get a word out of my choked up throat. "Cool."

I'm heading back to the garage when Xia asks if I'll come back for breakfast.

"I gotta go to the gym," I answer. "Didn't work out yesterday. Need to put in double today."

She chortles like I'm crazy. "You had a match yesterday!"

"A match is a match. It's not the gym."

Really, I just want to get back to Tommy before he wakes up alone in my ratchet bedroom. Between the house and the garage, my body finally settles on an emotion, and by the time I'm slipping back into my room, I'm grinning wide enough to ache my eye sockets.

Tommy is up, sitting off the side of my bed in all his naked glory, rubbing at his dreary eyes. There's spunk crusted to his abs, and his hair is a mess, sticking up at odd angles. It's the cutest thing I've ever seen. Makes me think about what Matt said. *Live a good life...* A good life has never really been in my purview, but as long as I've got a soccer match to train for, I've got a reason to live at all. I don't know what I'll do if Tommy becomes a second reason, but for now, he sure makes life more tolerable.

"Why are you dressed?" he mutters sleepily. "And why are you smiling like that?"

Drinking in the sight of him, I turn my smile to a smirk. "Not used to seeing your dick soft."

"Take your shirt off. That'll fix it." He bends forward, reaching for me, and his wingspan is long enough to capture my wrist and tug me between his legs. He pushes my tee up under my armpits and nuzzles his face against my chest.

Petting my puppy's hair, I say, "I reek like a gay sex club."

I probably shouldn't have said that. I know having sex with Tommy is the epitome of *gay*, but I've been trying to compartmentalize being gay and being with Tommy. Being gay has too much to do with how fucked up I am on the inside, and I don't want any of that touching this thing I have with Tommy. Whatever this thing is.

At the same time, one of the things holding me back from ever really considering myself *gay* gay is that I'd never found a man who made me feel comfortable before. And now, here's Tommy. My big, gay baby purring against my chest and curling his arms around my hips.

He murmurs, "If this is what a gay sex club smells like, count me in."

I know he's joking, but I still pick up his face and tell his blue eyes, "You better not. You're mine, baby boy."

Eyelids fluttering, Tommy asks, "Really?"

My nerves prickle. I press my lips to his parted ones so I won't have to answer, and I kiss him the way he kissed me last night. Slack lips and slow licks with sticky tongues. I want to roll around on his tongue until I'm slathered in his drool.

Finding my hand behind his head, Tommy brings it down between us and tucks my knuckles against his swelling cock.

"There he is," I whisper into his mouth.

"Told you."

I pull away from Tommy's mouth so I can put mine on something else. Gripping his growing shaft, I sink to my knees between his legs and sit low enough to nestle my nose in his pink scrotum. I hold his cock up and focus my mouth on his balls, licking and sucking each one into my mouth. He smells like musk and stale spunk, but I'm lapping it up like I'm the one in heat.

When his cock is perfectly stiff in my fist, I pinch my fingers below the rim of his cockhead and drag my tongue up his length. His skin is hot and tight, the vein pulsing against my tongue.

"Wait," Tommy exhales, cupping my jaw and coaxing my head back from his cock.

"Wanna eat you, baby," I tell him, rolling my fist over his cockhead and feeling pre-cum.

The little moan that chirps from his throat makes my dick twitch. When he tells me he wants us to eat each other together, I swear my cock salivates in my shorts. I'm up and shedding clothes while Tommy lies sideways along the mattress.

He reaches out and grabs my cock, rolling down my foreskin and thumbing my slit. I crawl my knees onto the bed and let Tommy guide my dick to his mouth. Propped on an elbow, he slurps me in and takes me deep.

"Deeper," I groan, watching him through a haze of pleasure. "Deeper, baby. That's it." I glide my palm down Tommy's side and around his hip, feeling for his cock. It's solid as stone, hot as a compress, and I stroke his length in the same rhythm Tommy bobs on my cock.

Tommy holds his throat around me as I swing a leg over his head and roll him onto his back so I can cage myself on top of him. Holding my hips high enough that Tommy doesn't suffocate, I lower to my elbows and wash my tongue all over the pulsing tool hovering an inch above his pelvis.

The way his lips suction my shaft while his togue sweeps across my glands has my hips begging to roll, but I keep them steady and focus on kissing a trail up and down Tommy's length. He was my first kiss, and he was the first person I ever went down on. After years of denying myself the fantasy of burying my face in a man's crotch and taking him down my throat, I finally found someone I'm not afraid to devour.

I mean... I was afraid the first time. Terrified. But, I couldn't stop myself. I was feeding an overwhelming hunger that wouldn't heel. I needed Tommy then, and ever since, I haven't been able to stop having him. I trace the tip of my tongue around the rim of his cockhead before slurping him into my mouth and sucking the precious pearls of pre-cum from his slit.

I take him halfway, then inch myself farther until my throat fills with his girth, stretching my jaw and tickling my gag reflex. Drool spills through my lips as I swallow around him. My eyes water and my lips pinch, but I take all of him in until my nose tickles his scrotum again. His thighs quiver against my palms, and he moans around my cock.

Caught up, I give in and rock my hips little by little. I hear Tommy gag, and I feel his hands grip my ass, but he doesn't still me. He slaps my ass before tugging my hips down and enveloping me in his hot, wet mouth.

My balls tease up tight, and I jolt up quickly, replacing my mouth on Tommy with my hand. Stroking him firm and quick, I pant, "Baby, baby, I'm gonna come. I'm gonna—"

Words fall away as my body racks with shocks of pleasure. I feel the rush of my balls emptying down Tommy's contracting throat, and I'm so delirious I don't even register Tommy is coming, too, until I feel warm globs of it hitting my face. I shut my eyes as one strikes my eyebrow, and I keep pumping him until his hips go jerky and he rolls us both on our sides.

Letting my softening dick out of his mouth, he fills the room with a sated moan.

I find a corner of my bed sheet and haphazardly wipe the jizz off my face, then we cuddle like this, for no other reason but we're too lazy to move. With our cheeks on each other's thighs and our arms slung around each other's hips, I hold him and he holds me. His cock really is adorable when it's soft and slightly wrinkled. I press little kisses to it while it shrinks up.

"Fuck, Rowan," he huffs. "I came so hard I thought I was going blind. Then I realized it was just your balls mashed over my eyes."

I snort, laughing hard enough to bring me back to reality. A reality where I can't be spending every second of the day tangled in bed with Tommy, milking orgasms out of each other like it's our job. I pull my leg from over Tommy's shoulder and sit up. Licking the taste of cum off my lips, I ask, "What time do you need to be at work?"

Tommy groans like that's the last thing he wants to talk about. "Ten."

"We can shower, and I'll drive you."

"If you drive me to work, someone will have to pick me up." He smirks. "Maybe that someone can take me back to his place so we can rub our boners together all night long."

I laugh some more. My boy is bold, and I can't say I dislike it. He can play shy boy around everyone else, but when I've got him alone, I want to see fire behind his blue eyes.

"I can pick you up and take you home, but we've got classes tomorrow. No sleepovers on a school night."

As sucky as it is to be the rational one, it's worth it the way Tommy pouts and says, "Okay, Dad."

Aroused all over again, I slip a hand behind Tommy's neck and bring his mouth to mine for a series of kisses that are so tender I nearly melt.

"I just love being with you," Tommy murmurs, his hand rubbing my thigh.

Even though he probably means he loves having sex with me, his words cause a flurry in my chest, and I feel the gears in my head churning. Overthinking is inevitable now, but I try to stay in the moment. I try not to freak out. I try not to say any of the bullshit things my mind comes up with on the spot, like *don't get used to it.*

Staying stolid, I squeeze the back of Tommy's neck and say, "C'mon, baby boy. It's bathtime."

20
Tommy

I miss the fourth match of the season because Erica guilts me into thinking it's more important that I drive her and Mav to Monterey for the weekend. In the grand scheme of things, it is more important. We're halfway through September, and this will probably be the last summer Erica ever spends on Earth with us. I take a ton of pictures of us at the beach, at the little café Erica loves, and at the seaside motel where we all stay up late on a king bed watching Pixar movies.

The whole thing does us all some good. I'm working on letting go of the resentment and cherishing the moment. The only thing that still doesn't sit right with me is that Mav doesn't know. Then again, I'm not sure telling him is the best thing either. Maybe it'll feel wrong no matter what. Maybe telling the truth can be just as bad as lying.

"You thought more on when you're gonna tell him?" I ask on the drive back home, somewhere around Gilroy.

Mav's got his big headphones on, tapping away at my old Switch that's basically his now.

The radio is spotty here, but I keep it on.

"I think I'll wait 'til I get real bad again. 'Til I can't hide it from him. Then, I'll just say the medicine stopped working, and there's no other options. It's not really a lie. The medicine wasn't working, and there's no other options."

I hold my tongue, seeing no use in parroting back to Erica what the doctors already have. That there was still a chance the chemo could make a dent.

"When are you going to introduce me to your girlfriend?" she asks at a normal volume, spider-crawling her fingers up my shoulder to attack the side of my neck.

"Ah!" I laugh, taking a hand off the steering wheel to swat her away. "I'm driving here, you nut. And there's no girlfriend to meet."

Oh, how true that statement is.

"Right, right. You're just *hanging out.*" She says the two words in a low, mocking tone. "You seeing her tonight?"

"Maybe," I sigh, only disappointed because of Rowan's no-sleepovers-on-school-nights rule. If I see him, it'll just be to train and trade blowjobs in his car before he drives me home. As much as I love the way he runs my ass into the ground before sucking me up into sweet oblivion, nothing beats a sleepover.

"It's okay if it doesn't work out. Rebounds rarely do."

"It's not a rebound," I say. A rebound presumes I'm using Rowan to help get over Lese, but there's nothing to get over. Even when Lese and I were good, I wasn't invested the way a boyfriend should be. The thought of staying with her forever was scarier than any thought of losing her.

"Then what's holding you back?"

So much it's unfair. I don't think Erica would suddenly think less of me if she finds out I'm dating a man, but I'm also not brave enough to take the risk when I'm not even sure if Rowan and I are dating. I want to date him. At least I'm brave enough to admit that. Even if we keep things discrete for a little while, I want to be with him. I want to be *real* with him.

"We've both just got a lot going on right now."

I must've sounded too melancholic, because Erica goes silent for a minute, probably thinking I mean her. I guess I do, but it's an excuse either way. Wouldn't matter what I have going on so long as Rowan wanted me back the way I want him.

"Maybe you should look into talking to someone. Like, a therapist."

"Why?"

"For grief."

"You're still here. Nothing to grieve." I'm saving face, and Erica lets me.

Even though I got the go-ahead from Coach to miss the match, he runs me during Monday's practice harder than Rowan ever has. More than two hours straight of laps around the track under a high sun, him whistling at me whenever my legs cramp up and hollering at me to pick it up. I run until I'm on my knees and dry heaving into the grass.

Rowan brings me a water, squats down beside me and asks if I'm good with sympathy in his eyes.

"I'm good," I pant, unscrewing my water and sloshing a third of it over my head before chugging the rest.

"Don't pop a boner just yet," Rowan says, a smirk in his tone. "Coach wants you joining drills. Need a hand?"

I take the one Rowan offers, and he hoists me up to my sore feet and slaps my back as I press the heel of my hand into my cramping side.

"Someone didn't drink his pickle juice," Rowan says.

Too tired to laugh, I give his ribs a lazy back-handed swat instead. "Tell you what," I pant as we cross the field to where the rest of the team is running footwork drills, "you drink enough pickle juice for the both of us, and I'll drink your salty cum once it reaches your balls."

Rowan laughs so hard he's got to clutch his side too, then Coach is screaming at us to get our asses in gear before he makes us both run suicides.

After practice, Rowan comes to my locker, sweaty and grass stained, and asks me how my classes are going. "I can tutor you," he says.

I'm taking a load off on the bench, too exhausted to even peel out of my soaked through t-shirt. Got just enough energy left to chuckle at how silly Rowan is. Whether it's training, yoga classes, morning runs, Sonic trips to cheer me up, and now tutoring, the dude is a scientist the way he's always concocting new methods to spend most of our free time together.

"I'm good. Thanks." It's early in the semester, after all. Mid-terms won't be for another couple weeks.

"It's important to keep your grades up now that you're on the team."

"Your lack of confidence in my intelligence is adorable," I tease, wishing we were alone right now so I could hold him against the lockers and kiss him.

And cue the boner.

I glance left and right before fixing my dick so it won't tent my shorts. When I look back up to Rowan, his eyes are on my lap, lips folded like it's a struggle not to smirk.

Pushing off the lockers, Rowan rustles his sweaty hand through my sweaty hair and says, "Gonna shower up. Lunch after?" He walks off toward the showers after I nod, and with my eyes glued to the contours of his back and the curve of his ass, my mind goes to wicked places. If I could get away with it, I'd follow Rowan into a stall and bury my finger inside his ass until he spurts all over the tiled wall.

I've got to rein it in, though, for the sake of our teammates and the men's basketball team who use those showers too.

There's a guy on that team who's nearly seven feet tall. If he stepped into the stall beside us, he'd get one hell of an eyeful over the divider wall.

Turns out, Rowan's idea of lunch is a salad place. Just salad. Sure, there's grilled chicken and chopped up hard boiled eggs mixed in, but it's still a damn salad. I can't remember the last time I paid for a meal that was just a salad. It does come in a pretty big bowl and served with naan, so it moves my hunger needle a good ways from starving. But, after we eat, all I can think of is what I want for dinner.

Walking back to the car, swinging a Vitamin Water at my side, I tell Rowan, "We should get dinner somewhere Friday night."

"Not gonna eat at Mommy's?"

"I'll just tell her I've got plans."

He chuckles, jingling his keys before sticking one in the driver's door. "Whatcha want, baby boy? In-N-Out?"

"Nah, I was thinking, maybe, Yard House."

Over the car, Rowan shoots me an odd look before swooping into the driver's seat. As soon as he pulls the lock on the passenger door, I slip in. Wearing my anxiety on my sleeve, I immediately stick a finger to my mouth, chewing on a hangnail that's been bothering me all day.

"Yard House is a fancy restaurant," Rowan says.

"It's not fancy. It's nice, I guess. I don't know. The food's real good."

"Expensive."

"I can pay," I offer, since it's my idea, and since Rowan's been driving me around so often, I've got extra cash I would've spent on gas.

Rowan takes a beat between turning the ignition on and buckling his seatbelt to scrunch his mouth like he's thinking it over. "Nah. Two dudes eating at a nice restaurant togeth-er on a Friday night? That's weird, man."

"I don't think it's weird." Okay, maybe I do think it's a little weird, but only because I've never done it before. I'm sure there are guys who do that sort of thing all the time. Like gay guys.

"Let's just go to Chipotle or something."

"What? For more salad."

"Hey," he smirks. "They put a lot of shit on those salads."

I smile, not totally forced, but it's masking a lot of neg-ative feelings bubbling inside my head right now. Things like, *he doesn't like you like that, dude, shut the fuck up.* In all my anxiety, I forget to think, and I blurt out something I heard Rowan say once. "It doesn't have to be gay."

Stilling his hand on the shift, Rowan turns his head and stares into me with that hauntingly indecipherable expres-sion he's mastered so well. Quietly, and without inflection, he says, "Except for the fact that you're gay."

Time stops for a moment, and it's a funny feeling. I can't count how many times he's called me gay boy, but I think this is the first time he's flat out said I'm gay without caveats. Despite the internet saying only I can decide what my identity is, hearing Rowan say the answer so bluntly and matter-of-fact feels like a weight lifted off me. Like I don't have to figure myself out anymore, because Rowan already knows exactly who I am.

As soon as time kicks back up again, I shrug a shoulder. "Gay dudes gotta eat. I can't survive on your dick alone."

The corner of Rowan's mouth quirks up in a smirk that vanishes just as quickly. I think he's going to say something snarky, like *you can try.* Instead, he says, "I can't. I'm sorry."

He turns face forward, and we lull into a silence that reminds me of the night of the party where I let jealousy get the best of me. What a shitshow. I decided then and there I wouldn't let anyone come between me and Rowan again, but it seems like I'm always coming between Rowan and the false reality he's created in his mind.

"You can talk to me, you know?" I move my hand on top of his. "I wanna understand you. I wanna know what you want from me. Wanna know who you are."

"That's beautiful," he mutters dismissively.

"If you don't wanna go out with me, then just say that, but don't tell me you can't, because you can."

Sending me a sharp look, Rowan says, "I can't go out with you, because I'm not gay."

I can't help but roll my eyes. "I'm sorry, but you're like the gayest dude I've ever met. You literally got on your knees for me the first time I kissed you."

I see the shift as soon as I get my careless words out. Feel it too, like the sudden drop on a rollercoaster that always has my mind half convinced I'm about to die for real. I don't think I'm about to die now, but I do think I might have just fucked everything up for real.

Somehow, Rowan's eyes seem to soften while his jaw goes rigid and his nostrils flare. The next thing out of his mouth is my worst fear. "Get out."

"What?" I ask dumbly.

He pulls his hand out from under mine and pushes my shoulder toward the passenger door. "Get the fuck out. Get out of my car!"

"Stop, Rowan!" I grab his forearms to keep him from shoving me out the door, and I hold them tight enough for him to try to fight against it. "I'm sorry. I'm sorry. I'm sorry." I apologize a dozen times, tugging on his arms until I'm close enough to whisper it into his ear.

When he feels less rigid, I let him go, and he slumps back against his seat. His hands jump to the steering wheel and white-knuckle it like we're going one-twenty. He's breathing hard, brows pinched, but at least he's not yelling at me to get out anymore.

I'll get on my knees for him right here in this parking lot if it'll help him forgive me.

After seconds that feel like hours, Rowan casts me a glare and says, "If you don't like anything I do to you, you can say it."

Exasperated, and halfway to tears, I exclaim, "I like everything you do to me! That's the whole point. I like you. I wanna be with you. I don't wanna fight. I just don't get it. I don't know what you're afraid of. I already told you, I'll never come between you and soccer. And your family seems like they'd be really supportive if we were—"

"They're not my family. I live in the back of their garage with all the shit they'd throw out on the curb if they weren't too lazy. They're not my family."

I understand the steel in his eyes for pain now, and even though I don't know why it's there, it settles inside me like a black cloud. I realize now that I'd been comfortable to treat the family Rowan lives with as his bona fide family because they seemed so much like a family anyone would want to be part of. But that's not really how it works. Just like I can't change the fact my dad is a deadbeat, Rowan can't change who brought him into this world.

"Who are your family?" I ask, my voice turning small and hesitant.

Eyes on the windshield, watching a couple with children hustle through the parking lot, Rowan mutters, "Don't have one."

"What about your parents?"

"Don't have any."

"Who raised you?"

Shrugging, he answers, "People. Here and there. Doesn't matter."

"It matters if somewhere along the way, someone taught you that it's not okay to accept yourself."

He heaves a long, shuddered sigh, but his hands loosen from the steering wheel enough to tell me he's calming down.

Careless again, I ask him a question I half expect him to ignore. "When did you realize you like boys?"

After a bit, he mumbles, "When I was...five or six, I guess. That's when my memories begin."

"Really?" I ask gently, wanting to reach out and take his hand, but too cowardly to follow through. Makes me think of when I had that boy crush at eight but hadn't connected the dots. Makes me think of when I was twelve and Rowan himself planted the seed that would gradually bloom into an acknowledgment that eventually lead me here.

"The family I was living with at the time had a biological son who was, maybe, sixteen, and he was always walking around the house in boxers. He was never very nice to me, but I was kinda obsessed with him."

Imagining that makes me smile, even though Rowan looks about as miserable as I've ever seen him. "When you were five?" I ask with some shock, since the human body hadn't appealed to me for many years past that age.

The moment Rowan breaks down is right after his broken voice asks, "Can we please not talk about this anymore?" Tears fall down his cheeks in rivulets, and he's full on sobbing when he says, "I'll go to the restaurant if you want me to."

My chest hurts so badly that I can only assume it's my heart breaking, and I pull on Rowan until he slings his arms around my neck and presses his face to my shoulder. He cries through my shirt while I hold him tight, whispering in his ear that he's alright—that I've got him. Even though I don't understand why he's so upset, I have an idea now why he's reluctant to tell the truth.

Something bad happened to Rowan.

He cries for a long time. The hard, choking kind that sounds like overwhelming grief. Eventually, his arms go slack, and he turns his head to swipe his wet eyes across my neck. He sits up, sniffles, and runs his hands over his reddened face.

I keep my hands on him, not wanting to let go. I put one on his jaw and spread my thumb across his cheek.

"Sorry," he mutters, like he'd accidentally fallen asleep during a movie.

"I got you," I whisper, looking into his bloodshot eyes, bordered by tear-speckled lashes. "You know I got you, right?"

Bottom lip quivering, he says, "Thanks."

"You don't need to be anything, Row. Just yourself. I got you."

"I just... I wish I could be more like you."

I exhale something close to a chuckle. "That's funny, since for half my life, all I've wanted was to be more like you."

"You don't wanna be like me, Tommy. Trust me."

"I do trust you. Do you trust me?"

After a moment, Rowan nods, sealed lips moving like he's chewing on the inside on them.

I smooth my palm past his ear and through his short hair. "Do you want to be with me?"

"Of course," he whispers.

"Then, you got me. I'm yours, Row. For real."

Eyes welling with fresh tears, Rowan whimpers, "I can't."

"Shh." I take his face in both my hands. "It's okay. Nothing's gonna change right now. You're still you, and I'm still me. We're gonna do the same shit we've been doing until you're ready to do more. Right now, we're gonna switch spots, and I'm gonna drive us to the nearest Dairy Queen for ice cream, because I know that's gonna cheer you up, and it's gonna make me feel a hell of a lot better after you made me eat that salad."

Rowan smiles and murmurs, "I like salad."

"I like your ass, but I don't make you eat it."

His smile widens, and on that note, I slip out of the car and round the hood as Rowan pops open his door. As soon as he's standing, he surprises me by circling his arms around my waist and laying his cheek on my shoulder. Right here, between the Legacy and a white Ford F-150, Rowan hugs me in the daytime hours, and I hug him back. I even touch a kiss to the side of his head. Risky, but he doesn't push me away.

Even when Rowan lets go, he feels closer to me than ever.

21

Tommy

When Friday night rolls around, I surprise Rowan by not inflicting a fancy, overpriced dinner on him. Instead, I take him to the movie theater to watch something I'd never get away with taking Mav to. There will be some violence, some sex, and hopefully some good quality filmmaking. What I'm most looking forward to, though, is spending the evening with...my boyfriend?

It's still up in the air, but regardless, we're together, and that's the most important thing.

Tommy and Rowan, leveling up. When I swing by his house to pick him up, I'm more excited than I ever was showing up for a date with Lese or any of the girls before her. I'm in my chino joggers and a denim jacket, trying to look good but casual. Rowan climbs into my truck wearing his tight black jeans and a velour tee with a fucking chain around his neck. As soon as his dreamy eyes are on me, it takes everything in me not to pounce.

At the theater, I pay for everything from the tickets to the sodas and nachos. Rowan teases me for that, saying I shouldn't be spending all my allowance on junk food. Such a jokester.

We pick two seats toward the back, fifteen minutes early to showtime. The screen is still projecting ads for TV shows and more junk food.

"You know," Rowan begins in a low voice as he fits his soda in his cupholder, "I heard that going to the movies is the worst thing to do on a first date. Both people are just sitting in a dark room, silent and not looking at each other or talking about anything for two hours."

"Hmm." I move my soda to the other cupholder so I can lift the armrest that separates us. "I don't know. Sounds like a good baby step to me."

I turn my palm up in the sliver of space between our legs, and as soon as Rowan shifts our nachos onto his lap, he lays his hand on mine and lets me lace our fingers together. I look sideways and catch him smiling toward the giant screen.

"All of your steps are baby steps," he whispers, "because you're my baby boy."

I snicker as I lean in close to his ear. "You look super hot right now."

"So do you."

We talk through the commercials but quiet down when the house lights go dark and the trailers play. By the time the *silence your phones* ad plays, my cheek is on Rowan's shoulder, inhaling whatever cologne he put on to smell so damn good.

It's true that movie theater dates make for lame get-to-know-you's, but I already know this is the person I want to be with. Whatever Rowan's hang-ups are, whatever trauma lies inside his stormy mind, I want all of him. Seeing a low-budget slasher movie is just an excuse to dip our feet into being intimate in public, and hopefully, by the time I'm acclimated to dating a man, Rowan will be a little less skittish about the idea.

After the movie, we walk around the promenade a bit, my hands shoved deep into my pockets so I'm not tempted to hold Rowan's.

"How're you feeling about tomorrow?" I ask him. "Will there be recruiters there?"

"Probably," he says. "Trying not to think about that, though."

"I bet you could've gotten into a club last year or even two years ago."

He shrugs. "I like school, and I always wanted to get my degree. And I dunno. I didn't feel totally ready before, I guess."

"You're good enough. You're incredible."

"That's easy for people around here to say, but there are incredible players all over the country. All over the world. I'm just a drop in the bucket."

"Do you know where you wanna end up?"

His smile turns wistful. "Whichever team wants me."

"I wish we could have a sleepover."

"Match tomorrow in Berkeley. Gotta be up bright and early for the bus."

"I know," I groan, knowing I'll be waking my ass up at five in the morning just to go sit on a bench for two hours at Cal. It'll be worth it to see Rowan do his thing, but I'd also really like to see Rowan do *my* thing in his bedroom.

"Tomorrow night?" he asks, because Saturday nights have become our thing. The only evening per week when Rowan isn't clambering to train, and the one night per week where neither of us have to wake up at dawn the next day. I'll take one night per week. It's a lot better than no nights per week, and we do fool around a lot in between.

"Totally." I tug on the hem of his shirt, coaxing him toward my parked truck, because the sooner we're not in *public* public, I can put my hands on him properly. "Is your, uh, your...people gonna be there tomorrow?"

"My people? Like, my posse?"

I laugh, but ever since Rowan's meltdown, I've been reluctant to call the people he lives with his family. Clearly, that's not how Rowan views them all the time, and I don't want to force a narrative that doesn't reflect his reality. "Yeah, your entourage."

"Nah."

"Well, I'll be there cheering you on."

Rowan's hand on my back, stroking my spine, is a pleasant surprise, since we're still finding our way to the parking lot. Baby steps. "Thanks, babyface. You're by far my favorite groupie."

"Fuck you," I cackle. "I better be your only groupie."

Smirking, he says, "Don't worry. You're definitely top ten."

The bus ride to Berkeley is a little over an hour, and I sit next to Rowan the whole way with one of his earbuds in my ear, watching compilation videos of sports movie monologues. All part of Rowan's away game ritual, but the vids do get my blood pumping a little quicker. I bunch my sweatshirt between us so no one notices I'm holding his hand beneath it, smoothing my thumb along his forefinger.

Berkeley is beautiful, and the weather already feels like fall. Overcast and foggy. I have to keep my sweatshirt on during warm-ups until exertion warms me up. The stands fill in, but there's no one here to watch me. My eyes scan the bleachers anyway, wondering which of the solo spectators are professional scouts here to see Rowan.

I briefly wonder where he'll end up next year, and if they'll help him accept himself, or if they'll only do more damage.

Three minutes into the match's second half, Connor goes down on a foul, and he doesn't get up. He doesn't look pained, but he stays on his knees anyway, cradling one hand on his lap and sticking the other high above his head, waving toward our line.

Rowan is the first to reach Connor. He puts his hand on Connor's shoulder and waves Coach over.

"Shit," I hear Coach say before he dashes from the sideline across the field. He hollers to the trainer to find Connor's bag.

I know where Connor left his bag. It's under the bench I've been sitting on since the match began. I hunch between mine and Malik's legs, grab it, and run it to the trainer.

When I turn back to the bench, Malik is shaking his head, sighing a curse word under his breath.

"What's going on?" I ask, feeling dumb.

Malik nods to the field and says, "Guessing the con-man got stung. Dude is deathly allergic to bees."

"Fuck, is he gonna be okay?" I turn toward the field to try to catch a glimpse, but all I can see past the bodies of those surrounding Connor is that he's laid up on his back.

"He should be good," Malik says. "He's always got an EpiPen in his bag, but last time this happened, they pulled him and took him to the ER, just in case. You never know with that shit."

Coach and the trainer walk Connor off the field to a chorus of claps, and the trainer takes Connor away while Coach snaps his fingers in my direction.

"You're in!" he calls to me, and my heart stops for a second. Concern for myself immediately replaces my concern for Connor. It all happens in a flurry, time moving too quickly for my mind to keep up. Coach is behind me at some point, saying words to me that should pump me up. My heart is sure pumping, but it's more nausea I feel. Then the ref gives the go-ahead, and I'm on the field, jogging toward Rowan on instinct but stopping short when I remember where the hell I'm supposed to be. I have to glance at the score cards just to remember what the score is. We're up 2-1. Not much room for error.

And just like that, the match is back on.

In a flash, I have to recall everything I know and everything Rowan taught me. Suddenly, it all comes back. Adrenaline takes the wheel. I focus on the ball, where the opponents are, and where my teammates are. I listen for their voices, and I track the plays.

The strangest part in all this is that I'm finally playing on Rowan's side. He doesn't chide me or tease me. When he tells me to stay on him, it's not to defend against him, but to protect him.

I got you.

He'd been working with me on my offense, but defense comes naturally, especially now, when I've got Cal on our asses, scouts in the stands, and our team is so far undefeated. I can't let the first time we lose be the first game I'm put into.

I take the ball when I'm open and get it to Rowan or Levi as soon as they're open and calling out to me. Then I'm doing everything I can to put my body in front of the opponents, making it harder for them to make a steal.

When a man in blue and gold has a ball dribbling between his feet, I'm on him like it's life or death while keeping my arms back to make sure I don't foul.

If I can just get the ball to Rowan—

The ball comes loose, and I make the pass, hoping like hell Rowan is still as open as he was two seconds ago. Like a hawk, he swoops in, takes possession, and flies across the field with his eyes on the goal. Cal's goalie readies himself for the attack, and just then, Rowan kicks the ball into the opposite corner, a clean strike right into the net.

3-1 now.

No time to celebrate, but inside I'm freaking out with joy.

When the game clock runs down, we're victorious. The elation on everyone's faces eclipses our sheer exhaustion, and a new sort of adrenaline kicks in. We cheer, pat each other on the back, and fuck up each other's greasy hair. We tell our opponents *good game* before hitting the locker room, then Coach gives us a rundown of what he saw out on the field, and how proud he is of us. The usual post-match pep talk I've gotten used to over the past weeks.

Mid-speech, Coach's hard stare zeros in on me. "And let's give a round to Tommy, who managed not to barf all over the field."

The team howls with laughter, and my face goes a shade redder.

"In all seriousness," Coach says, coming forward to clap me on the shoulder, "Good work out there, kid."

I nod the compliment away, feeling bashful, and I look at Rowan, because it's only his approval that means much to me. Across the aisle, standing against the lockers, he stares at me with a look that isn't hiding anything—all hunger and passion, like Rowan could swallow me whole at any moment. *Please do.*

Once we're all showered, changed, and back on the bus, Coach surprises us with lunch at a local pizza arcade, and we all become giddy like children. Connor and the trainer meet us at the restaurant, and Levi gives him an animated rundown of the match post-bee sting.

I'm holding my palm over my mouth to keep from cackling the pizza out of my mouth when Levi starts in on an impression of me.

"Tommy," Rowan's voice says above me, tapping my bicep.

I look up, and he's nodding for me to follow him. I take a quick swig of Coke to wash down my bite, then hop up and follow in Rowan's wake. It's a snaking path across the dining hall, through the arcade, and down a narrow hallway with doors leading to the kitchen and the restrooms. Rowan leaves through the door at the very end that swings open to reveal daylight.

Curiously, I follow him into what looks like an alleyway behind the restaurant, but I don't have many seconds to process where we're at before Rowan is shoving me against the brick wall.

Hands fisted in my shirt, hips digging against mine, Rowan kisses me like he's trying to scoop my tonsils out with his tongue. My reflex is to laugh into his mouth, but then he settles, slows things down, and I feel his bulge grind against my growing erection.

His hands move to my waist, locking our bodies together, and his mouth leaves mine to whisper in my ear, "You were so fucking hot out there today."

"Really?" I turn my head and lock my eyes on Rowan's fiery stare, like blazing hot coals between gorgeous black lashes.

"Yeah, baby. Can't you feel how hard I am?" he murmurs before putting his mouth back on mine. His head tilts, lips latching to mine as he sweeps his tongue along mine.

When Rowan turns his attention to my neck, I reach my head back against the wall to give him clearance to suck my throat and nip at my skin.

"Fuck." I grip Rowan's shoulders and push my ass forward to grind against his.

There's just enough sense left in my head that I look left and right, making sure no one's around. That's when I feel Rowan's hand slide beneath my waistband.

Oh my God. He grips me through my boxer briefs, kneading my balls before dragging his palm along my shaft.

I look left and right again, then tug my shorts and underwear down enough for my cock to spring out and slap Rowan above the bulge in his jeans.

He leans back enough to spit a line of saliva down, hitting the tip of my cock like a bullseye, and he spreads the wetness around with quick, skilled strokes.

"Are you gonna make me come?" I whine as Rowan pumps me like he's trying to finish me off fast.

Tucking his mouth to my ear, Rowan murmurs, "You want me to make you come, baby boy?"

"Fuck, yes. Please."

"Your cock is so hot, baby. Fucking burning my hand. My perfect fucking boy."

Losing myself in the moment—in this feeling—I take Rowan's face in my hands and kiss him while my body succumbs to his ministrations.

"I'm gonna come. I'm gonna come," I chant against his mouth, eyes shut and abs flexing.

"That's it." Rowan seals his mouth to mine, muffling my moans and milking me of everything I've built up since he sucked me off last night.

I cling to Rowan, steadying myself as my orgasm subsides. I moan as I soften in his fist, and I sigh when I look between us and find I've painted a large wet spot on Rowan's shirt. My breath catches in my lungs when Rowan uses the hem of that shirt to clean my dick before gently tucking it back into my shorts.

"You good?" he asks, putting a couple of feet between us.

I breathe a dazed chuckle, barely able to feel my legs. "Yeah, man. I feel awesome."

All he does is smirk and nod back to the door we left through.

"Wait." I take off my sweatshirt and give it to him.

"Thanks." He peels out of his own shirt, baring his killer body to the overcast weather to dress himself in my Sac State hoodie. He rolls up his soiled shirt and shoves it in the front pocket before tugging the back door open.

I get back to the team feeling jittery and euphoric, everything seeming to fall into place. I've got Rowan—not quite boyfriends, but baby-stepping closer to it each day. Got over a half hour of playing time today, helped secure a win, and even got some lukewarm praise from Coach. As for my family...we all love each other, and that's more important than anything.

Now that Coach is probably going to give me playing time now that I've proved myself, Erica wants to bring Mav to my matches. I'm excited over it, because I want them to see me play, and I want them to see how good the team is. I want Ma to come too, so she can see I'm not just wasting my time. That I'm actually good. Better than I ever was in high school. But I'm afraid that no matter what, Ma is always going to think there are more important things I should be doing than kicking a ball around.

After Erica's gone, Ma is going to need help with Mav like when Erica was real sick. She says Mav needs a male role model around so he won't grow up sideways. Not sure what that implies about me, since I never had a male role model around besides coaches and teachers who barely knew me outside soccer and school.

I don't know the first thing about being a father figure, but I try to be a good uncle. I want to show Mav he can do anything if he really puts his mind to it, so when the next home game rolls around, I ask Coach in his office if he thinks I'll get a few minutes playing time.

"You did well for us last weekend," he answers, but his tone is gruff, like he's not used to dolling out compliments to newbies. "But it'll all depend on how the match progresses and if I've got to relieve any of the guys.'

"I understand."

"Tommy." He stops me before I slip from his office. "Invite your family to the game. I'll see what I can do."

I realize way too late what the consequences are of Erica coming to the match. It hits me like a cold fish to the face when Coach puts me into the game during the second half, and I realize I'm shouting Rowan's name whenever he's in a jam, and I'm open.

Shit.

What are the chances Erica will believe my team captain just happens to share a name with the person Erica thinks is my girlfriend?

I fucked up. I never should have given her Rowan's name. Never should have told her I'm seeing anyone at all. I should have told her I get so dopey when my phone buzzes because I'm hooked on an online thirst trap from across the world who's sending me nudes and asking for money. I'm twenty. Erica would've bought that I'm that dumb.

Is Erica thinking I'm dumb really better than her finding out I'm gay?

It's not just about me, though. If she figures out that I'm gay and Rowan is Rowan, then she'll know Rowan is gay too. Rowan isn't even ready to tell *me* he's gay. He's definitely not ready for a complete stranger to know he's gay.

A palm slapping my shoulder wakes me out of an internal panic.

"You getting stage fright on me?" Rowan asks in the spare seconds before the opposing goalie tosses out the ball. "Pick it the fuck up."

My eyes dart from Rowan to the stands, where Erica and Mav are sitting, cheering me on like I'm back in high school.

I don't know how to protect Rowan from the damage I've already done, but I can protect him now, on the field. So I clear my mind and *pick it the fuck up.*

After we've won, Rowan jogs to where I am and slings his arms around me, hugging me firm and quick, but long enough to whisper in my ear that I'm amazing. It hurts that I have to shrug him off me, because all I want to do is tackle him to the ground and cuddle him to pieces.

As I'm walking toward our line, I exchange a wave with Erica. She takes Mav's hand and escorts him down the bleachers. The closer they get to joining me on the sidelines, the faster my anxiety heightens.

"Tommy!" Mav shouts, breaking into a sprint as soon as his shoes are on the grass. He flings himself at me, squeezing me tight. "That was so cool! You were so good! You won! You won!"

"Thanks, buddy." I rustle his shaggy hair with one hand while giving my sis a one-arm hug. "Sorry, I'm all sweaty."

"I think I'll live," Erica says before pecking a kiss to my cheek. "I'm so proud of you."

Mav slips from my side, and I hear him exclaim, "Dude, you're so cool!" I turn my head, and find he's tugging on Rowan's jersey, who is halfway through downing an entire bottle of Gatorade. Erica is saying things to me, but I don't hear a word over the sound of my heart thumping in my ears.

"Thanks, little man," Rowan says, fist bumping Mav once he's got his bottle capped.

"Are you the captain?" Mav asks, hopping on the balls of his feet like he's meeting Mickey Mouse for the first time.

"Sure am."

"Are you in the Olympics?"

Rowan laughs. "Maybe one day."

"I wanna be in the Olympics. I wanna be a striker! That's the coolest position, don't you think? I wanna start going to soccer practice soon. Mom says maybe next year."

"Maverick," Erica interjects. To my horror, she walks right up to Mav and Rowan. "Are you bothering people?"

"Nuh uh!"

Taking on that charming persona that never ceases to confound and arouse me, Rowan smiles at Erica, extends his hand and says, "You must be Tommy's sister. He was really excited for you and your son to see him play."

"Erica," she chirps, shaking Rowan's hand before planting it on Mav's head. "And this little rascal is Maverick."

"I'm Rowan."

My heart stops.

"Rowan?"

"Tommy and I train together a lot. He's an incredible player. Very talented. He'll be a starter next year, for sure. The team's gonna need him."

With a curious look cast between Rowan and I, Erica asks, "Rowan is sort of an unusual name for a guy, isn't it?"

Rowan chuckles, smiling with those dreamy eyes that are making me melt for all the wrong reasons. "I dunno. It's always been my name, and I've always been a guy, so it's a guy's name to me."

"Huh." Erica nods, a suspicious half-smile on her face as she tips her head toward me. "You know, Tommy has a girlfriend named Rowan."

This is it. This is what death feels like. The ground is opening up below me, sucking me down into a deep abyss of my own construction.

"Really?" Rowan puts his indecipherable gaze on me, but I'm stone solid. "That is some coincidence."

"I know, right?" says Erica. "I didn't think it was that popular of a name."

Still looking at me, Rowan says, "Didn't know you had a girlfriend, babyface. You should bring her around sometime. We can have a good laugh about having the same name."

"W—well, you know...it's complicated." I force a shrug and fold my lips after that.

To Rowan, Erica says, "We're about to go to lunch. Do you want to join?"

Thankfully, Rowan says he's got plans, then casually tells me, "See you at practice next week. Good job today."

I can't help but think the damage is already done. Even though Rowan acts chill, and Erica isn't fussing, I can feel it in the air that things are changing. But this isn't a baby step. This is a canyon-wide leap.

After Rowan walks off toward the locker rooms, I tell Erica I'll meet her and Mav outside the stadium once I change clothes.

When Rowan comes to me in the locker room, I expect the worst. That he'll be angry with me. So angry that he might break up with me.

"So," he says, leaning his shoulder against the locker beside mine. He's shirtless and still glistening with sweat, which only makes this harder for me. "You coming over tonight, or will you be with your girlfriend?"

"I'm sorry," I whisper, before I can process his question.

The smirk on his face takes me by surprise, because it doesn't look like an angry one. "Why are you sorry?"

"Well...for being a dumbass?"

His smirk becomes a thoughtful smile. "You're not a dumbass, Tommy."

"You're not mad at me?"

"She's your sister. You can tell her whatever you want. But seriously, are you coming over tonight? I got a present for you."

"Yeah?"

He answers with a waggle of his black brows and another smirk as he backs away from me, turning toward the showers.

I'm all smiles until I remember Erica's waiting for me. If not for Mav, I'd take my sweet time, but this isn't something I can wuss out on. I've got to face her.

In the parking lot, Erica acts like nothing's amiss, but I still feel that shift in the air between us. Mav is a good buffer, but he can only do so much.

The restaurant we go to is family friendly. They've got kids' menus with puzzles and games on them that Mav preoccupies himself with. It gives Erica enough time to notice how quiet I am, and how queasy I look.

"You okay?" she asks.

"Mhm," I lie. It's not all paranoia. The way Erica looks at me is off, and she's been a lot quieter than normal.

The server comes around, and Erica orders for herself and for Mav. I order a plate of parmesan boneless wings even though my appetite is trash.

"Rowan..." Erica says suddenly, her voice low and casual, despite the clearly discomforted look on her face. "He's pretty cute."

"I got to piss."

"Tommy—"

I'm already out of the booth, marching toward a placard against the opposite wall that reads RESTROOMS with an arrow left. I don't really have to piss, but I might puke. Thankfully, the feeling passes after I splash water on my face and take some deep breaths.

Jeez, how pathetic can I be? Erica is my sister, for crying out loud, and it's not like she's ever acted homophobic. Ma is a different story, but Erica wouldn't say anything to Ma that I tell her in confidence. Sibling code.

I go back to the table and slide into my side of the booth. My Coke is refilled, and Mav is playing make-believe with the salt and pepper shakers. Erica stares at me like she isn't sure who I am anymore. Not angry, just confused.

"I did tell you I don't have a girlfriend," I blurt out.

"So..." Erica looks beside her, like she's measuring how distracted Mav is before we embark on a conversation she considers *adult*. I try not to let it get to me, but it does. "Does this mean you've been...questioning?"

"Questioning?"

She pauses, and I can see the gears turning behind her eyes, like she's trying to choose her words carefully. "Is this why you and Annalese broke up?"

My eyes roll. "Lese and I broke up because she cheated on me. A lot."

"What the hell? Why didn't you tell me?"

"Because it doesn't matter. I didn't love her, and you knew I didn't love her, so it doesn't matter."

She pauses again. "Do you love Rowan?"

"It's—" I lose my words, my mind searching for an answer and coming up with a jumble of emotions I haven't properly dissected yet. "Maybe."

"Does that mean you're..? I mean, are you..?"

"Gay?" I say loud enough for Erica's spine to tease up. "Yeah. I am."

"H—how long have you..? When did you..?"

"I don't know, Erica. A while. Since I was a kid."

"Tom..." Her eyes look so sullen that it makes me feel like I made the wrong choice, like I should've kept it from her forever. Let her live blissfully ignorant that her little brother is queer until her time comes. "Why didn't you tell me?"

I answer honestly. "I wasn't sure. I thought I could be. I wondered if I was for a long time, but I didn't let myself fully accept it until...Rowan."

"He's the first guy you've..?"

"Yeah, pretty much."

"Well, just because you like one guy doesn't necessarily mean you're...*you know*. You're twenty. You're in college. This is the time when people experiment with who they are. You don't have to label yourself based on one person—"

"I'm gay, Erica," I tell her bluntly, because the sooner she gets it, the sooner we can change the subject. "Rowan's been there for me. I'm trying to be there for him too. I want things to work with us. But if it doesn't work out, I'm never gonna date women again. That's not who I am or what I want."

When Erica's eyes widen and shift toward Mav like I've just shouted a string of profanities, my temper rises. I compensate by lowering my voice and leaning in.

"I'm not saying anything inappropriate. I'm just telling you the truth."

"And I just want you to have a good life, Tom. You have so much going for you. You're talented, smart, compassionate, attractive. Why do you want to make life hard for yourself?"

"I'm not choosing this. I've spent my whole life choosing to be straight, but that's not real. I wanna live a good life too, and that means being honest with myself and being with someone who makes me happy. When I'm with Rowan, I'm the happiest I've ever been in my life. The way I feel when I'm with him is worth all the bullshit anyone else can sling at me."

"Are you fighting?" Mav asks suddenly.

"No," Erica and I answer in unison.

Just then, our food arrives, and Mav has a grilled cheese and fries to distract him. Erica and I leave our plates to cool, stuck in a contest to see who can look the most defeated.

"Does Mom know?" Erica asks.

"No. Hell no. You're the only person I've told, besides Rowan."

Exhaling a sigh, Erica reaches her arm across the table and sweeps her hand across my hair. "Just be careful. Be safe. Men are horrible, present company excluded. Just when you're convinced they love you, they leave."

22

Rowan

Sneaking Tommy into the garage sight unseen doesn't go as planned when Xia is sneaking hits off her nicotine vape in the backyard when we roll through.

"You guys can hang out in the house if you want," she offers like she's hoping we'll agree. "The girls are watching a movie in their room, so they won't bother you if you want to hang in the living room."

"We're good, thanks," I answer, already holding the side door open for Tommy.

"Breakfast tomorrow morning, okay? Around eight-thirty."

"We might sleep in," I answer, then immediately wince at how fucking obvious I am.

"Breakfast sounds great," Tommy says to Xia. "Thank you so much."

"Of course, sweetheart. Like I said, you're welcome here anytime. Rowan doesn't even need to be here. You can just drop by. I mean it."

"Goodnight, Xia!" I send her a pointed look I hope tells her she's laying it on way too thick.

Thankfully, she backs off, and I pull Tommy into the garage with me.

"Sorry," he says with a small chuckle. "I know they're not your real family, but I still want them to like me. Plus, I really love breakfast."

"I'm worried they're gonna like you too much." Once we're in my bedroom, I flick on the lamp and shut my door. "I shouldn't have said that shit about them the other week, though. They've done a lot for me, and they really are the closest thing to a real family I've ever had."

"It's okay, Row." He smiles at me in that way he does a lot lately, like he can see through me to my fundamental particles. He used to call me an enigma, but when he sets his eyes on me, I feel them inside me like they're reading the walls of my soul. "There's only one universal truth about all families. At some point, they're gonna disappoint you. You're allowed to feel disappointed in the way they treat you and still be grateful for everything they do for you. And you're always allowed to vent to me about anything."

"Thanks for the insight, Dr. Tommy." I cross what little floor space there is in this place and plant my hands on Tommy's waist so I can feel his hard body when I kiss him. "Speaking of families, how did things go with your sister? Did you tell her?"

"Yeah," he murmurs between soft pecks to my lips.

"What did you tell her?"

"That I'm gay, that I'm dating a man, and that I really want to be with that man, and I have no interest in dating women ever again."

I lean back enough to study Tommy's beautiful face, remembering the times we crossed paths as kids and thinking about how wrong I was about the sort of person he was. "You're really brave, Tommy. I'm proud of you."

He tugs me in for another kiss, then murmurs against my lips, "Where's my present?"

Snickering, I take a step back and shake my head. "Can't give it to you yet."

"Why not?" He pouts a little, like the precious baby he is.

"Because you're wearing too many clothes."

A big grin stretches across his face. "Oh? This is a naked-only present?"

"That's right. So, c'mon, gay boy. Strip for me."

He takes his time, flexing every muscle in his torso as he peels his t-shirt up and over his head. A purposeful rake of his fingers through his soft hair fixes his effortless, heartthrob cut, and a swipe of his tongue along his lips makes his kissable pout glossy. I trail my eyes down his wide chest and rippled abs to where his fingers pluck at the buttons of his light-wash jeans. He slips off his shoes and pushes his pants down muscular legs.

When he's in nothing but boxers, he hooks his thumbs in the waistband and smirks. "Why does it feel like I'm the one giving you a present?"

"It'll be mutually beneficial in the end."

Chuckling, he strips out of his boxers, freeing his bobbing, half-hard cock and low hanging balls.

I stand my pillow up against my headboard. "Lie down. On your front."

Tommy has a hand stroking his cock until the moment it's wedged between his body and my mattress. With his head turned toward me, it's his turn to watch me strip. I don't put on nearly the show Tommy did, but his eyes drink me in like I'm Magic fucking Mike.

"Put your arms at your sides," I tell him before grabbing the bottle of baby oil I found among the junk Matt and Xia were fixing to toss.

The bedframe creaks when I add my weight to it, and I straddle Tommy's thighs. Staring at the expanse of his back, I'm tempted to lick him from the bottom of his spine to the top. Instead, I dribble a line of oil in the same formation.

"What's that?" Tommy asks, flinching slightly from the sensation.

"Shh." I spread my palms through the oil trail and fan it across Tommy's back. I press my hands firmly into places I know he must be sore from how hard he's been working.

A soft moan in my baby's voice tells me he likes it. I press my thumbs into knots between his shoulder blades and spine, and he moans even louder. The sound makes my cock throb and my foreskin retract.

"Fuck, Row," Tommy moans, as I drag my palms parallel to his spine. I press down on the dimples above his ass before kneading those pale, firm globes.

I add more oil and repeat every motion, focusing on the areas that produce the most noises out of Tommy.

"You're good at that," he says, his hips shifting against the mattress ever so slightly.

"It's easy once you understand the muscle groups. You've been working yourself hard, baby boy. You're so fucking tight."

"Yeah?"

I press my hands to each of Tommy's butt cheeks and spread them apart, getting an eyeful of his pink puckered hole. I find the baby oil beside my knee and dribble a small amount right onto that hole, reveling in the sound it elicits from Tommy's throat. Somewhere between excitement and worry. I use my finger to spread the oil along his crack and around his hole. When he's slick, I massage my palms into his cheeks and tease his hole with my thumbs.

"Don't worry, I'm just touching," I tell him, but there's so much pleasure in Tommy's moans, I almost ask to breach him. Instead, I smooth my hands back up to his shoulders and knead the muscles there. While I do, I let the length of my cock nestle along Tommy's crack, and I can't stop myself from humping him.

It's hard to believe Tommy's mine, even when he's naked and underneath me, supplicating to me, groaning a shortened version of my name that only he's allowed to call me. I lean down and graze my lips against his ear. "Turn over, big boy."

"Look who's talking." He flips onto his back as soon as I give him clearance, and when I'm sitting back on his thighs, he clasps a hand around my cock and gives a few slow strokes.

Selfishly, I let him work me while I dribble oil across his chest and down the center of his abs. I let a few drops touch the underside of Tommy's cock, too, laid out across his hip.

This time, I massage him gently. Just an excuse to run my hands over every inch of him. From his biceps to his chest, my fingers taking time to rub his soft nipples to nubs, then down his sides and along the v-lines sculpted into his physique. I thread my fingers through his brown pubic hair, and glide my thumbs up the length of his cock.

"Oh, fuck," Tommy sighs, eyelids fluttering and his mouth doing that frowny thing it does when I edge him.

"You have such a beautiful body. I can't get enough of it. When you came onto that field in April wanting to kick my ass, I swear I almost popped a boner you were so hot. I thought you were cute in high school, but now I can't get you out of my mind if I try."

"Don't try. Think about me, and I'll think about you. That way, we're always together."

"Such a romantic." I cup one hand around Tommy's balls, rolling them and caressing them with my thumb while my other hand makes languid passes over his cock.

"I love you."

My mind skips a beat along with my heart, like my body freezes in time for just a moment. But even when my head forms thoughts again, I can't make sense of them. I can't make sense of *that*. Love?

"I'm sorry," Tommy murmurs, squeezing my thighs and staring at me through half-lidded eyes. His abs are flexing, legs twitching, cock pulsing in my gentle grip.

He's close. That's why he said it. He loves being with me, and he loves the things I do to him. That's all it is.

"Shh," I whisper. "Relax. You know you're mine, right?"

"Your baby boy?" he asks in a small whimper that goes straight to my yearning cock.

"That's right. My perfect baby boy." I stroke him quicker, firmer. "You gonna be a good boy and come for me?"

Bottom lip trapped between his teeth, Tommy nods fast. "Mhm."

I climb off Tommy's thighs and squeeze myself between him and the wall. I wrap an arm beneath his head while I keep my other hand stroking his dick.

Tucking my mouth close to Tommy's ear, I tell him, "Listen to my voice. You're not allowed to come until I tell you to. Understand?"

The sound Tommy makes is a lovechild between lust and desperation. I cover my mouth with his so I can drink up every little moan and whimper. He's so lost in his own pleasure, his lips can hardly move with mine, but his tongue makes lazy attempts to mingle, and I lap it up.

I pump quicker, my room filling with the sloppy sound of my oiled up hand working his oiled up cock. "Not yet," I murmur into Tommy's slack mouth.

When his pleasure-sounds turn urgent, and his body trembles, I squeeze my thumb and forefingers under his raging crown and hold it there until Tommy settles.

"Not yet," I repeat, before dragging my fist over his cock.

"Oh my God," Tommy breathes up to the popcorn ceiling.

I jerk him fast, faster than before, until Tommy's legs jitter across my comforter, and I stop to pinch his head again. "Not yet."

Again, I resume with a few slow strokes before rubbing him full-force. When I sense Tommy on the verge, I stop and revel in the sight of his fat cockhead pulsing. "Not yet."

He's panting, quivering, and humping my fist in a gloriously untamed fashion.

"Not yet." I let his cock lie along his abdomen. Tracing his length from stem to tip, I find his frenulum and massage the glands with my forefinger while my thumb caresses his blinking slit. I touch my forehead To Tommy's sweaty one and tell him, "Come for me, baby. Right now. Be good for me."

His shuddered whimper rises and falls with the heaving of his chest, and to my absolute amazement, his cock twitches and warm fluid sluices over my thumb.

Eyes wide and heart pounding, I stare into his dazed eyes and murmur, "That's it. That's it. Let it out."

"Rowan," he whines as opaque fluid pools between his flexing abs.

"Good boy."

He shudders, eyelids fluttering, but as soon as my tongue is inside his mouth, he comes alive. A growl rumbles from his throat, hands grabbing for my hips, and he flips me on my back so quick that I yelp. He's between my legs, hunched over, and he swallows my cock deep. He gags and slobbers all over me, gripping my base and bobbing on my shaft. The sight alone is enough to rile me up, but it's all the feelings Tommy produces that threaten to push me over the edge.

"God, Tommy, you're gonna make me—"

He pulls off, gasping in a breath while strings of saliva and pre-cum tether his mouth to my dick. He breaks the strands with a few strokes over my head before he sits up and brings his hand to his stomach.

"Look what you did to me," he says, smearing his fingers through the fluid streaking down his abdomen.

"Looks good on you," I pant, rising to my elbows.

When he brings his fingers to my mouth, I take them in. He knows how obsessed I am with the way he tastes. I suck him in to the knuckles, wash my tongue under his fingers, and swallow down his salted spunk.

There's hunger in Tommy's eyes as he pulls his fingers back, a fierceness I only see in bed or on a soccer pitch. Next thing I know, he's got the baby oil in one hand, and he's slopping it all over the same fingers I'd been sucking on.

My legs open wider before my mind knows what's going on. Tommy grips me under one knee and pushes it up toward my chest.

"I'm not just gonna touch you," he says, pressing his oiled fingers to my asshole. "I'm gonna fuck you."

Holy shit.

The air leaves my lungs as a shiver courses down my spine to wrap around my balls. My cock feels harder than it ever has been, my heart beating faster. I glance at Tommy's crotch and see his cock hasn't deflated at all. Long, thick, and so much larger than anything I've had inside me before.

"Just my fingers. Promise," he assures.

I must look as terrified as I feel. Part of me wants to know what it's like to have Tommy inside me. Would he fit inside like a nesting doll, making me feel whole? He said he loves me, and even though he couldn't have meant it, I think I might love him for real. I think I might want to be his. Completely.

But it's too much. I'm not ready. Not ready to love. Not ready to be loved. *What the fuck do I know about love?*

Tommy is already pressing his fingertip through my pucker when I nod my head in urgent consent. Whether or not I'm capable of love, *I need him.* He buries his finger to the hilt in one slow, smooth motion, and he holds it there while his other hand plays with my cock.

"So tight," he murmurs as he pumps that finger through me at an equally slow and smooth pace.

I lie back, shutting my eyes and focusing on the stretch and the fullness that's so unique to being penetrated. I feel cool liquid splash down my ass and realize Tommy is adding more oil. Soon, his finger pumps easy and rhythmically, twisting this way and that. I pick my other knee up, and tug at my ass cheek, widening myself for him.

Momentary fear passes through me when he pulls out, and I tighten myself up on instinct. Then, there are two fingers probing me, stretching me and sinking deep.

"Oh God," I moan, hugging my knee like a security blanket.

"How does it feel?" Tommy's low, devilishly deep voice asks.

"Incredible," I sigh, and that's before Tommy curls his fingers in such a way that the sizzling fuse inside me ignites my nerves like fireworks on the Fourth of July. My eyes go wide, but I don't see a thing. My toes curl and my hand flies to my dick, seeking reprieve while desperate to not let this feeling end.

"Right there?" Tommy asks.

"Don't—don't—don't stop."

There's fluid drooling from my cock, but whatever orgasm this is, it isn't quite like anything I've felt before. When I feel Tommy's tongue on my cock, all I can do is make sounds I've never made before and shake in a way I never have before.

I've never been more afraid to come, and the build-up has never felt so good.

My climax hits as Tommy wraps his lips around me, and I ball my fist in his hair to hold him steady while I fill his throat. "Yes, yes, yes," I moan. "Fuck me, Tommy! Fuck!"

Tommy's throat swallows around me, his tongue fluttering against me, his fingers rubbing some place inside me that makes me feel like I'm soaring.

Everything inside me fills Tommy's mouth before he lifts off my dick and kisses me. But it isn't just a kiss. My lips part along with his, and my mouth fills with my own viscous release. Our tongues play together amid the fluid, sharing licks and trading my cum back and forth until we both swallow what we're left with.

"Holy fuck," Tommy exhales, his face hovering over mine, bleary eyes locked with mine.

The drag of his fingers pulling out has me in a brief panic, and I tell him to be slow. When I'm empty, I miss him, but then he tackles me in a firm embrace that rolls us sideways and seals our bodies like Velcro.

Our hands roam freely, and I hike a knee over Tommy's hip while he shoves his thigh up against my balls. We kiss and poke each other with our noses like pecking hens, for no other reason except we're both fuck-drunk and happy. I can't feel his erection, but I remember how wild it looked just a handful of minutes ago.

"Lemme finish you off," I murmur.

After a bashful groan, he says, "I already did."

"Really?"

"You were just too fucking hot. Watching my fingers disappear in your ass, your cock leaking like that, the sounds you were making... I can't believe I wasted five years of my life having straight sex."

I can't help it. I burst into laughter against his shoulder, howling until my eyes water. Tommy's own laughter fills my ear, our bodies vibrating against each other with mirth. It rolls us so I'm on my back and Tommy's propped on an elbow beside me, looking down at me like I'm a marvel of the world.

"I really thought you were gonna fuck me," I say.

"Would you be into that?"

God, yes.

I shrug one shoulder. "Never done anything like that before."

"Never bottomed?"

"Either or..."

His brows do a small hop, like he pegged me for someone who fucks even though he was my first kiss. "Not with anyone?"

I shake my head. "Only shit I'd done with anyone else was a few handies and blowies from girls when I was too weak to stop it, and like...moments of desperation."

"Like what we were doing in the beginning?"

"No." I rake my fingers through his hair to push it off his forehead. "You're different. You're mine. I've never really had anyone before."

His eyes searching mine like runes etched into ancient rocks. It almost has me regretting telling him that. *So pathetic.* "I'm sorry," he says.

"For what?"

"Sounds like you've been taken advantage of before."

My face falls, not liking this shadow drifting overtop us when all I want to do is be fuck-drunk and happy with Tommy. "Nah. It's not like that. I let that shit happen. I don't blame anyone."

He nods, then leans in and kisses me.

Ah, yes. This is what I wanna be doing.

"You weren't just a moment of desperation for me either," he says. "I think you're the first person in my life to make me feel like I'm lucky."

I force myself not to grin, suddenly feeling like I've shared too much emotion for one night. "C'mon," I say, sitting upward. "Let's get a shower and wash all this jizz and baby oil off of us."

Tommy complies with a groan. "Fine, but only 'cause when I eat your ass later, I don't want to taste anything except you."

And now, I'm grinning.

23
Tommy

Mid-term week means no Rowan, and no Rowan makes Tommy a sad, sad boy. I have to drink my fill of him through casual glances during practice and the many, many dick pics the dude texts me. I don't know how he's writing all his papers with his cock always hard as a rock, because I'm sure struggling.

To make matters worse, Eve has been blowing up my Instagram inbox. Now that word is spreading that I'm getting decent playing time, her interest in me has skyrocketed. I try playing nice, but as soon as I text something accidentally halfway flirtatious, she responds with a mirror selfie of her in a skin tight singlet.

Eve

> Got some new gummies that are hella potent. Cum over and vibe w me we'll listen to music and u can help me lotion my legs

Eek.

Meanwhile, I'm waiting on bated breath for Rowan to text me back. As soon as he says it's okay for me to touch myself, I'll head into the bathroom for my second shower of the day.

Rowan

> You need to give yourself small rewards during mid-terms so you don't go insane. How long have you been studying for your poli-sci exam?

Me

> Forever.

Rowan

> Lol aww baby boy. Do another half hour then you can take your horny shower. Send me a vid. I wanna see you cum for me

Me

> Every time I cum it's for you

Rowan

> Don't tease me. I gotta submit this fcking paper before I can jerk off to the vid you'll send me

Oh, he's one to talk about teasing. The motherfucker pushes my buttons like I'm a slot machine. Now I understand why Lese was always so disappointed in me. The way I am with Rowan is how she wanted me to be with her. Obsessed.

And then there's Eve...

Eve

> When u get here u can help me decide if I should get my nipples pierced

Great. Now I'm just picturing Rowan with pierced nipples and it's not making studying any easier.

Fuck this.

It takes five minutes of typing, deleting and retyping before I hit send on a rejection message to Eve.

Me

> Sorry, studying. Don't really have time for girls atm. Lots going on

Just when I think I've done the diplomatic thing, I get an unsettling response.

Eve

> Lol too busy sucking Rowan's dick u mean

What of it? But I can't fall into the trap. I can't out Rowan. I can't out myself in a catty DM to a girl I don't give a shit about.

Me

> Not even but ok

Eve

> Bye homo

What the fuck?

"Tommy?"

I look away from my phone at the sound of Mav's little voice.

"Hey, bud," I say as Mav climbs up onto my bed. I'm on my stomach, textbook open, pen lying idle on my notepad. I click my phone screen off while Mav climbs onto my back like I'm a jungle gym, his boney knees digging into the knots Rowan had rubbed so well that one night. "Ouch. Careful."

"Sorry." He plops his butt on the center of my back, forcing the air from my lungs.

"I'm not a bench," I choke out.

Mav giggles and slides off me, planting himself on the vacant side of my double bed. There's a picture book in his hands that he opens and picks at the page corners. When he says my name like a question again, I assume he's about to ask me to read to him. Instead, he asks, "What's gay mean?"

"Uhh, why are you asking?"

"You said to Mommy you're gay."

My head snaps toward my open bedroom door, and I pray the living room TV is loud enough that Ma didn't overhear. In a whisper, I tell Mav he doesn't need to worry about that now.

"Does it mean you're sick like Mommy?" he asks, pouting like he could cry.

"No, no, no. I'm not sick. I'm fine, buddy."

"Mommy says she's fine, but then she's always crying."

"It's not a sickness, and it's not a bad thing. It's nothing you have to worry about. I promise."

"But what is it?" he presses.

Heaving a sigh, I push myself up to sit facing Mav. "It's complicated, and it's really personal. So you can't tell your grandma, okay?"

"I won't tell, I swear."

I tell him to shut the door, and he quickly obeys. Once he's scrambled back onto my bed, I give him as simple a summation as I can think up on the fly. "Gay is when a boy can only have crushes on other boys, or when a girl can only have crushes on other girls."

"You have crushes on boys?" he asks.

"I do. Sometimes."

"How do you know if you have a crush?"

"Well usually, if you have a crush on someone, you think about them a lot, you want to be around them a lot, and you sometimes wanna do special things with them that you don't wanna do with other people, like holding hands, hugging them for no reason, and giving them presents."

"What if I don't have a crush on anyone?"

I chuckle. "That's fine. Like I said, you don't need to worry about it right now. A lot of people who are gay don't figure it out until they're in high school, or college, or even later, and that's okay."

"Are you gonna get married to a boy?"

"One day, maybe. Would that be weird?"

"Kinda, 'cause if you marry a boy, whose tummy makes the baby?"

"Uhh," I laugh discomfortingly. "No one would. That's not how it works."

"How does it work?"

"That...you're gonna have to ask your mother."

After the last of our mid-terms are in, Rowan finally lets me take him to Yard House. Lunch, though, not dinner. There's a lot less pressure on lunch than there is dinner. Still, when I pick Rowan up, he looks like he tried hard to fix himself up nice. That chain around his neck is a dead giveaway, since he only wears it when he wants to impress. Impress *me*. Like he even needs to try.

While we wait at the hostess stand to be seated, I finally ask Rowan where he got that chain.

"Just a gift," he says, "from a guy I used to see in high school."

A guy? He told me I was his first kiss. Was this guy just a fuck buddy? Were they sucking each other off under the bleachers between math and science class?

Chortling, Rowan slaps my shoulder and says, "You should see your fucking face right now. Jeez, babyface. My social worker gave it to me when I graduated. Can you believe that? On that dude's shitty salary, he bought me this?"

My relief survives only until I realize why Rowan had a social worker. Whoever his biological family is, they either couldn't care for him or didn't want to. I always thought I had it rough with a deadbeat dad, but Rowan didn't have half of what I did growing up.

I put my hand on Rowan's back and hope he won't shrug it off. "That's really nice of him. He must've really liked working with you."

He scoffs but allows my hand to linger. "Don't know about that. He was nice, though. Too nice for the shit he was dealing with."

What shit did you have to deal with? I almost ask, but the hostess returns with two bound menus and takes us to a two-top. She leaves a drink menu for us too, and I wonder if she'd card me if I order an IPA. When Rowan orders an iced tea, I follow suit. Sounds more adult than a Coke, at least.

Eyeing the lunch menu, Rowan asks, "So is this the date where we ask each other about our hopes and dreams, what we're gonna name our kids, and whether we wanna live in a Craftsman or a mid-century modern?"

I know he's teasing, but my face feels hot at the mere reference to future-plans. "Or we could just play *I Spy*."

"I spy a french dip that looks promising."

Interest piqued, I turn my menu over and skim the choices.

A young woman in fitted, black clothes trots over with our iced teas, introduces herself, and asks if we know what we'd like to order.

"A couple more minutes?" Rowan says.

The woman nods sweetly, eyes flitting to me and staying there long enough for it to feel intentional.

After she's gone, I see Rowan is eyeing me like he saw exactly what I saw. He smirks a little, turns his menu face down and asks, "When did you start thinking you were a little gay boy?"

I don't know what it is about Rowan that makes me ingest that question like it's a compliment, but I'm all smiles when I answer, "When I was twelve, I was playing a juniors club match. Almost won, but the opposing team had this one guy who was just unstoppable. Rowan fucking Hughes. I thought he was incredible and the cutest boy I'd ever seen. I was star-struck when he shook my hand after the match. Then, he called me a faggot and told me to suck his dick. Made me wonder if maybe I really was gay."

The smirk that was fixed on Rowan's face falls along with his shoulders. A jarring shift from playful to downright morose. It isn't the reaction I expected, but maybe I should've.

Just above a whisper, he says, "I'm sorry."

I lean forward. "It's okay—"

"It's not okay. I was fucked up then, Tommy. I never should've called you that, and I sure as hell didn't really think you were gay. I was just angry and hating the world, and I took it out on you. I took it out on a lot of people. I'm sorry."

"It's okay." I reach my arm across the table, but I pull it back when I remember that while this is a date, it's still a baby step. "I forgive you, Row. I forgave you a long time ago. Now it can just be a funny story we tell our grandkids one day, in our mid-century modern."

While his eyes stay soft, his mouth offers a bit of that smirk back. "You better cut that shit out."

I breathe a chuckle through a fresh grin, and I decide what I'll order for lunch. Whatever Rowan's having.

There's just enough time before our server comes back for me to tell Rowan about Anthony, about the kiss and the kids who jumped me. As hard as it is to see Rowan sad, it's comforting that I can talk about this with someone who receives it with genuine sympathy. Like he gets it.

"I'm sorry that happened, baby," he says. "I'll never let anyone fuck with you, okay? You might be stronger than me, but I'll go feral on any motherfucker who comes at you for anything."

Our server saunters back to our table side, touching her fingers to the table and leaning forward like she's trying to elongate her slim form. Her cat eyes fall to me, putting me on the spot before she's even asked what I'd like to order. When she does ask, it feels like she wants me to say her name.

Ick.

"I'll get the french dip," Rowan interjects, handing over his menu.

"Same," I say and hand her mine.

She takes both and stacks them in her hands, glancing between the two of us. "You two brothers?"

"No," I answer immediately.

Rowan helpfully adds, "But we do share a bed sometimes, if you know what I mean."

My eyes widen for no other reason than I'm stunned Rowan would go so far as to even insinuate intimacy between us. A baby step of his own, maybe?

"Oh, really?" The woman's expression grows devious now, and that's when Rowan's expression changes from amused to annoyed.

"And we're one hundred percent not interested in sharing one with anyone else," he says firmly enough that the woman gets the hint and leaves our table with her tail between her legs. "I can't stand people."

"Says the communications major."

Between sips of iced tea, we talk about the emails Rowan has traded with recruiters, and the meetings he's scheduled at coffee shops and Matt and Xia's dining room table. We talk about sports, of course, and I ask him about how he grew up, because I'm desperate for any morsel of backstory Rowan is comfortable enough to share.

All he says is that his upbringing wasn't very interesting. "Only difference between my childhood and the average kid's childhood is no one ever even pretended to love me, and it was a heck of a lot easier for my guardians to kick me out when I became inconvenient."

"Is that what happened? They kicked you out?"

"In one way or another. Either way, they walked me out the front door, and I never saw 'em again. Can't even remember some of my foster parents' names, and those were the decent ones."

"Shit."

Holding a steak fry in his fingers, Rowan sends me one of his disarmingly charming half smiles and says, "Don't look at me like that. I'm fine."

I think he's lying, though. He's broken down in front of me too many times for me to think he came out of the Sacramento County foster care system unscathed. I can't imagine anyone who has tried taking their own life is *fine*. He said he's past that now, but suicidal ideation must linger like its own sort of trauma, right?

"Do you ever have contact with your biological parents?"

"Told you, babyface. I don't have parents."

I nod like I understand, but I don't. Maybe I never will. Maybe it's better for Rowan that I'm here for him even when I don't understand. "Thank you for coming here with me."

"I'll do anything for you." He says it so casually, while swiping two fries into a porcelain dish of ranch dressing, but my heart hears it loud and clear. "I might be a little bitch about it first, but I'll eventually do it."

I stare at his dark, steely eyes until they meet mine, and the connection alone is enough to make me blush.

After lunch, we drive around until we end up at Douglas Field, and I park in the same lot where we jerked off together and where I tasted his dick for the first time. This time, we leave my truck and meander up the concrete steps in favor of the tip top. There's a pee-wee tournament taking up the field, but most of the spectators are down below. Up here is quieter, warmer, and the air settles better in my lungs.

Mine and Rowan's fingers lace together in the sliver of space between our legs, and I feel a small rush of adrenaline every time someone walks far enough up the bleachers that they might notice us. Still, I won't let go, even if someone does see.

Watching Rowan watch the tournament, I tell him I've been thinking about going to a Queer Alliance meeting on campus. Other than various on- and off-campus activities, there's a weekly gathering in the meeting hall under the freshman dorm. Got no clue what to expect, or if I'll even get anything out of it, but I figure it's worth checking out.

"Thought *queer* was a slur," Rowan says passively.

"Not anymore, I guess. Seems like more of a catchall term. A broad umbrella to fit a wide variety of identities under."

Eyeing me sideways, Rowan asks, "Like *freak?*"

I smirk back. "Or, weird-o."

"Well, let me know how it goes."

"You could come with me." I feel a little guilty suggesting something I know Rowan won't be into after he admitted he'd do anything for me. Last thing I want to do is take advantage of him. I may not know what all he's gone through, but I know it's a lot more than anyone should, and I've already pushed him so much.

"Nah. That ain't me."

"Okay." I don't press. Just squeeze Rowan's hand and tap the side of my head to the side of his.

"I've been thinking about Pavloving your dick."

"S'cuse me?" My face reddens as my eyes widen.

"Like anytime I'm wearing a particular color, or if I do a particular action or say a particular phrase, your dick is trained to get hard instantly, and you're possessed by the sudden uncontrollable need to fuck me. What do you think?"

My face hurts from how wide I'm grinning, my body clearly loving this idea more than my wary mind is. "You've been watching too much porn."

"That's not a no."

"I'll think about it."

"Good boy." He reaches his neck until his mouth is beside my ear. "Think *long* and *hard.*"

Something close to a moan escapes my throat, and I turn my head to stare at Rowan's mouth when I say, "You want me to fuck you, huh?"

"I said I want you possessed by the urge to fuck me. Didn't say I'd let you."

"You're amazing," I murmur before kissing his oh so inviting lips.

He kisses me back so easily that I forget we're in public until Rowan leans back, releases my hand and fixes his face to neutral, head angling back toward the field. It's all because of a couple with the same idea as us, reaching the top landing and carrying on to a bench a little ways down the row. A normal looking, young-ish couple. A man in cargo shorts holding hands with a woman in yoga clothes. They don't seem to pay us any mind, but when they're well enough away, Rowan says, "That guy looked at us weird."

"Think I give a shit what a dude in cargo shorts thinks?"

A small laugh from Rowan is enough to bring him back to me for another kiss.

24

Rowan

The day before Halloween, I agree to go with Tommy to one of his little gay boy meetings. Queer Alliance, or whatever the fuck it's called. He didn't ask me necessarily, but he did that thing where he subtly suggests something and his face not-so-subtly begs me for it. It's those puppy dog eyes, wide and blue and melting me into a cynical puddle.

If it were up to me—and it usually is—we'd be running wind sprints right now. Instead, I'm following Tommy's lead down into the bowels of the freshman dorms. A carpeted stairwell takes us to a subterranean lobby with doors to a few banquet rooms of various sizes. The only door that's open is what must be the largest room. Huge and carpeted, with a stage and everything, fold-out chairs organized like we're about to be pitched on a time share rental, and way too many people for my liking.

I hope it's not homophobic to think this would be easier if everyone were straight. I grew up surrounded by straight people. Jocks and dudebros of varying degrees. I know how to talk to those people. I am those people, besides the straight part. Tommy wants to find some place where he "fits in," and that's great for him, but I can't help feeling like I'll fit in here even less than I do around my usual crowd.

Even Mustache Jack is more comforting than this place. At least at the gay bar, the lights are dim, there's alcohol to settle my nerves, and there's an abundance of visual and auditory stimulation to distract everyone from my existence. There, I can sip my drink, people-watch, and maybe inch myself closer to a more comfortable headspace.

Here, the lights are high and all there is to do before everything kicks off is acknowledge each other. As soon as I walk in, I feel a deafening sense that I'm being acknowledged. I hear Tommy's name being exclaimed, and my proximity to him is suddenly a barrier. When someone pops up in front of us like a bouncy denim Smurf, I think to make a break for it.

"Hey, I know you." The Smurf in question points a tatted finger at me, and the double-take between them and the door gives me whiplash. It doesn't hit me at first, but then I notice the pins on their jean vest lapel. A memory of Oscar and his buddies at Mustache Jack flickers in my head.

"Andy?" I question.

"Indy, but close enough." They smile like a teenager meeting a popstar in person, eyes scintillating in a way that makes me itchy. I'm scratching the back of my neck when they say, "You're Oscar's friend."

"We're not friends. I tutored him once, and he hit on me. That's it."

"Who did what?" Tommy asks in that quick, breathless tone he adopts when he's jealous.

"Don't worry. I hate that guy," I tell him before it dawns on me Indy is Oscar's friend. Grimacing toward them, I say, "Sorry. I don't hate him. I just think he's...annoying."

Thankfully, all Indy does is laugh, then asks Tommy, "Boyfriend?"

Further proving what a jackass I am, I interject, "We're just buddies." I even slap Tommy on the back like I'm burping a baby.

"Uh huh." Indy nods, looking between us like they've already seen what we do together naked. "Well, we're running a little behind. Technical issues with the PowerPoint, so hang out."

Once they've bounced away, I send a wary look to Tommy. "A PowerPoint?"

"It'll be fine, *buddy.*" The way he smiles tells me he's not upset, only teasing. I want to apologize, but I also can't promise I won't do it again. I told Tommy we can be boyfriends, but I figured that'd still stay private. Maybe he told all these people. Maybe he's telling everyone.

He's come here enough times that a handful of these people are on first name basis with him, and every time someone says hello, I feel like the most out-of-place third wheel ever. It almost compels me to hold Tommy's hand.

Tommy winds up in a conversation with a wiry dude with a septum piercing who asks if I'm "the boyfriend." I toss my arm around Tommy's shoulders and say, "I'm his dad. Had him real young, but he's my pride and joy."

I missed this dude's name, because I wasn't paying attention, but whatever his name is, he laughs just like Indy did. "Good for you guys."

He moves on after dapping Tommy's fist, leaving me alone with Tommy's very unamused expression. Behind his folded lips and lowered lids, though, I know he thinks I'm funny. I hope.

The next person to gravitate toward Tommy's magnetic aura is a better-than-average looking guy. Doesn't hold a candle to Tommy, but he's tall-ish, fit-ish, and his shoulder length hair is bouncy and wavy. If he were on the soccer team, I'd chat him up a bit and play nice, but he's not on the team. He's here. At a club for gays. Chances are good he's probably gay, or at least likes dick.

I hate him.

Tommy calls him Chuck and slaps his palm like they're buds or something. "This is Rowan," Tommy introduces me.

"His boyfriend," I state plainly, slipping my arm around Tommy's waist this time.

"Cool." Chuck's head bobs, fists on his hips. "Mine couldn't make it. He's got a frat thing tonight. He wanted me to go with him, but I hate that sorta shit, so I came here. Beats sitting in my dorm watching my roommate clip his toenails all over our rug."

"Frat boyfriend? I didn't know frats let gays in."

Chuck chortles. "They don't actually ask if you're gay or not, but either way, most of them don't give a shit. There's actually an all-gender queer fraternity here, but Javi went and joined the one his wrestling buddies are on."

Wrestling boyfriend? I didn't know there were gays on the wrestling team, although there are a lot of "wrestlers" in the gay porn I watch. "Interesting."

Clasping his hand on my shoulder, Tommy says, "Rowan is captain of the soccer team."

Chuck's eyes pop, grin expanding. "No shit? Damn, we're going to have to go to a game then. Show some support. I had no idea the captain of our soccer team was queer. You guys any good?"

"Undefeated," I grumble, deciding to let the *queer* thing slide.

"He's gonna go pro," Tommy boasts, like I'm his pride and joy. "Gonna get drafted this winter and become a big shot."

"That's fucking awesome." Chuck swings his arm, tapping my bicep. "An openly gay pro soccer player? I'm telling you, it's true what they say. The future is gay."

No matter how lame that slogan is, I'm not dwelling on that as much as I'm reeling over "openly gay." That's not what I am. I'm not openly anything. I agreed to be boyfriends with Tommy, because he's my baby. I agreed to come to this queerdom, because I want to make Tommy happy. I didn't agree to be an openly gay whateverthefuck.

Before I can force my mind to think rationally, I blurt out, "I'm not gay, dude."

"Oh." His face falls. "That's my bad. I'm still learning how to not assume shit about people. Which you'd think I'd be good at since I've been a flaming homo my whole life, but everyone assumes I must be straight because, I dunno, the way I dress? The way I talk?"

"Just talk about how much you like dick. Then, people will definitely not think you're straight."

I'm being an asshole, but Chuck laughs anyway. Even taps me on the arm again and says I'm a riot. There's a riot in my head right now, and I want it to get the fuck out. I'm too afraid to look at Tommy, because he's probably disappointed in me. I don't know why it's easier to say I have a boyfriend than it is to say I'm gay. Maybe it's because I can undo a boyfriend, but an identity is fundamental. I don't want my boyfriend to be undone, though. I want him to stay, and I want him to keep being proud of me like I'm proud of him.

After Chuck trots off, Tommy's voice fills my ear, telling me he's sorry. I whip a confused look at him and tell him *I'm* sorry.

He slips his arms around my neck, turning me to face him. "Do you wanna just go?"

Yes.

But I glance around us and realize that, while I might feel out of place among this crowd, we can put our arms around each other here and not worry that someone will look at us funny.

"Nah. Let's stay," I tell him. "I'm, like, super invested in whatever this PowerPoint is gonna be about."

Though he doesn't believe me for a second, Tommy smiles and hugs me like the tender boy he is. I don't deserve it, but I take it for all it's worth before we find two chairs in the back row and hold hands on top of my leg.

I might be bad at being gay, but I'm good at being a student, so I find the lame ass PowerPoint on the queer history and culture of Sacramento to be more enjoyable than I'll ever admit to Tommy. He can tell anyway. The discussion is interesting, especially when others express the same feelings of fear and paranoia that I'm well acquainted with. Resentment, too, that life has to be more challenging for us. More uncertain.

Being gay isn't the only thing that makes my life challenging, though. It's not even half of it.

On our way out of the building and into open air, I forget to let go of Tommy's hand, and we end up walking hand-in-hand halfway through campus before I think to let go.

"It's still early," he says. "We could go get ice cream or hit the gym."

Wishing I wasn't too chicken to hold Tommy's hand all the way to his truck, I ask, "Can I take you somewhere?"

He smiles and says, "Anywhere."

I must be in a great fucking mood, because I'm actually excited when I park Tommy's truck in the narrow lot beside Mustache Jack.

"Is this a gay bar?" Tommy asks incredulously. The row of rainbow flags bordering the flat roof probably gives it away. "Have you been here before?"

"Once or twice."

He looks at me like I've morphed into a different person, and I guess that's fair. I've been closed off with him. More open lately, but still closed. Before we reach the door, his face shows a grim expression. "Is this where you would do the desperate stuff?"

"No. Definitely not. Honestly, I'm not really sure why I'd come here. Maybe I was doing my own baby steps, and this was one of them. All I'd do is sit at the bar drinking fruity margaritas and people-watching. Thought maybe you'd like being here with me."

"Totally." He's beaming now, proud of me again. "I've never been to a gay bar. Shit, I'm not even twenty-one."

"It's cool. I've never been carded."

For a Wednesday, Mustache Jack is packed. Then again, it is the night before Halloween. From the looks of it, some people are already in the spirit, done up in costumes that are weird and a little sexual. A group peels from the bar and we snag two of the stools they left vacant.

While Tommy scans the place looking half-enthralled and half-terrified, I order us two blackberry margaritas.

"Brought a friend this time," the bartender says with a wink, and I realize he's the same dude who usually serves me. He's in a leather kilt tonight, his eyelids painted neon green.

Tommy notices and smirks at me. "Only been here once or twice, huh?"

"A handful of times. No more than a dozen."

He chuckles, the disco ball over the dancefloor putting sparkles in his eyes. A Prince song plays through the speakers while the accompanying music video shows on big screens around the hall. The air feels crisp and smells like liquor and leather.

Leaning his elbows on the bar top, Tommy says, "We look like two straight guys who accidentally wandered into a gay bar."

I laugh, because he's right, and that's usually exactly what I look like when I'm here by myself. No one ever questioned me, though. Everyone left me be to stew in my self-loathing surrounded by people who wouldn't bat an eye if I chose to actually be honest for once.

"Who cares how we look?" I tell him. "No one else does."

Grinning, he sticks his hand to my head, kneading my scalp until my eyes roll.

"Where'd you find this one?" the bartender asks when he sets two purple margs in front of us, on the rocks with sugar on the rim and a skinny straw to sip.

"We're on the Sac State soccer team together," I answer. "I'm a forward, and he's a midfielder."

"I don't know what that means, but I love it!"

Me too.

For a while, Tommy and I simply chill at the bar, drinking, roasting the music, and staring at each other until one of us blushes first.

"Wanna dance?" Tommy asks when our drinks are down to ice cubes, and the bartender has already swiped my card.

I balk. "I can't dance. Don't got any rhythm."

"Are you kidding me? I watch you when you play. You're a fucking work of art out there."

"That's different. That's soccer."

"C'mon." He takes my hands, scoots off his stool and tugs me off mine. "I can't dance either. We'll suck together."

Now, sucking together sounds more up my alley.

Tommy pulls me into the fray. Thankfully, only a few people are full-on dancing. Most are just vibing, swaying, bobbing, and mouthing the words to whatever Cher song this is. That's pretty much what Tommy and I do, minus mouthing the words, since neither of us knows them. We vibe, and it feels nice. His hands on me always feel nice. My hands on him feel even better. Our foreheads touch, then our mouths. Right under the disco ball like it's a mistletoe on Christmas. I'm happier now than I ever have been on any Christmas day.

Finally, I realize what's so great about this place I've been coming to once a month since last year. It's not the ear-splitting pop music, the flashing lights, the half-naked people, or the fruity drinks. It's the freedom. The freedom to choose whether I'm left alone or noticed, and the freedom to kiss my boyfriend and not feel like the world is going to fall apart around me. Even if outside is doomsday, this place is a bunker. Being in here, avoiding Armageddon with Tommy, feels like the epitome of happiness.

This time, when Tommy puts his mouth to my ear and tells me he loves me, I actually kind of believe him.

It's the last match of the regular season, and even though our team is undefeated, I need this win like I need air in my lungs as my team fights to break a tie against UC Davis in their home territory.

I think I spot a few scouts in the stands, and I don't want to disappoint them. Even more, I don't want to disappoint the team, who've put their blood, sweat, tears, and EpiPens into this season. I don't want to disappoint Tommy, who's got my back right now, making sure the opposing team can't make their plays. Hell, I don't want to disappoint McDonough either, because I'm sure the dude could use a raise with how much child support he's on the hook for. Another benefit to only liking dick.

The second half is flying by. Players are faking fouls just to catch their breath and buy some time. Levi intercepts the ball. I call out his name and receive the pass. I dribble it between my feet, racing for the enemy's goal, but their defenders are dogging me. When I look for Raisel, I find my baby instead.

"Row!" he hollers in that voice that will never not send a shiver down my spine.

In a split second, I decide to take a chance on him the way I've been doing this whole time, and I make the pass. No sooner than Tommy has possession of the ball, he's striking it toward the goal. The Davis goalie dives the wrong way, and the ball hits net.

"Yes!" I shout, the adrenaline pulsing through my veins screaming for joy, and I run straight to Tommy.

He's grinning like he can't believe it, like he just walked on the moon and made all his childhood dreams come true. I don't know if it was his childhood dream to secure our spot in the championship round, but he sure as shit made it come true.

"That's it!" I shove his chest and he stumbles back, dazed and elated.

Our teammates on the field and along the sidelines cheer Tommy on, but he zeroes in on me. Before I can blink, he lunges forward, grabs my face, and shoves his mouth against mine in a firm, impassioned kiss.

My heart stops, and my adrenaline turns sour. I don't have to push him off me. By the time I realize what he's done, he realizes it too.

Jumping back, his bulging eyes meet mine, and it's like we're caught in a vortex. Time stands still, but only in the immediate space surrounding us.

What the fuck do I do?

Before I can figure out an answer, the ball is back into play, and I switch my mind to game-mode where nothing else can touch me.

The clock winds down the final minutes of the match, and we secure our win. Yet, there's nothing celebratory inside me. Inside, it's all paranoia and fear, and in my effort to mask that, I turn to stone.

When Levi claps my shoulder and says, "Congrats, Cap. Did y'all say *I do* first?" I stiff-arm him, and tell him to fuck off.

I try not to look pissed, but there's only so much I can do when my whole body is on fire, and I need to get the hell out of here. It's Armageddon, and I'm right here in the thick of it. Unprotected. Every single eye in the stadium feels like it's on me, but I don't check to verify. I beeline for my bag and retreat into the Davis locker room.

The guys filter in behind me, but I gather up my shit and head toward the showers. Just over the sound of my racing heartbeat, I hear Levi's voice bouncing off the walls. "Yo, Tommy! You the Romeo to his Juliet, or is he the Romeo to your Juliet?"

Under a searing hot water spray, I brace my hands against the tiled wall and hang my head. I stare at the drain like it's a hypnotist's watch, letting the sight and sound of drizzling water lull me into stasis until my heart rate lowers to baseline.

Don't be mad.

Don't be mad.

Don't be mad.

I can't let myself be mad. Tommy did a dumbass thing, but I can't be mad. For him, I can't be mad. Tommy is more important than what Levi or anyone else thinks. Tommy is more important than everything. Except soccer. I need soccer like I need Tommy. More, actually. Because when I inevitably lose Tommy, soccer will always be there. It's the only constant. If the scouts saw him kiss me, they could think I'm gay, and I don't know if they'll want a gay player over a straight one when it comes down to it. The smallest things can make the biggest impact. Tommy swore he would never come between me and soccer.

Don't be mad.

I leave the shower with a towel around my waist, and I tug on a pair of underwear and shorts from my bag before going back to my team's segment of the locker room. Of course, Tommy and I had picked lockers right next to each other, so when I get back to mine, there Tommy is.

Still in his jersey, he sits on the bench with his elbows on his knees. When I get close, he looks up at me with his innocent blue eyes that silently beg me for forgiveness. I gulp, not knowing what to say, silently or otherwise.

"Hey, Tommy!" our douchebag goalie calls out, voice already laced with laughter. "If you wanna get on the volleyball team next, I hear their captain is also a homo."

Something clicks in my head, and now I'm fucking livid. My body moves on autopilot, leaping me over the bench and barreling me into the goalie. His name is Brandon. I've never met a Brandon who wasn't a piece of shit. I force him against the lockers with my forearm jammed into his chest.

"Shut your fucking mouth," I seethe. "Don't ever talk to him again. You got shit to say, say it to me, motherfucker."

"B-bro, it—it was a joke," Brandon sputters.

"Rowan, Rowan." My name in Connor's voice coupled with his hands pulling me back has me releasing Brandon and a fraction of my anger. "Relax. It's cool. No one's gonna say shit anymore." Keeping an arm around my shoulders, he sends everyone a pointed look. "Right, guys? No one's gonna say shit anymore."

I shrug away from Connor and march back to my locker. Head still in a flurry, I plant myself on the bench beside Tommy and hook my hand on his shoulder, kneading his tensed muscle. The voices of our teammates fade to the background of my mind so I can focus on Tommy's pouted mouth as they form the words, "I'm sorry," softer than a whisper.

"Don't worry," I tell him, even though I'm so chock-full of worry I can hardly stand it. I just don't want Tommy to worry. He's mine, so whatever consequences come from this, it's on my back.

"Hughes!" McDonough's gruff voice shouts from the doorway.

The chatter in the locker room simmers, and I pop my head up over Tommy's bowed one. "S'up, Coach?!"

"Your mom's here!"

So Xia is going around telling people she's my mom now? And what the hell? I thought she and Matt had a Girl Scout thing to go to with Olive. Maybe Matt took Olive on his own and Xia came to watch the match?

Oh God, she saw the kiss. She's never going to let me live it down. At least I know her exuberant gushing will be encouraging. That's the thing about Xia. Her most annoying trait is how relentlessly encouraging she is.

Quickly, I put on a shirt and slip into my Converse. Tommy asks if we're good, and I tell him of course. I want to say more. I want to make sure he's really okay before I leave him, but there isn't much I feel comfortable saying here in the lion's den.

As I'm headed toward the exit, McDonough asks if my "mom" is giving me a lift home.

"Yeah, we usually get lunch or something after matches," I answer.

"I don't need to know your daily agenda, Hughes. Just if I can cross your name off the bus log."

"Cross away." I roll my eyes, hoist my bag higher on my shoulder, and dip.

The crowd in the stadium has dwindled. I walk part of the perimeter to get to the gates leading to the pavilion.

Expecting to see Xia, and maybe Lena and Bruno, it's jarring when I don't see any of them. If I don't see them, I usually hear them. Xia's got a cut-through-walls voice, but I don't hear her through the milling crowd.

"Rowan?" An unfamiliar voice draws my attention to a petite woman clutching a purse strap across her chest. She looks older than Xia, but not by much. Short, pale, and the shadows under her eyes are even worse than Xia's were when Bruno was just born. She smells weird too. Not bad, just weird. Makes my stomach turn a little, and I don't know why.

I tip my chin. "Yeah?"

"Oh my gosh." She looks me up and down like I'm a de-ity, shuffling in closer. "Look at you. You're so handsome."

"Uhh..." My lip curls, and I take a big step back. "Thanks, lady, but I'm actually waiting for—"

"Rowan." She takes two steps forward, white knuckling that purse strap like there might be a weapon in it. "You don't recognize me, do you?"

Am I about to get Lennon'ed? I'm featured on one ESPN weekend morning segment that no one saw, but it was enough to get me a stalker? *Just my fucking luck.*

Backing up the way I came, I start to tell her I've got to get back to my team, but she interrupts me again.

"I'm your mom," she says, dripping earnestness from every line and freckle on her face and the tears in her gray eyes. "March twenty-second at five o'clock in the morning, I gave birth to you in the backseat of your daddy's car on the way to the hospital. You looked just like a doll. Didn't even cry none. Don't think I heard you cry 'til you was a week old, and only after some trying. That's how I knew you was an angel sent to me. Did you hear me? I'm your mom."

My eyelids blink and my lungs take in air, but inside my head, I'm paralyzed. Might as well have been shot dead.

25
Tommy

The bus ride home from Davis is a half hour at most, but time moves like molasses. As far as I can tell, none of the bickering on the bus is about me or Rowan, but my ears aren't working tip top right now. All I know is, I've finally humiliated myself enough to die in it, but the worst part is that I took Rowan down with me.

"Hey, man." A few taps to my shoulder draw my attention up to Malik, standing and swaying slighting in the bus aisle. "Scoot over."

I'm in the aisle seat. Same one I sat in on the way here so Rowan could have the window seat. Even though he went back with his family, I left his space vacant, mostly so I wouldn't have to sit next to anyone else.

Since Malik's been a buddy since high school, I push my bag to the floor and move over.

He takes a load off in my spot and sizes me up lazily. "'Sup?"

Confused and anxious, I answer, "Uh, 'sup with you?"

"Just wondering if you're good."

"I'm fine."

"You don't look fine, and I'm wondering if you're freaking out more over what the team thinks or what Cap thinks. 'Cause if you're worried about what the team thinks, you shouldn't. No one cares. They'll rib anyone for anything the least bit unusual, but underneath the shits and giggles, no one cares if you've got a thing for Rowan."

"But," he continues, "if you're worried about what Rowan thinks of your crush, that all depends on what y'all already got going on."

It's a trap. One I won't fall into easily.

"We just train together."

"You sure?" he asks.

"My feelings for Rowan have nothing to do with however he feels about me. I'm the gay puppy dog following him around everywhere, okay? He puts up with me. Not the other way around. It's all on me."

"Dude." Malik interrupts me with a funny smile. "That's sweet of you to save face for your boy, but finding out Rowan is a repressed gay dude has been on everyone's Bingo cards since I joined the team. No one's surprised. A lot of guys are just hyped they called it right. Think Levi won fifty bucks off one of the assistant coaches, so he's pumped."

Bitterly, I turn away from Malik and scowl at the back of the seat in front of me. "Well, I'm glad everyone's having such a great time because of us."

Malik sighs in that way people do when they're getting comfortable. Makes me think he's planning on sticking by me until we get back to Sac Town. "You think Cap is pissed at you?"

"I dunno," I mutter, because I truly don't know. He said he's not. He said we're good, but then he left my orbit before I could help him through whatever he's feeling. When I'm not with him, his reality is out of my control. I'm helpless.

"How bad will it be if he's pissed?"

"Monumentally." I look down at my lap—at my hand that I wish was holding Rowan's right now. "He's more fragile than he let's on, you know? He's been through some shit, and I've been trying not to push him too far too fast. I don't want him to shut down because of something stupid I did without thinking."

"You serious about him?"

I chuckle mirthlessly. "As serious as anything in my life."

"Well, if he's serious about you, he'll get over it. He'll man up, reach out, and everything'll be chill. If the worst thing a girl ever did to me was kiss me at a match, it'd be the best relationship I ever had."

I try to force a smile, but I can't. Not now. I'll text Rowan when I'm home and hope for the best, because that's all I can do now.

It's Monday afternoon, in the thick of practice, and I'm keeled over clutching my stomach as the turkey and cheese sub I had for lunch threatens to barrel back up my throat. Coach's drills aren't what's making me nauseous, though. It's that not only has Rowan not answered a single one of my texts or calls since the Davis match, but he didn't show up for practice either.

It's a bad sign.

A very bad sign.

If he's not pissed, then he's spiraling. Probably feels how I feel right now. Like the world is tumbling off its axis and any second now we'll fly off into a limitless abyss.

The guys are still teasing me, which doesn't help matters, but I'm brushing off as much as I can. After practice, I nearly lose it the way Rowan did in Davis when Levi asks, "Yo, Tyson. When you and Rowan have sleepovers, who takes the top bunk and who takes the bottom bunk?"

Before I can react, Coach is hollering my name through the locker room, and he doesn't sound happy. I follow him to his office where he sits behind his desk, then I pull up a chair and prepare myself to be reprimanded for something. Anything. For that embarrassing display at the Davis match, for nearly puking during drills, or for existing at all.

"Where's Rowan?" he asks me point blank, like I'm hiding him in my back pocket.

"I don't know." My voice comes out hoarse, and I realize this is the first time I've spoken all day. "Maybe he...needed a sick day."

Coach blinks his hard stare at me long enough for me to fidget. "Rowan doesn't take sick days. I've had that kid come to practice with a hundred-and-two temperature. Last spring, he rolled in here with a shiner as big as my fist and his eye half swollen shut. So where is he?"

The idea Rowan would be better off right now if I'd punched him again rather than kiss him makes me feel like crying.

"C'mon, Tommy. Either he's in jail or laid up in a hospital bed incapacitated, because those are the only reasons I can think of why he'd skip practice without so much as a text. Which is it?"

I shake my head, because there's no way Rowan's in jail. He may act like a little pit bull sometimes, but he's not actually a fighter, and he wouldn't put his future in jeopardy by doing something illegal. The only reason I can think of why Rowan might be hospitalized is one I can't bear to consider. He wouldn't have harmed himself because of me, would he?

"I don't know where he is," I say.

"Wrong answer."

"I'll find him." I stand up so abruptly, the chair tips over behind me, and I scramble to set it right.

"You better," Coach snarls, "because if he's not here tomorrow, he's benched for the quarterfinals, and you can tell him that when you find him. Tell him I'm not bluffing!"

In a panic, I race from Coach's office in favor of my locker, gathering my shit as quick as I can. As soon as I'm out of earshot of the team, headed toward my car, I call Rowan's number for the first time since yesterday.

This time, it doesn't even ring. Straight to voicemail.

I call again. Straight to voicemail.

I text him.

Me

> Please lmk your ok. Coach is pissed you missed practice. I need an excuse to give him so he won't bench you on Sat.

Me

> Just lmk where you are. I won't bother you, just need to know

Me

> I love you

All my messages are turning green, which makes me think Rowan's phone died. Or he blocked me. No, I wouldn't have gotten his voicemail had he blocked me. Right? I have a class in an hour, but that's the last of my priorities. If I had Matt's number, or Xia's, I'd call one of them and see if Rowan is at home, but I don't. I drive to the house instead.

By now, I've got the route memorized, and when I get there, I see the black Legacy parked at the curb. Unsure if this is a good or bad sign, I park behind it and go to the driveway gate before remembering it's padlocked. Reluctantly, I switch directions and walk around to the front door.

The door peels open quickly after I hit the ringer, revealing a skinny little girl in a stained school uniform. Her eyes pop, and her cheeks flush, bare feet shuffling her halfway past the door like she's trying to hide.

"Hey, Olive." I wave awkwardly. "Is, uhh, your mom or dad home?"

In a flash, she runs off through the house, leaving the front door half ajar. I think to follow her, but decide that's creepy as hell, so I stay standing out here. A minute later, I spot Matt coming across the foyer.

"Tommy?" he asks, pulling the door open the rest of the way.

"Hi. Sorry to just drop in. Rowan missed practice today, so I came by to see if he's okay. I tried texting and calling, but I think his phone's dead."

"Wait." Matt lifts his palm toward me. "Rowan missed practice?" After I nod, Matt sticks his head out of the door to study the street, probably looking for Rowan's car, but it's exactly where he usually parks it.

The perturbed look on Matt's face has me anxious.

"When's the last time you saw him?"

"Saturday morning, I think?" Matt waves me inside the house, shuts the door, and leads the way through the kitchen and out the backdoor. "We knocked for breakfast yesterday morning, but he didn't answer. Figured he went for a run or to meet you somewhere."

My heart rate climbs and climbs as I follow Matt through the musty garage and wait behind him while he knocks on Rowan's shut door. By the time it's clear no one is going to answer, my heart is beating so loud in my ears I barely hear Matt telling me to stand back.

Stand back?

Stand back for what?

In case the room explodes when Matt opens Rowan's door? Or, in case he opens the door and finds Rowan swinging from the ceiling fan?

"What the hell?" Matt mutters as soon as the door is open.

Screw standing back. Rowan is mine. I shove past Matt and shimmy into the room to find what Matt is so confounded by. The bed is empty and unmade, Rowan's backpack is on the swivel chair, his gym bag stuffed under the desk, and the plastic storage bins normally stashed under his bedframe now clutter the floor space.

"Help me?" I say to Matt, and we both carry the bins out the door one by one until there's enough space for me to climb down to the floor beside Rowan's bed and peer underneath.

My heart stops as it drops into my gut. Wedged between the floor and the metal slats of his bedframe, Rowan's body lies limp on his front, his head turned toward the wall.

"Row?" I flatten myself to the carpet and reach for Rowan's lifeless hand. I hold my breath as I lift two fingers under his downturned wrist, waiting to feel a pulse.

Just as my eyes fill with tears, Rowan's hand twitches, fingers curling. My heart spasms as I shift to hold his hand. The fact he's alive at all has all the feeling returning to my body. His head turns, and I can just make out the whites of his eyes through the shadows.

"Tommy?" His voice is small, rough like gravel, and emoting that sleepy sort of confusion like I just woke him from a long sleep.

"Hey, buddy," I meekly coo, like he's Mav after a nightmare.

"What're you doing here?" he rasps.

"I'm here to see you. You weren't at practice today, so I came to make sure you're okay. Are you okay?"

After a beat, Rowan grumbles, "What day is it?"

"Monday. Four in the afternoon."

A low, groggy groan rumbles quietly from Rowan's chest. He's smells like he hasn't showered since Davis, and his dreary face looks like he hasn't shaved since that morning either.

"Let's get you out from under there, okay? Can you move?"

When Rowan doesn't answer for a while, I look up to where Matt lingers fearfully in the doorway. He pushes his hair back, then comes over to help.

With a lot of coaxing and some tugging, Matt and I squirm Rowan out from his hidey-hole. In only a rumpled t-shirt and boxer briefs, Rowan drops his butt to the bed, and Matt grips him by the shoulders to keep him sitting upright.

"Rowan." Matt shakes Rowan a little. "Did you take anything?"

Rowan's head shakes.

"Did something happen?"

Lightheaded from how infrequently my lungs have taken breath, I watch in worry and guilt, expecting Rowan to say this is all my fault. Isn't it? I fucked up, and now I fucked him up. I broke him, and as selfish as it is, I don't want Matt to know this is my fault.

Rowan nods, and I gulp.

"What happened?" Matt asks. "Did someone hurt you?"

When Rowan's eyes flit to me, I want nothing more than to burrow myself under that bed and never come out. But then he looks back to Matt and mumbles, "My mom showed up in Davis. My real mom."

After an achingly long time, Matt murmurs an, "Okay," pats Rowan gently on his bicep, then stands and asks me if I'm planning to stay.

Takes me a few blinks to process the question. I have that class, but I still don't care about it. I don't know what good I'll do here, or if Rowan even wants me here, but I can't leave. The thought never crosses my mind to go.

I nod, and Matt sidles past me and out the door.

"Wait." I chase after him and catch up as he's crossing the threshold into the backyard. "Where are you going?"

"Need to take care of some things," he says, much too casual for my comfort.

"He missed practice without calling Coach. He missed his classes—"

"I'll take care of it. I'm a dad, Tommy. I know how to handle this stuff. Just stay with Rowan and make sure he's okay. If you need anything, I'll be in the house. The backdoor's unlocked."

As confused as I am anxious, I find a pack of room temp water bottles on top of the dryer and take one into Rowan's room.

He's slouched forward, face between his knees and his hands behind his head, like he's suffering motion sickness on a turbulent plane.

"Hey, hey, hey," I murmur, uncapping the bottle and lifting Rowan upright. "Drink this, okay?"

He doesn't speak, but he parts his lips when I touch the rim of the bottle to them. With a slight tilt of his head back, he drinks.

"I've been so worried about you," I say. "Is your phone off?"

He doesn't answer, just hands me the bottle. I cap it, set it aside, and in the time it takes me to turn back around, Rowan is standing. His arms open, and I walk into them to cradle him to my chest.

"Is it really Monday?" He asks with his eyes on my shoulder.

Sweeping my palm along his spine, I tell him not to worry about a thing.

I take him to bed and unfurl his blankets so I can pull them up to his chin. After toeing off my shoes and pulling off my jeans, I slip under the blankets with him and draw his back to my front. Spooning him and kissing the back of his oily head, I tell him everything's going to be alright, that I won't leave him, and that I love him.

Inside, my mind tries desperately to work a puzzle I barely have any pieces to.

His mom showed up in Davis. His *real* mom...and somehow, she did this to him.

Two hours pass since Rowan drifted off, and I'm on my back reading PDFs for school when there's a light knocking on the door. It's gotten dark enough outside that not much light passes through the window, so I switch the lamp on after standing, and I put my pants back on for the benefit of whoever's knocking.

I open the door and find Xia there, looking just like a worried mom would.

"How is he? Is he alright?" she asks.

"Sleeping now, but he's in bad shape. Feels like he hasn't eaten in days."

"I'm about to start on dinner. I'll make plenty for the both of you. You two can eat with us, or wherever you'd like. Does he need anything right now? Do you need anything?"

I glance back at the bed, where Rowan hasn't moved a muscle. "This might be a weird request, but do you have a bathtub we could use?"

"Of course, honey. You can use ours. Come inside when you're ready, and I'll show you where it is."

"Thanks." Before she leaves, I step halfway out of the room and whisper, "He thought it was you. In Davis, when Coach told him his mom was there to get him, Rowan thought it was you. Do you know who his real mom is?"

The same heartache I feel seeps through Xia's dark eyes. "I only know what Matt told me."

Back in Rowan's room, I find him a pair of basketball shorts for now and a change of clothes for him and myself.

Second thing I do is put a knee on the mattress and a hand on his shoulder to nudge him awake. "Hey, sleepyhead? Time to get up."

A groan clears his throat while a fist scrubs his eyes. "Tommy?" he asks in the same way he did two hours ago, while still wedged under the bed.

"C'mon, sweetheart. Gotta get you cleaned up."

Another groan, and he turns onto his back, blinking up at me with his face scrunched oddly. "Am I what that smell is?"

Being an athlete for half my life, I've been around some funky smelling dudes, and Rowan is about as ripe as they come right now, but it's nothing I can't handle, and it's one thing I know I can fix. It might be the only thing.

I lean down and press my lips to his, even though I'm pretty sure he hasn't brushed his teeth in as many days as he hasn't showered or eaten.

"Is it morning?" he asks.

"It's about six in the evening. Monday."

"Shit." He brings a hand over his eyes like he could cry, but I just press kisses to his salty forehead and tell him again that everything's going to be alright. "I missed practice. I missed my classes. You have class."

"None of that matters right now. All that matters is that we get you washed up and fed, okay?"

I get him up and into his basketball shorts and slides. I put my own shoes back on, gather our changes of clothes under an arm, and put my other around Rowan's shoulders to walk him to the house.

"Where're we going?" he asks when I take him outside the garage.

"Gonna give you a bath for real." I kiss the side of his head before taking him up the back porch steps. I only let go of him to open the back door for us.

Xia is starting on dinner in the kitchen but drops everything to show me the way through the house. She takes us past the kids' bathroom and through her and Matt's room to their en suite.

"Towels are in the cabinet. Products are in the shower. Check the vanity drawers for anything extra you might need." She wrinkles her nose, giving Rowan a once over, then cups his whiskery face in her hands. "We love you, alright? This is your home. Don't forget that."

When I have Rowan alone in the en suite with the door shut and locked, I find everything I need and pile it all within arm's reach of the large tub, then I turn the water on to hot. Meanwhile, Rowan's a statue. Standing, breathing, but completely still. His dreary eyes are on the floor, staring, as cooperative as a mannequin while I undress him.

"You can talk to me, you know?" I tell him before tugging my shirt off. "Whenever you're ready, you can tell me anything."

He doesn't answer, but his eyes have shifted to my body, so I know my Rowan is still in there.

November has chilled the air. It seeps through the walls and makes the near scalding bath water feel all the more comforting when I help Rowan into the tub with me. I'd found a bath bomb and tossed it into the water, so the water looks milky and smells like vanilla and honey.

I leave the faucet turned to a trickle to help keep the water hot, and it's the only sound in the room besides the gentle slosh of the water as I dunk a fresh washcloth into our pool. First thing I do is bring the steaming cloth to Rowan's head to wet his hair and massage his scalp.

Eyes fluttering shut, Rowan moans gently and leans into my hand.

"So this is what baths are like," he mumbles.

"You'd never taken a bath before?"

"Not that I can remember."

I take my time with him, lathering Matt and Xia's fancy products all over him. Not that 3-in-1 shit he buys at the grocery store, but moisturizing shampoo and conditioner, exfoliating body wash and facial scrubs. I run my hands over almost every inch of Rowan's body. Sometimes there's a washcloth in between. Sometimes it's just my skin caressing his.

"Does this mean I'm the baby now?" Rowan asks, coming back to himself little by little.

"Only if you wanna be." I stroke my thumb along Rowan's jaw and consider how dreamy he'd look with a beard. How stunningly masculine.

Like he's reading my mind, Rowan asks, "You think I'd look good with a beard?"

"You'd look super hot with a beard."

He groans. "Itchy, though."

"I'll shave it for you." I hear him breathe a small chuckle as I turn and reach an arm over the lip of the tub, finding Matt's shaving cream and a disposable razor from a pack I found in a drawer below the sink.

"Gonna make my face baby smooth like yours?" he asks.

"Just wait 'til you find out my face is this smooth because I can't grow a beard."

Slight chuckle turning to a bright laugh, his smile reaches his ears. It's a healing sight, as if I'm the one who needs to be healed.

I bring Rowan's legs over my hips and pull him close to shave his face with the same focus and delicacy as if I were shaving his balls. The whole while, Rowan keeps his arms slung around my waist and his dark eyes locked onto mine.

When I'm finished, I wet his washcloth and clear his face of excess cream until he's back to looking as young as he is. I take time studying his face, memorizing it, because moments like these are fleeting, and time with people we love is never as long as we want it to be. *I want it to be forever.*

"Tommy?" he quietly asks.

"Yeah?"

"I'm gay."

Not wanting to make a huge deal about it, I just smile and say, "I know."

"I know you know," he says, his mouth forming a rare pout, "but I never told anyone before."

Curling my arms around his shoulders, I pull him into me, smooth cheek to smooth cheek. "I'm so proud of you."

"I didn't do anything."

"You did so much."

He leans back, reconnecting our eyes before he leans in and kisses my mouth, gentle and sweet. "Are you gonna wash my dick next?"

I laugh suddenly. "Want me to?"

"Hmm." His mouth twists and eyes shift like he's mulling it over. "Nah. That's more of the sixth date sorta thing."

I'm still snickering when he finds the washcloth in the water and climbs to his feet. Standing between my legs, rivulets of water cascading down his lean, muscular form, Rowan turns his ass to me and does the job himself. I keep my legs spread to the sides of the tub, and I lean back against the slope. When Rowan is through, I coax him back down so he's lying against me, his back to my front, and his head on my shoulder.

Hugging him tight, I kiss the side of his head and tell him I love him, not because I need to hear it back, but because I need him to know I'm still in this. I've still got him.

26

Rowan

Not sure how long we've been soaking in this tub like a milky gay soup, but it's hard for me to move when Tommy whispers in my ear that it's time to get out. I feel weak, and empty, and pathetic. Also, wet. Tommy gets me standing, and water spills from my body like rainfall.

"Gonna wipe me down like at the car wash now?" I'm trying to be cheeky, like that'll make up for how monumentally useless I am.

"Now, we're gonna get in the shower," Tommy answers, holding onto my arm while he steps out of the tub and onto the bath mat. From there, he's able to reach his arm into the shower stall and crank the water on.

"Am I not pruny enough?"

Smiling, he says, "I've bathed my nephew enough time to know that when you're real filthy, you got to do an extra rinse off afterward."

Shit. "Was I really that bad?"

He holds my arms, smile drifting to something more thoughtful. "Well, I did find you sleeping under the bed with all the dust bunnies and cobwebs."

A shock of humiliation settles in my chest, pinching my heart and stirring a pressure behind my eyes. "I was under the bed?"

"You don't remember that?"

Delving into my memory, I come up short. I remember Davis, and I remember...that woman. Remember the first panic attack and ending up somewhere I'd never been before. Remember ordering an Uber and hoping someone would pick me up before my phone died. Then it gets even more hazy and fragmented, like waking up from a dream and not really knowing what happened. I don't even remember Tommy showing up, just that I woke up, and he was there, telling me it was bathtime.

"Did you take anything, Row?" he whispers. "You can tell me. I won't judge you or nothing."

"I don't know. I don't really have anything to take. Sometimes, I take Benadryl to sleep when I'm really upset and trying not to do something stupid. Maybe I took some of that?"

Tommy wraps me in his arms, hugging me like we've been apart for too long. Then he takes me into the steaming shower stall, adjusts the temp, and hugs me under the rain head with the same fervor. Not much rinsing, just a lot of hugging.

"I think you just wanted an excuse to keep me naked longer," I murmur beside his ear.

"Caught me," he murmurs back.

"Fucking gay boy."

This is the first time I've really been in this bathroom. Sure, I've passed through it a few times when I've babysat the kids and had to go searching the whole house to find them, but I never lingered longer than a glance. It always felt off-limits. Bedrooms that aren't mine, bathrooms that aren't mine, a house that's not mine... Last thing I want to do is overstep, start taking shit that's not mine and encroaching on spaces I've got no business being in. I kind of remember Xia telling me this is my home, but she probably just meant the garage.

Yet, here I am, brushing my teeth at Matt and Xia's double sinks next to Tommy, like we're playing house or something. Fucking weird, but I like it. I like being clean too. I like wearing clean clothes and seeing Tommy wearing my clean clothes. His ass looks amazing in my joggers, probably because they're half a size too small on him.

We tidy up the bathroom as best we can and leave the wet towels in a laundry basket, then Tommy takes my hand and holds it while we leave this bathroom that suddenly feels like a sanctum. Walking through the hall is jarring. New scents and new sounds, like I'm a newborn having to adjust to life outside the womb, and it feels like too much.

Too much family.

Olive and Lena are playing dolls in the living room while Matt's got a hockey game on, and Xia is giving bites of baby food to Bruno in his high chair between cleaning up the dining table.

"Oh, good!" she exclaims as soon as she spots us coming out of the hallway. "Come here. Pick a seat. Both of you. I've got plates in the oven."

I don't know why she's being so nice. She's always nice, but still. It's not like someone died. I'm just a giant baby who can't handle his emotions well enough to keep the people around me from freaking out. It's clear that I scared Tommy, and that's the only reason he's here on a school night, tending to me like I'm an invalid.

Still hand in hand, Tommy guides me to the table, because my legs are still sort of stiff from going unused for multiple days. We sit next to each other, chairs pushed up close, and when Xia brings us two plates of meat loaf and extra buttery mashed potatoes, Tommy moves his hand from mine to my thigh.

"Your favorite, honey," Xia tells me, and she's right. She's always right. "There's frosted oatmeal cookies in the pantry when you finish dinner. Just for you."

Figures she knows what my favorite cookies are. It's stupid, because I'm a twenty-two-year-old man, but my voice cracks when I tell her thank you, and my traitorous eyes fill with tears. It's bad enough Tommy's seen me cry. I don't want Xia getting an eyeful and thinking I'm even more messed up than what all Matt has told her.

Tommy moves his hand from my leg to my head, raking his fingers across my scalp. It's enough of a distraction to keep the tears from falling, and right now, that's more important to me than keeping my relationship with Tommy hush hush.

When Xia is through doting on us with glasses of water, cans of soda, and extra napkins, I shovel food in like I haven't eaten in days. I guess I haven't.

Is it really Monday?

"You missed class," I tell Tommy, feeling an odd sense like we've already had this conversation.

"You're more important," he says.

"Nothing is more important than your grades."

"Alright, Dad." He sends me a small wink before scooping potatoes into his mouth and washing it down with a swig of Coke. "Eat your food," he says when he catches me staring.

"Tommy? Will you stay tonight?"

"I'm not going anywhere."

Both relieved and terrified, I focus back on my food to try to fill my stomach before I become too queasy to take a bite. Tommy thinks telling him I'm gay is a big deal, and maybe it is, but it's a drop in the bucket compared to what else I've been hiding away to fester. What's really amazing is that Tommy is here at all, without even knowing a thing.

Perfect Tommy Mathison... He even changes my sheets for me after dinner and helps me get all my crap back under the bed where it belongs. I can't believe I was under there when Tommy showed up. It's mortifying. I don't remember crawling under there, but I have a good idea why I did it.

He cracks the window, letting crisp autumn air into my musty space, then he sits himself cross-legged on my bed and asks if I want to watch something.

Since I don't really watch anything besides sports and game film, I shake my head. "We can watch something if you want, though."

"C'mere." He reaches out, and I put my hand in his so he can tug me onto my bed with him. Onto the fresh, cozy blankets that smell like fabric softener. He tries to cuddle, but I pull away and scoot toward the foot of the bed. If I don't do this now, I never will.

Drawing an invisible line across the mattress, I stick to my side and kick off my apology parade. *Sorry for disappearing. Sorry for worrying you. Sorry for being so fucking pathetic.*

"Stop." He leans forward, finds my hands and holds them in my lap. "You don't need to apologize. I'm just glad you're okay, and that you're not mad at me."

My voice cracks. "Why would I be mad at you?"

Pouting like he does, Tommy mumbles, "What I did in Davis."

"What?" Oh. The kiss. I completely forgot about that. Nothing like a whirlwind of post-traumatic stress to make me remember which problems are actually worth giving a shit about. "Tommy, that's nothing. I don't care about that. I'm not mad at you, I promise."

"It's okay if you are. I fucked up."

Squeezing his hands in mine, I cry, "You're the best thing that's ever happened to me. I'm not mad at you. I'm just a broken person, and I try really hard to hide that from you so I won't scare you away. I'm sorry you have to see me like this."

Humiliated by my quivering, whimpering voice, I drop my chin to my chest and silently curse myself for being such a fucking loser. My chest hurts as if Tommy has already given up on me, and my mind is already preparing myself for the inevitability that I'm going to lose him.

Warm hands stroke the length of my outer thighs as Tommy's voice tells me, "You're not broken."

"Tommy." I lift my chin to show him the mess I am as tears streak down my face. "Look at me."

His hands jump from my legs to my jaw, swiping away those tears with his thumbs. "I am looking at you. I see you, and I don't see a broken person. I see someone who's upset and hurt, and I see the boy I fell in love with. If you trust me, you'll know I'm being honest with you."

"I do trust you. It's just hard. This whole thing is hard. I wanna be good for you. I wanna be a good boyfriend. I wanna take care of you. I wanna deserve you—"

"Row, what did your mom say to you?"

My heart stops, and my tears dry when I forget to blink. "What?"

"When Matt and I got you out from under the bed, you told him your mom was at the match on Saturday. What happened?"

Hands shaking in my lap, Tommy finds them again and grips them firm.

"I—I don't know," I mumble meekly. "As soon as she said she was my mom, I sorta fell out of myself. I don't think I heard one word she said after that. Then, I was running like I was being chased until I realized I was lost."

"You should've called me. I would've found you."

I want to tell him I didn't want to put all my baggage on him, but the truth is, I just wasn't thinking. When I quit running, my body went numb and my mind was in such a flurry I could hardly make sense of my phone screen while I ordered the Uber. I wasn't thinking about Tommy. I was thinking about getting as far away from that woman as possible and burying myself into a hole so deep no one would ever find me.

But Tommy found me anyway.

"Did you recognize her?" Tommy asks when I stay silent too long.

"Yes, and no. I didn't know who she was when she came up to me, but then she felt kinda familiar at the same time. Like maybe she was in some of my dreams growing up."

Nightmares, I should've said.

Tommy nods but doesn't speak, waiting for me to keep going, but the only thing I can think of to say is the thing I'm the most afraid to tell him.

Looking away from Tommy's eyes, I focus on the rise and fall of his chest instead. "I know you think it's dumb that I have such a hard time saying that I'm, *ya know.*"

"I don't think it's dumb," he insists. "Look at me. I don't think it's dumb. I just wanna understand, so I can help make it less difficult. That's all I want."

I try looking back into his eyes, but it's too hard right now, just like everything else. "I think the reason it's so difficult is 'cause of what happened to me." Fear clams me up, unable to speak anything more until Tommy asks me what happened. It's like my body won't do what my mind wants it to until Tommy coaxes it out of me. Looking at him is suddenly impossible, so I turn my head to the wall instead. "I was, like, exploited."

There's a pause before Tommy asks, "Exploited?"

"You know. Molested."

There's a longer pause, and I can hear Tommy's breaths grow louder and more purposeful, like each one is a conscious effort not to suffocate on what I'm telling him. "How old were you?" he eventually asks.

"Little. Like, really little. Too little for me to remember it happening. But I'd have dreams—*nightmares*—all the time when I was a kid, and that really fucked me up. I didn't know why that stuff was in my head, or what it meant. I thought maybe it meant I was a bad person, because I thought only bad people had bad dreams, and I had bad dreams all the time. Dreams that would make me puke as soon as I woke up. Dreams that made me hate myself and make me wanna die.

"When I was in, like, eighth grade, I tried looking for my parents. That's when I found out what happened and why I was taken from them. It made sense of my dreams, but it didn't make me feel any better. It actually made me feel a lot worse. Realizing my biological father was in prison for doing the worst shit you can do to a kid, and he did it to me. That my biological mother had been locked up, too, for helping him do it.

"All I ever wanted was for someone to love me and to know what that feels like. I thought that because I'm gay, no one would ever love me. Until you. But now I'm scared that I can't be what you need me to be, because I'm too fucked up. I'm scared I won't love you right, because I've never loved anyone good before. I'm scared I'm gonna lose you, because I love you so much. I didn't think I could love anyone like this. I didn't think—"

The air expels from my lungs in a choked sob when Tommy collides himself against me, hugging me tight and holding my head to his shoulder.

"You're not fucked up," Tommy speaks against my head, his lips grazing my scalp with each word. "You're mine. Hear me? You're mine, and you always will be. I will always love you, Row."

He says more things, but I don't hear them over the retched sound of my crying. Even if I could hear them, I don't know if I'm in the right headspace to process it all. All I know is that I told Tommy something I swore I never would, but somehow, he still wants me. Somehow, while I'm breaking down all over him, he makes me feel whole.

With Tommy's hands rubbing stripes across my back, it shocks me how quickly I recover. How quickly my heart calms, my eyes dry, and my lungs breathe easier. When he leans back, he takes me with him, and he lets me lie half on top of him, my cheek on his shoulder and his lips against my head.

"Sweetheart," he whispers, like that's my name now. It feels ironic, since my heart only feels sweet when it's beating for Tommy.

"Hm?"

"You know you didn't deserve what happened to you, right?"

"I know."

"You know you're not a bad person, right?"

"I guess."

"You're lovable, Row," he tells me. "You're generous, supportive, protective, and beautiful. That's all you. I've never met anyone as special as you. What happened to you...what those people did...that's not who you are, and that's not why you're gay. You're gay because you're supposed to be loved by a man, and I'm gonna be that man. I'm gonna love you. I'm gonna take care of you whenever you need it, and I'm gonna help you get through this. Anytime you're feeling any type of way about what happened, I'm gonna be here for you."

Takes me a while to process all that. A minute, but maybe more. As long as I focus on the sound of Tommy's heart gently beating beside my ear, I keep myself from crying again.

"As long as I never see that woman ever again, I'll be okay."

Stroking his palm up and down my arm, Tommy says, "Then that's what I'll work on. I won't ever let her near you."

I pick my head up and stretch my neck until my lips touch his. "Thank you."

"I got you. Always."

The kiss we share soothes my soul and tells me things are going to be alright.

"Will you do me a favor?" I ask.

"Anything."

I uncurl my arm from around Tommy's waist to pinch the t-shirt he borrowed from my stack of clean laundry. "Can you take this off?"

"Yeah." He sits up enough to tug the shirt off, drapes it over the headboard, then lies back down.

Now, when I put my cheek on his shoulder, it's only Tommy I smell, and it's only his flesh I feel against mine. I lay my palm in the center of his smooth, bare chest and feel for his heartbeat.

"I love you," he murmurs against my hair before kissing my head.

For the first time in my life, it's easy to tell someone, "I love you too," because it's Tommy. And Tommy really is special.

27

Tommy

We stay up half the night, and for the first time, Rowan answers every question I ask. He tells me about his childhood, starting where his memories begin—the house with the hot teenager who pretended Rowan didn't exist. He tells me about the bad families. The ones who starved him, neglected him, and called him names. He tells me about the good families. The ones who remembered his birthday, left gifts under the tree for him at Christmas, gave him lunch money, and got him to his soccer matches on time. He tells me about the in-betweens too. The families he was with for a month at most while he bounced around aimlessly, searching for another landing spot. They were kind, more or less, but open about not having the space for him in their home or hearts.

What a crazy notion...not having space for Rowan. While I spend these hours curled against him on a narrow bed fit for one, I know that making room for Rowan is the easiest thing in the world.

He tells me how he always knew he was gay, from as early as his memories begin. He always liked boys, never girls. Never even tried to date girls besides a handful of begrudging hookups that only made him feel worse about himself.

It's another crazy notion to think that our relationship began with my ex-girlfriend basically forcing herself on him. Every extra detail of Rowan's backstory makes me hate myself a little more for ever going after him. I dance my fingers down the side of Rowan's face and wonder how I could have ever hurt this beautiful boy.

He tells me about Matt too. His tenth grade history teacher and the assistant men's soccer coach at McClatchy High when Rowan started there.

"To be honest," Rowan muses, "I had a crush on him my freshman year, but I eventually realized that's because I had a very warped perspective on authority figures. He was the first adult to really give a shit about me in a way that resonated and felt good. He was like the older brother I never had, 'cause he was always looking out for me. Until you, Matt was the only person I ever told about what my parents did.

"I turned eighteen during my senior year, and the family I'd been with wasn't the best, so I was sorta homeless of a while. Couch surfing at friends' houses or sleeping in the school when I could get away with it. I'd been spending the night in the locker room at school for a few days when I tried killing myself again, this time with a few hydrocodone and a bottle of Vodka I stole. I don't remember this, but right before I passed out, I called Matt. He came and found me, and he took me to the hospital where I had my stomach pumped, and I was put in the psych unit for two weeks.

"After that, Matt let me come live with him and Xia, and I've been here ever since."

"I hate you had to go through all that," I tell him, even though it doesn't come close to expressing the whirlwind of emotions spiraling in my head right now. Anger, sadness, and love in equal measure.

He shrugs like it's no biggie, but behind his eyes, I know there's a lot of hurt there. Not just from what his parents did, but that it took until he was already an adult to find something halfway stable, and that it took until now for him to feel safe enough to baby step out of the closet.

"It's always darkest before the dawn, right?" he says. "I can feel it now, though. The dawn."

Eventually, I fall asleep wrapped around Rowan, and the first thing I do when I wake up is research how to file a restraining order.

Rowan and I play hooky this morning and stay in. Xia brings us breakfast before heading out to work, and she says Matt got the kids' pediatrician to write a doctor's note explaining Rowan's absence from practice and his classes. That's some Dad-level magic if I ever saw it. But Rowan is determined to go to practice today. He doesn't even seem anxious about it despite how juvenile our teammates have been about the kiss. Then again, Rowan isn't one to let anything get between him and a soccer ball.

What's shocking is when we get out of my truck in the student lot, Rowan glues his hand to mine and laces our fingers.

Submitting to the butterflies in my chest, I let it be. But when we cross from the parking lot to the Student Union side of campus, I ask Rowan if he's sure about this.

He shrugs the shoulder that's holding up his gym bag. "It's my last semester here. Season's almost over. We're undefeated. Only person whose opinion I care about is yours. Everyone else can think what they want." Sending me a small smirk, he adds, "Feel free to let go, babyface."

"You kidding? I finally get to know what it's like to walk through campus holding hands with the cutest boy in school. I might never let go."

"Cutest?" Rowan shows me those teeth, cheeks looking about as pink as mine feel. "Look in a fucking mirror."

"Only if you're standing next to me."

Rowan tightens his smile the way he does when he's flustered, but he asked for this. Submerged in the foot traffic milling through campus, I reach my mouth to Rowan's temple and smooch him there, giving him just what he ordered.

That grin comes back to Rowan's face in the form of a sudden laugh. "Alright, gay boy. I think they get the picture."

Ah, but I don't care about whoever may or may not be noticing our PDA. I'm too giddy to care. After such a rough and emotionally taxing few days for the both of us, I realize just how important it is not to squander the love I've earned. That passionate, protective love Erica said doesn't happen to everyone, but it's happening to me. How could I dare to shove that in a box?

"I love you," I tell him, loud enough I'm sure he'll hear it over the surrounding chatter.

"Love you too."

Rowan doesn't let go—and I sure as hell don't—until we're at his locker, and we break off so I can head to mine. Other than a few cat-call whistles from our more immature teammates, no one says shit to us until Connor comes up behind Rowan and asks if he's feeling alright.

From my locker, I just make out Rowan's answer. "Had a mean stomach bug from some bad chicken, but I'm good now."

Can't miss Levi's obnoxious voice calling out, "Hope lover boy did a good job nursing you back to health, man, 'cause this match on Saturday is gonna be a dog."

Lover boy? It's better than "butt buddy," so I won't complain.

"You getting nervous on me?" Rowan asks.

"Like hell! I'm more worried if those cameras are gonna catch my good side." He swings an arm around Rowan and says, "Just got one more question, Cap."

"What's that?" Rowan asks passively, focused on digging his gear out of his locker.

"You're gonna make me Best Man at the wedding, right? 'Cause, if it weren't for me knocking lover boy out with that high kick, y'all wouldn't have had your little meet-cute in the middle of McKinley Park."

"Our little *what?*"

"Just letting you know, man," Levi says, patting Rowan on the shoulder, "I look fire in a navy tux."

"Noted." Rowan's eyes roll so wide they land on me, and I swear to God, he's blushing.

After practice, I take Rowan to his treasured salad joint and watch him go ham on a bowl of spring mix and grilled chicken. If I didn't have work later, I'd take him for ice cream. Maybe a movie. I just don't want to leave him. I'm scared to leave him, like dropping him off at his and going on my way is akin to giving up on him. To losing him.

Get a grip, Tommy.

"Hey." I stop Rowan before he can hop out of my truck in front of his place. "You gonna be okay? I can come back tonight."

"You don't need to babysit me anymore," he says with a somber smile. "I won't do anything stupid. I promise."

Slipping my hand behind his head, I tell him, "As soon as you fill out that paperwork, I'm gonna take you to the courthouse."

He's silent for a few beats, searching my eyes. "Love you, baby boy."

"Love you too."

One lingering kiss and a promise to text me later is all I get before he's dropping out of my truck and heading up the driveway to that padlocked gate.

Like a lovesick puppy, I already miss him, but I've got to get home to change clothes for my shift that starts in less than an hour.

Pulling up to the house, I'm too busy calculating if I've got enough time for a second lunch to notice there's a man standing at the curb, staring at the house. An odd feeling comes to me when I'm halfway up my front stoop. It makes me turn around, tip my head to the guy, and ask wassup.

The dude leans against a white SUV, but kicks off it as soon as I speak. I can't place him, but something about him feels familiar. A young-ish man, definitely older than me, but not old enough to convince me he's my long-lost daddy, finally crawling back home from wherever the hell he's been for over a decade. Whoever this guy is, though, he knows me.

"Tommy?" he says, sizing me up like I'm an alternate version of myself he can hardly fathom. "Hell. Last time I saw you, you were just a lanky kid with acne and braces."

"Uh, who are you?" I come back down the walk cautiously. It doesn't hit me until the guy introduces himself as Paul Hammel that while he's not my deadbeat dad, he's Mav's.

The front door opens behind me, and there's Erica coming out the doorway. My first thought is, *where's Mav?* But I get too caught up on my second thought to ask my first, *what the fuck is Paul Hammel doing here?*

"Tommy." Erica comes down the porch steps looking like I caught her stealing money out of Ma's purse. "Y-you remember Paul, right? We'll be out for a bit. I thought you had work today."

Looking between the two of them, I don't know how to react. Here's the man who left my sis high and dry when she was pregnant, never to show his face around his own son, and now he's here. Doing what? Picking Erica up for a date like they're back in college?

"What's going on?" I ask Erica.

As if it's no big deal, she steps past me in favor of Paul Hammel and says, "Paul's in town, and we're going to grab an early dinner and catch up."

Grab an early dinner and catch up?

"Where's Mav?"

Her eyes turn slightly pointed. "I'll talk to you later, alright? After you get home from work."

"Good seeing you again," Paul says to me before leading the way for my sister to get into his SUV.

The feeling in my gut tells me something's off, but it's probably my hatred for Paul that's causing it. I just don't know where Erica's hatred for him went off to now that she's sneaking off into his Durango to *catch up.*

By the time I change into my work shirt, I've got two texts. One from Erica telling me Ma took Maverick to Costco with her, and one from Rowan—a fresh addition to my endless bank of dick pics.

At least he's feeling better.

While Rowan is the one I'm texting in each of my spare moments at work, as soon as I get home, the only thing on my mind is finding Erica to take her up on her promise to "talk to me later."

It's almost ten o'clock. Mav's asleep and Ma is in her room with the TV on. She texted saying she put my dinner in a Tupperware in the fridge. When I go into the kitchen, Erica is coughing up a lung in the sink with the water running.

"Hey, hey, you alright?" I give her middle back rhythmic pats that make a dull, hollow sound as Erica retches speckles of crimson into the white porcelain. I whip a dish towel off the oven rung and have it ready for Erica to take and clean the blood from her chin.

"Erica—"

"It's okay," she says, shutting off the water.

"You're not okay. Let me take you to the ER—"

"Tommy." She grips my biceps and looks up at me with earnestness in her sad eyes. "It's okay. It's going to get worse now. That's how it works, but it's okay. I'm okay. I don't want to go anywhere, and I don't want you to worry."

"How long have you been coughing up blood?"

She answers by darting her eyes around, like checking to make sure Mav isn't hiding behind a cupboard. "Want to go for a walk?"

The nights are getting cold. I wait on the front porch for Erica to find a coat, then we pick a direction at random and head down the street. We walk slowly, but Erica still stops me three times to tell me I'm going too fast. I end up heel-toeing down the sidewalk with Erica's hand on my elbow, neither of us speaking what's on our minds until we're a block and half from the house.

"Where were you last night?" she finally asks.

The answer comes out easier than I expect. "Stayed with Rowan."

"You never used to stay over at Annalese's."

"That was different. That was Lese. Besides, her mom's got all those cats, and I'm more of a dog person."

"You've never had a dog," Erica chuckles.

"Well, I know I'm not a cat person."

"Does it feel weird?" she asks. "Being with a man?"

"You mean dating a man or having sex with a man?"

Eyeing Erica in the yellow glow of the streetlamps, she's blushing and scrunching her nose like she'd rather live her whole life blissfully unaware that I've ever had sex. Or maybe it's just the gay sex she's flustered by. Either way, I get a sinister kick out of discomforting her.

"Both, I guess," she says, smiling through her shyness.

"It is weird, but in a good way. I actually wanna go on dates with him, plan things and take him places. Even if we're just sitting on a bench watching grass grow, I could do that for hours and be happy. He doesn't make me feel like I have to be any sort of way. Like, all I have to do is exist as myself, and he treats me like I'm perfect."

Erica swoons, hugging my arm with both of hers and laying her cheek on the ball of my shoulder. "Aww, Tommy, you are perfect."

Now I'm the one blushing, and I've got no one else to blame but myself. To even the playing field, I tell Erica, "As for the sex...*mind blowing*."

"Really?" her eyes scintillate, grinning ear to ear.

"Yeah. It's just... He's so... He's fucking hot, for one thing. But everything he does to me—everything we do together is..." I make an explosion sound with my mouth, realizing my mind isn't poetic enough to conjure an accurate description of how incredible Rowan makes me feel.

"Oh my God," Erica snickers. "You really are gay."

"Lese thought I had erectile dysfunction."

That's got Erica laughing so hard, she's coughing again, and all our mirth dies on impact. She crouches so her hands touch the sidewalk, and she splatters the cement in blood.

"Erica." I pat her back again until she settles. "Let me take you somewhere."

"I'm fine," she croaks, swiping her coat sleeve across her mouth. "Let's start back home."

I take her hand and help her back up. We turn around, and she hugs my other arm on the way back toward the house. This time, it's my turn to ask the questions. "What was Mav's dad doing here? I thought he fucked off to Oakland."

"He did, but he drove in so we could talk."

"Talk about what? All the child support he's never paid?"

"It's complicated, Tommy."

"Yeah, everything's complicated. I'm gay, you're dying, and Mav's never had a dad a day in his life, because that loser couldn't be man enough to accept his fucking responsibilities."

"He didn't know," Erica mutters.

"He didn't know what? That he's a loser?"

"He didn't know about Maverick."

"What?" Stunned immobile, I halt in the middle of the sidewalk.

Erica lets go of my arm and turns to face me. Not meeting my bulging eyes, she mumbles, "Like I said. It's complicated."

"Complicated? You told me he ran off because he didn't want a kid. You told me he said Mav wasn't his. You told me he refused to take a paternity test. You lied to me? How is lying to me complicated?"

"You were thirteen when I was pregnant, Tom. Of course I lied to you. You were a child."

"You lied to Ma. After all she's done for you."

Rolling her eyes, Erica says, "Mom didn't do shit for me or Mav until I got sick. First thing she told me when she found out I was pregnant was to pack my shit, because she wasn't going to raise another baby."

I crane my head back and heave a hard breath up toward the hazy sky, willing myself to calm down. "So you made sure Mav was out with Ma so you could go relive the glory days with the dude you've been lying to for seven years?"

"No. I asked him to meet up so I could tell him the truth."

When I look back at Erica, she's a mix of somber and hopeful.

"I've been stalking his socials for the better part of a year. He's in a good place. Got a good job and his own place near some good schools."

"So?"

"Mav is going to need somewhere to go when this thing inside me does me in."

My heart drops to my feet. "I thought Mav was gonna stay here."

"Ma doesn't want to—"

"I want to," my knee-jerk emotions blurt out. "I'll take Mav. Leave him to me. I'll take care of him. You know I can take care of him."

"You can't, Tommy."

"Seriously? I've been Mav's uncle for six years, and Paul's been his dad for half a day, but you think he can do a better job than I can? 'Cause he's got a good job? I'll get a better job, Erica. I'll get my own place for us if Ma is who you're worried about. I'll be Mav's guardian."

"Absolutely not."

"Why not?" My eyes water, like Erica's death sentence has suddenly become Mav's too. When she goes, he goes.

"You're a kid, Tommy. I don't care that you're legally an adult. You're a kid. I am not going to turn my baby brother into a parent at twenty because of my bad decisions and my bad fortune. You were never an option. You hear me? Never."

"I get it," I mutter through my tears.

"I'm sorry." She hugs me, and it takes a moment before my body will hug her back.

"Is Paul gonna take him?" I ask against the top of her head.

"He wants a paternity test to make sure. Then, he obviously wants to meet Mav, but yeah, he said he'll work on getting his place ready for when the time comes. Hopefully, not 'til summer, so Mav doesn't have to switch schools mid-year."

Trying to hold in my emotions for the sake of Erica's, I muse, "Oakland isn't that far. I could visit him a lot. Every weekend even."

Pulling away enough to look up into my eyes, Erica asks, "Will you take him? When it's time, will you take him to Oakland? If you take him, it'll be easier for him."

"Of course. I'll do anything for him. I'll do anything for you."

Erica falls back into my arms, and I squeeze her as tight as her frailty allows.

When we finally make it home, I tell her to head inside while I linger on the porch. As soon as the front door shuts between us, I put my ass on the top step, pull out my phone and tap Rowan's name into my contacts.

"Hey, baby boy," he answers, voice a little groggy. *"You miss me?"*

"Hell yeah, I miss you," I tell him. "Didn't wake you, did I?"

"Nah, I'm just lying in bed watching game film. It's late for you. Need me to read you a bedtime story? Heads up, though. It's gonna be my paper on the history of broadcast media."

Breathing a chuckle, I say, "I totally wanna hear it. You think we could talk for a little while first?"

"For sure. You can talk to me about anything."

28
Tommy

Last time I was on a plane, I was twelve, going to the little league championship. Now, I'm crammed into a tin can with the rest of the Sac State team, getting ready to take off for round one of the NCAA College Cup in Utah. My nerves are ablaze, and it doesn't help that every seat in this plane is full. Never thought of myself as claustrophobic, but something about not being able to move my legs is brewing a panic inside me. Doesn't help either that I'm in a middle seat between some dude who smells like soup and Raisel, who's been up near the cockpit, flirting with the flight attendant since we boarded.

"Hey, roomie."

My head turns up at the sound of Rowan's voice, and he's flashing me a sneaky half smile before dropping into Raisel's aisle seat.

"Really?" My anxiety immediately wanes as Rowan's shoulder presses against mine. Being wedged in doesn't feel so bad when it's Rowan's doing. If he also got us roomed together in Utah, I'm dubbing him my hero.

"Switched room assignments with Raisel. Also switched seats with him, so you can hold my hand the whole way to Utah." He says it like he's teasing me, but when he flips up the armrest and holds his palm upward, I clasp it eagerly.

"How'd you swing all this?"

"Told him you snore like a lawnmower."

Frowning, I ask pathetically, "Do I?"

"Nah," he coos, lacing our fingers. "You sleep like an angel."

"You two are adorable!" Levi's cringe-worthy tone seeps between our seats from the row behind us.

Rowan twists and cranes his neck tall enough to shoot Levi a glare over his headrest. "Put your headphones on and mind your business."

"Aye aye, Captain!"

I'm red-faced and snickering, embarrassed but in a giddy way, where being teased starts feeling like praise.

Most of the flight, Rowan and I watch game film on his phone, sharing his Bluetooth earbuds. When we get close to Utah, and the dude to my left is snoring against the window, Rowan plucks the buds from both our ears and leans close to my ear.

"When we get to the room, I've got a present for you," he murmurs.

"Oh, yeah?" I turn my head, and our noses nearly brush. "Is this a mutually beneficial present?"

With soft eyes, Rowan's mouth smirks, and he says, "That depends on how you decide to use it."

Shit. And here I thought he was going to let me get through this entire flight without popping a boner.

The sneaky bastard sticks a bud back into my ear, then his own, and taps play on his phone like he didn't just plant that seed in my head. I lay my cheek on Rowan's shoulder, focus on his phone screen, and will my dick to deflate in my travel sweats. I fall asleep waiting for myself to go limp.

At Salt Lake City International, the assistant coaches corral us all into a chartered bus that takes us to a Best Western near the campus of our opponents.

"Damn, Coach. Couldn't have sprung for a Marriott or something?" Raisel complains as we're dropped off with all our luggage in front of the hotel.

"You're welcome to book alternative accommodations for yourself, Mr. Cruz," Coach answers before addressing the lot of us. "Dinner will be in the banquet hall at six o'clock sharp. If you're not there on time, and everything's gone, you're on your own 'til breakfast. I think there's a 7-Eleven down the street."

Six o'clock. So, we've got two hours to get settled in our rooms. *How many times can I make Rowan come in two hours?*

Our room is on the second floor, smack between Levi and Raisel's room and Connor and Zeke's. It's a small room with two queen beds, one for Rowan and one for me, but the first thing I do is tug Rowan onto the bed closest to the bathroom and ravage him. Our shoes thud to the floor as we kick them off, and we shed our clothes in a flurry of wet, desperate kisses and roaming hands.

I get him naked, sprawled out below me, and I kiss him all the way from his smirking mouth to his flexing abs. I pick up his turgid, pulsing cock and roll his foreskin down to swipe my tongue across his glistening slit.

"Shit," he huffs, fingers threading in my hair and his knees parting wide.

One hand on his pelvis and the other on his thigh, I take his cock down my throat without regard for my gag reflex. Lying between his legs, I rut against the duvet and moan around Rowan's cock.

He grunts on every exhale, fingers pressing into my scalp as I bob on his shaft.

"Fuck, c'mere." He hooks my ears and draws me off his dick

After a moment of disappointment, I'm filled with more excitement than my raging cock can contain when Rowan pushes me on my side then rotates his body so he's lying with his face at my crotch. He wastes no time taking me into his mouth, but I taste him with patience. Licking him, kissing him, nuzzling my nose into his scrotum. It isn't until Rowan is moaning around my dick and trying to hump my face that I open my jaw and suck him down. I snake my arm around his hip, hugging him at first, then sneaking a devilish finger between his cheeks.

Without the baby oil Rowan keeps next to his bed in Sacramento, I stick to petting the outside of his little pucker until I've gagged enough times on Rowan's cock that I've got a plentiful cache of saliva in mouth to spit onto my fingers.

While I rub my wet fingers along Rowan's crack, he strokes my shaft and sucks on my crown, like he's trying to finish me off already. I jerked off in the shower this morning, after promising Rowan it wouldn't make me late to the bus bound for the airport, but I still feel myself getting close.

Burying one slick finger knuckle deep inside Rowan's ass interrupts the steady rhythm he had going on my dick. Groaning from his chest, he spits me out of his mouth just to praise me.

"Fuck, baby. That feels so good," he pants against my thigh. "Don't stop. You're gonna make me come in your fucking mouth, baby."

His ass squeezes my finger in a death grip, but there's just enough room for me to rub his walls while he grinds between my hand and my mouth. He jerks my cock with strength and vigor, but it isn't until he engulfs me back into his hot mouth that I know I'm about to come. It's the feel of him groaning around my shaft as the first shot of his fluid hits the back of my throat that pushes me over the edge. My orgasm hits while

Rowan is bucking against my mouth, feeding me enough of his seed that my eyes water and my stomach flips.

I drink down every drop, and Rowan swallows all of mine. And when we're both spent and full, we turn onto our backs beside each other and heave breaths up at the ceiling.

Savasana.

The thought makes me laugh. For some reason, Rowan laughs too.

As soon as I've caught my breath, I turn back onto my side and turn Rowan onto his, too, facing away from me this time. I push on his hip and squeeze his ass, pulling his cheeks apart so I'm eye to eye with his tight hole. It winks, daring me to have a taste. I dive in, wanting to eat my fill, and I lave that little pucker with my eager tongue until it's relaxed enough I can dig my tongue through his rim.

"Oh my God," Rowan breathes. His hand finds the back of my head and rests it there, not holding me in place or pulling me further in. Just resting there, sometimes finger-combing my hair. "Feels so good," he softly moans. "Why does it feel so good?"

"Why do you taste so fucking good?"

He breathes a chuckle that becomes a pleasured sigh as I return my tongue to his hole.

It isn't until my jaw feels sore that I pry my mouth from between his cheeks, and by then, my cock is half hard again.

"Tommy?" Rowan turns onto his delicious ass and sits up. He hugs his knees to his chest the way he does when he's nervous, but the look on his face is pure wickedness. "I wanna give you your present now."

Perfect timing. My hand instinctively wraps around my dick, coaxing it to swell. "Oh yeah? I'll be honest, it's gonna be hard to top the present you just gave me."

His wicked smile becomes a devilish smirk. "It's in my bag," he says before scooting himself across the bed and padding across the charcoal carpet.

In his bag? Curious now, I sit up and watch him dig through his luggage with a giddy flutter in my tummy. If this is anything like the FitBit he gave me, I'll hate that he wasted the money on me, so I hope it's only a simple pleasure. Jelly beans maybe, or a cock ring so I can last longer the next time we sixty-nine.

A second after Rowan zips his bag back up and stands, he's saying, "Catch," and tossing me something no larger than my palm. I catch it, feeling a plastic bottle and seeing clear gel inside. The label spills the beans clear as day, and my eyes go wide as my smile stretches. *Anal lube.*

I look from the travel size bottle up to Rowan, who's staring back at me thoughtfully. What I once interpreted as stoicism, I now know is Rowan's thoughtfulness—his inquisitive mind working overtime with not enough energy left over to make his face emote all that he's feeling.

"For real?" I ask.

He shrugs one shoulder. "You're always saying how bad you wanna fuck my ass."

Leaving the lube on the duvet, I climb off the bed and circle my arms around Rowan's waist. The way we are, my dick pokes at his, and I feel him grow against me. Touching my forehead to his, I say, "I want to so bad, but only if you want me to."

The corner of his mouth ticks up. "I bought the damn lube, didn't I?"

I gulp, head swimming, and my heart pumping all my blood down to my dick.

"Or...do you want me to say it?" He tilts his chin and grazes his lips against my ear. "I want you to make me come while your long, fat cock is inside me as far as it'll go."

I shudder, my hands gripping Rowan's ass and pulling his hips against mine. Rubbing my cock against his pelvis, I let out a needy moan.

The heat of Rowan's mouth covers mine, and we kiss with languid sweeps of our tongues while Rowan's hand slips between us, just enough room to wrap his fingers around my shaft and tug me loosely.

"C'mon, baby boy," he whispers into my mouth before stepping back. He holds my cock like a leash, guiding me back to bed. He falls to the center of it, head on the pillows, and I fall on top of him, kissing him, touching him, loving him.

"I should stretch you more first," I murmur against his lips.

"Yeah?" He combs his fingers up and down my back, his legs already hooked around my hips. "Did Google tell you that? You look up a step-by-step guide on how to fuck your boyfriend's ass?"

I blush, because he's sort of right. "I just don't wanna hurt you."

"You're not gonna hurt me."

"Still." I press my lips to his before begrudgingly peeling my nakedness off of his. Sitting on my heels between his legs, I tell him to flip over.

Biting down on his bottom lip, Rowan maneuvers onto his hands and knees, the top of his head inches from the headboard. I crawl backward and pull him along with me to give him more room, then I spread his cheeks and lean in to pet my tongue across his hole until he's purring.

Sitting back, I reach for the Astroglide, pop the cap and squeeze a line onto two fingers. The gel is cool and thicker than I would have expected. I bring it quickly to Rowan's ass and smear it along his crack before doling out another line to my fingers. This time, I spread the lube all around my fingers, then press both to Rowan's hole. Hoping his ring is still relaxed from the one finger I already fucked him with, I burrow my middle and index fingers in together.

Rowan's breath hitches and his hips jerk slightly, but he doesn't protest when I bury my fingers deep, rather he moans. He even rocks back against my fingers like he's already ready for more.

I'll never tire of watching his adorable asshole bloom for me, sucking my fingers in and hugging them tight. Seeing my fingers pump steadily in and out of him has my cock throbbing and raring to take its turn.

Patience.

"What?" Rowan drowsily murmurs, quirking his head back to look at me through the corners of his eyes.

Shit, I said that out loud. "Sorry, was talking to my dick."

Rowan laughs, but the way his body wiggles around my fingers quickly has him moaning again. "Don't be patient. I need you, baby boy."

No matter how many times Row has called me that, it's got my mouth hanging open now, nearly drooling. "Yeah? You need me?" I ask needily, kneading his ass with one hand while I pump and twist my fingers inside his tight hole.

"God, yes," he moans toward the pillows. "I want you to fuck me so bad. Don't hold out on me."

"I won't."

"I want you to come in my ass, Tommy. Promise me."

"I promise," I answer quickly and breathy, lust-drunk and hazy.

"God, you're gonna feel so fucking good. I'm gonna come so fucking hard while you're fucking me, baby."

"Shit," I hiss, my cock already twitching out a string of pre-cum on my thigh. I stand up on my knees and pull my fingers from Rowan's depths as slowly as my desperation allows.

Every nerve in my body ignites, skin blazing, as I grip Rowan's hip with one hand, my cock with the other, and press my tip to his hole. A few firm rocks of my hips pops my head inside, fogging my head and blending my thoughts into incomprehensible pulp.

The sounds Rowan makes as he slaps his palm against the headboard are guttural and indecipherable. He's so tight and warm and perfect that I almost can't stop myself from plunging into him fully, but I still myself with just my head buried into him and ask if he's okay.

"Mmmm," his gut-sounds produce.

My eyes roll back as I push my hips forward, burrowing deeper. "Holy shit, Row," I whimper.

He whimpers along with me, and I reflexively glide my palm up and down his spine to soothe him. When I realize I never lubed my cock, I draw back and pop my head out of him slowly.

"Turn over," I urgently command.

While I slather my dick in Astroglide, Rowan hastily flips onto his back. I pick his legs up and press his knees close to his armpits. *So fucking flexible.* I lift his balls and roll them in my hand as I line myself up to his asshole again.

This time, when I press forward—*oh my God*—I'm sucked in like I belong there.

Rowan gasps, eyes popping as I nearly bottom out in one thrust.

I plant my hands on either side of his head and look down into his eyes. "You good?"

"Mhmm," he hums, but his face screws up in a tight grimace, and his fingers dig into my sides like he's afraid of blowing away.

"Tell me if you need to stop," I murmur through a type of pleasure I've never felt before. Another inch or two and I'm grinding my hips against Rowan's ass, fully submerged in his heat. "God, you feel incredible."

Rowan's mouth hangs slack, his eyes wide but barely focused. I'm not sure if he's looking at my mouth or my nose, but I lean down and touch both of mine to both of his. His whimpers become mine, and mine become his. I buck my hips, and he mewls like he's in pain while murmuring words like, *"yes, yes, fuck, more, yes."*

Sweat covers my body as I feel my temp skyrocket. I bury my face in Rowan's neck and seal my torso to his while I hump inside him harder and quicker than I probably should. I'm seeing red, but it's not anger. It's all the blood my heart is pumping in overdrive to keep my cock swollen and my stamina up.

"T—Tom—Tommy!" Rowan cries, pushing on my shoulder and shoving his arm between our perspiring bodies.

Between us, Rowan takes hold of his shaft. That raging, purple tip is dribbling fluid. My stomach and his are glistening with it, and more drools over his abs now.

"Fu—Fuck, I'm—" he whimpers before biting hard on his bottom lip.

I prop myself higher and replace Rowan's hand with mine so he can clamp both his hands over his mouth. I pump his length twice as fast as I fuck him. In a matter of seconds, he's grunting into his palms as cum sluices from his pulsing cock to join the puddle of pre across his body.

The sight enraptures me, ironically keeping me from climax with how intently I'm focused on providing Rowan's. When he's spent enough to gasp and tug my hand from his shaft, I reseal our bodies together, glued with his spunk, and I moan into his ear that I'm close.

Hugging his arms around me, Rowan breathlessly murmurs, "That's it. That's it, baby boy. Come for me. Let it out."

"Fuck!" I grunt against his cheek as I feel an electrical current of pleasure overwhelm my senses. My hips go wild, rutting inside Rowan with abandon while I empty my balls as deep inside him as I can reach.

Time ceases to exist. There are no seconds, only heartbeats. I melt on top of Rowan like I'm made of water, and I count each soft thump from Rowan's chest like I'm counting sheep at bedtime. As sweaty and sticky as I am, nothing beats this feeling. The euphoria of just being *here*, with *him*.

"I love you, Tommy," Rowan says before kissing my heated cheek.

I hum, testing out my post-coital voice box. I turn my head and kiss Rowan's lips. "I love you too."

29
Rowan

It takes only minutes for Tommy to fall asleep on top of me, drowsy from the travel and that monster of an orgasm he had. He's still nestled inside me when he drifts off. As he softens, I'm able to wiggle my hips enough that he slips from me, and I seal up tight like nothing ever happened. *Oh, but it happened.* I feel the ache in my bowels and the soreness in my anus. There's pleasure in the discomfort, though. I grind my ass against the mattress just to amplify the sensation.

I let Tommy drool on my shoulder until the chill outside seeps inside, and I'm shivering despite Tommy's body heat. I nudge him awake, and we clean up our mess with a washcloth I wet in the bathroom sink, then we burrow ourselves under the comforter and sheets, taking full advantage of a bed that's actually equipped for two bodies. Still, we don't stray far from each other. We stay tangled. Touching, kissing, breathing against one another like we're melding into one.

Sometimes, I'm tucked to Tommy's side, sticking my nose in his armpit and rubbing my thigh against his soft dick. Sometimes, Tommy's tucked to my side, mouth on my shoulder and his fingertips swirling in the hairs across my chest.

When Tommy cages himself over me, the memory of us fucking is enough to harden me, but my dick is still too tender to be touched. I keep my hands on Tommy's body, and he keeps his on my face, cradling my jaw as he dips his tongue into my mouth.

We make out slowly, one lazy kiss morphing into many more.

"Marry me," Tommy murmurs so quietly I'm almost convinced I imagined it.

My chest vibrates a quiet chuckle. "In Utah?"

"Wherever." There's a sneakiness behind his bashful smile as he pokes the tip of my nose with his. "When we get back home, I'll drive us to Vegas."

"Damn, that was some fuck, huh?"

"I'm serious," he claims, and his sparkling eyes make me think maybe he actually is serious.

I jitter my fingertips up his sides to make him laugh, and I tell him to cut it out.

"It doesn't have to be a mid-century modern, you know?" he says. "It could be a Craftsman, or a Spanish Colonial. Hell, I'll even settle for a split-level, or just some shitty studio apartment. As long as it's ours."

It's easier to assume he's joking, because believing him makes my heart beat painfully in my chest. It conjures all sorts of thoughts I've been trying not to dwell on. Future-thoughts. One-year-from-now thoughts. Five-years-from-now thoughts. Twenty... Tommy has a way of making all my worries disappear while simultaneously overloading my mind with quandaries I never anticipated. I've been so used to being alone that this is the first time I've been able to imagine my life with another person.

But Tommy's my baby. No matter what. Nothing's going to separate a dude from his baby, right? Only thing I can think of is soccer. The thing that I've let rule my life so the horrors wouldn't. The thing I still convince myself is more important than anything, even Tommy. Soccer is my passion, but Tommy is the love of my life. Both of them are my heart and soul, and I don't know how to rectify that yet.

All I know for sure is that I'm never leaving Tommy, so until he gives up on me, he's stuck with me.

When I stay silent longer than I should, the sparkles in Tommy's eyes sober, and he says, "I'm sorry. I'm just joking. Swear."

"Hey." I peck his pouted lips and splay my hands across his back. "You're mine. Don't need a marriage license to prove it."

"If we ever get married, then I would be your family, and you would be mine. For real."

Oh, babyface.

My chest feels impossibly tight, my whole body warm and tingly, spreading heat to my face that I'm sure is turning red. Speechless, I answer Tommy's musing by wrapping my arms around him and flattening his body on mine. I hug him tight, my nose under his ear and my fingers pressing into his back muscles.

Trying to lift the mood, I murmur, "We're already family, remember? I'm your dad."

Thankfully, he giggles at that while nuzzling his face into my neck.

I tell him I love him, and he says it back, then I whisper, "Will you do me a favor?"

"Anything."

Once we reluctantly separate from one another, I tug on some shorts from my bag, then find my electric trimmer in one of the inner compartments. I hand it over as soon as Tommy finishes dressing in a pair of boxers.

Quirking a curious brow, Tommy asks, "And what body part am I shaving tonight?"

Blushing, I say, "My head, fucker."

"Yeah?" He steps close, sticking his hand to my head and running his fingers across my hair that I've let grow out too long. "I've been waiting to find out what your hair looks like grown out. It's almost long enough for me to know if it's curly or not."

"It is. I don't like my hair, though, and I hate going to have it cut, so I usually just buzz it myself."

Hand drifting to the nape of my neck, Tommy agrees to buzz it for me.

I take the chair from the writing desk and move it into the bathroom, and Tommy makes quick work trimming my hair down to stubble. Through the mirror, I watch him dust the stray clippings from my head with his palms.

"Why don't you like your hair?" he asks.

"When it's grown out, it looks just how my dad's looked in his mugshot."

Tommy's eyes connect with mine in the mirror, a somber expression I wish I hadn't put there. Still petting my scalp, Tommy says, "It's not his hair. It's on your head. It's yours. No matter what it looks like."

"I know," I sigh. "Still like it better this way."

Thankfully, he smiles. He presses a kiss to the top of my head and says, "I like it too." He hugs his arms around my shoulders and touches his lips to my temple. "Fucking hottie."

I blush and snicker, turning my head and tilting my chin to kiss his mouth.

Then, it occurs to me... "Shit, man. We missed dinner."

"Fuck." He straightens up and darts his eyes around the small bathroom like there might be food stuck to the walls. "7-Eleven?"

Ick. "I guess. Shower first?"

With a funny waggle of his eyebrows, Tommy drops his boxers.

While Tommy washes my back for me, his hand slipping between my ass cheeks, I realize I just lost my virginity. Getting fucked for the first time by someone who loves me has been on my bucket list for years, and for years, it seemed as unattainable as climbing K2. I never thought, in all those years, the man who would fuck me and love me in tandem would be the baby-faced midfielder from Emerson Middle School and Johnson High.

You're gay because you're supposed to be loved by a man.

I still think about that. Right now especially, as Tommy curls his arms around me and presses his half chub against my ass, warm water speckling our bodies in a cloud of steam. Maybe I'm not gay because of the abuse, but because my soulmate is a boy. Maybe I'm gay so that I can know this indescribable feeling of love at the hands of the most incredible person I've ever met.

In the hallway, we run into Levi and Raisel, who also missed dinner. Raisel brought his PlayStation, and they got caught up playing Madden. Hopefully they had the volume up loud enough that they couldn't hear me and Tommy fucking.

The four of us make the trek to 7-Eleven together, talking shit the whole way about this and that. I'm trying to be social and charming, keeping Levi and Raisel occupied on topics besides the obvious one. I've decided it's fine to be out-of-the-closet gay so long as no one's making a big fuss about it. So we talk about tomorrow's opponents, their strengths and their weak spots. Levi's been Snapchat stalking a few of the Utah boys, so he's got some quality taunting material up his sleeve, if we're ever in a bind.

At the store, I go straight for the refrigerator section and find pre-packaged sandwiches, Babybel cheeses, and hard-boiled eggs. Tommy is so tall, his head sticks up over the aisles, so I find him quickly. Go figure, his arms are laden with snack cakes and chips.

"Really, Tommy?"

He sends me a timid smile, shrugging his shoulders. "Every dinner needs dessert, right?"

"We've got a match tomorrow. You eat all that shit tonight, you'll be wearing it on the pitch tomorrow. I got you a sandwich."

Groaning, Tommy concedes, shoving the chips back on the rack in front of him. "Fine, but I'm getting the Trolli's and the mini donuts, and you're gonna thank me later when we're in bed and you've got a sugar craving."

I laugh, because sugar cravings are all Tommy. Okay, sometimes I crave the occasional slushy, but the only thing I crave in bed is Tommy's delicious body. "Alright, hand it over. I'll pay."

Figures Levi and Raisel are ordering a giant pizza from the hot foods menu. I swear, if we lose tomorrow, I'm blaming it on those carb addicts. Waiting behind them in line, Tommy slips his arm around my waist and tightens me to his side. Probably notices me shivering. I'm not used to Utah weather, and it's just as chilly in here as it is outside, only less windy.

I must be fuck-drunk still, because it doesn't occur to me how we must look until we step up to the counter in tandem and the big dude behind the register is eyeing us with a wrinkled up nose like he's smelling something foul on us.

Fucking bigot. But I hate myself the most right now, because I shrug Tommy's arm off when I drop our haul on the counter. While the bigot rings us up, he's trading glances between me and Tommy like we're a math problem, and my guess is this dude didn't get very far in grade-school math. "You two broth-ers?" he asks, and I roll my eyes.

"Yeah, man," I deadpan. "Just treating my baby brother to some snacks before I tuck him into bed and sing him to sleep."

Off to the side, I hear Levi and Raisel snickering.

Under the cashier's breath, he mutters, "Damn queers," and it makes my skin bristle with rage.

"What the hell did you say?" I seethe in the moment before Tommy tugs me back. He puts his broad body between me and the counter.

"How much, man?" Tommy asks, his voice as deep as al-ways, but dull now. No inflection, all business. It pisses me off. Not because of him, but because he's got to play nice with this neanderthal who's eyeing me over Tommy's shoulder like I'm scum.

Tommy takes his wallet out of his back pocket and hands the dude his card, which only pisses me off more. Tommy is perfect, but the situation sucks ass. To make it worse, Levi and Raisel are watching, and they're shaking their heads at me as if to say, "It's not worth it." I know it's not worth it, but worth's got nothing to do with how livid I am.

"Y'all from California?" asks the neanderthal.

"So what?" Tommy says.

The neanderthal scoffs, for whatever reason, and asks if we'd like a bag for all our shit. When it's all bagged and in Tommy's hand, I sidle up and take it from him while slipping my free arm around his waist. "Thanks, baby," I tell him, while glaring daggers at the sour-faced dickhead.

"Let's go," he says, slipping his arm around my shoulders, and we head for the door, not waiting for the pizza twins.

We let go of each other as soon as we're outside, and I scowl into the night as I march toward the Best Western.

"Hey." Tommy jogs to catch up, and his palm closes around the nape of my neck. "Don't let that asshole get to you."

"I'm not," I grit, jaw tight and my eyes still aching in their sockets, because that asshole clearly got to me. At least I'm not cold anymore. No longer shivering, but I'm shaking with anger. "Just wanna get back to the hotel. I'm fucking starving."

"It's my fault. I shouldn't have put my arm around you like that."

"Don't do that. It's not your fault. That dude is a miserable fuck."

"Yeah," Tommy agrees, throwing his arm around me. He slows me down by pressing me to his side and smooching my temple. "But, we're not. We're great fucks."

A blush heats my face even more. "You think I'm a great fuck?"

"Words cannot describe the caliber of your ass, Row. That dude in there was just jealous he'll never experience an orgasm half as good as the one your ass gave me."

Flushed and grinning, I still somehow complain. "That prick doesn't deserve even the weakest of handjobs."

Tommy takes my hand that's not gripping our food bag and brings my palm to his crotch. He's hard, bulging against the fly of his jeans. "What do I deserve?" he asks hotly.

Smirking incredulously at his devilish babyface, I answer, "Anything you want, baby boy. Just you name it."

Suddenly, I'm only starving for one thing, and it's not among the many snacks weighing down the bag around my arm. As soon as we get back to our room, that bag gets tossed on the desk and forgotten, and our clothes become heaps across the carpet. I've got Tommy sprawled across the unmade bed, and I'm sitting on his thighs, slathering his pink, raging cock in clear lube. My fist moves so effortlessly along his thick shaft, and I can't decide which sight is more arousing, his cock weeping in my hand or his face all twisted in pleasure.

"Tell me what you want," I rasp.

His hands are on me, roaming my bare thighs and gripping my knees. "I wanna fuck you. Wanna live inside you."

I gulp, my boner pulsing, the tip tapping against Tommy's balls with each twitch of arousal. I'm still full of his cum from earlier, well aware that he pumped way more inside me than leaked out onto the duvet. My guts still ache from the pounding he gave me when he was past the point of no return, yet my body still craves him.

Fuck, I really am a bottom bitch.

"Baby, I can't be too sore for tomorrow."

He moans through his teeth, hips bucking against my fist. "C'mon, I'll make it hurt so good."

A wimpy little moan squeaks past my gaped mouth. Tommy's language tells me he's too close. I force my hand off his cock and massage his balls instead, lifting and kneading them, stroking my thumb between them.

"You're insatiable," says the pot to the kettle.

"Didn't used to be," he whines. "My ex had to guilt me into fucking her."

My nostrils flare, a sudden twinge of anger clenching my heart at the allusion to a time when Tommy had been with someone else. He may have fucked that girl, but she never had him. Not really. Not the way I do. I lean over him, planting my elbows beside his head and touching my forehead to his. Our eyes connect, and so do our cocks. I feel his jump against mine, and he moans from just that simple touch.

"That's because you're a little gay boy," I grit, a fire in my eyes that's only one percent jealousy, and ninety-nine percent lust. "And you're mine. Even when you were with her, you were mine. You've always been mine. Ever since I first laid eyes on your pretty face. The prettiest boy I ever saw. *My boy*. Do you understand?"

"Mhm." He nods quickly, lips pouted and his eyes blazing with desperation. His hands are already on my ass, fingers touching me where he claimed me earlier. Where I claimed him.

"I might be your bottom bitch, but I'm still your daddy. Understand?"

"Row," he whimpers. "I'm gonna come."

The admission widens my eyes, and I look down between us to see his cock raring red and drooling.

Holy shit, he's about to come.

I sit up quickly and plant my ass back on his thighs.

To calm him, I first calm myself.

"Shh," I coo, gliding my hands up his body. I trace his pecs and thumb his perfect pink nipples to nubs. "Relax, baby. It's not time to come yet."

His hands grip my knees, and I can tell they're itching to touch his cock, but he's too good of a boy to try something like that. "I'm sorry," he whispers, before clamping his teeth over his plump bottom lip.

"Nuh uh. Don't say that." I run my palms down his sides and along the v-shape of his pelvis, stopping short of his cock and skating over his abs. "I got you too worked up."

"You're perfect," he breathes.

"I'm the one who should be sorry. For getting so mad earlier. I just don't like when people disrespect you. And us."

Looking into my eyes, Tommy says, "People are gonna do what they're gonna do. As much as it sucks, we're the lucky ones, because we're happy. Right?"

"I'm happy," I say, and the words sound shockingly sincere, like maybe I actually am happy. Not just happy with Tommy, but *happy* happy.

"Me too." Tommy smiles like he means it, too, despite all the shit life has been throwing at him. "I think you came into my life at exactly the right time. When I needed you the most."

My heart jumps, my arms covered in goosebumps. "Oh, baby boy," I sigh wistfully. "I think I've always needed you."

"You got me."

I lean forward, capturing Tommy's mouth the way he's captured my heart, tender and timid, but ripe with desire. Our lips part together, and our tongues dance. His hands are back on my ass, and I moan when his fingertip circles my rim.

So needy.

But I'm needy too. I never thought I'd meet a man who's as needy for me as I am for him. Is that what a soulmate is? Because my soul feels tethered to Tommy in a way that makes me understand why his mind would impulsively go to marriage and family. Those things are forever. I meant what I said, though. He already is my family.

I trail my mouth down to Tommy's chest, kissing the taut flesh stretched over firm muscle, and I take a nipple between my lips. Sucking gently, I flick the tip of my tongue across the nub as I locate its twin with my thumb.

"Feels so good," Tommy sighs, a warm palm cradling the back of my head.

Picking my chin up, I look into Tommy's eyes and repeat, "Tell me what you want."

"Wanna fuck you all night. Over and over until there's no more cum left in my body, because it's all inside you."

I'm blushing, eyes wide with lust as I imagine that exact scenario. My thumb is still circling his nipple. I lean my hips down just enough to press our cocks together. "Ask me nicely."

"Can I fuck you, please?" he sighs.

Sitting up, I reach for the Astroglide and pop the cap, but I still myself before dolling out a line onto my fingers. Eyeing Tommy pointedly, I say, "That's not good enough, baby boy. If you want me to let you shove your pretty cock up my ass, you're gonna have to try again."

He moans and squirms, hips shifting to creating a modicum of friction between our cocks. *"Please,"* he begs. "Please, *daddy?"*

My nostrils flare for a different reason now. Shock, joy, and overwhelming lust. "That's it," I praise as I squeeze a healthy amount of lube onto my fingers. I bring them around to my ass and smear it along my crack before wrapping them around Tommy's cock to add to what's already coating him.

Hips bucking from that simple contact alone, Tommy moans, "Please, daddy. I need to get inside you."

"That's it, baby." I stand up on my knees and crawl forward until I'm straddling his hips and holding his cock between my cheeks, wedging the tip right up against my still tender hole.

"Fuck," he grunts as his hips jerk upward. The force causes a sudden splitting of my ass as he breaches me in one quick thrust.

"Unnnnnghh!" I whimper toward the ceiling, my legs quivering as they struggle not to collapse below me. I fall forward, caging myself over Tommy while he fucks the first few inches of his dragon dick inside me. "Shh, shh, shh. S-slow, baby. Slow." I press my forehead to his shoulder, catching my breath as his hips steady, and his hands roam the length of my back.

"So close," he whines in my ear before swiping his tongue across the shell.

Planting my palms on his solid chest, I push myself upright, and in the same motion, I ease my ass down over Tommy's pulsing cock. "Holy fuck, you're huge," I moan, having to tug on my ass cheeks to ease him all the way in.

For the life of me, I don't know how he fits, but he does. I feel his dick reaching places inside me that shouldn't feel as good as they do. How do I love this? How do I impale myself on Tommy's humongous steel-rod cock and feel more pleasure than I ever have in my life?

His girth presses against my prostate, rubbing me in a way that creates fireworks under my skin. My eyes roll and my chest heaves. I'm gripping Tommy's chest and grinding my ass on every single inch of him.

"Oh, fuck!" He grabs my hips and lifts me high enough that he can pump his cock inside me and control the pace.

"T-T-Tommy." My chin drops and I check on the state of my dick, swollen so stiff my foreskin feels tight and my crown is throbbing. Clear fluid dribbles from my tip, pooling on Tommy's body, and my balls are so tight it's almost painful.

I make sounds I barely hear over the thump of my heartbeat in my ears, and my whole body is shivering despite how red-hot I am. Just like the first time, this all feels like an orgasm, but it's been minutes since it began, and somehow, my body knows a bigger climax is pending. I'm almost afraid of it, like my cock might actually explode.

"I'm gonna come!" I cry, actual tears obscuring my vision.

"Yes, yes, fuck yes. Me too," Tommy grunts as he bucks his cock in and out of me.

Arching my back, I angle my cock downward enough that with every thrust inside me, the underside of my cockhead grazes Tommy's washboard stomach, and the lights flashing behind my eyes suggest it's just enough to get me to the finish line.

I'm fucking delirious with how badly I need to finish.

"Fuck me. Fuck me," I whimper like a nymphomaniac.

Tommy tugs my hips down, pressing all of himself inside me as he growls, "I'm coming, daddy," and I'm fucking done for.

Fucked.

Fluid jets from my cock, and this time it's the good stuff. The stuff that empties me out to make room for unbridled euphoria. Waves of bliss crash into me, turning me into a mewling, quivering mess until I collapse on top of Tommy, but even then, my body is still grinding on his lap like it's stuck in a loop. Every time my ass reflexively clenches around Tommy's girth, another shock of pleasure racks through me, and another grunt escapes Tommy's throat.

Even after I'm sated, my hips still rock. I don't quit grinding on Tommy until he's flaccid and slipping from my hold. A trickle of Tommy's hot seed rolls down my scrotum.

Tommy holds me, kissing the top of my head like I'm the baby now. I don't mind it sometimes. Giving up control. Truth is, I'll let Tommy do anything to me. He can have all of me whenever he wants it. I might make him work for it, but I'll always give him what he wants.

"My boy," I whisper, so spent I could pass out right here and now.

Only problem is, now that I am sated, my body remembers how starved I am. For the sake of my grumbling stomach, I force myself to stay awake.

Reluctantly, I peel my body from Tommy's and find a familiar mess coating both our bodies. I check his face, and he's smiling crookedly at me, like he's admiring something new about me. It flusters me, and I look away.

"Can I ask you something?" I whisper, turning onto my back beside him.

His head turns so he can keep his gaze glued to my face. "Of course."

"Do you think I'm weird?"

Tommy laughs suddenly, turning enough to press his face into my neck. He kisses my pulse and says, "You're a total weird-o, Rowan Hughes, and I love it."

30
Rowan

I hate Thanksgiving and always have. Are there any foster kids who like Thanksgiving? It took until my tween years to decide holidays weren't for people like me—people with no family, no real friends, and no purpose for living outside of a daily routine of school and soccer.

Now, I still hate holidays, but I sort of have a family, my best friend says he wants to marry me one day, and I've got more reasons to live than I ever did before. Reasons to be thankful...

It's backwards maybe, but when a dude in a black robe at the Sacramento Court House granted the no-contact order against *that woman* without even a hearing, I've felt more thankful than ever knowing my birth mom has to stay the fuck away from me, or else. There's no forgiveness in my heart for her, only resentment, and everyone I've talked to about it says that's okay, which is basically Tommy, Matt, and Xia. I've been thinking, though, and after the NCAA tournament, win or lose, I'm going to try going back to therapy. It did fuck all when I was a teenager, but I'm not a kid anymore. I actually want to get on with my life now. I want to enjoy life. Not just soccer and porn, but *life*.

Unfortunately, life is chock-full of anxieties, even when everything is going pretty well. Got the restraining order, lost my virginity, I'm about to graduate a semester early, and my team is still undefeated. But it's Thanksgiving, which is a huge deal for Matt and Xia, and they somehow convinced me to invite Tommy and his whole fucking family over for the party.

Now I'm pacing, stress-sweating in the backyard, because the warmth inside is too much to bear. Too much heat, too many people, too many ways this could all blow up. It's not Erica or Tommy's adorable nephew that I'm worried about. It's his mother. I'm clearly not good with mothers as it is, but from everything Tommy has told me, his mom is a great woman so long as she thinks Tommy is straight, which means she needs to think I'm straight too.

Even when I was lying to everyone about being straight, people still thought I was gay!

This is a mistake.

I hate this.

There are so many people here that they've filtered into the yard, so now I can't even pace by myself. Xia's got more relatives than I've got teammates, and it seems like they all showed up, and Matt's side is a bunch of macho, country dudes from Redding wearing camo ball caps with their dress shirts. I barely know any of them, and whenever I get caught up in their small talk, they treat me like I'm Matt and Xia's charity case.

Even if Matt and Xia are my family, their families are not my families, and nothing makes me feel like more of a foster kid than extended family members constantly asking me how long I'm planning on sticking around.

At least now I have a bona fide answer for them. Leaving in a few months, to the city of whatever MLS team wants me. I'll be gone like a final gust of winter wind, and I won't miss this place at all. Except Matt, Xia, the kids and…Tommy.

When I get drafted, what am I gonna do about Tommy?

It's a question I've been asking myself a lot, but I keep pushing it away, turning it into something I'll worry about later as if later will never come. But the draft is next month, then we've got until February to figure it out. February isn't much time, but it might be enough for Tommy to smarten up and move on, find someone better who's not so fucking weird. Just because I'm the first dude to touch his dick doesn't mean I'm going to be the only one.

Don't think about that.

Don't think about that.

Don't think about that.

"Rowan!" Xia's half sticking out of the open back door, hollering to me over the sounds of her cousins' kids running around in the driveway. "Tommy's here!"

Shit.

I've been so busy pacing and mentally freaking out that I forgot to check my phone for his "on my way" text.

"Where's your sweater?" Xia asks, tugging on my t-shirt to stop me on my way into the house.

"Too hot."

She gives me that *boy please* look that makes me feel like she's my real mom. Real moms are always pressed about their kids not wearing sweaters when it's cold, I guess.

"I'll put it on before dinner. Promise. You remember what we talked about, right? Be cool."

Folding her arms across her chest, she says, "Rowan. I don't need to *be cool*. I am the definition of cool."

"Yeah, sure." No time to challenge her, so I skate past and sidle through everyone packed into a too-small house, keeping my chin lifted until I spot the top of Tommy's head poking up over everyone's.

The first glimpse I catch of him, my stomach flips and I can't help the grin that stretches my cheeks. Doesn't matter that we worked out together just yesterday. As good as he looks in joggers and a sweat-stained tee, there's something princely about him in a cardigan and chinos, his hair blow-dried and fluffy like he's some sort of boy band pop star. When he smiles back at me, he glows like there's a spotlight permanently fixed above his head, putting sparkles in his sapphire eyes.

"Hey," we both say at the same time. His arms open first, and mine follow, and he hugs me for real. Like he missed me. Like eighteen hours apart is just too damn long now. I can't imagine what he could have missed about me, but I know I missed him. Missed him enough that I forget we're supposed to be playing shit cool.

"You're freezing," he says beside my ear.

"You're so warm," I say back.

I let him go, clear my throat and shove one hand in my pocket like that'll make all the difference, and I turn to the woman beside Tommy who I recognize as his sister.

"Nice to see you again. Thank you for coming." I shake her hand and pretend like Tommy hasn't told me a laundry list of personal details about her. She's beaming, even brighter than Tommy, like she wants to pinch my cheeks and tell me how precious I am.

I lean down to the kid hanging onto her arm and hold my fist out toward him. "Hey, lil' dude. Hope you're hungry."

"He's feeling shy," Erica says, laying her palm on Maverick's head.

"That's cool," I say to him. "I'm shy sometimes too. I was just hanging out in the backyard where it's a little less crowded. You wanna kick a ball around? I bet you're already a soccer star like your uncle, huh?"

Mav's head shakes against Erica's hip, but he's smiling. Not bright, but enough.

It's not like I'm dying to be scrutinized by Tommy's mom, but I do notice she's not around. Besides Erica, the only women around us look related to Xia or Matt. No one that looks like Tommy.

"Where's your mom?" I ask Tommy, and I watch while his light dims to a somber half smile and a shrug.

The look he gives me speaks a million words, but without time to hear them all, I just slip my hand into his and hold it between us. Fuck being cool. I'd rather be with Tommy. He laces our fingers together while I play host, not giving a shit if Matt's hick half-brothers have a problem with it. Only times they talk to me are to tease me about how gay soccer is anyway, so it shouldn't shock them I'm actually gay.

I take them around, introducing Tommy's family to mine. Matt is as outwardly emotional as a potted plant, so I don't worry about him embarrassing me. When I introduce him as my dad, he doesn't correct me, and that feels better than I ever thought it would. He pats my shoulder, squeezes the back of my neck, and tells Erica how proud he is of me, like I really am his kid.

Xia is still in the kitchen with her mom and aunties working on the sides while her brother grills up meat in the backyard. Her family is the definition of *a lot,* but they're more open-minded and open-armed than Matt's side. When I introduce Xia as my mom, her aunties coo over me like I'm Bruno, rattling my shoulders and calling me *mijo.*

Face red, I shut my eyes to spare myself from their giddiness while Xia wraps her arm around me and tells Erica all sorts of embarrassing shit.

"Your brother has been so good for Rowan," she gushes. "I don't think I've ever seen him as happy as he's been since these two started seeing each other. Rowan would tell me they were just training, but this kid turned into a lighthouse any time he mentioned Tommy. He was so obvious."

"Okay, okay," I tell her, finally opening my eyes to give her a warning look. *You're not being cool.*

"Tommy too!" Erica exclaims, swatting Tommy's bicep. "I swear, every time he looked at his phone, he was blushing. Tommy told me Rowan was a girl, though."

"That's not exactly what I said," Tommy interjects.

"I had no clue Tommy was gay," Erica says. "I mean, he got teased a little in elementary school, but kids can be like that. He'd only ever dated girls."

Xia answers, "I don't think Rowan's dated anyone before Tommy, but we've known he was gay for a while. Since he was fifteen or sixteen. There was just something about him—"

Needing to escape this hellish conversation, I zero in on Maverick and ask him if he'd like to meet some of the other kids. I know Lena is in the backyard playing with her little cousins, and she's right around Mav's age.

"That sounds fun," Tommy quickly exclaims, letting go of my hand to scoop Maverick up into his muscular arms. "Let's leave the grown-ups alone to talk about how gay your uncle is."

"Tommy, I'm sorry," Erica laughs.

"We'll be out back." He plants a smooch on Erica's cheek like the tender boy he is, and he carries Mav through the front door, checking over his shoulder to make sure I'm following.

Right behind you, baby.

Stepping out into the late November chill, I realize how cold it actually is. My skin tightens beneath my white tee, and I tell

Tommy I'm going to grab my sweater from the garage. While I'm at it, I grab one of my soccer balls from the bin under my bed.

Mav's brown eyes glow when he sees me bouncing it between my hands, and Lena breaks away from her cousins to throw herself at me, asking to play.

"We're all gonna play," I tell her, bowling the ball across the grass toward Mav. "You wanna be on my team? You and me against Tommy and his nephew."

Being a soccer coach and all around sports nerd, Matt already has two pop-up goals set up on either end of the long yard. Sidelines are the flower bed against the perimeter fence and the cement path along the garage.

Takes about two minutes for our little match to be overrun with kiddos, and I'm not good enough of a babysitter to play referee to a full-blown youth league match. I let the kids' parents take over, and Tommy and I slip off to the side. I lean my back against the stucco wall of the garage, and Tommy puts his shoulder to wall beside me.

"This is cute," he says, pinching my crimson knit pullover. Xia bought it for me while out shopping for the kids' Thanksgiving outfits, and I immediately thought it looked dweebish. I'm not used to looking nice. My idea of nice is black on black, and my chain so I don't look poor. Tommy grazes his fingers across my neck, fishing my chain from underneath my sweater and laying it down overtop. "So cute," he murmurs, like he's saying it to himself.

I turn my gaze from the chaotic match and look into Tommy's eyes. "Why didn't your mom come?"

Those stunning blues flit downward, studying my chain as his fingers continue to play with it. "Didn't wanna lie. I know we agreed to tell her you're my best friend, and you are my best friend, but that's not all you are. And she's got to know eventually, before she starts setting me up with her friends' daughters."

"You told her about us, baby?"

"Told her we're in love. That you're my person. That I've been gay ever since those kids beat me up in school." He chuckles, a small bit of morbid humor behind it. "Told her it's ironic she signed me up for team sports so I wouldn't grow up to be a sissy, and now I'm dating my team captain."

Reaching up, I cup Tommy's jaw and press my thumb under his chin until his eyes meet mine. "You're not a sissy. Did she call you that?"

"Nah. It was just...the way she looked at me, I guess. Like I'm not the man she wanted me to be. Not mad, but disappointed. She doesn't wanna meet you. I think she'd rather just pretend I never told her. I think she'll come around, though. In time."

I'm compelled to apologize, but I'm also trying this new thing where I stop acting like I'm a terrible person. I didn't turn Tommy gay, and I didn't create all the turmoil in his life, even though I certainly play a role in it. My job as his boyfriend is to protect him when I can, to comfort him when I can't, and to love and support him.

"She will come around," I tell him instead. "You're a great man. She'll remember that, eventually."

Tugging me into his arms, we finish that *I missed you* hug, and he tells me he loves me.

"I love you too," I hum with my cheek against his. "My beautiful boy."

Dinner is a marriage as oddly complementary as Matt and Xia's. Asada and grilled chicken, beans and rice, with warm tortillas, plus the traditional fixings of mashed potatoes, stuffing and mac and cheese. Maybe it's blasphemy, but there's little better than Xia's brother's asada coupled with Matt's mom's mac and cheese.

Shamelessly, all I really want to do is take Tommy to my room and ravish him. Nuzzle my nose all over his clean, smooth skin and eat his cock for dessert. But with Erica and Mav here, there isn't a great time to sneak away, and I think it's important to Tommy that his sister likes me. It's important to me too. I show her all of my practiced charm, and show Mav all of my practiced child-tolerance, and by the time the Mathison clan is heading for the door, I think I've won them over.

I walk them to Tommy's truck and say goodbye, but before Tommy can climb up into the driver's seat, I ask him if he wants to hang later. I want to take him back to Mustache Jack. They're open tonight for a Thanksgiving event, but I don't really care what the event is about. I just want to take Tommy some place where he'll feel accepted, where we can drink a little and kiss a lot.

"Hell yeah," he whispers, eyes flickering down to my mouth. He hooks a finger on my chain and draws me forward, kissing me in the street with his family in the car behind him. Just a soft, lippy kiss after sundown, but it's a public kiss, nonetheless. An *I don't give a fuck* kiss that has my heart fluttering like crazy.

"Sleepover after?" he murmurs.

"You think I'd pick you up just to drop you back off?" I smirk. "I'm gonna help clean up here, then I'll text you."

It takes an extra two hours for Matt's more obnoxious family members to leave while I help Xia and her mom clean up. At one point, Matt's drunk cousin, Frank, slapped my shoulder and called me "one of the ladies." No one else heard, and I chose to clench my jaw and let it be, but it makes me think of what Tommy said.

Am I a sissy?

What the fuck does that even mean?

I'm not a sissy. Frank just doesn't like me. Unlike Xia's side, a lot of Matt's family members dislike me and always have. They think I'm a degenerate parasite, and now I'm a fag on top of it. It's one of the many reasons why, even if I call Matt my dad, he never will be. If he were my dad, his family wouldn't treat me like an interloper.

It's almost nine when I pick Tommy up, and we head straight for the bar. On the way, Tommy says his mom's avoiding him now—leaving the room when he enters, not answering when he speaks right to her. While he vents, I'm trying not to hate her. I just keep my hand on Tommy's thigh and tell him to be patient.

"You were patient with me when you didn't have to be," I say. "That's what I'm thankful for today. You."

He snickers despite our sober mood, grinning at my profile. "Rowan, you literally chased me down and gave me back something I love, asking for nothing in exchange. And that's after I punched you in the face. I was gonna be as patient with you as you needed. Even if you never kissed me back that day, I'd still be waiting for you. I'd wait forever for you."

It's hard to keep my eyes on the road when he's saying shit to make my heartbeat quicken and my face turn red. "Shit, baby boy. You think I'd let a sucker punch get in the way of us?"

"I like that. *Us.*" His hand slips behind my neck, gently kneading me there. Not the fatherly squeeze Matt gave me, but something tender and soothing. "Tommy and Rowan," he breathes.

Grinning like a madman, I turn my blinker on and roll into the lot beside Mustache Jack. "Alright, Mister Romantic. Let's get you a drink."

Turns out, the event tonight is a fundraiser for a local non-profit called the Found Family Project, a free, inclusive after school camp for queer and gender non-conforming youth to connect with mentors and peers that reflect their similar experiences. It feels serendipitous, almost discomfortingly so. It's not like I want to be reminded of how I had no one growing up, but it also feels important to realize there are a lot of kids today who might feel just as hopeless and alone as I did.

It's not preachy either, or a seminar like what we sat through at the Queer Alliance meeting. It's a drag show, the first one I've ever been to. Drink sales go to the organization, so I feel even better about the ten-dollar margaritas I buy for Tommy and myself. There are giveaways too. Who doesn't love free shit?

"Well, well, well!"

My spine stiffens as a familiar, grating voice fills my ears, and a second later, I'm flinching as a long, pale arm drapes over my shoulders. The face of an incredibly tall Swedish man pokes between Tommy and I, smirking like a sneak while we're waiting for our drinks at the bar.

Oscar.

"I heard a rumor there were a couple straight boys from the soccer team here, and you two are the straightest looking boys I've seen all night."

Rolling my eyes, I shrug Oscar away and lean over the bar to grab the two purple margaritas the bartender just set down. I pass him a twenty as Tommy tells Oscar, "We're not straight."

"No? You finally come out of the closet, Rowan?"

I shoot a glare at Oscar and hand Tommy his marg. "I was never straight. I just don't share my business with random people."

"Random people? After everything we've been through?" Oscar clutches his chest, feigning offense before telling Tommy, "We used to date. He broke my heart into a million pieces."

"No, we didn't. Don't tell him that."

Chortling, Oscar says, "No, no. I'm just joking. We're just friends. I'm Oscar."

Looking equally amused and perturbed, Tommy shakes Oscar's hand before taking a small sip. Then he snaps his fingers. "Men's volleyball captain?"

Oscar beams. "So Rowan has told you about me."

"Uh, yeah. Totally," Tommy chuckles, reaches out and hooks his arm around my waist.

"You must be Tommy," Oscar says. "I remember seeing your texts while I was putting my number into Rowan's phone, which he never used. Talk about a tease."

I'm glaring daggers at the flamboyant ass, but he is amusing. If it wasn't so flirtatious, I'd appreciate his snark a lot more.

"When was that?" Tommy asks me, one of his perfectly thick and golden brown eyebrows lifted.

Sighing against Tommy's side, I send him an apologetic smile. "While I was making you wait for me."

Like the angel Tommy is, he purses his lips against the side of my head and says, "You're good, sweetie. I seem to remember you making it up to me. In the outdoor weight gym."

My eyes widen at Tommy's mischievous smirk, and I glance at Oscar, who's snickering like a villain.

Oscar claps his hand on Tommy's shoulder, but puts his sight on me. "Have to say, Rowan. I can see why you turned me down. This might be the most beautiful man I've seen in my life. You two open, or..?"

"Dude, it's not gonna happen," I laugh, still blushing from what Tommy said.

"Fine, fine." He steps back, giving up the shtick. "If you guys want, my group is over at the booths. We're also planning a Denny's run after the show. So catch up with us if you're hungry."

"Thank, man. Nice to meet you." Tommy lets go of me to shake Oscar's hand again, a sweeter boy than I'll ever be despite his pet name for me.

Reclaiming me with his arm, Tommy leans in close to my ear, his fruity breath asking, "You didn't do anything with him, did you?"

"With Slenderman?" I balk. "Nah, I draw the line at six-two. I don't wanna look like a shrimp."

Tommy chuckles, tickling my cheek with his nose. "You know, in cleats I'm six-three."

I turn my head, grazing my lips against his. "In that case, I meant to say six-three."

We kiss, but it feels like making magic, and I can't wait to take this man home and make love to him. The night is young, though, so we'll finish our drinks first, watch a bit of the show, and be gay in public for a while before we go be even gayer in private.

"You make me feel lucky," I murmur the words Tommy told me not that long ago, but he smiles like I just came up with it myself.

31

Tommy

We're here. The NCAA championship match. The whole shebang. Winner takes all. Loser takes jack shit, except the honor of being second best, I guess. Who wants to be second best? I wouldn't be stressing as much as I am if not for how badly Rowan wants to win. Needs to win.

Soccer is his life, after all. Not just something someone stuck him into to teach him to be a man, but ended up loving. It's his purpose, and it's his last chance to win the College Cup for Sac State. Sure, it's a team effort, but none of us would be here without Rowan, and everyone knows it. Even Levi cooled it with the teasing. He and Rowan are more like friends than I've ever seen them, and it makes sense despite their contradictory personalities. Levi is the second best player on the team, after all. Rowan's right-hand guy in a lot of ways. If I'm being real honest, I'm sort of jealous about it. Can't be the Tommy and Rowan show if Levi is Rowan's go-to.

On top of my jealousy, I'm straight up stressing. Coach tells me I'm a starter today. For the biggest match, on the biggest stage, of my entire life.

"Think you can handle the pressure?" Coach asks like there's a right and wrong answer.

"Y-yeah. Totally. Thank you, sir."

"Don't let me down, kid." He walks off, and I walk in a daze until meeting Rowan halfway along the sidelines.

"Did you do this?" I ask him.

Still smiling, he shrugs. "It's McDonough's decision, not mine. All I did was tell him I need you on that field with me. That you're the best defensive midfielder we got next to Connor." He clasps his hands behind my head and draws my forehead to touch his. "This is it, baby boy."

"I know," I breathe, heart pounding in my chest.

"You got this."

"I'll try."

"You got this," he repeats, eyes pumped and fiery. "Say it."

"I got this."

His mouth covers mine, right here on the sidelines as our guys ready for a match of their lives and the stadium steadily fills. He smooches me firm where scouts are watching. Hell, where fucking ESPN is watching. It makes my spine tingle and my cock twitch. I have to separate myself from him just so I won't cause a scene in my shorts.

"I got this," I promise again, more to myself this time.

Walking the sidelines, I spot my family in the stands. They flew all the way here to see me. Even Ma. Another reason I can't fuck this up. They spot me, too, and wave like mad, like I'm a celebrity all of a sudden. I wave back, scared shitless but smiling anyway.

It's been two weeks since Thanksgiving, and between training, finals, and stealing as much time with Rowan as possible, it's gone by in a flash. Still, the hours where Ma and I sat on the porch, finally hashing out my life like filling in the gaps of a soap opera she missed too many episodes of, seemed to drag on for an eternity.

The worst part was when she asked if she'd done something wrong—if it was her fault, or someone else's fault. If Dad had done something before he ran off. Made me think of Rowan and all the shit he's got to cope with that I'll never understand, because the first person who touched me was a girl at a pool party when we were both fifteen and awkward, fumbling around in a laundry room.

"No one did anything," I insisted. "It's just part of who I am. Who I've always been. And I'm glad this is who I am. I like being gay. I like being myself. I like being able to tell you the truth, even if you're disappointed in me."

She never denied being disappointed in me, but she hugged me and told me she'll always love me. That I'll always be her son.

For now, I guess that has to be good enough.

On the field, before the whistle, Rowan shakes hands with the captain of the opposing team, a school out of Ohio. After the whistle blows, everything moves lightning fast, and I have to trust my muscle memory to remember where to be and when. There's so much going on, and the sheer amount of people around us amplifies the stakes to untenable heights.

"Focus, Tommy," Rowan tells me in passing, a quick tap to my shoulder like he caught me dozing. I'm not dozing, just dizzy.

Focus, Tommy.

Focus on the ball. Where is it? Stay on it.

Focus on your teammates. Where are they? What are they doing?

Focus on Rowan. Does he need you? He always needs you.

Focus on the opponents. Who's on them? Who are they on?

Focus on their goalie. Is he focused?

Focus on Coach. Why's he waving his arms? Stop focusing on Coach. He's not important.

Where's Rowan?

"Row!"

The second our eyes connect across the field, he torpedoes the ball across the grass and it smacks me right in the side of my cleat. I don't hesitate. I can't. The Ohio guys are coming for me, but I'm faster than them. Because of Rowan and his obsession with running, I'm faster than them.

"Tyson!" Levi calls out to me, which is helpful, because at this point, if Levi yelled my actual name, I'd assume he's talking to some other Tommy.

I knock it to him, and he makes the shot, but the Ohio goalie is always focused. Dude is a beast. Like the big boss in the last level of a video game.

How are we going to get through him?

By halftime, we're down 0-1. I'm not a fan of Brandon, our goalie, but he feels like shit for giving up the only goal in the game so far. Rowan pulls him aside for a pep talk, which is awkward, given that time Rowan shoved him against the lockers for talking shit.

Maybe teams are like families that way. They can talk shit, piss us off, disappoint us, but we're still a team. We need each other.

With the score the way it is, Coach can't afford to sub anyone who's still got fight in them, so when it's time for the second half to kick off, we all go back out.

One of the Ohio guys tips his chin toward me from across the half line. "Heard you suck your captain's dick, pretty boy," he leers through a nasally tone.

The hairs on the back of my neck stand up, and I'm flush with something close to contempt. That's what he wants.

Wants me to lose focus until the only thing I'm thinking about is how much I hate him for bringing up Rowan like that. If I stay contemptuous, he wins. If I don't give a fuck, maybe I win.

I tip my chin back at him. "Only when I'm hungry."

The dude seethes, muttering something under his breath. My ears don't catch it, but my mind hears *faggot*.

So what?

The whistle blows, and I focus.

Whatever Rowan said to Brandon worked, because he's not letting the ball touch net again, and Rowan's able to fake out the Ohio goalie just enough to put a point on our board.

1-1 now, taking a smidgen of the pressure off, but when it's anyone's game, it could still easily tip the other way.

Time is winding down, and the team is gassed. Coach subbed Connor out and put in Zeke. Even Levi looks like he's waning. But I'm good. I feel good, and as long as Rowan's still out there, I'll stay good.

The leering dickhead from Ohio has suddenly made it his mission to close me down. He's scrawny, but quick as a ninja.

"So which one of you has to take it up the ass after we beat you?" he rasps through his labored breaths. He's losing steam, which is good for me, but I'll let him think he's got me covered until the very last minute.

"You sound jealous. Your boyfriend dump you for someone with a bigger dick?"

"I'm not fucking queer like you," he spits.

"Sure about that?" I'm timing the play, eyes on Rowan, Levi, Raisel, and Zeke. "'Cause, you sure look like a cocksucker."

Raisel passes the ball to Rowan, and with a clear path between me and the goal, I see an in. But, just as I make my break from this sniveling creep, something sharp captures me in the ribs, jabbing at my kidney and knocking me on my ass.

"Fuck!" I roll over, trying to stand, but I only get as high as my knees before I'm crumpling over, clutching my side, and digging my forehead into the grass.

I hear a whistle blow, and I hear my name in Rowan's voice.

"Tommy!" He's at my side in seconds, on his knees with his palm on my back. "Tommy, you good?"

"The little cretin elbowed my fucking kidney," I groan into damp blades of grass.

Gripping my arm, Rowan pulls me to my feet, and I shake the pain off best I can. The ref is in my ear, telling me I'm due a penalty kick.

A penalty kick? I had a clear path before I went down. I was going to ditch the cretin, call for the ball, and win this fucking game for us while the goalie was looking the opposite way. I had it all mapped out in my head. Now I have to risk it going head to head with the final boss? *By myself?!*

Rowan has worked with me a lot on offense, but it's still a weak point. Rowan is way better at tricking goalies and faking directions.

"You got this, baby," Rowan pumps me up.

I got this.

The field clears for the showdown. Me versus the goalie. He stares me down like it'll rattle me, but it's nothing compared to Rowan's smolder. I count my strides backward. I steady myself. I swipe my wrist across my sweaty brow, and I plot my strategy.

It happens in a whirlwind. My heart lodges in my lungs, holding my breath hostage, and I kick the ball as hard as I can toward the right corner, and—

Net.

I fall back to my knees, gasping in a long breath that I then expel through an incredulous laugh. My head throbs with how loudly the stadium cheers, and I hear my teammates' voices doing the same. They're on me, shaking me, slapping my back, and calling me the G.O.A.T.

Someone helps me up. I don't know who, but Rowan's corralling us to finish the match. There's only a minute left, plus two for overage. Ohio is exhausted and demoralized while we're riding high. My side doesn't even hurt anymore. 2-1 feels so much sweeter than it ever has before, and when the time runs out, that's where the final score sits.

The field is mayhem. Our bench clears, everyone celebrating. Confetti falls from the rafters like it's the Super Bowl. I'm looking up at it all with as much wonder in my eyes as if it were snowfall in Sac Town.

I yelp as something like a punching bag smacks into my side, landing me back on my ass, flat on my back.

"You did it!"

I blink, and it's Rowan on top of me, caging me on his hands and knees, staring into my eyes the way he does before asking me to fuck him. The adrenaline, the elation, the atmosphere, and Rowan's fucking eyes. It all accumulates in my shorts, and I'm actually getting hard right now, in the center of the field surrounded by everyone.

"You did it!" Rowan repeats before colliding his mouth onto mine, latching our lips and kissing me like I'm food and he's starving. It only lasts a few seconds, but it's enough to steal the air from my lungs.

Standing on his knees, Rowan looks like an angel with gunmetal eyes as multi-color confetti sprinkles his head and shoulders. "You did it."

I sit up, snatching the back of his neck and touching our foreheads together the way he did before the match began. "We did it," I tell him. "*We* did it."

Throughout the draft process, Rowan kept the details of his convos between him and the clubs interested in him on the down-low. He didn't want to talk about it with me, and as far as I know, he never even talked about them with Matt. Rowan isn't a superstitious athlete, but everyone has their quirks. I assumed he didn't want to jinx anything.

The nagging, insecure voice inside my head is worried Rowan's tight lips mean he's fixing to go far away. Miami or New York maybe. Someplace far away from Sacramento and everyone in it. Wouldn't blame him. He's felt like he's had nothing here for so long that I imagine he's dreamt up a million fantasies about being some place else and starting fresh. But, starting fresh usually means starting *single.*

ESPN taps into a camera mounted over Matt and Xia's living room TV, because they know Rowan will be drafted. It's only a matter of when, and by which club. We all hang on bated breath, watching the draft coverage live. I'm beside Rowan, gripping his hand, almost as anxious as he is right now.

Last night, Rowan got in his head. Started talking nonsense, saying he won't get drafted by anyone on account of him being gay. Supposedly, there were some trolls in online forums saying cruel shit about my Row after our College Cup win, but they can fuck themselves. If people want to talk shit, they can do it to our faces so I can pummel them to the ground.

But I've also seen some supportive chatter about how special Rowan's draft will be because he's gay, like he's a true trailblazer. With all that comes a heck of lot more pressure, though.

There's so much sitting on Rowan's shoulders, he's vibrating with nerves beside me, but when the MLS commissioner steps up to the podium and announces that the San Jose Earthquakes are using their first round pick on Rowan Hughes of Sacramento State, I've never seen my boyfriend so fucking happy.

Grin reaching his ears, he leaps up from the sofa like he won the lottery. He lets go of my hand so he can swing his arms around me and hug me like we're both winners.

San Jose.

It's far, but it's not *far* far. It's not on the other side of the country. It's a two-hour drive. That's nothing. He can visit me all the time, or I can drive to him. We can make this work. Can't we?

I swallow all my anxieties down and focus on the moment—on Rowan's happiness, because he deserves this. No matter what comes of it, no matter what it means for us, Rowan deserves this, and I'm so unbelievably proud of him. My boyfriend is a pro soccer player!

As if he can read my mind, the first thing Rowan says to me when we have a second to ourselves is, "How's it feel that your boyfriend is a pro athlete?"

Staring into the warm depths of his eyes, I answer, "I think you know how it makes me feel."

Scared and horny.

The way Rowan's eyes flicker down to my crotch tells me he only suspects the latter, which is good. I don't want him to know I'm scared. Don't want to make this moment about me and my neediness.

He tosses a couple glances over his shoulders, probably making sure his family isn't watching, then he draws me close and leans his mouth beside my ear. "You know what this means, right?"

Circling my arms around his neck, I lean into him and relish his warmth, like it's another thing I'm about to lose come February. "Means you're a superstar."

"Means I'll be able to take care of you. For real."

My eyes blink in tandem with the flutter in my chest. I lean back enough to study Rowan's eyes, because I clearly can't read his mind as well as he can read mine. "What do you mean?"

Smile turning to a smirk, he asks, "What do you think it means?" That smirk falls as quickly as it appeared. "Unless...you wanna stay here."

"Stay here?"

"I know you'd have to change schools and uproot yourself, and you'll probably miss your family and your friends, but you'll be about the same distance from Oakland as you would be staying here. When Mav is living up there, you can still visit him whenever you want, or he could come stay with us even. I worked really hard to make sure I wouldn't take you too far away from him, but I'll understand if you need to stay put. At least we won't be separated by much."

While my stomach tumbles, my mind spins. "You chose San Jose for me?"

His smile widens, and his eyes soften with the amount of awe in them. "Of course I did. Chose it for me too. For us. I know you really love a mid-century modern, but how about a modest townhome in a boring suburb?"

All the joy in me busts loose, and I end up laughing with my forehead dropped to Rowan's shoulder. When I catch my breath, I lift my head and hug him tight. "Sounds amazing."

He chortles like I'm losing it, but in his voice, it's all hope. "You'll come with me then?"

"Fuck yeah." I smooch his cheek so many times he has to wipe my saliva off with the sleeve of his nice sweater. Then I smooch his mouth with the same vigor.

"Boys!" Matt's voice separates us. Rowan's face is as red as mine feels as I shove my hands in my pockets and hang my head bashfully. "Time to go out and celebrate. Olive Garden?"

"Matthew," Xia starts. "We need to go someplace nicer than Olive Garden. Where do you want to go, Rowan? Anywhere."

"Honestly..." Rowan's shoulders hop, and he sends a timid smile across the room, "Olive Garden sounds pretty dope right now."

The kids cheer, and I'm just happy to be invited. It's too cramped for all of us in the minivan, so I follow them in my truck with Rowan in the passenger seat, holding my hand over the center console.

We can't stop talking about San Jose, a city neither of us has spent much time in. Rowan's been researching it like mad, though, and he's telling me about everything he's read and all the things we'll be able to do there. He's an encyclopedia of San Jose running trails, and I can't help but laugh that even in Rowan's fantasies, we're working out.

"And you can do whatever you want," he says, glimmering at me like I'm artwork. "I mean it, baby. I'm gonna take care of you, so whatever you wanna do, I'll support you."

I snicker at the windshield, trying to stay close to Matt's bumper without being a total tailgater. "Like a sugar daddy?"

"Sure. Doesn't that sound hot?"

I send him a glance, and of course, his brows are wagging.

"Clearly, we know who the breadwinner is about to be in this relationship, but I'm not just gonna be your arm candy.

I do wanna finish my degree. Maybe since we just won the freaking College Cup, San Jose State will be open to giving me an athletic scholarship, and I can finish up there. Been thinking about changing my major anyway. Only reason I picked Business Administration is 'cause Ma says it's practical, but I think I wanna be a physical therapist."

"So you can rub me down every night?"

I snort, letting go of Rowan's hand so I can snatch his thigh and squeeze it. "You're thinking of a massage therapist."

"Oh," he laughs. "Well, how about you be a physical therapist, and I'll be your massage therapist?"

"Or I could even be a sports trainer. Work for a pro team one day."

"I think that'd be perfect," Rowan says, laying his hand over mine. "Whatever you decide to do, you'll be perfect."

"I'll figure it out. *We'll* figure it out." I send another glance sideways, and Rowan's smile matches his hopeful tone, nodding in agreement.

This is the first time we've really talked about our future, other than me half-joking about getting married when I'm fuck-drunk and Rowan telling me to knock it off. Come to realize Rowan's been thinking about this a lot. About where he'll end up, where we'll end up, and how he's going to make it happen. How he's going to keep the Tommy and Rowan show on the air for good.

After our celebratory lunch, I kiss Rowan goodbye outside the Olive Garden and promise to call him tonight. As much as I love "family time" with Rowan's crew, I promised Mav I'd take him to the movies tonight to see some kiddie Christmas thing he won't quit talking about. Now that the future is becoming more defined, I need to spend as many moments with Mav as possible while we're still living in the same city.

As soon as I get in the door, he's cheering. Excited that I'm home in time for the movie, I think, but then he shouts, "I saw you and Rowan on the TV!"

"You watched the draft?" I snatch Mav up and swing him around like a rag doll until he's cackling and Ma is shouting at me to be careful. I set him on his feet, and he reaches out his arms like he's a zombie, swaying through his dizziness.

"Is Rowan famous now?" Mav asks.

"Nah, not famous. He just worked really hard and got a big promotion. Maybe he'll be famous one day. Might even see him on the front of a cereal box."

Coming out of the kitchen with a plate and dishtowel in her hands, Ma says, "They've been talking about him on the news."

"What? Why?" I don't watch the news. Too bleak, but I'm not a cave dweller. My mind manages to guess what Ma's talking about before she explains.

"A lot of people think it sends the wrong message, drafting a man who is...you know."

"Who is *gay*," I state.

"Not only that, but making a big fuss about it. Putting him on camera like that, on ESPN, talking about how he's the first openly gay kid to be drafted, as if that makes him more valuable than those other kids. You being there didn't help, holding his hand like that and making it so obvious. People are talking about you too—"

"I don't care what people say about me, and Rowan *is* more valuable, because he's the best. He earned what he got despite being gay, not because of it. Whatever comments people have, positive or negative, it doesn't matter. He deserves a spotlight for his accomplishments, and he deserves to sit with the people who love him. I want it to be obvious I love him, because I do."

"Don't fight!" Mav whines, throwing his arms around my legs.

Ma turns around with a heavy eye roll, but she stops short of the kitchen and flips around for a second round. "So you're perfectly fine with everyone seeing you as nothing more than one of those alphabet-salad people?"

I scoff, finally tossing my keys on the coffee table and dropping my overnight bag on the floor. "I don't even know what that means."

"That video is going to be online forever," she says. "All anyone has to do is Google your name, and there pops a video of you holding hands with a man. A man you're probably not going to still be with a year from now. Any employer you have after this is going to see it. Anyone you try to date is going to see it—"

"Stop talking." I shrug Mav off because I can't linger in the same space as my mother for one second longer.

In my room, I start a text to Rowan, but I delete every word before sending it. The last thing Rowan needs is to hear how homophobes on the news are criticizing him after the most significant achievement of his life.

I flop onto my bed and hug a pillow to my chest. Just when I start thinking Ma is coming around, she changes course like the wind, more concerned with what bigoted talking heads think than what her own son is going through.

San Jose.

I keep my mind settled on that until the anger washes away and I feel good again.

When there's a tapping at my door, I nearly convince myself it's Ma coming to apologize, but it's Erica who slinks in and shuts the door behind her. "Hey. I can take Mav to the movie if you're not up to it."

"No, no. I'll take him." I check my phone. "If we leave in fifteen minutes, we'll still be there in time for the trailers."

Erica nods and toes out of her slippers.

I roll over and make space for her on the vacant side of my bed. Taking the pillow from my arms, she tucks it under her head and turns to face me.

"How're you feeling?" I ask, noticing the bags under her eyes.

"Like shit," she mumbles, eyelids drooping like she could fall asleep at any moment. "Managed to shower, though. When I got out, Maverick said something about you and Mom fighting."

"We weren't fighting."

"You know he hates fighting. He's sensitive. Like you always were. Any time Mom and I got into it, you'd burst into tears. Didn't matter what we were talking about. Just the tones of our voices were enough."

"She just says the dumbest shit sometimes. Pisses me off."

Raking her slim fingers through my hair, Erica says, "I know. Let it roll off your back."

"Trying."

"She's going to need you when I'm gone. To love and to judge. Don't give her all of you. Give her some, but take the rest with you to San Jose."

Ah, the magic words. I can't help but smile, even as my eyes fill with tears.

"You're going with him, right?"

I nod, smile widening. "But I'm not leaving you. I'll stay until it's time, and I'll take Mav to Oakland like I promised. Then, I'll go to San Jose."

Chapped lips stretching to show a tired grin, Erica whispers, "I'm proud of you."

"For what?"

"Being a good person. That guy is lucky to have you."

"I'm the lucky one. Trust me."

My phone buzzes under my ass, and my first thought is that Rowan's texting, but then it keeps on buzzing. I pry it from underneath me and see a number I don't recognize.

Swiping to the green call icon, I answer with a tentative, "Hello?"

An unfamiliar voice fills my ear, asking if this is Tommy Mathison. "That's me."

The voice introduces themselves, and the very next phrase out of their mouth is one that stops my heart cold and stuns me into sitting upright. "Are you serious?" I ask them.

They are. No joke. They bid me goodbye, and when the line goes cold, I stare at my screen and wonder if I just dreamt that.

"Who was it?" Erica asks, picking herself up on an elbow.

Looking back at her over my shoulder, I can't believe what I'm about to tell her. "I got drafted."

"What?" She hauls herself up and grips my shoulder to keep her sitting straight. "Seriously?"

"Seriously. Last round pick, but I got picked," I mutter, my head in a flurry. I swallow a lump that forms in my throat and it sits like a log in my gut, making me feel sick.

"You don't look happy," she says. "This is incredible."

"Yeah," I sigh, shaking with an anxious adrenaline. The most dreadful sort of excitement I've ever felt.

"Then what's wrong? Which team is it?"

I gulp, scratching at the back of my neck. "Toronto FC."

Toronto...also known as *really fucking far away from San Jose.*

32

Rowan

When I get the ESPN notification with Tommy's name right beside the words Toronto Football Club, I wish I could say my first feeling is pride. I wish I were that selfless. I wish I were that good of a person. That good of a boyfriend.

Toronto...

I wish I could say I don't cry as much as I do, but once the first tear falls, the rest just won't quit until I'm so drained of energy I pass out fully clothed on my unmade bed.

What wakes me is Xia knocking on my door to tell me she and the girls baked cookies, if I'm interested. I hate the look on her face when she sees me, like she just found me behind a dumpster digging for scraps.

"Think I'll pass tonight, but thanks," I tell her.

"Have you talked to him yet?"

I shake my head.

"Honey, just because he's drafted doesn't mean he has to commit."

"Yes it does," I sigh, raking my hands across my scalp and taking a small bit of comfort in that my hair is too short to muss. "This is his shot, and he earned it. No way I'm letting him turn his back on this opportunity just because of me."

"You say that like you're not just as big of an opportunity."

"I'm not an opportunity. I'm just...the first guy he fell for. You know what they say. First loves never work out."

"Oh?" Her arms fold and her brows go crooked. "Is that what they say?"

"I'm not hungry, Xia, but thank you."

She stays staring at my eyes, but I've long since averted mine. Eventually, she resigns, dropping her arms and leaving me to wallow.

If I were a good boyfriend, I would have called Tommy the second I found out, congratulated him, and told him how proud I am of him. Instead, I wait for him to call me, because I need the extra time to rehearse the aforementioned reaction.

The call comes close to nine o'clock, and I'm almost too scared to answer.

"Yo," I answer, immediately wincing at how stupid that sounds.

"Yo," Tommy parrots on the breath of a chuckle. *"You're not busy right now, are you?"*

Not unless lying motionless in bed for hours counts as busy. "Nope. Wassup?"

"Were you, uh, keeping up with the rest of the draft at all today?"

Be cool. Be cool.

"Not after you left. You know Xia and her family time. No phones allowed."

"Well...as fucking crazy as it sounds, I got drafted."

Be cool.

"What?" I feign shock. "Are you serious?"

"Nuts, right?"

"It's amazing. Shit. That's amazing, Tommy. W-who drafted you?"

The line is quiet for a few torturous moments. *"It was, uh, Toronto."*

Pinching the bridge of my nose to fight back the emotion, I say, "Toronto is a good club, and they see what I see in you, which makes them a smart club."

Amid Tommy's silence, I can barely make out the sound of his throat swallowing. *"So, you think I should commit?"*

"Absolutely," I answer quickly. "This is your shot, and you deserve it. You won that match, Tommy. You won us the tournament. That was you."

"I called a homophobe a cocksucker, and he elbowed me in the ribs. That's why we won."

Even in my misery, I can still smile at that. My baby boy, calling a homophobe a cocksucker. I'm just sad I wasn't right there to hear it. "Still counts."

"What about...us?"

The question is a fist, squeezing my heart to a fine pulp. "We've still got time to figure us out."

"Okay," he sighs, and I wish I could tell which emotion it's laden with. *"But...what about San Jose?"*

"It's not going anywhere. I'll be there, and you can come visit me whenever you can. I'll visit you too." I try holding my breath to keep the tears in, but I need my breath to speak, so the tears dribble down the side of my face freely. "Maybe it'll be better this way. I'm probably going to be so busy in San Jose, you'll never see me, and you'll resent me. I don't want that. And this way, we'll still be connected through soccer. We'll be doing the same shit, so we'll always have things in common to talk about, and our off-seasons will always be in-sync. We'll see each other a lot during the off-seasons, and we can train together like we do. Doesn't that sound better?"

No. It sounds fucking horrible, but Tommy doesn't say that. He's silent for a while.

"I'm so—" we both say in tandem, and we both cut ourselves off on the same syllable.

I'm so proud of you, is what I was going to say. "Sorry, what were you gonna say?"

Tommy expels a long breath, then says, *"I was gonna say I'm scared."*

"Baby, don't be scared. There's nothing to be scared of."

After another drawn out pause, Tommy asks another daunting question. *"Do you promise?"*

"Yes, I promise," I answer quickly, and now he'll really know I'm a liar, because there's always something to be afraid of. Even when times are better than usual, there's always horror right around the corner.

Tommy's been distant. Or maybe it's me who's being distant. Pre-grieving, maybe. Eight weeks is a long time, but it's time I'll only spend growing more and more in love with him and, by the end of it, I don't think I'll survive saying goodbye. I'll let him go, and without him, I'll do something stupid. I'll hurt myself, and I'll hurt him, and I can't let that happen. Maybe letting him go now will be better for us in the long run.

This is why relationships are bogus. Promises don't mean shit in this life. Everything we put into it gets taken away. Only sure thing is that the sun's going to rise the next morning. No guarantees on what the light's going to unveil, or what sort of people we'll be when it does.

It's only been a few days since the draft, but with how sporadically I've found sleep, it feels like weeks. Either way, I've spent way too many hours binge watching sad movies that only solidify my opinion that love is an illusion and life is meaningless. I take it as a sign when most of these tragic tales are about gay men and boys.

I'm halfway through an erotic sex scene between two depressed hotties and trying not to get turned on, because I know how it's going to turn out. One man will die or realize he's better off alone, and misery will prevail. This is when Xia taps on my door and tells me Tommy's here.

Tommy?

"Uhh, okay! I'll be out in a minute!" I pop out of bed, shut my laptop and scramble to put together a clean outfit. Something that'll make it look like I still give a shit about myself, Adidas and my coat for the short trip from the garage to the house. I'm already shucking the coat off as I pass through the kitchen, and I drape it on a dining chair.

In the living room, Tommy is shooting the shit with Matt over something or another, standing half a head taller than my pseudo-father. He spots me and smiles, then lets Matt finish his thought before slapping his palm and stepping toward me.

"Hey, Row," Tommy murmurs, sizing me up like it really has been weeks since we've been in the same room. His hand cups my jaw, thumb smoothing across the stubble I've been ignoring.

"Sorry," I mumble, noticing how kempt Tommy looks, stunning as ever.

He smiles curiously, like I'm being weird. "For what?"

"I didn't know you were coming by."

Taking his hand back, he sticks both into the pockets of his perfectly fitted jeans. "I tried calling a couple times and—I dunno—got the feeling maybe your phone died. Got kinda worried, I guess, 'cause of last time."

"Shit. That's my bad. I'm good, I swear. Just been binging a bunch of depressing ass movies and forgot about my phone. I'm sure it's dead somewhere."

He chuckles quietly, taking his hands out of his pockets to lay them across my shoulders. "Why are you binging depressing movies?"

Because I'm a depressing person living in a depressing world, and I like to keep on theme.

"Caught up in the algorithm, I guess."

Olive and Lena zip from the hallway, prancing around the main room like they're ponies, and Xia calls to them to wash up for dinner. "Are you eating with us, Tommy?" she then asks.

"Um..." He sends me a perfunctory glance before answering her. "I think we're gonna go out for dinner." Looking at me again, he asks, "You wanna go out?"

"For sure. I should probably change then."

"You look fine." He runs his palms along my shoulders and down my arms, pulsing my biceps. "Let's talk first, yeah?"

Talk?

"Sure." I grab my coat off the chair and slip it on as I leave the house the way I came, Tommy in my wake.

It's already dark out, but the motion sensors trigger the backyard lights to flicker on, illuminating the yard and half the driveway. My soccer ball is still chilling in the grass from Thanksgiving, and Tommy heads for it like a moth to the LEDs. He dribbles it a little between his Vans and shoots it into the kiddie goal.

"Nothing but net," he exclaims, swinging his arms up toward the sky in triumph.

Hands in my coat pockets, I cross the grass but stop short of arm's reach. "What did you wanna talk about?"

He does a slow one-eighty, showing me a smile that emotes the antithesis of what all I've been feeling the past few days. Soft and serene, not wide enough to make his babyface dimple, but enough for me to feel warm, even out here.

"I've been thinking a lot since the draft," he says, not one hint of waver in his deep tenor, "and I wanted to tell you in person I'm passing on Toronto."

It's crazy how he can say the exact words I need him to, but hearing them aloud evokes only indignation. "Tommy, don't—"

"Hey." Long legs cross the boundary I left between us, and Tommy's powerful hands clasp around my arms. "It's done. I made the call today."

My body wants to crash into Tommy, but my fucked up mind forces me in the opposite direction. Pulling away from him, I ask, "Why would you do that? Call them back. I'm serious. I'm not letting you quit because of me."

"I'm not quitting. I'm making a choice, and I choose to go to San Jose with you."

"Well, I won't let you."

"Then I'll stay here, but I'm not going to Toronto. It's done."

Heart knuckle-punching my chest, I pace just to keep from jumping out of my skin. "This is a dream come true opportunity, and you're throwing it away for what? Some guy you've been dating for a few months?"

"You sound like my mom."

"Maybe your mom is right this time."

"Or maybe you're projecting." He lurches forward, capturing my arm and holding it firm enough that I can't just shrug him off. Keeping me still, he halves the gap between us, close enough that the scent of his body wash alone is overwhelming. "I love soccer," he says, "but it's your dream, not mine. It was always just a placeholder for me. Something to keep me distracted from what was going on inside me and the things I thought I had to hide from everyone, but it was never my dream."

Flushed with the heat Tommy radiates, I tilt my gaze and allow myself to see the resolve in his eyes. The stubborn sincerity.

"You're my dream, Rowan," he murmurs. "It's always been you, and I will never give up on you. Ever. Not for anything."

The heat is overwhelming. It makes my face crumple and my eyes sweat. Tommy grabs me and hugs me to his chest before the rest of me crumbles, and I sob against his shoulder without rhyme or reason.

"Shh, shh, it's okay," he soothes, cradling the back of my head with his other arm slung around my back.

"Thank you." I choke on the words, turning my face into his neck and nuzzling my weeping eyes against his pulse.

"I love you, Rowan," he speaks, rocking me in his arms as if we're floating in the center of the sea.

"Thank you," I breathe from my heart.

Laying his cheek on mine, he hums, "Can we be happy now?"

I pick my face out of his neck and blink until the tears on my eyelashes fall. My arms stay cinched around him, hands locked behind his back to make sure we can't part. "It's hard for me sometimes," I croak, hardly any air left in my lungs.

"I know." A warm palm cradles my jaw, a coarse thumb dragging across my wet cheek. "That's why I'm here. For you. I'll always be here, so *I* can take care of *you*."

33
Tommy

The summer heat finally showed itself this week, as if spring had held out just for Erica. It always was her favorite season. When all the flowers bloom and the trees get green again.

Today is the eighth day of the post-Erica world, and I still don't feel totally human yet, but I'm not the hollowed out shell I was on day one. The heat helps, because I actually prefer summer, and the morning sun blazing through my bedroom window right now is helping my body to sweat out all the darkness and soothe the demons from my mind. The voices telling me how ugly life is when, in my heart, I know the opposite to be true.

I'm alone now, but only right now. Only in this room and in this bed. I'm not really alone, though, because as I sweat it out in basketball shorts on top of the sheets, I still smell Rowan around me. Even after a week of him using my soap, my shampoo, and stealing my clothes, I still smell *him.* His skin, his breath, his cum, his sweat, and that cologne in his bag that he spritzes on sometimes because he thinks it'll help win Ma over.

I hear Rowan just as clearly. By now, I know his footsteps from anyone else's, so I know it's him moving around in the kitchen. I hear dishes rattling, silverware clanging, and water periodically running. I hear his voice. Muffled, but it's there. I hear Ma's voice, too, more shrill and discernible.

They've been getting along, kind of, which has been nice, but I still don't like leaving them alone together too long. Rowan is a sweetheart, and anything Ma has to say about him rolls right off his back with minimal damage, but Rowan is fiercely protective of me. If Ma utters a single critical word about me, Rowan won't shy away from setting her straight, and Ma isn't a fan of being set straight.

Just in case, I unglue myself from the mattress after nearly an hour spent staring at the ceiling since waking up. I find a muscle shirt on the floor that probably doesn't smell much better than my bare skin does, and I tug it on as I leave my room.

I'm yawning and rubbing the lingering sleep from my eyes when I come through the hall, and Rowan's voice says, "Hey, you. Sleep okay?"

He's sitting at the dining table, Mav on his lap, and he's smiling that somber smile at me. The one he offers before he's sure I'm in a mood to be smiled at for real. I'm always in the mood to be smiled at by Rowan, even when it feels like there's a hundred pound weight pressing down on my shoulders.

Because Ma sits right across from him, I forgo a more honest answer in favor of a white lie. "Yeah, it was okay." Standing at the head of the table, I scan my family and notice they're all in their pre-planned outfits already. Ma in her black dress, Mav in his black button down, and Rowan in his black polo shirt and chain.

"Shit, you're all dressed," I mumble, hearing the hoarseness in my voice. "Am I late?"

Rowan's head shakes as he uncurls an arm from around Mav to tap the next placemat over. "There's plenty of time. Sit down and eat something."

While my room smells like Rowan, this one smells like breakfast, and my stomach growls, which I count as a win considering my appetite has been hovering just above *none* since Erica left us. On the table is a platter of pancakes and plates of bacon and scrambled eggs. Mav uses Rowan's lap as a booster seat while he picks at his plate with a kiddie fork, and Ma is cradling a mug in her hands.

"There's coffee in the kitchen," she says, and I beeline for it. Hot coffee sounds like just the thing to help expel the darkness inside me.

I take a mug of coffee and cream back to the table and drop into the seat Rowan had directed me toward. There's a clean plate out with a fork and knife. I go straight for the pancakes, still warm, and slap two on my plate. It takes until now for me to recognize these pancakes as the ones Erica would make—the ones from the recipe box Grandpa left to her.

"Full disclosure," Rowan says, palm stroking across my shoulder blades, "I made these, so they're not very good."

Despite how dull and drained my body feels, my eyes well with emotion as I stare at the thin, whole wheat pancakes that somehow always taste better than the boxed, buttermilk ones. "You made my grandpa's pancakes?"

"Tried to. Your mom helped me."

I gaze at my boyfriend before shifting it to Ma. *They were cooking together?*

Sensing my surprise, Ma answers my unspoken curiosity. "If you're going to be living together now, he's going to need to learn how to cook. Twenty-three and the man can hardly crack an egg."

Directing my incredulous smile at my perfect boyfriend, I say, "Thank you."

"Don't thank me yet. Like I said, I messed 'em up a little."

Under Rowan's watchful eye, I butter my cakes and douse them in syrup before carving out a big bite and shoveling it in. Even better than the taste is the comfort of familiarity. Maybe they're a little clumpy, but they're *everything* right now.

"So good," I hum, swiping the stray tear from beneath my eyelid. "Thank you so much."

Rowan's hand slips up to my neck, thumb stroking the short hairs at my nape.

Laying my hand atop Mav's head, I say, "You okay, buddy?"

"I guess," he shrugs, staring at his eggs.

"Gonna see your dad today."

Tone perking a bit, Mav answers, "Yeah, that'll be nice."

Ma tells Mav to come sit with her so Rowan can eat, and the simple acknowledgment of Rowan's comfort level from my mother gives me another reason to smile.

As soon as Rowan's lap is empty, I can rest my hand on his leg and keep it there while my other one works on getting some food into my empty belly. I try to eat quick. Regardless of Rowan's patience, I'm pretty sure I'm running behind. The service is at noon sharp. At the church where my family would go to every Christmas and Easter.

I must be making my nerves especially obvious, because Rowan firms his hold on the back of my neck and says, "Take your time, baby. Nothing's gonna start without you."

Feeling more appreciation for him than I can ever properly express, I have to settle for leaning sideways and pressing a syrupy kiss to his cheek. Just the fact he's taking all this time away from his club to help me wallow through the greatest loss of my life means the world. I'm sure pro soccer clubs aren't typically amenable to letting their star rookie players take a three-week hiatus in the middle of the season, but Rowan pulled it off like a magician. As soon as I called and said it was time, he was here the same day. Said he would stay as long as I need him.

I'll always need Rowan, but we settled on three weeks, to give us time for a funeral and to pack up Mav and take him to his dad's the way I promised Erica I would. Then we'll pack up my shit, and I'll finally move into the condo we picked out together.

A change of scenery will be good for me. It'll be good for Mav, too, and the fact that we won't be far apart calms my soul when I start to worry. Whenever he needs me, I'll be there. An hour in the car is nothing. Just like Rowan has been visiting me every week, I can visit Mav just as often if he needs it, and there will always be space for him in San Jose.

To save time, I brush my teeth and shave my sad excuse for facial stubble in the shower, and I dress in the bathroom, sweating anew in itchy dress clothes. I wear my Vans, even if it's inappropriate, because I can't stand clunky dress shoes, and I really don't think Erica would give a shit what's on my feet at her funeral.

Mav rides with Ma in her car to the church, and Rowan takes us in his car. Still driving that old Legacy despite his new pro status. He says the clunker is too sentimental to part with; a speck of my year-old cum still stains the upholstered ceiling above my head.

We arrive just in the nick of time. Rowan always says fifteen minutes early is on time, but today, he doesn't say a word about us rolling into the church at five past noon. He was right too.

Nothing began without us. Everyone here is still milling about, quietly chatting and settling into their seats. While Ma talks with the pastor, I pick Mav up and walk with Rowan to the first pew of the quaint church.

There are people here I know, I'm sure of it, but I don't acknowledge anyone. I'll let Ma be the designated mingler if that's what she wants, but I'm just not interested. Not interested in thanking everyone for being here when it's such a monumentally shitty thing that we have to be here at all. That my sister is dead.

The only people I hold focus on are sitting on either side of me. Got an arm slung around Mav's shoulders to keep him at my side, and I've got a hand holding Rowan's on top of my thigh.

The other day, the pastor asked if I was preparing to say a few words at the podium, but I can't. I'm no public speaker even on a good day. It's not something I'm cut out for, and I don't think Erica's spirit will mind if I keep my thoughts of her tucked in my heart where they'll always be safe.

"Hey," Rowan whispers beside my ear. "If you ever need a break, it's okay."

I get what he's saying, but even if everyone understood, I can't be the guy who leaves in the middle of his sister's funeral because he can't handle his emotions. "I'm good."

Giving my hand a pulse, he smiles tentatively and nods.

Ma speaks. It's beautiful. Erica would have appreciated it, especially the part where Ma apologizes for not being a more thoughtful and well-equipped mother, but despite their combativeness, Ma and Erica loved each other.

I don't cry. I already did all that. Shed so many tears it's a wonder I didn't wither up and die of dehydration. Days and nights spent huddled in bed, sweating and crying, with Rowan holding me like a baby, even after I'm certain his limbs went numb from my weight. I was lost, but I found my way back with Rowan as my guide. The first time we made love after Erica's passing, I burst into tears as I came. Not from grief, but from how fucking grateful I was to have him here. I'll never forget that.

After the service, everyone stands, and I become more aware of the surrounding faces. Some are strangers to me, some are semi-familiar, and some are so familiar it puts an extra pang in my chest. Some guys from the team showed up, and they play the awkward dance of apologizing to me for my loss while congratulating Rowan on his success. But I'd much rather talk about the Earthquakes than my grief and how I'm "holding up."

Some of my friends from the Queer Alliance appear and offer similar sentiments to the ones they texted to me in the group chat last week. Feels better in person, when I can see it in their eyes that they really are sorry for my loss. I get hugs from Indy, Chuck and his boyfriend, Javi, and Oscar, who swings his arms around me and Rowan at the same time. The fact Rowan is enduring a group hug right now shows he's on his best behavior. Doesn't even squirm.

Rowan's family is here, too, and the hugs keep on coming. Olive gives me a picture she drew for me. All happy things. Flowers, sunshine, and her whole family. Including Rowan, plus me. There's no sorrow in my tears as I say thank you and give Olive an extra hug.

When I realize Annalese is here, I'm not sure how to feel. While I've been content not having her in my life anymore, the fact of the matter is that Erica really liked Lese. Hell, Erica wanted me to *marry* Lese. Turn her into a Mathison to keep me from ending up a lonesome wreck. But a lonesome wreck is exactly what I was until I tethered myself to the love of my life the night I punched him in the face over something Lese did.

"Tom," she calls me, hands tucked into the pockets of her plain black dress, her plain black heels carrying her cautiously toward me. "I'm so sorry."

Still holding Rowan's hand, I send him a glance to gauge his discomfort before I commit to a convo with my ex. Lese looks the same as when we dated, though less flashy maybe. She's not trying too hard to look hot anymore, but in hindsight, she was probably doing that for me, because she thought I'd want her more if she kept her makeup on point and her fashion trendy.

"Thanks," I mutter. "Thanks for coming. Erica would appreciate it. You helped her a lot for a while there."

With a tight smile, Lese nods like she's well aware. She looks beside me, and her smile drifts away with the words, "Hi, Rowan. I saw your premier match on TV. Seemed like you did really well."

"Thanks," he mutters with about the same melancholic disinterest as my tone is laced with.

"The announcers were saying you could be the next Messi."

"Hopefully I'll start getting paid like Messi soon," Rowan answers. "San Jose ain't cheap, and I've got a growing boy to feed."

My eyes tick wider, and my face reddens, knowing he's talking about me. Thankfully, Lese just looks confused and doesn't press for context.

Looking back at me, Lese asks, "Can we talk for a sec?"

The glance I send Rowan seals the deal. He gives my hand a pulse and nods toward the side door leading outside. "I'm gonna check in with my parents before they leave. I'll be right outside."

I nod, but as soon as his hand slips from mine, I regret it. Still, I let him go, and I shove my hands in my pockets, committing to a longer convo than I have the mental will for.

"Is he always that funny?" Lese asks, eyes lingering on Rowan as he leaves out the courtyard exit. All it does is remind me that for a brief blip in time, she was all over Rowan. Even though I spent four years reciprocating Lese's come-ons, I still feel an odd sort of jealousy that she'd touched Rowan before I knew I could.

"It comes and goes," I shrug, knowing full well Rowan's feeling a twinge of jealousy, too, over those four years Lese laid claim to me. In his weird way, he was letting her know I'm his now. Marking his territory with a half-jest the same way he does when someone hits on me in public. It's always mildly embarrassing and semi-amusing, but I never tell him to stop, because it's also oddly comforting. After all, *his* is exactly what I want to be.

"Are you moving to San Jose?" she asks, a look in her eyes like she might hope I'll say no.

"Yeah. Next week actually. I only stuck around here this long for Erica and to finish up the semester. I've already finalized my transfer to San Jose State, and I'll be playing soccer there. Got a full ride, even. The coach over there loves that I got drafted and turned it down to stay in school, and he especially loves that I've got three years of eligibility left, which is good since I'm also changing my major. It'll be at least another two years before I graduate."

"Sounds like you got it all figured out," she says with a wistful smile. "I'm glad. I'm glad you're not alone."

Speaking of not alone, over Lese's head, I notice a particularly beefy man staring at us from a few yards away. "He with you?" I ask my ex.

She tosses a look over her shoulder, then swishes her hand dismissively. "Sorry, that's just this guy I've been seeing."

"You brought a date to your ex's sister's funeral?" I pop a small smirk because it's just too funny.

"Well, you know me. Class act."

I breathe something close to a laugh, which feels strange in my throat and a little inappropriate given the venue.

"Can I ask you something?" she murmurs timidly. "I don't want to make today all about me, but I figure I'll probably never see you again."

"What is it, Lese?"

"So..." she stalls, pursing her lips to either side of her face to make her nose wiggle. "How gay are you?"

"Uhh." A hand leaves my pocket to itch at the back of my neck. "Like, a hundred percent."

"Did you know the whole time we were together?"

Heaving a sigh, I suppose Lese deserves to know, so instead of brushing her off, I answer as honestly as I can. "It's complicated. I didn't *know*, but I kinda knew."

She nods, sucking on her bottom lip.

"I'm sorry," I offer.

"You should be," she says evenly, "but I should be sorry too, so I think that cancels it out."

"Beef squashed?"

Her mouth quirks a half smile. "Yeah. Beef squashed. Can I give you a hug?"

I'm a little burnt out on non-familial hugs, but I nod and accept Lese into my arms for the last time. A loose, passionless hug, with my hands on her upper back. I pat her when it's been long enough, and we separate.

"Take care of yourself," I tell her, because I'm not sure her current man is up for the job, but that's not my business anymore.

Feet taking me where my heart guides them, I end up in the courtyard, draping my arms around Rowan's waist and burying my face in his shoulder. If I weren't forty pounds heavier than him, I might try clinging to his body like a koala. He was in the middle of talking to Xia about something, but I know she won't mind my intrusion, and I guess I'm just too needy to care right now. Rowan is quick to hug me back, palms sweeping my spine and lips pecking my temple.

"Wanna go home?" he whispers.

Home. Home sounds glorious, but not the home he's referring to. I want to go to San Jose. I want to go to the king size bed I've been sleeping in a couple weekends out of the month like mini vacations, yearning to turn those vacations into *life.* Life with Rowan.

"Can we get ice cream?" I hum, hoping Xia can't hear how clingy and whiny her son's boyfriend is.

"Absolutely."

Ma is going to lunch with the pastor and his wife, and Mav's dad is taking him some place fun where he can be a kid away from all this sadness. Rowan and I go to Sonic and eat ice cream and Coney dogs in his car like old times. Even after those pancakes at breakfast, I'm still hungry, so I eat two dogs and half of Rowan's ice cream while he giggles and gives me his *I love you, dork* looks.

"Music?" I ask with a mouth full of Rowan's cookie dough ice cream.

"Pick your poison." He sticks that dated ass aux chord into his phone like this is 2014.

"Play me some of your shit. Like, uh—what do you like? JPEGMafia."

Rowan snorts a laugh that tickles my nearly full belly, and he taps at his phone screen until the car fills with the sweet sound of Rowan's taste.

Swirling my spoon in Rowan's cup, I ask, "Are we gonna jerk each other off after I finish this?"

Rowan grins madly. "If that's what you want."

"Hmm." I roll the vanilla and toppings around in my mouth, letting it all melt on my tongue and chill my teeth. "As much as I love your hand, it's not my fave body part of yours to stick my dick in."

"Just tell me what you want, baby boy. Anything. I'll give it to you."

I touch my cheek to the headrest and stare into Rowan's dark, dreamy eyes. The eyes of the boy who called me *faggot* when he was at his lowest, and the eyes of the man who calls me *baby boy* because he needs me to be his just as badly as I need to be his. As badly as I need him to be mine.

"Don't spoil me," I tell him, skimming my palm along his thigh and wishing he was wearing his flimsy running shorts. "You'll turn me into a brat."

Expression soft, he lifts a hand to brush his fingers along my jaw. "If you turn into a brat, I get to punish you."

A scared little moan escapes me, and I shift my hips to soothe my dick as it swells in these uncomfy pants. Like a real baby, I whimper, "You punish me enough."

Rowan's eyebrows flicker with a moment of confusion.

"I just miss you so much." My eyes go misty again, and I hate that I'm doing this. Hate that I'm being this way, but I can't help it. Not today. Not for the past eight days.

"I'm right here."

"I mean when you're gone," I cry, the words gurgling from my throat like muddy water. "I miss you so much when you're gone. I try not to, but I can't help it. I need you."

"Hey, hey, hey." His large, warm palm pets the side of my head, over my ear and down my neck in gentle swoops. "That's gonna change. The next time I leave, I'm taking you with me. I'm not leaving you again. You hear me?"

"Mhmm," I whine, but it comes out some pitiful, anguished cry. I turn and keel over, and Rowan somehow slips my tray off my lap before my forehead touches the dash. "I'm sorry, I'm sorry."

"Don't apologize." His hand is on my back now, stroking my spine. "You're allowed to feel what you're feeling."

But my feelings don't make sense. Why do I miss Rowan so much it physically hurts, even when he's sitting right next to me? When he's been with me nearly every hour of every day since last week? When next week, we're loading up my truck and convoying to San Jose together, finally?

He's right here.

But it fucking *hurts,* and the only explanation for the pain my mind can fathom is that *I miss him. I need him. Where is he?*

Oh... This isn't really about Rowan, is it?

I suck in a harsh breath, allowing my lungs to fill fully for the first time in minutes, and I slump back in my seat.

"Breathe, Tommy," I hear Rowan say, and I have a feeling he's been repeating that phrase for a while. His palm presses my chest, rubbing me there, right over my heart, and I breathe against it as evenly as I can while holding back the tears.

"I'm sorry," I heave. "That wasn't about you. I'm sorry."

"It's okay," he implores, another hand on my forehead, smoothing away the sweat and my bangs that stick to it.

Even though it's okay, I'm overtaken by shame that I let my emotions run rampant like that. Sobbing to JPEGMafia at a Sonic Drive-In is about as embarrassing as it gets.

"I have an idea," Rowan says. "Let me take you someplace pretty. A pretty view for a pretty boy."

He drives us to school, of all places. Parks in the lot beside the horticulture building, and he holds my hand until we're at the gate to the public garden. My stomach aches from too much food and all my memories of Erica and I. There aren't a lot of places in Sacramento I'm going to miss, but I'll miss this place.

I stop at every informational plaque, even though I've read them all dozens of times over, and I marvel at every lizard that scurries across the path. Soon, we pick a bench under a shade tree, and I lean against Rowan's side like he's a damn stone pillar, completely stable. He wraps one arm around my back and the other rubs my arm that's slung around his waist.

"Don't let go," I murmur, eyes closed, heart and soul completely at his mercy.

"I won't."

"Promise?"

"I promise, baby." And even when I hear voices nearby and footsteps crunching down the path in front of us, he doesn't let go.

"Marry me."

His chest vibrates as he exhales a quiet chuckle against my head. "Cut it out."

"I'm serious," I whine.

"I know," he whispers, touching a kiss to my head. "You're mine, okay? You're already mine. I love you."

"Mmm," I hum, suddenly unable to do much else. My body relaxes into the feel of Rowan, into his scent, his touch, and the sound of his heart beating close to my ear.

By nightfall, I'm feeling more like a functioning human being. Mav has been staying in Ma's where all of Erica's things make him feel safe, so my room has been a small paradise for Rowan and I. It's cluttered and there's no AC, but my bed is big enough for two and my box fans muffle any noise we make after bedtime. It's not San Jose, but as long as I'm with my man, I'm good.

We shower separately, which sucks, but there's only one bathroom here, and it would freak Ma out too much to see us head in for a shower together. While Rowan showers, I'm already on my bed in boxers, hair still damp, and I'm scrolling through the San Jose State class catalogue for the hundredth time, considering my options. Thinking about school distracts my mind from thinking about Erica, and it puts a drop of excitement back into my nerves.

It was a no-brainer to settle on kinesiology as my new major, but I'm still wavering on whether I want to track myself toward physical therapy or sports management. Either way. I'm thinking I'd like to get my Masters after graduating, so I set myself up for success with a good career. Rowan loves the thought of being our breadwinner, but I have my heart set on us being a team.

He comes into my room already dressed in cotton sleep shorts and a tank top, but he pulls the top off after locking my door so he can press our bare chests together when we cuddle, I hope. He crawls over me and straddles my hips, a dangerous position that invites more than just cuddles and kisses.

I let my phone slip free of my fingers as Rowan's parted lips touch mine. It thuds on the rug, but I don't give a fuck. My hands grip Rowan's ass and pull him down flush so his crotch fits against mine.

We kiss and grind, and my cock swells in my boxers enough to feel wet. Sticking my hands inside Rowan's shorts, I squeeze and tug on his taut ass. Underneath the scent of my body wash, I find that Rowan scent that drives me up the wall. I lift my knees, plant my feet on the bed, and buck my hips up to match his gyrations.

Moaning and grunting in my mouth, I know I've got him on the hook. It doesn't take much, but Rowan is better at denying himself than I am. He finds pleasure in denial, and I find pleasure in his control. Tonight, though, I could really use his control without any of the denial.

His mouth devours me. First my lips, then my neck, then my poor little nipples that are far too sensitive for the joys Rowan gives them. They tighten under his lips. Soft kisses each to harden, then he picks one and nurses from it like it's the very tip of my cock. I shiver and moan, legs flexing and dick twitching.

"Fuck, Row," I sigh, tracing my finger around his tight, little rim. It never ceases to amaze me the amount of times I've gotten my cock all the way up there when his hole is so deliciously tight.

The closest bottle of lube is in my nightstand, but I know from experience that horny-Rowan can take one finger dry so long as I just hold it inside like a plug rather than fuck him with it. My sweet boyfriend loves to be filled. It's his favorite thing in the world next to soccer and cuddling. My favorite is watching him come all over us while I pump him full of mine. Perfectly complementary.

But I'll admit, being especially needy has also made me increasingly curious.

"Row," I whimper as his tongue flutters across my nipple.

"Tell me what you want," Rowan growls against my chest before pinching that delicate nub between his lips and tugging.

A layer of anxious fear on my tongue, I breathe, "Will you top me?"

His tongue sneaks back into his mouth, and he darts his chin up, touching it to my chest and staring at me with his eyes as big as I've ever seen them.

"Are you sure you want that right now?" he asks, quiet and haunting.

I take his face and draw him up to press our mouths together. I lick the drool from the corner of his mouth and suckle his bottom lip, then I move my mouth to his ear. "I wanna feel what you feel when I'm inside you."

His moan shudders, and I can tell by the way his hips keep grinding that he's mulling it over seriously. "I just don't want to risk hurting you. Not tonight."

"You won't," I rasp, though the inside of my head knows I'm lying. I think I want it to hurt, just a little. What is Rowan always saying? *It hurts so good.* Will it hurt as good as when Rowan drills me on the soccer field or pushes me to run harder and faster and longer, even when I feel about ready to crumble? "*Please,* sweetheart. I want you to feel what I feel when I make love to you."

A devious smirk crawls across Rowan's face, his cock still mashing against mine in an agonizing rhythm. "That's beautiful, baby," he teases.

Tugging a hand out of his shorts, I skate it up the valley of his back and thread my fingers in his short hair. He's been letting it grow out, just an inch or so on top, but it's enough to show off a curl pattern and natural color. Not black, but a rich brown that looks like molasses in the sunlight. I rake my fingertips through the soft thicket and draw his mouth toward mine.

"Spoil me," I dare him softly before kissing at his bottom lip. "You can punish me later, but right now, I want all of you. Every last inch."

A low, rumbling moan accepts my terms, and his mouth seals the deal with an open-mouthed kiss like he's trying to suck the lips right off my face. Without unlocking our mouths, Rowan's body shifts and I hear my nightstand drawer slide open. Then, a cap pops.

"Take your fucking boxers off," Rowan grits.

Shit... What's that saying about being careful what you wish for? But as anxious as I am, I'm rock fucking solid, tenting my boxers and wetting the fabric with pre-cum. I can't get them off me fast enough.

By the time I'm naked for him like a damn offering, Rowan's fingers are wet with lube. My pouty eyes and weeping cock beg him to take all of me in a way he never has before. When I grab my dick, he swats my hand away and tugs on my thighs to pry them apart.

"Put your feet on my shoulders," he says, hunkering down between my legs like he's going to give me head.

The position exposes me, terrifies me, and comforts me all at once. Rowan's slick fingers massage my rim while his tongue tastes my inner thigh down to my balls. He's touched my ass before, but never with the intention of entering me until now. Now, I bite down on my bottom lip and will my body to relax.

"If you ever need to stop, let me know," Rowan whispers up at me, his gray eyes glinting like silver.

"Mhm," I nod, and in that moment, with Rowan's gaze synced with mine, he drives one finger through me with more ease than I imagined. Still, it feels like so much more than it is. Stretching, pinching, pushing on my walls and reaching somewhere deep within them.

I'm trembling, eyelids fluttering, and I can't tell whether I hate this feeling or love it, but I decide to roll with it for now either way.

Hissing a breath in through his teeth, Rowan croons, "So tight, baby. You've really never tried this alone? Just to see if you'd like it?"

My head shakes, my back and forehead percolating with sweat. I watch in wonderment as Rowan skims the tip of his nose along the underside of my cock before touching a kiss to my tip, dispelling a fresh bead of pre-cum onto his upper lip. His lubed up finger drags inside my ass mischievously slow. All the way in, then a little bit out. All the way in, then a little bit out. And while it still feels like an intrusion, the way Rowan worships my cock with gentle kisses and a dancing tongue has my hips rocking between his finger and mouth.

"Oh my God," I sigh, combing both my hands through his hair now. "You love my cock, don't you?"

The eyes that flicker up to mine are darker than they were a minute ago, and the finger inside me drags out completely. "I love every part of you," Rowan murmurs as two fingers pry my hole open and fill me to the last knuckle.

Holy fuck, holy fuck, holy fuck.

"Holy fuck," I whine, squeezing my eyes shut.

"You okay, baby boy? Is this too much?"

"Huh uh." I shake my head, but I know my face is a picture of pain. It does hurt, but the pain is nothing compared to the strangeness of it. The *'I can't believe Rowan enjoys this shit'* confusion mixed with the *'holy hell, Rowan is inside me'* excitement. And this is just two fingers, and while Rowan's hands are big, they aren't as big as mine. His dick isn't as big as mine either, but it's big enough that I can't fathom expanding enough to take it.

Oh, but I'm dying to try.

Rowan takes his time with me, though, fingering me in languid motions while his mouth continues to pleasure my dick just enough to keep it aching, but not enough to get me to the edge. That is, until Rowan hits a pressure point inside me that shoots a spark of electricity up my spine. I hop up onto my elbows in shock as my body quakes with what feels like a spontaneous climax.

"I'm coming," I warn him breathlessly, eyes wide with concern as my cock drools clear fluid into my navel.

"You're not coming," Rowan says, squeezing my thigh and standing up onto his knees. "Not yet. Not 'til daddy pops your cherry for real."

I whimper submissively as Rowan massages what I can only assume is my prostate until I'm pleading for an orgasm that will end this euphoric torture. "Please, Row. Fuck, I need you. I *need* you. Fuck me, please."

The consequence of my request is that Rowan's fingers leave my body and that delicious spot inside me. My anxious excitement returns when he shimmies out of his shorts, wets his cock with lube, and presses his tip to my hole.

Wearing a breathtaking look of determination, Rowan takes my ankles and plants my feet on his chest as he grinds his hips forward. One hand lifts my balls while the other grips his shaft. A firm push pops the top of his cock inside. My back arches, and I slap a palm over my mouth to keep from crying out in a mix of overwhelming fear and pleasure.

This is how Rowan felt the first time, in that hotel room in Utah. He'd told me afterward that it was as if his whole life flashed before his eyes in a split second until his body understood that the pain was the good sort, not the bad.

I feel it. Exactly that.

I feel that lightning bolt crack of terror and the subsequent wave of blissful relief as Rowan takes his sweet time rocking an easy rhythm against me. Like a slow dance—just vibing—until I'm relaxed enough for him to fuck me.

Instead, he nudges my feet out, and he folds himself on top of me, caging me and colliding our mouths together in a kiss that's more like CPR. Him breathing into me while I breathe it back into him. His eyes are half-lidded, and I'm seeing stars. I wrap my arms around him and hold my knees as high as I can.

"Oh my God," I moan, not feeling that same electricity Rowan's fingers produced, but it's something even better. *Comfort.* The comfort of being filled, of being taken, and of being his.

Reading my thoughts, Rowan rolls his forehead against mine and grunts, "You're mine."

His control is hypnotic. He takes every itch of pain away from me and replaces it with love. It's *indescribable.* Just as he described.

When he loses control, it's awe-some. My mouth gapes and my eyes widen as I watch and feel him succumb. He lasts all of a minute, from the moment he entered me to the moment he squirms, grunts, and bares his teeth on my pec. He bites me as my ass floods with warmth, and I pray it leaves a mark.

He ruts inside me a few times, his hips going rogue from the tenderness of our lovemaking, and I clench my jaw and take it, loving every second of Rowan's orgasmic abandon until he's left heaving on my chest.

Somehow, I've forgotten about my dick. I'm not even sure I'm still totally hard, but feeling Rowan let go inside me feels game-changing.

As he softens, my muscles coax him out of me, then seal his seed inside.

"Fuck." He picks himself up on hands and knees above me. Hanging his head, he mutters, "That's fucking embarrassing."

Immediately, I let out a full body laugh I can't control. My hands are more sympathetic, stroking his sides and around his back. "Why are you embarrassed?" I coo.

Grinning bashfully at me, he says, "I lasted about as long as a teenager losing his virginity."

"Well, you did sorta just lose your virginity. Your top virginity."

"I guess." He flops onto his side and glues himself under my arm. "Was it good for you, at least?"

"Are you kidding?"

His chin lifts, eyes staring into mine while his fingers skate along my cock, reminding me I'm definitely still hard. "I wanted to make you come."

"I hope you still will."

Leaving me in suspense, he lays his cheek on my shoulder and moves his fingers up to the indentations his teeth made in my flesh. "Do you think you're vers now?"

I hum, mulling it over. "I wouldn't go that far, but you looked so beautiful."

Huffing a giggle through his wrinkled nose, Rowan stretches his neck to reach my mouth. I turn onto my side so we're face to face, and I tug his leg over my hip while we kiss.

"How did it feel for you?" I murmur with our noses touching and my palm holding the back of his head.

"Incredible," he whispers. "Never felt anything quite like that."

"Yeah?" I stroke my boyfriend's gorgeous head and decide I'll bottom for Rowan whenever he wants it.

"Mhm," he hums, eyelids fluttering as I hold his gaze. "But honestly...I come even better when you're inside me."

A grin tightens my face, my heart fluttering. I'm so giddy I flip Rowan onto his back and pin him down with my hands around his wrists. "There he is," I snicker above his mouth. "My bottom bitch."

"You motherfucker," he seethes through a smirk and reddened cheeks.

I smooch his lips and tease his tongue with mine, pulling back before he can suck it into his mouth. "I'm sorry, daddy," I pout. "I just wanna know what it's like to fuck you while your cum is still hot in my ass."

"Holy fuck," Rowan sighs hotly, tongue licking his lips and eyes going wickedly wide the way they do when he's horny beyond belief. Sure enough, when I look down between us, his cock is swelling up anew.

In seconds, I lube my dick and flip Rowan onto his elbows and knees, ass up and taunting me. I slap one cheek, and Rowan tosses me a glare that quickly morphs into a smirk.

I lube my thumb and bury it in Rowan's hole while I grip his hip. I stretch him just enough that I know he'll open for my dick. Enough that he'll still feel our friction like bolts of lightning, clawing at him with all the comforting pain he craves as much as I crave inflicting it.

Trading my thumb for my cock, I push my way in, reveling in the squeeze of Rowan's tight muscles around me. So tight I can hardly move, but I pump and pump, and gradually loosen him enough to fuck him right.

Rowan clamps his mouth over his forearm, muffling all the sounds his body yearns to project. The firm muscles along his back flex under my roaming palms. *My man,* I think as I beat my dick into him. Firm flicks of my hips have Rowan mewling into his arm, then into my pillow when he bunches it up under his chest.

As crazed as my lust is, I last much longer than Rowan's one minute. I stay fucking him until we're both sweating and panting by the time I finish—when I fill him like he filled me, and I jerk his cock until he's painting the top sheet in his climax.

I tug the sheet onto the floor then pull Rowan's spent body against me to cuddle among the warm breeze of the whirring box fans. I trace his placid bottom lip with my thumb, and he purses a kiss to it.

"Imagine," I murmur, "doing that every night for the rest of our lives."

A dazed chuckle rocks Rowan's chest as he tightens his arms around me, picking his leg up over my hip again. "Fucking gay boy," he rasps.

"One-hundred percent." Not even one percentage point of doubt left over.

34

Rowan

We travel to Oakland in Tommy's truck, adding miles and memories to the old Tacoma. It's been a week since the funeral, and though Tommy will mourn for a long while, I feel his depression lifting with every day that passes.

My brave boy.

It's hard for me to keep my hands off him, needing to soothe him constantly, just in case the hurt grows overwhelming. In the car, I keep my hand on his leg, or his shoulder, or holding the back of his neck. While we're stretching our legs and shopping for road snacks at the gas station, I hold his hand and don't let go. Only time I leave Tommy's side is when we reach Paul's building in Oakland, and I offer to haul Mav's things from the parking garage while Tommy escorts Maverick to the third floor.

The condo is spacious for this side of the city. Probably the same size as Tommy's house in Sacramento, but with humongous windows, an open floor plan, and a TV that screams Super Bowl watch party. Mav has his own room, already painted his favorite color—lavender—and already fixed up with new kid-sized furniture and toys from the list Tommy had texted Paul. The rug is a big soccer ball, and the framed promotional posters on the walls are all from the NCAA championship match.

"It's Uncle Tommy!" Mav cheers, hopping and pointing at the poster showcasing Tommy's picture perfect babyface, trying to look hard in his Hornet's jersey.

"Thought he'd appreciate that," Paul chuckles, proud of himself but not smug about it. Dude already has that dad vibe going. Dorky, slightly disheveled and adorably uncool. Reminds me of Matt, and I hope that's a sign Mav is in good hands.

I'm holding one-third of Erica's ashes in a wooden box the size of a watch box with a small latch and lock on it. While Mav is distracted rummaging through all his new toys, I trade the box into Tommy's hands, and he trades it into Paul's.

"It's my sister," he says, low voice turning lower. "For Mav, in case he wants it. You can give it to him now or when he's older, but it's for him."

Paul nods with a sympathetic look. "I'll keep it safe."

I chime in, telling Paul there's some of Erica's things in the blue storage bin I left in the living room. Some things Tommy and his mom thought Mav might like one day as keepsakes.

We spend a few hours here, helping Mav get acquainted with his new home, and we all have lunch together at the table. Tommy leaves Mav his Switch and makes sure it's hooked up to the massive TV before we say our goodbyes. But it's not really goodbye. We'll visit often, and our second bedroom in San Jose can become a room for Mav in a pinch.

The day after Erica passed, when Tommy could hardly get out of bed, he asked me if I could help him raise Maverick if that was what Erica had wanted. It felt like a trap when he asked. While I knew it was grief and guilt provoking the question, I feared that saying the wrong thing during such a tender time would set a fissure in our relationship. I needed to support Tommy in any way I could, but I also promised to always be honest with him.

"I don't know," I had answered, lying with him on our sides in the middle of his bed. There were tears in my eyes, because there were tears in his, and because I was scared he'd be upset with me. "I love him, but...I don't think I'm capable of raising a child right now. Maybe one day. Maybe never. I think I have a lot of work to do before I can be a good parent."

He'd set his palm on the side of my face, stroking away my tears as if he was there to comfort me and not the other way around. "I understand," he'd whispered. "Honestly, I don't think I could do it either. I would try if I had to, but I'm glad I don't have to. Does that make me a bad uncle?"

"Absolutely not," I had implored. "You're an incredible uncle, Tommy, but you're also twenty-one. You're still in school. Your life and your future are just as important as Mav's. Paul is the one who's meant to raise Mav now, and I'm gonna raise you."

He'd huffed a quick chuckle that morphed into a sob as he'd crashed his face against my chest so my shirt could soak up his tears.

Now he hugs Mav fiercely, lifting the munchkin off his feet and swinging him around until he's dizzy. Tommy smooches Mav's cheek about a million times before letting him go and shaking Paul's hand goodbye.

When Mav runs into my own arms, my heart melts a little. Makes me wonder if Tommy was this sweet when he was seven, and I think the answer is pretty obvious.

It's wild to think that if I'd grown up different, and I hadn't been so broken, maybe Tommy and I could have been friends most of our lives. By the time he started soccer, I was ten. I would have gone up and talked to him after the first ever match where our teams went head to head, and I would have asked to be his friend. I would have beaten the everfucking snot out of those kids who jumped him for being gay. I would have told him I was gay, and we could figure it out together. We could have been together all this time. *Childhood sweethearts.*

Instead, I feared his beauty and his perfection, and I called him a terrible word because I hated myself too much to allow myself a friend.

It still hurts to think about. It hurts a hell of a lot. More than I ever let on to Tommy, because I don't want him to have to keep proclaiming his forgiveness. Regret doesn't go away just because there's forgiveness, and regret is one of the many things I'm learning to cope with in therapy.

"Ready?" I ask Tommy at the door, just in case he needs more time. I'll give him all the time he needs, even if it means camping out on Paul's living room floor tonight.

The smile Tommy gives me is wistful, a little sad yet certain. "Yeah. Let's go."

On our way down to the parking garage, I ask Tommy for his keys so I can drive us. He doesn't question it, probably because he drove us all the way here and wouldn't mind a break. Thankfully, he doesn't seem to suspect I've got ulterior motives.

I guess, sometimes, I still keep secrets from Tommy. But just the one, and today's the day to spill the beans.

He gets curious early on, when he realizes I'm driving into San Francisco instead of backtracking inland toward Sacramento. There's a lookout point Paul told me about a while back, behind Lake Merced and up an easy cliff trail.

"What are we doing here?" Tommy asks me as I park the truck at the base of the cliffs.

"Thought we could go for a walk. Enjoy some sights before we head back to Sac."

Chuckling, he says, "The sooner we get back to Sac, the sooner we can get to San Jose."

"C'mon." I click my belt before reaching over and clicking his. "We'll have years to enjoy San Jose. Let's enjoy a little San Francisco now."

Blue eyes full of suspicion, Tommy climbs out of the truck and follows my lead up the winding, paved trail. We're back to holding hands, and everyone we pass either politely ignores us or pays us a friendly hello. I'm passed giving a shit if Tommy and I receive wayward glances, but it's calming to be in a location where I know people won't hassle us for existing. San Jose is like that. Not as outwardly flamboyant a city as SF, but I don't worry about our safety there, either. I think our life is going to be really good there.

At the top of the cliffs, a concrete tunnel leads to the promised views. We're a skyscraper's height above the ocean, and it goes on for more miles than I can possibly guess until it meets the horizon in a stunning melding of blue. Reminds me of my lover's eyes, which I get lost in just as easily.

The grin across Tommy's face tells me he's happy I brought him here. I tug him along, meandering down footpaths along the cliff until we're far enough from other visitors that I'm not overwhelmed by nerves.

"This place is beautiful, Row," Tommy says, eyes glued to the view.

"Just like you," I tell him, projecting all the mush in my heart out to him.

He blushes and eyes me oddly, since I'm rarely so cutesy out in public. "Should we keep walking?"

"Hang back a sec." I squeeze his hand and bring him back to face me. "I wanna talk to you about something."

"Okay." His suspicion turns to worry lines, which I hope means he isn't expecting what I'm about to reveal. "What do you wanna talk about?"

I release his hand and swipe the nervous sweat off on my hip before fishing into the pocket of my bomber jacket and taking out the small box I've had in there since we left Sacramento early this morning. Fiddling with it in both hands, I begin, "So—"

"Holy shit," Tommy breathes, completely vexed.

Smiling at his dopey, star-struck expression, I start over. "So I know we've joked about it—"

"I wasn't joking," he quickly states.

I exhale a small laugh as the butterflies in my gut flap around tirelessly. "I know you've mentioned it, and I always tell you that you're mine, no matter what, and that's the truth. But now that we're finally, officially, about to move in together for real, I don't want you to just be my boyfriend anymore. I want to take you to San Jose with me tomorrow as my fiancé."

Fully committed, I drop to one knee and lift the black leather box between us. Flipping the lid open, I show Tommy the ring I picked out six months ago when my check from the Earthquakes cleared. A white gold band with small, black diamond inlays.

"Tommy Mathison," I utter, staring up into the limitless pools inside his eyes, "will you marry me?"

"Row," he breathes, face twisted in something that looks like anguish but somehow evokes the opposite, and it sends my heart into a frenzy. "Sweetheart... Are you kidding? Of course I'll marry you. You actually got me a ring?"

Beaming so bright my head feels hot, I pick the ring out of the velvet lining and pocket the box. "Hell yeah, I got your ass a ring. I'm not some deadbeat."

Releasing a breathy, emotion-filled laugh, Tommy holds out his left hand, and I slip the personalized engagement ring onto his proper finger. On the inside, I had the band engraved.

'Forever Yours.'

I stand, and Tommy barrels into me, nearly knocking me on my ass when he crashes our mouths together.

"God damn, I love you," he mutters between impassioned kisses.

"I love you too, baby boy."

We kiss for minutes, arms around each other with the coastal breeze wrapping us up in a summer chill.

"I'm gonna get you a ring," Tommy speaks against my mouth.

"You don't have to."

"Yes, I do."

"I'll pay for it."

He snorts. "Like hell you will."

We're laughing and holding each other, and it just feels so damn *right*. There isn't a single doubt in my mind about this man being the one I'm meant to be with, and the clarity feels like freedom.

If Tommy gets me a ring, I'll have it engraved as well, and it'll say what my heart screams whenever I look into Tommy's eyes.

Never Give Up.

Now Available

Salt (Like Teammates Book 2)

CONNOR

Getting accepted into the same post-grad university as my girl-friend seemed like a solid reason to stay together. Now that I'm in San Diego, living with Thalia's family, all I want to do is go back to Sacramento. Back to my family, my friends, and the sport I love like crazy.

When I stumble upon a pickup soccer match on the beach, it stirs something in me. My eyes, and my camera, obsess over the dark-eyed forward with a body straight out of a fashion magazine.

Dane Calvo...tall, untamed, and unabashedly gay. He hits on me, and I reject him. Then I find out he's Thalia's younger brother—the one who sleeps in the bedroom next to ours. Maybe it's a bad idea trying to be friends with a guy who is clearly into me, but I'm straight. At least, I think I am.

DANE

The only thing worse than my sister moving in is that she brought her stupid boyfriend with her. Now I've got both of their crap taking up valuable counter space in my bathroom, and my dad is making me eat dinner with the family.

When I discover Thalia's boyfriend is the same drop-dead cutie who was taking stalker-pics of me at the beach, I know I can have fun with it. The problem is, he knows I'm gay and my family doesn't. Even worse, he wants to be friends—wants to train me even—but the more time we spend together, the more I want him all to myself.

He keeps saying he's straight, but I have my doubts. But even if he's not, how could someone as good as Connor Whitlock ever want a train wreck like me?

SALT is a spicy sports romance that deals with themes related to identity, infidelity, mental health, and family trauma. It is the second book in the Like Teammates series but can be enjoyed as a standalone. This book is intended for readers age 18 and up.

Acknowledgements

To Jess, you are a writer's guardian angel. I'm not sure this book would have ever seen the light of day if not for your support, kindness, and unwavering encouragement. You are a beautiful person, and I am so incredibly grateful for your friendship.

Thank you Ellie and Nova for your detailed beta-reading, and thank you Rachel for lending your artistry in creating such a beautiful book cover. Your time and dedication were bright spots in this process, and this book is so much better due to your respective involvement.

To the online community where my writing journey began, y'all gave my work a home, and I wouldn't be the writer I am today without your support and feedback.

To Ms. Hill, who told sixteen-year-old me that I "write different," thank you. It was the most valuable maybe-compliment anyone had ever given me regarding the thing I love more than life, and I'll never forget it.

About The Author

Jonah Yorke is a born-and-raised Californian with a degree in Cinema from San Francisco State University. With a passion for storytelling, he specializes in writing contemporary queer romance with ample spice, angst, and catharsis. When he is not writing, he is likely watching baseball, daydreaming to sad music, or out looking for more caffeine.

www.ingramcontent.com/pod-product-compliance
Lightning Source LLC
Chambersburg PA
CBHW031956130726
47903CB00013B/1118